FORBIDDEN LOVE

Her eyes shone in the aftermath of tears as she raised her face to him. "Ben" she whispered.

His lips found hers eagerly parted, as hungry and insistent as his. The past and future forgotten, Lacy lived only in the present, in his embrace. Her arms tightened, holding him closer. He answered her urgency, crushing her against his chest.

They parted, breathless, stunned by the naked passion of the moment.

"Lacy . . . ." He tasted her name, savoring it.

She stared at him, her eyes wide as the enormity of what she had done washed over her, overwhelming in its implications.

Lacy pulled from the safety of his arms. One slender hand to her mouth, she stared at him in horror. "No," she whispered in painful realization. "Dear God, no!"

Passion clouded his mind. He moved to embrace her once more, not comprehending the new terror that haunted her. "Lacy!"

"No!" she cried. With a strength born of anguish and fear, she pushed him away. Blindly, she turned and ran back toward the barn, the bonfire, and the sanctuary among the townspeople.

ELIZABETH DANIELS

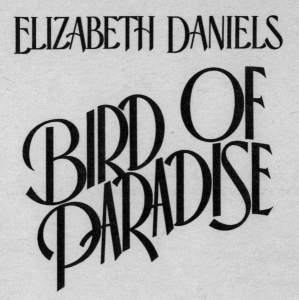

BIRD OF PARADISE

LEISURE BOOKS NEW YORK CITY

To my best friend, Janet Hafner,
Who's a mite partial to Ben Paradise.

A LEISURE BOOK ©

December, 1991

Published by

Dorchester Publishing Co., Inc.
276 Fifth Avenue
New York, NY 10001

Printed in the United States of America.

BIRD OF PARADISE

CHAPTER I

April 1848

Society titled her "the untouchable heiress," a misnomer William Quire felt Lillian Marie Phalen courted out of pure viciousness. If her heart was untouched, he doubted the same could be said of her exquisite body. He'd often witnessed her disheveled appearance after a turn in the shadowed garden with one of her admirers, Caleb Innes. And he had noted how her soft red lips, bruised with passion, often curved invitingly for that young seaman.

Harrison Kilmartin also received special attention, Quire thought. As her current partner on the ballroom floor, Kilmartin was the recipient of those secret, seductive smiles, of her calculated blushes and rash, unfulfilled promises. Quire watched them as the movements of their dancing brought her full ivory skirts swaying intimately against Kilmartin's ebony pantaloons. He drew her close, closer than propriety allowed, and Quire imagined that his rival feasted on the sight of her white, full breasts rising from the low neckline of her gown. Quire could almost feel the yielding softness of her tiny waist, feel the tumult of desire that inevitably rose in the pit of his stomach. He pictured her dark-lashed, gypsy eyes luring her victim on with glimpses of forbidden delights in their Lorelei depths.

Kilmartin bent closer, his cheek nearly brushing her pale ash-blond curls as they clustered in attractive disarray at her temples and along her graceful throat.

She was etheral, breathtakingly beautiful, angelic.

Angelic? Quire smirked. She was a daughter of Satan with her free ways. The woman was too open, too familiar with the employees of her father's shipping concern, illiterate swabbies, all of them. She encouraged the advances of men like Innes and Kilmartin despite their reputations as womanizers. She was an opinionated bitch who took pleasure in crushing a man's reputation, of destroying a man's ego. What grated most was her intent to run the Puritan Shipping Line in Captain Phalen's absence, a resolve Quire found far from proper or feminine. Sometimes he felt she acted more like a damned suffragette than his intended bride.

Once she bowed to fate, accepted his proposal and married him, her trips to the docks would end. He would not have his wife clambering aboard the scrupulously maintained triple-masted Puritan barques anchored in the harbor. The mere memory of the day she'd accepted a wager to scale the rigging of the *Puritan Paramour*, the newly launched clipper, made him furious. The fact that she'd done so effortlessly, in spite of her skirts, had not made him proud of her unusual accomplishments. She should have been practicing the pianoforte or needlework as other young ladies of her status did, not scrambling the ropes like a common seaman. Once they wed, she'd leave the shipping business in his hands and content herself with raising a family.

Quire gulped at the goblet of brandy in his hand. No matter how many times he repeated the litany of changes he'd make in her life, he couldn't actually picture Lacy reforming.

Lacy. Her father's pet name suited the girl far better than her given name. She'd been exquisitely feminine, frail in build, fragile in appearance even as a gangly chit who exasperated the captain's attempts to keep her out of boys' clothing. She'd scrapped with the cabin boys, her thin legs poised in a fighter's stance, her tiny fists raised menacingly, determined to prove to her male peers that she was their equal. The tomboy had evolved into a temptress without losing any of that earlier determination. She'd never hand over control of the Puritan Line to any man. Lacy considered no one more capable of running the Line than herself. She was certainly far more capable than Harry Phalen, her cousin and his brother-in-law, Quire admitted. As long as Lacy kept her thumb in the pie, it meant profits could never be siphoned into Quire's own pockets. Gaining her as a wife would be only a temporary success. It was the fortune the Line represented that was his long-term goal. Money could open doors, could save face.

The last, of course, was the most important. Pride for the family name demanded he marry money. His sister, Abigail, had failed to secure the Line in marrying Harry Phalen and producing a son. Who would have expected old man Phalen to slight his male relative and deed controlling interest in the business to his daughter? Abigail believed adamantly in her plan to wed her brother to Lacy Phalen thus securing the inheritance to rebuild the deteriorated Quire estate. As Lacy's chaperone, Abigail had discouraged a number of suitors already, leaving the field clear for William. Only Caleb Innes was immune to her hints.

Quire finished his brandy quickly as the dance ended. Innes was first mate aboard the *Puritan Temptress*, a barque on the Liverpool packet run. Innes had shipped as a cabin boy with the Line and industriously worked his way into the position of first mate. There was talk that as a favorite of Miss Phalen, Innes would soon have a ship of his own to command. To insure the promotion, Quire expected Innes to propose to Lacy. If the man had any ambition at all, he would have wed the girl long ago. At nineteen, some considered Lacy on the shelf.

Abigail Quire Phalen sat on the far side of the crowded ballroom, along the wall with the other chaperones. Her brown hair was bound in a neat chignon, and her unassuming gray silk dress blended with the other soberly clad matrons.

Matriarchs of Boston's elite, the seated women resembled a row of crows, scavengers eager to pick apart the reputations of any debutante rash enough to gain their censure.

Abigail had lost the tentative claim she'd had on beauty. Fortunately, she had managed to trap a husband before the softness had disappeared and had left an angular, sharp-faced woman in its place. She had singled Harry Phalen out, not for love of his attractiveness, but because he was biddable and easily led. After living with the ever-current threat of financial ruin, the Phalen money had beckoned, luring Abigail into marriage before she realized Harry would not inherit the vast resources of the Phalen assets. It had taken the last of the Quire capital to launch Abigail. Failure to rebuild her family's fortunes had grated on her, causing Abigail to become possessed by a single dream—that of claiming the Puritan Line for her brother through Lacy Phalen. Until her schemes reached fruition, only Abigail's strength of will and quick mind managed to keep William solvent.

Abigail stared intently at her tall, broadly built brother, willing him to glance her way. If force of personality alone could accomplish her ends, the Line would have been in her control long ago. Resentment had grown into a desire for revenge, not against her sheep of a husband or the enterprising Captain Phalen. Her hatred centered on the one person she saw as an obstacle between herself and the Line: Lillian Phalen.

William tore his gaze from Lacy and Kilmartin as if in response to a silent command from his sister. A slight, barely perceptible nod of her head directed his gaze to the entrance hall where their hostess and a stocky, bearded man had just entered the room.

The arrival of Captain Sean Phalen at the ball was unprecedented. The man rarely made an appearance, and his presence now made Quire uneasy. The captain was not opposed to his suit, but Quire was determined to secure Lacy as his betrothed before her favorite, Innes, returned to port. Creditors aside, William burned to possess her, to join battle with the beautiful spitfire and, if necessary, crush her spirit. Once he'd subdued her, he was sure the fever in his blood would be cured and he could concentrate on rebuilding his estate.

Abigail would divert the captain's attention, buying Quire time to coerce the girl.

Quire tugged his waistcoat down over his slightly paunchy waistline and moved onto the dance floor.

Lacy Phalen cursed inwardly as she realized William Quire was striding purposefully toward her. It had been a very pleasant evening so far. Her dance card had been fought over and rapidly filled. There had been many good-natured comments from the eager men determined to take advantage of Caleb Innes's absence. They might decry his ability to monopolize her dance card but none dared dispute the fact that he was her favorite. She doubted anyone would be surprised when she married Caleb. She'd been planning to do so ever since he'd stolen that first kiss from her five years ago. No, longer. Since she'd met him. She had been nine, he ten and preparing to leave on the *Temptress's* maiden voyage, his first sailing as a cabin boy. Caleb had radiated excitement for all his cocky manner in patronizing the furiously jealous little girl she'd been.

She smiled softly, unaware that her escort recognized the expression, a special smile she reserved for the absent Puritan officer.

"Ousted again." Harrison Kilmartin sighed and lifted her slender lace-gloved hand to his lips.

Lacy laughed, a light twinkling sound. "I'm sorry, Harrison," she murmured unconvincingly. "Thank you for the dance."

The tall blond man lingered over her hand. "Does Innes know he's a lucky man?"

"I doubt it." She grinned. "You must tell him."

He smiled sardonically. "Heartless creature. I see Quire bearing down on us. How the devil did he get his name on your card? I thought you detested the man."

Manners demanded he nod civilly to Quire and hand her over. As if she were goods for sale, Lacy thought, angry. Kilmartin was barely out of hearing before she turned on the large man before her.

"I'm otherwise engaged for this dance," she declared. "If you'll excuse me, William . . ."

The cool verdant gaze irritated him. The least she could do was act civil when they were in public. As her chaperone's brother, he deserved courtesy.

He smiled as if she'd made a jest. "I had hoped you would have saved a dance for me, Lacy."

How could the man be so dense! Every slight,

every cut, slid off his back. She had ceased throwing hints at him. Such kindness had been met with this same dogged disregard for her feelings.

Quire welcomed the burning spots in her cheeks, signals of her rising temper.

Lacy's hands gripped her fragile ivory fan. Her white even teeth bared in a polite grimace. "I believe I have made it extremely clear that I do not wish to dance with you or talk to you." Contempt colored her forest-green eyes almost black.

The man before her was immune to her show of emotion. "My dear Lacy," he purred, "I don't know why you have conceived a dislike of me. I have only your best interests at heart. My intentions are quite honorable as I think you know."

Damn the little bitch! Abigail was correct, naturally. The only way to achieve their end was to compromise the girl, force her into marrying him for the sake of her reputation. If he could coerce her into the garden and keep her there long enough, their goal could be accomplished that night.

Lacy glared at him as if she could read his thoughts, daring him to put his plan into action. "If Caleb were here . . ." she began.

Quire hid his irritation and chuckled. "But he isn't, my dear. I doubt the inestimable Mr. Innes plans to marry you. Unless he has suffered a bout of ambition on this voyage, I fear Caleb Innes will be content to sail for the Puritan Line rather than own it."

Her eyes flashed with fury. "But you have no hesitation in taking over control, do you, William?"

Bitch! His face suffered a slight spasm as he controlled the anger her statement inspired. "I wouldn't dream of it, Lacy. I know how much the Line means to you. I only wish to cherish you as my own. If in time your interest changes, I would be willing to undertake the responsibility of overseeing . . ."

He was smooth, always rolling, sailing before the storm of her refusals, conveniently ignoring her outbursts, ever pushing to drive her into the shoals, to throw caution to the winds and lose her temper. Well, she wouldn't! Disaster lay in that direction. A mistake she feared would find her wed to him.

The orchestra played the opening bars of the next dance. To whom had she promised it? Mr. Answorth? Mr. Latimer? William stood blocking her view of the ballroom. Her court had dissipated, claiming other partners long ago. Even Harrison, knowing her dislike of Quire, had deserted her. She needed someone to distract him, someone to force him to exchange pleasantries with rather than to court her.

Thinking she searched for her father, Quire took her arm, intent on proceeding with his plan. "You're flushed, my dear. I wouldn't recommend exerting yourself in this heat. Perhaps a walk in the garden? I believe the Forsythes are known for their beautiful roses."

Lacy tried to shake off his guiding hand. "I've said I won't accept you, William. Look for a bride elsewhere. I'm sure there are other heiresses who are not as fastidious in their tastes."

The hand on her arm tightened. "Lacy, Lacy.

15

Elizabeth Daniels

You are such a child in these matters. The fascination you have for Innes will fade. Your father and Abigail will undoubtedly choose your husband. And it will be me." He smiled, sure of himself.

Others found her attitude unreasonable, Lacy knew. William Quire came from an old Boston family. He was personable, respected, accepted everywhere. Any number of her friends would have eagerly accepted his suit. Handsome in a fleshy sense, his pale brown hair was styled and sleek. His appearance was always the height of fashion.

Yet she could not explain the repulsion she felt toward her chaperone's brother. That circumstance alone threw them together often, placing her in a position where she could not refuse him as her escort. She could not shake the feeling that he was a predator and she the prey he stalked. William's patience and persistence knew no limits. But she was reaching the end of her endurance.

The captain's plan to leave Lacy in her cousin Harry's care during his voyage to China would place her in Abigail's home. Under the woman's eye, Lacy's life would be restricted by more than just the unreasonable strictures forced upon a young unmarried woman by society, and to have her freedom so limited was what Lacy chose to avoid, no matter what the cost. All her arguments concerning her sailing with the *Paramour* when it pulled anchor for Canton and Hong Kong had fallen on deaf ears as far as her father was concerned.

Her only other hope was that he would allow Polly MacGuire to be her companion while he was

16

gone. If he refused, she was desperate enough to ask Caleb to run away with her. Surely her childhood friend would not refuse her request.

Quire's thumb stroked the soft inner side of her arm as he gripped it above her elbow.

The caress sickened her. "Leave me alone, William. Please." She bit each word savagely. "Papa will not discount my desires when it comes time to choose my husband."

The passion in her voice made the blood rush in his ears as he delighted in his power to raise such a strong emotional response from her. Even hatred. Reveling in her resistance, he forced her out the terrace door into the welcome coolness of the garden, guiding her along the walk away from the lighted windows. A last backward glance assured him that the matrons had noted their departure.

"I mean to have you," William said in her ear. "You and the Line, Lacy. Your father looks favorably on the match. You would do well to accept that fact."

Chinese lanterns were placed about the garden to illuminate, yet conceal lovers' rendezvous. Earlier rain showers had dampened the most adventurous of young spirits. Now only shadows danced among the carefully tended hedges and flower beds as a breeze swayed the lanterns to a silent tune. Lacy turned her face into the wind, tasting the tang of salt in the air, finding in it the courage to withstand William yet again.

Quire inhaled the fragrance of spring that clung to her white-gold ringlets. Gently, he drew her resisting form into his arms. "Your friend, Celia Hancock, will wed next week," he reminded her.

"Doesn't that make you think of your own future?" The feel of her stiff and unyielding yet warm body so close to his made him mad with desire. Her palms were pressed against his chest in a futile effort to curb any further advances on his part. As if her meager strength could deter any man intent on claiming those tempting lips for his own!

She had fantasized her own wedding, endeavoring to place Caleb's beloved face in the bridegroom's place. It was elusive, evading her in her reveries, although she knew his every feature as well as her own. She would never admit to Quire she even thought of marriage. Somehow, she knew he would find a way to trap her into saying something he could twist to his own advantage.

She pushed against the gold embroidered silk of his waistcoat, trying to loosen his binding embrace. "Excuse me, William. I really must go. I have promised this dance . . ." she began.

"Lacy," he murmured, a frightening new tenderness in his voice.

She found herself drawn closer and his brandy-tainted lips descended to claim hers.

She would definitely have to exchange strong words with the gardeners, Agatha Forsythe decided surveying the drooping petals in the large flower arrangement in her entrance hall. No matter that the rooms were stifling in her attempt to thrust spring upon her winter-locked guests. Bowers of wilting hot-house arrangements competed in beauty with the ladies' pastel ball gowns, and their delicate fragrances were cloying and distasteful in the overheated rooms. If one did not look

closely, however, the effect was still quite charming. Soft candlelight danced in reflected glory in
the numerous gilt-edged mirrors placed on the
ballroom walls to lighten the atmosphere. It was of
paramount importance that her guests forget that
spring was elusive, as evidenced by the steaming
windows.

Perhaps if she ordered the sashes thrown open
. . . No, there would be an outcry against the ill
effects of night air. She would order more champagne. If the guests didn't feel the need for a
restorative, Mrs. Forsythe certainly did.

Coming in from the damp night's cool embrace,
the two men found the warm, heavily perfumed
air repulsive. The elder stocky, bearded man with
the rolling gait of a seaman glanced at his companion ready to suggest a hasty retreat to the more
piquant atmosphere of a tavern. Damn the promise
he'd made Lacy. She knew he hated these society
parties. If she hadn't railed at him for neglecting
her, he wouldn't be standing here dripping on the
Forsythes' carpet.

Unhappy, he handed his coat and hat to the
waiting lackey and grimaced at his tall comrade.
He'd only met the fellow that afternoon when he'd
shown up unexpectedly at the warehouse office.
Yet there was something about the cut of the man's
jib that he liked. "Good of you to bear me up,
Paradise. Detest these sort of things, but my daughter insists I put in an appearance."

An amused smile creased the younger man's
tanned face. He removed the high-crowned beaver
hat, and brushed his dark hair back in place. "Not

Elizabeth Daniels

at all, Captain. My travels have been rather un-
eventful since I left Virginia."

Captain Sean Phalen chuckled. "I wouldn't put
this shindig in the same league as the stories your
granddad used to tell of ye, lad," he said, a soft
Irish brogue coloring his deep voice.

"All exaggerated, I'm sure, Captain," the young
man said, his blue eyes sparkling merrily. "I was a
lousy trapper."

"Not the way the colonel told it, lad. Said you
were the luckiest young cub ever spawned."

Agatha Forsythe surveyed the late arrivals, a
pleased expression on her flushed plump face. It
was a feather in her cap to have Captain Phalen at
her ball. The wealthy owner of the Puritan Shipping Line rarely accepted invitations, and here he
was with a very attractive man in tow!

It crossed her mind that the stranger was merely
another member of Lacy Phalen's court of admirers. Extremely good-looking, his well-cut dark
evening clothes hugged broad shoulders and muscular thighs. The snowy-white shirt and tie ac-
cented a deep tan.

"Captain," she cooed, holding her hands out to
grip Sean's rough, weathered ones. "Miss Phalen
did promise you'd be here but I hardly dared
credit it!"

The captain found himself drawn uncomforta-
bly against Mrs. Forsythe's well-fleshed form. "A
pleasure, Agatha," he mumbled, gruff. "Hope you
don't mind that I brought you another guest."

"How could you think I'd be anything but
pleased, Captain?" she scolded, her small eyes

covering the tall young man's lean form with appreciation.

What startling, beautiful eyes the stranger had. They fairly leapt from that dark face. And the things they did to a woman! The insolent puppy was surveying her as frankly as . . . as . . . Well, she'd never felt so flighty or giddy at any man's perusal of her body. Certainly Mr. Forsythe had never made her feel so attractive. She felt almost girlish.

"Let me present Benjamin Paradise," the captain said, recalling her from the most improper course of her thoughts. She was a married woman, after all. A pillar of society, she hoped. Still, no one ever said Agatha Forsythe hadn't nourished romantic dreams as a girl.

"It's always a pleasure to welcome another unattached gentleman, Mr. Paradise," she enthused.

The stranger took her hand and kissed it softly. "Please, the name's Ben, ma'am," he said.

The flush on Mrs. Forsythe's face heightened with pleasure. She liked the soft, drawling quality of his voice. If she were younger, she would have admitted to chills at the seductive sound of it or perhaps to the look in those merry blue eyes.

The captain exchanged an amused look with Paradise. The man had a way with the ladies, that was clear. In his younger days in Dublin, Sean had cut a swath with the colleens himself. That had been before he'd shipped to America and met Amelia Wainwright, of course. Delicate of feature and gentle in bearing, Amelia had captured his roving heart. Her father hadn't much cared for an

Irish swabbie as a son-in-law. Figured him for a fortune hunter. But Amelia had been adamant. In the end, old Wainwright had relinquished not only his daughter but her considerable dowry to the penniless Irishman.

He'd proved the old man wrong by buying his first ship with the money and building up a very successful shipping business.

He missed Amelia. Their daughter, Lacy, was the image of her late mother. Fortunately, Lacy had not inherited Amelia's delicate constitution. She was a bonny lass who would bear many grandsons for the Puritan Line, and he had his precious Polly to pamper to his other needs.

"Miss Phalen tells me you plan to sail soon to China, Captain. Are you in the shipping business, Mr . . . er . . . Ben?" Agatha purred.

"No, ma'am." The young man smiled giving her an excellent view of blinding white teeth.

"I imagine Miss Phalen has saved you a dance on her card," she said. If only she were young enough to dance and not receive the censure of her friends. To have this attractive man gazing down at her as he guided her through the intimate figures of a waltz would be . . . absolute foolishness on her part. She was the mother of grown children. How could she even think such thoughts!

"I've not had the pleasure of Miss Phalen's company," Ben drawled.

Her eyes brightened with interest. She'd long disparaged the affect Lacy Phalen had on men, particularly when Agatha's own daughter was overlooked. Men worshipped at the heiress's feet. It was embarrassing, Agatha thought, to have her own son one of the biggest fools in that court. This man would definitely turn the Phalen girl's head. Perhaps Lacy would break her heart over him. Agatha was certain that by the end of the evening there wouldn't be a female heart that Benjamin Paradise hadn't won.

"Are you planning to make your home here in Boston, Ben?"

"No, ma'am. I'm lately from Virginia but my home is on the frontier."

Again that devestating smile! He simply had to meet Lacy Phalen!

She took the arms of both men in a proprietary grasp and dragged them toward the ballroom, intent on holding both prisoner until every matron noted her success in securing the two most attractive men in the room. Let them gossip about that!

"Allow me to introduce you to some of our attractive ladies, Ben. I doubt you'll find any as lovely on the frontier. Such a wild, desolate place, I understand. And dangerous! My goodness, yes, don't you have wild Indians there?"

Sean Phalen listened to his hostess ramble on, amused at her interest in his companion. He noted with pleasure the petite form of Polly MacGuire floating about the room in the arms of one of her young admirers. Thank goodness Polly wasn't as stuffy as others of their generation! He liked the touch of gray in her hair, the smile lines about her eyes and mouth. Most of all he liked the way she welcomed him into her bed. Ah, Polly, the most enchanting little widow in Boston.

"Oh, dear." Agatha sighed. "There's Mrs. Hawthorne waving at me again. She's been asking for you all evening, Captain. I'm afraid you'll be forced to listen to her accounts of those British relatives of hers. It's all she can talk of since she got the letter announcing the arrival of her nephew this fall. You'll have to excuse us, Ben. I hope you don't mind being abandoned for the moment." She fluttered. "I will be right back to introduce you, I promise."

Ben grinned. "I will be desolate until your return, dear lady."

She flushed, coloring as brightly as her pink gown. "Do try to be nice to Mrs. Hawthorne," Agatha urged Sean, and impelled his resisting form across the crowded ballroom.

Ben Paradise accepted a glass of champagne and relaxed just inside the wide double doors of the ballroom. He was amused by the glances thrown in his direction. The feminine stares were openly admiring, even come hither despite his being a stranger in their midst. Or perhaps because of it. The men were hostile, prickling, ready to defend their territory from the intruder.

Ben sipped his drink, allowing his eyes to travel slowly around the room. A year ago he would have given anything to be in a home such as this. Any home for that matter. Huddling in a leaky lean-to, he had stared at the poor showing of pelts he'd accumulated after a season in the mountains. Game had definitely been trapped out. Travis had said as much before leaving for California. But Ben'd been too damn stubborn to believe the old fur trapper. After a quick depressing sale in Saint Louis, he'd managed to double, then triple his profits at cards before returning to the plantation in Virginia.

The colonel had welcomed him with open arms on his arrival, just as he had every time Ben returned. The old man had seen to Ben's education following Ben's brother David's death, sending him to William and Mary. It had given him a veneer of sophistication and the manners and speech of a gentleman, but the need to be on the move was deeply ingrained. Or had it just been that plantation life lacked the excitement, the danger, he had grown up expecting?

When the colonel had died two months ago, Ben had set about disposing of the old man's estate. The decision to travel north to terminate the contracts his maternal grandfather held with the Puritan Shipping Line and the cotton mill had been based more on Ben's restlessness than in personalizing the terminations. Soon enough he would run out of options and return to Missouri.

The glittering perfumed and pampered women swaying in the stiffly extended arms of their black-suited escorts were a far cry from the women he usually met. Were they as wanton as the speculative glances promised?

Peaches-and-cream complexions, careful chignons and bounding sausage curls were the rule rather than the exception. The mousey wall-flowers were plentiful. Some looked his way hopefully. Others seemed embarrassed by his presence. They knew as well as he that Mrs. Forsythe would soon return to introduce him to each of them in turn. Politely, as expected, he would request the pleasure of a dance. A painful experience for all concerned. Fortunately, he was a man who enjoyed female companionship, even the platonic variety on occasion.

His glance moved back to the revolving color of gowns on the dance floor. Perhaps if he played his cards right, one of those seductive smiles would result in something more satisfying than merely a dance. There were always bored young matrons eager to ease a man's needs without threatening their comfortable position as married women.

The little brunette in the blue dress was lively enough. The red-haired man with whom she was dancing wore a proprietary air as he swung her around the floor. The absence of a wedding band on her hand and the adoring expression with which she favored her companion quickly ruled her out.

There was the blonde, of course. She had drawn his eyes the moment he had entered the room. Now he wondered idly if she was married. She was easily the most beautiful woman in the room. Her pale blond, almost white hair, gleamed in the candlelight. Her creamy breasts rose temptingly from a froth of ivory lace on her low-cut dress. Her waist was impossibly small, and she was taller than the other women, a fact that he, a six-footer, appreciated.

It was her dark-lashed eyes that had drawn his attention. The sooty, gypsy look was sultry in her otherwise pale face. No, pale was the wrong word. She was light complected, naturally. Women of her age were very concerned about darkening their complexion with exposure to the sun. There was an animation to the perfect oval face that denied the use of the term "pale." The girl had spirit; he could feel it across the length of the ballroom.

She wasn't dancing with her escort. Her face was flushed with anger as she pulled her arm from the man's grasp. They seemed to be arguing: the man insistent, the beauty determined and resistant. At length, she succumbed to his demands and allowed him to lead her into the garden.

Ben finished the champagne and set the thin-stemmed crystal next to a vase of wilting flowers. An amused grin played about his lips. Why not? What did he have to lose? The lady obviously needed a gallant to rescue her. There was no telling what she would offer as a reward for his services.

Lacy twisted in Quire's arms so that his kiss missed its mark, landing on her temple. She itched to slap his face, to kick his shins, but the tight embrace held her captive. Panicked, she searched the garden and encountered a pair of startling blue eyes.

The stranger towered over the majority of men she knew yet stood shoulder to shoulder with Quire. He was slimmer, leaner, more muscular than William, and there was grace in the easy way he moved.

"Am I interrupting anything?" he asked, his voice a lazy drawl that belied his alert stance.

Quire regarded the intruder, wary. His arms relaxed their hold on the squirming girl. She broke free and moved away, putting the stranger between them.

In the ballroom, the orchestra began a new selection.

"My dance, I believe," the newcomer drawled, giving Quire a polite smile.

Lacy stood to one side, her breasts rising quickly as she tried to control her frantic emotions. One long strand of golden hair hung down her back as a result of the struggle and she had managed to drag her skirt through a puddle. "I thought you'd forgotten," she answered huskily, taking her cue from the stranger.

Quire did not intend to lose his chance to be alone with Lacy. His future depended on it. "I don't believe Miss Phalen should indulge at the moment," he said, measuring the intruder.

Ben's smile widened. So this was Lacy Phalen. A neat armful for any man. He liked the stubborn set of her jaw, the fury that burned in the green depths of her eyes as she prepared to rebuke the fellow's statement.

"Don't think we've met," he said, offering his hand to the other man. "Benjamin Paradise. I arrived a little while ago with Captain Phalen." He wasn't surprised when the hand was refused. With barely a pause, he offered an arm to the blond beauty.

Lacy pointedly ignored the bristling Quire. Her smile was warm, eager, as she took Paradise's arm, dazzling Ben.

Quire burned with impotent rage. The stranger was an obstacle, an untested opponent at present. He would have to retreat from the contest, for a contest it certainly was. He recognized the carefully banked expression in the other man's eyes.

There was danger lurking in those icy depths. The man moved like an animal, unconsciously graceful and alert.

Quire straightened his waistcoat, and ran a hand over his hair to insure its perfection. "Excuse me," he said, and brushed past the couple.

Lacy sighed as William returned to the house. "Thank you, Mr. Paradise. Mr. Quire can be quite insistent."

He smiled down into her upturned face. "A pleasure, Miss Phalen. Feel free to use me any time."

She grinned at his comment. "And did you really come with my father, Mr. Paradise?"

"Strangely enough, yes, I did. Although I will confess it was a pleasant surprise to find you were his daughter, Miss Phalen."

"And if I hadn't been? Would you have played Galahad then?" she inquired.

He smiled. "It eliminates the prospect of an irate husband or indignant parent taking me to task. I have a feeling the captain won't be upset with my intervention."

She laughed, a delightful crystaline sound, deep, throaty, full of promise. "No, you won't have any problem with Papa."

She floated rather than walked, Ben noted as he led her back toward the house. The daughters of neighboring plantations in Virginia had not possessed the gracefulness he recognized in Lacy Phalen's step. He wished the dance hadn't been a ruse, that he could actually claim her, feel her melt in his arms, moving with the music, his guiding hand at her waist. The full curve of her hip and generous display of bosom were enticing and when added to the straightforward expression in her incredible green eyes and the lush fullness of her lips, he could well understand Quire's determination to discourage competition for the lady.

Was he competition? A stranger, here today, gone tomorrow.

The feel of Lacy Phalen's slender hand on his arm tempted him to extend his stay in Boston.

Lacy stole a glance at him. His eyes were such an unusual shade of blue. Icy, yet they warmed her. "I'd best go in by a side door," she said. "It wouldn't do to return to the ballroom together."

He nodded. "Perhaps I'll claim that dance yet."

Her face tilted coquettishly. "I hope you do, Mr. Paradise."

It was a full thirty minutes later when Lacy made her way down the stairs from the ladies' retiring room to the ballroom. The hemline of her gown was irreparably damaged, the water stain prominent among the tiers of lace that decorated her wide skirt. Ordinarily, rather than appear in the soiled dress, she would have sent a message to Abigail requesting they leave. But the mysterious stranger, Benjamin Paradise, beckoned. She couldn't explain why she was drawn to the man. Perhaps it was the laughter in his eyes, or his bronzed skin so like that of her father and Caleb, who spent their days in the sun.

Lacy searched the ballroom, easily locating his tall figure on the dance floor. Patience Rowley was having trouble following the wide sweeping circles of the waltz, and Ben shortened his steps to accommodate Miss Rowley's tiny form. Yet his partner could not overcome her awkwardness and obviously was overwhelmed at her good fortune of dancing with the most attractive man in the room.

Lacy had more difficulty finding her father who had wandered into the card room. When she found him, it took all her powers of persuasion to pry him from the table.

"Aren't you going to introduce me to your friend?" she demanded as they reentered the ballroom.

The captain studied her a moment, one hand stroking his beard. His hair, once blue-black, was now liberally sprinkled with gray which Lacy thought made him look rather dashing. He was still very handsome and youthful despite having passed his fiftieth year. His skin was weathered from years at sea to an attractive warm olive tone. His brow was creased in a perpetual scowl, yet his eyes danced, giving him a devil-may-care air. He was not a particularly tall man, but his shoulders and arms were quite powerful.

"Friend?" Lights twinkled in his sea-green eyes, reminiscent of sun flecks glinting off waves as the tide rolled into shore.

"The one I understand accompanied you this evening."

He looked thoughtful. "A man, you say, colleen?"

Lacy gave her father a disparaging look. "With Polly here tonight, I doubt you'd be foolish enough to bring a woman."

Sean sighed. "You aren't supposed to know of Polly at all. Proper girls don't."

"Thank goodness I'm not proper. I love Polly dearly. Now, about the stranger . . ."

"Nice boy," the captain said. "I think you'll like him, too, Lacy."

Her face softened as she readily agreed. "I do. I met him in the garden. Now, introduce me to him properly so I can dance with him."

The captain chuckled. "How fortunate that your dance card is empty."

"I saved these dances for you," she countered saucily. "Promise not to tread on my toes?"

He nodded and took her in his arms.

"Colonel Webber is dead," the captain informed his daughter, guiding her energetically across the highly polished parquet floor. "Paradise is his grandson. Came to let me know personally."

"I hope he's continuing the shipping contracts," Lacy said.

"No, he's sold the plantation."

Her pale brows rose in surprise. "To whom? We'd best send Harry down to convince the new owner to ship with us."

When she did dance with Paradise, Sean wondered whether his daughter would flirt or talk business. It still amazed him that she had such a comprehension of the shipping business, but it shouldn't have. He had trained her as if she'd been his son. He'd only drawn the line at letting her sail. It had always been her heart's desire. If she married Caleb Innes, he would be the last to be surprised if she set up housekeeping on board ship. After all, other skippers' wives and families traveled with them.

After Amelia's death, he had elected to remain landlocked, determined to give Lacy the kind of life her mother had wished for her. But he missed the sea and was now looking forward to his voyage to China. Since the end of the Opium Wars and the opening of Hong Kong Harbor, he'd been itching to go. With the *Puritan Paramour* complete, it was only Lacy who kept him in port. He'd once hoped she would marry before he sailed. He knew she'd set her heart on Caleb Innes but he worried all the same. Innes would probably break her heart. An excellent sailor, he'd make a good captain one day, but it was the young man's roving eye that bothered Sean.

Perhaps she wasn't set on Innes. A glow of excitement, of almost breathless anticipation, radiated from Lacy as they worked their way near the dancing forms of Benjamin Paradise and Patience Rowley.

The music ended. "Good evening, Miss Rowley," the captain greeted. "Paradise. Don't think you've met my daughter, Lillian. Lacy, Benjamin Paradise."

Patience Rowley was heartbroken as the Phalens joined them. She'd been lost in fantasies, glowing as her friends glared jealously from their chairs along the walls. Fairy tales did come true. Prince Charming indeed lived. He had danced with her and made her feel beautiful and fascinating for a short while. Now that Lacy Phalen stood next to her, reality rushed back with depressing swiftness.

"Enchanted, Miss Phalen," Ben said. His eyes flickered over her, warmly noting the imperfect rearrangement of her curls, the becoming blush that rose along her throat and colored her cheeks at his perusal.

"I believe you've been promised a dance, Mr. Paradise," she said. "I only hope I can follow you as easily as Miss Rowley. You dance beautifully, Patience. I'm afraid Papa leaves much to be desired as a partner."

"Only because my daughter tries to lead," the captain allowed. "I'd be honored if you would dance with me, Miss Rowley."

Patience looked uneasily to where her stiff-backed mother sat with her equally erect elder sister, Charity, who would despise her for dancing more than a single dance. Especially after Mr. Paradise had asked *her* to dance rather than Charity.

"I must thank you, Miss Rowley, for your forbearance," Ben murmured, lifting her gloved hand to his lips. "Especially since my clumsy efforts must have crushed your feet innumerable times."

She would never wear these gloves again. She'd sleep with them under her pillow, Patience decided. It didn't matter what Charity said. She would dance with Captain Phalen, too! This was a night to remember!

Lacy watched a glowing, triumphant Patience Rowley waltz away in her father's arms. "Patience looks different tonight," she mused.

"My wizard's touch," Ben said whisking her into the sensuous movement of the dance. "Would you like me to do the same for you?"

She eyed him warily. "And what would I have to

do in return, Mr. Paradise? I already owe you a token of gratitude for intervening in the garden earlier."

"Really?" His tone was soft, caressing. "Wasn't a dance my reward?"

"A paltry reward, surely."

"Perhaps not. I am collecting a number of murderous looks from your other beaux. Have I usurped one of their dances?"

She glanced over his shoulder to the guests watching the dancers. It was the envious looks of the women that she noticed, however.

"We are dancing rather close," she said.

He didn't loosen his arms. If anything they tightened, drawing her closer until they were almost touching.

"Do you mind?" he challenged.

His eyes were such a lovely shade of blue, the icy brilliance startling in his sun-darkened face, caressing her with an intimate touch. She enjoyed the feel of his hand at her waist and the way it made her very aware of his masculinity. The faint woodsy smell of his cologne was intriguing and sharp in contrast to the tang of sea spray that clung to Caleb and her father. And he was far from awkward on the dance floor. He danced beautifully, guiding her in wide swooping circles.

Pale blond ringlets moved softly on either side of her face. "No, I don't mind," she answered, her husky voice filled with the purring quality of a contented cat.

"Are you sure you don't mean that you don't mind causing trouble, Miss Phalen?"

"Perhaps."

"I've made an enemy or two, have I?"

"I wouldn't put it that strongly, Mr. Paradise."

He had read the expression in Quire's eyes, though. If he were staying in Boston long, he'd need the sixth sense that had guarded his back in the wilds. The streets of any town harbored predators more vicious than the dangers encountered in the wilderness.

Yet, he liked living on the edge of danger, and the lovely woman in his arms courted it. He could see the excitement glittering in her eyes. Eyes that were innocent shining emerald stars.

A tangible scent of danger emanated from Paradise, an air of mystery that seduced Lacy, and his magnetism drew her. She wished to melt against the hard breadth of his chest as his arm encircled her waist.

"Don't tempt me, Miss Phalen."

"To what end, Mr. Paradise?"

"Perhaps a dance with the most beautiful woman in the room isn't sufficient payment for rescuing her."

Her soft lips parted expectantly, as if she had forgotten they were in the center of a crowded room. "What sort of payment, Mr. Paradise?"

He could hear the anticipation in her voice, saw a gleam of mischief flare behind her thicket of black lashes.

His smile widened wolfishly. She was an accomplished flirt. Those full, lush lips were made for kissing. It would serve her right if he accepted their sweet invitation.

"Are you planning to be in Boston long, Mr. Paradise?"

He had planned to leave the next day. "Why do you ask?"

She considered her answer. "There is much to discover in Boston. We are a very old city, you know."

It was incredible that her lashes were so long, so dark under her pale brows. It would be difficult to leave this enchanting minx whose eyes promised fulfillment he sensed she was inexperienced to give. Still, he was on no schedule. What did a few days matter?

"Stay," Lacy whispered seductively, then laughed at his expression of surprise. "I intend to give you a tour of the city, Mr. Paradise. Nothing more."

"Nothing?" His eyes dropped to her lips.

His forwardness made her giddy, breathless. "Nothing, sir. Surely the historic sights of Boston are a sufficient lure to make you extend your stay."

"Absolutely, Miss Phalen," he murmured, and drew her infinitesimally closer.

CHAPTER II

The anchor's resounding splash in the waters of
Boston Harbor sent a skittish gull sailing skyward,
his white wing catching the last rays of the setting
sun before he wheeled away from the tall masts of
the *Puritan Temptress*. The crew worked quickly,
their faces turning often to inhale the scent of the
city.

Caleb Innes leaned on the gleaming rail watching the gull, his nose wrinkling at the taint of
civilization that stretched its way across the water
from the shore. Dusk hid the soot-stained buildings from closer inspection, yet he saw the scars in
his mind's eye.

Why was it he always returned feeling guilty?
Who had told him that it was unnatural for him not
to miss the women he left in Boston? Was it that
odd for a man to prefer the sea to the home he

shared with his widowed mother and younger sisters? Or was it incomprehensible that he should find pleasure in other women's arms when Lacy Phalen waited for him?

Innes sighed. The truth of the matter was he loved the sea far more than any woman. The sea was the siren that drew him as no mortal woman's arms could. He had found a temporary harbor in many beds, had tasted sweet lips aplenty from Boston to Liverpool and back. None could hold him, although many tried.

The longboat smacked the water far below him, recalling Innes to his duties. Late it may be but there were passengers eager to disembark and officials to notify of their arrival. He scrambled down the rope ladder.

Lacy stared out the window of the small, converted storeroom at the Puritan Warehouse. The two male clerks with whom she shared the tiny office had long since left for home. Their absence made it much harder for her to break her disturbing new habit of daydreaming. She found herself repeatedly gazing out, unseeing at the small patch of sky visible just over the next rooftop. Had the day been sunny or leaden gray? She could not recall. Ben Paradise's departure should have signaled a return to normal, a return to busy days spent bent over her cousin Harry's precise notations on the manifests. A full week had passed since Paradise had left, yet she still experienced a glow of contentment because of the hours she had spent in his company. But the pleasure resulted in twinges of guilt. Caleb was the man she planned to wed, yet she had not given him a thought, had not missed him at all once she met Benjamin Paradise. She would make it up to Caleb, show him he was the one with whom she wanted to spend her life. She would think only of Caleb from now on.

The window beckoned her once again, her mind rebelliously painting a memory of laughing blue eyes rather than Caleb's warm brown ones.

Only when the light faded was she drawn from her reverie to turn up the lamp. The warehouse could be far too quiet at night, the sounds of ships rubbing in their moorings or the noise of mice scurrying among the neatly stacked crates ominous in the stillness. Shadows grew, flitted, as ghostly drafts played with the flames of the oil lamps.

Her father was late returning from the docks, fortunately giving her more time to complete the ledger. Her shoulders ached from leaning over the large oak desk, and her eyes burned from frowning over columns of figures that stubbornly refused to balance.

She'd get wrinkles from frowning. Who had told her that? Celia or Abigail? Most likely it had been lighthearted Celia Hancock, now Mrs. Edward Clary, as Celia fretted about her looks.

Lacy smoothed nonexistent lines from her brow with ink-stained fingers. One column of numbers totaled. Pleased, she stretched to ease the taut muscles of her shoulders. The action pulled the brown-and-gold striped silk of her gown tight across her breasts, outlining their fullness and the natural slimness of her waist.

From the darkened doorway, Caleb fought the

quickening of desire in the pit of his stomach as he surveyed the girl at the desk. She was undoubtedly the most desirable woman he knew. Her soft, rounded body cried out for a man's caresses. He would be a fool not to want her. Perhaps if she were anyone but Lacy Phalen his conscience would have allowed him to seduce her, to be the first to teach her the wonderous ways of love.

Unaware that she was observed, Lacy rubbed her nose and bent once more to worry over the neatly etched figures in the book.

Lacy worked far too hard to prove her abilities, Caleb thought. She was alone in the warehouse, the hour growing later, time passing unnoticed as she studied the spidery handwriting that detailed the cargos of the Puritan ships. She should be dancing, drinking champagne, flirting with the men who vied for her attentions, enjoying life. Because he was fond of her, he hoped she would find a husband to cherish her. Would it be Harrison Kilmartin? The man had long been his rival for her affections.

Rival? Now why had he used that word? He had always known Lacy was not for him, that she belonged in another man's arms.

At the desk Lacy frowned as the second column of figures eluded the solution she sought. She chewed thoughtfully on the pen.

Caleb moved, quietly circling the desk, stalking her from the shadows. A fond smile played about his rugged face. There was a very pleasant traditional welcome to be played out yet, one they had reenacted after countless voyages. One he would certainly miss once she married.

Lacy sat back with a sigh of relief. At last the accounts balanced. She reached to replace the pen in its notch only to find a pair of strong arms enfolding her from behind. Startled, she knocked over the bottle of ink.

The arms quickly released her to save the ledger from disaster.

"Not a peep out of you did I hear, little puritan. Does that mean you have gotten in the habit of being embraced by strange men during my absence?" demanded a soft voice in her ear.

"Caleb!" she cried, and jumped from the chair, nearly upsetting it. "When did you get back? I didn't think you were expected yet! Does the captain know you're here? How was the voyage? Did all go well?"

Caleb righted the spilled ink bottle and dropped the ledger on the seat of the chair she had vacated. "Such a chatterbox she is," he said to the walls. "But never a word about me poor self. Do I hear, Caleb, how are you? Caleb, I've missed you?"

"Caleb," Lacy said belatedly, "I've missed you." She looked at his bronzed face, his teeth white and sparkling as he smiled. His black hair seemed almost blue in the light cast by the lamp. His shoulders seemed broader and more muscular than she had remembered. How could her memory have played her false? How could she have allowed another to take his place, even temporarily, in her affections?

"What? Can it be possible?" Caleb demanded. "The dear little puritan says she missed me and there is no one around to hear?"

She smiled provocatively at him. "Yes. And there really is no one else around, Caleb."

He needed no further urging and swept her into his arms. His kiss was as she remembered or perhaps it was a little more experienced.

"Faith," he declared when they parted, "you've not forgotten a thing I taught you, Lacy. Or have you been practicing on someone else while I was away?"

A warm flush colored her cheeks. "And I was about to ask you the very same thing, Caleb Innes," she countered on the defensive.

His smile was slow and teasing. "'Tis wicked you are, Lacy Phalen."

"Aye." She sighed, a twinkle in her deep-set emerald eyes. "'Tis a curse, I'm thinkin'."

Caleb cocked his head to one side. "Don't go giving me your father's blarney, my girl. Did you truly miss me?"

"Caleb Innes, are you calling me a liar?" She pulled out of his encircling arms. "I don't believe I heard you say you missed me! Now that you're in line for a ship of your own, I suppose there will be no talking to you." She moved out of his reach to the far side of the desk, her striped skirts swaying provocatively.

"Don't be hairbrained, Lacy. Of course I missed you," he lied.

She gave him a coquettish look across the wide expanse of wooden desk. "Sure and I'm far from knowin' it."

Caleb smiled fondly. Ever since they had been children, she had teased him with an imitation of her father's broque. He was always surprised how easily she fell into it all these years later. Her tone and the set of her pretty mouth reminded him of a saucy English barmaid in whose bed he had spent much of his shore leave in Liverpool.

Caleb started around the desk; his arm outstretched to catch her. Lacy dashed around the far end, carefully keeping the chair between them, enjoying the game.

"Sure and I'm far from provin' it at this rate," Caleb mimicked. "Stand still, you little vixen."

"No," she said stubbornly. "I've heard far too many tales of your other girls. I don't think I should believe a word you tell me, Caleb Innes."

"It's true, every word of it is true."

"Which of it is true? The part about your conquests or of your devotion to me?"

"Oh, the conquests, of course."

"Caleb!" She flew at him in mock anger.

He enclosed her tightly in his arms as she beat at his broad chest. He was still dressed in his Puritan Line uniform, his dark blue jacket hanging open, his black cravat loosened to hang down over the bleached white of his shirt front. "Caleb, how could you!"

He laughed. It was a hearty sound much like her father's chuckle.

Lacy kicked his shin and he released her as he clutched the tender spot. Lacy pushed him, sending him tumbling into a stack of empty crates in the corner.

"Let that be a lesson to you, Caleb Innes. Don't tamper with my affections," she retorted, her hands on her hips, the picture of indignation.

There was no reply from the reclining form. He didn't move at all.

"Caleb? Caleb, are you hurt? Caleb?" Anxious,

she knelt beside him. "Caleb, I'm sorry. I didn't mean for anything to happen to you." She touched his brow with her hand, smoothing back his tousled hair.

Caleb's hand gripped her wrist, and his other arm pulled her down on top of him.

"Caleb, of all the disreputable things you have ever done, this is the *worst*," Lacy declared, squirming in his arms.

"Stop wiggling."

"Why should I?"

"So I can kiss you, that's why." He sounded exasperated.

"Well, why didn't you say so? Welcome back home, Caleb." Gently, she leaned down to brush his lips but he forestalled her.

"Welcome back home, she says," he told the partially demolished shipping crates. "That sounds like a sisterly peck on the cheek."

Lacy narrowed her eyes. "Sisterly! Is that what you think of me?"

"Now did I say that I think of you as my sister, little temptress?"

"I'll show you sisterly," she declared, and pressed her lips to his.

Caleb's arms tightened around her but he did not move.

Lacy raised her head. "It wouldn't hurt you to cooperate, Mr. Innes."

Caleb smiled and he pulled her down, his lips parting hers, his tongue beginning a slow exploration of her mouth. Once again, Lacy felt the delicious sensations his kisses evoked. She could feel his heart pounding against her hand.

She pulled back from his kiss, gasping for breath. "Oh, Caleb, I *have* missed you."

He touched her cheek tenderly, his eyes glowing with aroused passion. Then suddenly, he scrambled to his feet, leaving her in a tangle of skirts on the floor.

"Sir, I was just looking for you to report the *Temptress* is back."

Sean Phalen's brow raised as he looked from the tousled form of his daughter on the floor to the young officer standing stiffly at attention above her. "So I can see." Phalen smiled. "We spotted you earlier today. I take it you have been welcomed back properly?"

Caleb flushed. "Yes, sir. Most properly."

Lacy pushed her golden curls from her eyes. The enjoyable tussle with Caleb had left her a prisoner of her twisted skirts, her cheeks flushed, and her hair tumbling from its careful knot. She looked pleased with herself and slightly mischievous. She lifted a hand toward Innes for help in rising.

The captain's grin widened as the young man hesitated. "Caleb, if you wouldn't mind assisting the lady, I would appreciate your service."

Lacy took Innes's hand and came swiftly to her feet. She caught her balance against his broad chest. Caleb's arm came around her for a fraction of a second before he released her.

"Was it a smooth trip?" the captain asked, eyeing the fresh ink stain on the desk top.

Caleb cleared his throat. "Aye, sir. The hold was quite full this trip. There were a number of passengers as well."

"Good, good," Sean answered, distracted. He

picked the ledger off the chair, looked at the damp surface of the desk, and dropped the book back on the chair.

Lacy perched on a packing case, her feet dangling a few inches off the floor. "I think we should invite Caleb home to dinner. Then we can discuss the *Temptress*'s voyage at leisure, Papa."

Her father's dark eyebrows rose in a silent question.

Belatedly, Lacy included Caleb's superior, Captain Carpenter, in the invitation. "It's far too late in the day to think about unloading the cargo. I'm sure the crew would by far prefer to be with their families."

The captain surveyed Caleb's disheveled appearance, then his daughter's. "Is that so? And just who is running things here?"

Lacy's eyes twinkled with suppressed laughter. "Just now, I am."

Sean chuckled. "It's up to you, Mr. Innes. If you prefer to dine with a woman with rumpled hair and an ink smear on her nose than with your mother and sisters, I welcome you at my table."

Caleb carefully kept his gaze on his superior. "Thank you, Captain. I'll accept your kind offer. Mother will understand."

Undeceived by the young man's serious demeanor, the captain winked at his daughter. "Then if you will see to Lacy, I'll see to a carriage," he said, and tapped Lacy on her nose before ambling out of the small office.

Lacy scowled, her eyes crossing as she tried to locate the offending spot. "Is there really ink on my nose?" she demanded.

"Yes," he answered. Then hearing the outer door shut behind Captain Phalen, he kissed the black smear. "But you are the only woman of my acquaintance who still looks beautiful in such a state."

Her eyes twinkled at him, as her hands slid to his shoulders. "Well, if it's up to me, Caleb Innes, you will be made captain in no time at all. Especially if you keep showering me with compliments like that." Lacy paused and tilted her chin, considering him. "Or do you shower all your conquests with the same honeyed words?"

Caleb noted the game was rejoined. "Faith," he cried to the empty room, "will the woman never be satisfied?"

Lacy smiled sideways at him. "Sure and wouldn't you be wantin' ta know that, Caleb Innes?"

Caleb looked as if he was strongly tempted to turn her over his knee. "Lacy Phalen, you are enough to try a man's patience."

She sighed. "Aye. So the captain says. Will you be agreein' with him, then?"

For an answer, Caleb pulled her back into his arms.

Ben Paradise stared out past rain-spattered windowpanes at the tranquil countryside. He stood hunched over in the confining area, his hands braced against the low sloping ceiling. Dark stubble shadowed his clenched jaw, and brown hair ruffled forward over his troubled indigo eyes.

It was time he went home, he thought as the sinews of his naked back flexed in irritation. Unrelieved civilization made him itch for the untamed beauty of the mountains, for vistas that denied a man the comfort of seeing the smoke of his neighbor's cook fire curling lazily into the brilliant blue sky.

Or was it just that the spell of bad weather that had dogged his footsteps since leaving Boston depressed him? He didn't want the total isolation he'd known as a trapper. He wanted to settle among people who were his own kind, people he knew, and to return to the town his parents had founded. A return to simple pleasures like toasting his feet on Charlie Delaney's stove at the general store this winter. Or fishing and hunting in the rich forests of the Ozarks, for pleasure now rather than out of necessity. Then, at the end of the day, he'd have the comfort of the saloon and the girls in the upper rooms.

A soft mewing drew his attention to the tangle of sheets on the bed as the woman turned in her sleep, one slender arm outflung as if searching for him. The sight of pale yellow tresses spread over the pillows suddenly repulsed him. Not that the girl wasn't comely. He had found her so the evening before. She'd been energetic, imaginative in bed. Yet she had been unable to satisfy the strange yearning that possessed him of late.

Weary, he turned back to the window no longer seeing the neat hedges or rain-splattered puddles in the yard below.

He was an ass to tarry in the East any longer. The girl in the bed brought home that realization with crushing clarity. He'd rarely taken a woman just because she was available and willing. A gleam of avarice in a flashing eye dampened his enthusiasm for a tussle in the sheets. Yet the woman in the bed had brightened visibly at the color of his money and she hadn't minded, or perhaps even heard, when he called her by another woman's name. A slip of the tongue of which even he had not been cognizant until he'd heard his own voice murmur it.

Mentally he caressed the name again.

Lacy.

Yes, it was past time to return home. If he lingered longer, he'd find himself back in Boston, back on the doorstep of the narrow three-story red brick house, prepared to resign his freedom. Perhaps if she was willing to relinquish the Line . . . No, just in the short time he'd spent in her company, he realized the Puritan Shipping Line was Lacy's life. He was the one who rebelled at the bounds a desk at the warehouse entailed. He preferred a fast and chance-ridden future at a card table, forced to live by his wits rather than by inflexible schedules. He missed the feel of his Colt strapped to his thigh, the flow of cards through his fingers.

He should have left weeks ago, should never have dallied. If he caught the first train, or if necessary, the stage, for Pittsburgh, he'd be down the Ohio halfway to Missouri in a week's time.

CHAPTER III

The winds had been steady for two days when Sean Phalen surrendered to the temptation to put to sea. It would only be a short voyage, to New York and back, he had insisted to Lacy. Just long enough to acquaint the crew with the *Puritan Paramour*'s caprices.

Lacy stood at the docks, watching the clipper's sails fade from sight. She was disconcerted that her father had remained inflexible in his decision to place her in Abigail Phalen's care during his absence. The captain's pronouncement rang a death knell in Lacy's ears. She and Abigail had never been comfortable together. The older woman's ideals were confining and old-fashioned, a direct contrast to Lacy's upbringing. Thrown into such close proximity, a battle of wills was inevitable.

Both women tolerated the social necessity of being seen together, and they spoke to each other only when conversation could not be avoided. Then their voices were stilted and polite. In the narrow quarters of her cousin's home, Lacy strove to avoid her hostess. She spent long hours at the warehouse, determined to merit the trust her father had placed in her abilities.

The captain had left Lacy and Harry in joint control of the Line during his absence. It would be a shakedown cruise for the cousins as well as for the *Paramour*, he'd explained. Soon he would sail for China, a voyage he planned to expand to two years in an effort to set up Puritan offices in the Far East. The two young Phalens would be left in complete control during his voyage.

The arrival of the *Puritan Belle* prior to the captain's departure insured the Line offices hummed with activity. The *Belle*'s skipper, Owen Ransom, was the only Puritan officer Lacy had not been able to influence with her wiles. He was a hard man who disliked women. His bull-like voice issued forth from a short-necked, stocky body. His thinning hair was metallic in color, his eyes red-rimmed and small in his jowled face. He had a weakness for good food and the Good Book. His strict sense of religion made him unpopular with his crew, for he limited their activities in port. But in Sean Phalen's opinion, Ransom was the best sea captain ever to pilot a Puritan ship. He trusted Ransom and ordered his daughter in particular to take Ransom's advice to heart when it was given.

Although the crew of the *Puritan Temptress* was equipping to sail with the tide two weeks hence,

Lacy rarely saw Caleb. She was busy keeping account of the merchandise from the *Belle* as it was purchased by local businessmen. This was her chance to prove to both her father and Harry that she was a capable working member of the Puritan Line despite her gender. The added incentive of not wishing to return to Abigail Phalen's home until absolutely necessary goaded Lacy to working longer hours.

Owen Ransom found her bent over the books long after everyone else, including her cousin, had departed.

Despite his bulk, Ransom moved with the lightness of a cat. He stared in disgust at the slight frame of the girl at the desk. It offended his sensibilities that Phalen allowed his daughter a free hand in the daily workings of the Puritan Line. Although he had never found fault with her work, Ransom felt Lacy Phalen would do well to learn more feminine pastimes than how to balance a ledger. He moved toward the dimly lit office, a scowl on his face.

"It is time you went home, Miss Phalen."

Lacy started at the harsh order. She blinked at the shadowy form in the office doorway, relaxing when she recognized the speaker. "Oh, Captain Ransom, I thought everyone had gone."

"I doubt your father expected you to be this devoted to the Line." His tone was insulting. Ransom moved his bulk just inside the door. Light reflected off the polished buttons of his waistcoat. His face was in shadow. "It is time you returned to your cousin's house, Miss Phalen."

Used to getting her way with men, Lacy was not disturbed by his gruff orders. She nodded in brief acknowledgment and pushed back the books. "Yes, I suppose you are right, sir. I just want to do a good job while my father is gone." She stretched to ease the stiffness in her shoulders and stifled a yawn. She apologized to the heavy-set man for her shocking lack of manners, but he waved it aside.

"I'll see that you are escorted, Miss Phalen."

She knew it was useless to argue with him. Ransom didn't believe women were people. The way he treated her in particular had always made Lacy think he associated her actions with those of a freak in a circus side show.

Lacy stood and reached for the cloak she had tossed on a crate earlier. "There really is no need for anyone to see me home, Captain. Mrs. Phalen sends a carriage for me. I suppose I've kept the driver waiting quite some time now. I'll be perfectly all right in his care."

"Nevertheless, you will be escorted home," Ransom said.

Lacy's chin came up, determined that he shouldn't push her needlessly. "Captain . . ."

Ransom paid her no heed. "Innes!" His voice boomed out over the stacks of packing cases, echoing faintly in the recesses of the warehouse.

Lacy relaxed as Caleb's muscular form stepped from the shadows. He held himself smartly at attention. "Yes, sir."

In the shadows, Ransom's face was expressionless. "Mr. Innes, you will accompany Miss Phalen in her carriage before you return home. I hold you accountable for her safety."

56

Caleb's answer was quiet in the still, barn-like atmosphere. "Yes, sir. You can trust me to see to Miss Phalen's welfare, Captain."

Irritation flickered briefly on the man's features. "I'm sure I can, Innes. Fortunately, Miss Phalen, you are not the only one trying to prove something with your late hours."

If Caleb noted the implied slur, he ignored it. He placed Lacy's cloak around her shoulders.

"Thank you, Captain," Lacy said. "You can be sure I will tell my father of your concern for my welfare." Her voice was brittle but Ransom did not seem to notice. His enormous shoulders hunched in what might have been a shrug of indifference.

"Good night, Miss Phalen." He moved off, dismissing the couple.

As she climbed inside the worn interior of Abigail's hired coach, Lacy's next yawn was impossible to hide. She leaned back in the seat, her head against the tufted upholstery. "Oh, I am sorry, Caleb. I guess I am more tired than I thought. There really is no need for you to come with me. I'm perfectly safe with Knapp."

Knapp was the usual coachman sent from the livery stable. A silent man, he was usually muffled to the eyes in a long woolen scarf no matter what the weather. Lacy had never heard him utter two words other than to his horses. All she received was a nod in greeting. Still, she trusted him completely.

Caleb brushed aside her protests. "I have my orders, Lacy." He climbed in and slammed the door closed. Knapp called to his horses. The carriage lurched forward, throwing Lacy against

Caleb. He gathered her close to nestle in his arms. "Here, this is far more comfortable, isn't it? I never thought I'd thank old Ransom for stopping me tonight. But damn if I'm not glad he did."

Her head rested trustingly against his shoulder. His arm around her offered an added warmth against the damp chill that invaded the carriage. Lacy sighed and let her hand stray to rest against his chest. The rocking motion of the carriage was very soothing. She yawned again and snuggled closer to him.

"Mmm, I'm glad he did, too. This is far nicer than riding alone. But I hardly think Abigail will approve."

"We'll cross that bridge when we come to it," he assured her as his lips brushed her hair.

Lacy dozed, unaware of the silent battle that raged within her companion. The faint scent of lavender rose from her soft hair to befuddle his senses. The intimate feel of her warm body curving so naturally into his as she slept made it difficult to remember who she was, and that she was untouchable as far as he was concerned. He was more than willing to sample the delights of her wet, eager mouth and of stolen embraces. He could hardly believe that Lacy was oblivious to the temptation she presented. At times he could almost swear she was set on seducing him.

Caleb breathed a sigh of relief when the carriage stopped, and he gently shook her awake. "You're home, little puritan. Much as I hate to leave, I'm afraid your cousin would frown upon my continuing to act as your pillow."

Lacy sat up, loath to leave the comfort of his arms. "Oh, I am sorry, Caleb. Did I fall asleep?"

"Ransom's right, Lacy. You are working too hard. Things are running smoothly at the warehouse. You don't have to oversee every shipment personally." He opened the door and climbed out of the coach.

Ignoring the carriage step, Lacy leaned out, going into his arms. "You know how much the Line means to me, Caleb. I want to prove to Papa that I can do just as good a job as any man."

Caleb lifted her down, his hands tight around her slender waist. "If Captain Phalen didn't think you could handle it, he wouldn't have entrusted you with the job while he is gone, Lacy," he insisted as her feet touched the ground. "You don't have to prove anything to him."

Her hands were still on his shoulders, and his remained on her waist. She looked up at his shadowed face. "Yes, I do. Even Papa doesn't think my interest in the Line is . . . well, feminine."

The glow of the gas street lamp highlighted her upturned nose, the soft curve of her cheek, luring Caleb. She was so innocent, so beautiful. With a will of their own, his arms enfolded her, one hand sliding slowly up her back, drawing her close. His other hand came up to caress her face, his fingers tilting the determined set of her chin until his lips met hers. "Nothing you do would ever be unfeminine, little puritan."

On the driver's box, Knapp cleared his throat. Reluctantly, Lacy slid from Caleb's embrace. "Knapp, you will return Mr. Innes to his home

59

before going back to the stable, won't you?"

The man nodded, his face almost disappearing within his muffler.

She walked up the path to the front door, the wind whipping her cloak, plastering it to her back. Caleb's boots sounded loud and echoing behind her.

"Perhaps I should escort you home every evening, little puritan. Since it has old Ransom's sanction, no one would look askance."

"No one but Abigail." Lacy sighed. "There really is no reason for you to go so far out of your way, Caleb. I'm perfectly safe with Knapp, you know."

Caleb's hand shot out, catching her wrist as she reached for the door knocker. "There's a perfectly good reason why I should continue to see you home."

"There is?"

"There is." His voice held the hint of mischief that she remembered so well from their childhood escapades. But the gleam in his eye was one she had discovered only since his ship had returned from its last voyage. When his arms gathered her close, Lacy entwined her fingers behind his neck and lifted her lips to his.

She pressed closer to Caleb, enjoying the hardness of his body against hers, knowing his exploration could go no further than a kiss on Abigail's doorstep yet letting him know that she would welcome further attentions were the circumstances different.

Their kiss had barely begun when the door opened and Abigail pulled Lacy from the young officer's arms and into the hall. Stunned, the young woman shrugged off Abigail's restraining hand. She turned again to Caleb only to find an expression of cold, calculated fury on Abigail's angular face as she closed the door firmly in his face.

"How dare you!" Abigail hissed.

Lacy shook the cloak from her shoulders and dropped it over a straight-backed bench in the entrance hall. "I'm afraid I don't understand you, Abigail."

Abigail's claw-like fingers closed over Lacy's arm, forcing her into Harry Phalen's study. "How dare you use business as an excuse to carry on your affairs and then have the audacity to bring your lovers to my door! I've warned your father where your wild ways would lead," Abigail raged.

Lacy stared at her cousin's wife. "I worked late over the books as Harry often does, I believe," she stated coldly. "Captain Ransom ordered Mr. Innes to escort me home."

Abigail's voice was heavy with sarcasm. "And did Owen Ransom also order Mr. Innes to kiss you? *On my doorstep?* I imagine further improprieties were invited in the carriage!"

Lacy's silk skirts whispered ominously over the carpet as she glided to Harry's desk and lit a lamp. As the wick flared, she could see the other woman's face, its sharply defined planes ghastly in the half-light. She turned the flame up to bathe the room in light.

"Nothing went on in the carriage, Abigail. I was tired. I fell asleep on Caleb's shoulder."

Abigail was in no mood for appeasement. "And what excuse do you have for your behavior on the doorstep?"

"Excuse?" Lacy settled herself in Harry's large chair behind the desk. She met Abigail's fury, her eyes innocent. "Do I need one? I'm sure other women kiss their suitors. If you had had more than one, even you might have been tempted, Abigail."

The older woman's fingers turned white as they gripped the top rung of the ladder-backed chair opposite the desk.

"No," Lacy cooed, confident that she held the upper hand. "You would never have been tempted to kiss a man, would you, Abigail?" She shifted in the chair, leaning on the arm, clearly at ease. She straightened the pen wipe, heedless of Abigail's venomous glare. "I've never ceased to be amazed that you presented Harry with a son. I wonder how that could have happened? Did he have to get you intoxicated?" Lacy paused long enough to pave the way for the next insult. "Or did you allow *him* to get drunk?"

Abigail's body stiffened. Yet when she spoke her voice was crisp and controlled. "You will regret those words one day, Lillian."

Lacy's eyes flashed at the use of her given name. Only Abigail ever used it, her tone implying admonishment of a school child.

"Really?" Lacy forced her voice to sound politely bored. "Much as I would like to chat with you, Abigail, I have had a tiring day. I don't suppose you waited dinner for me. But do you suppose your kitchen could supply me with a light meal? I'll send my maid, Becky, down for it."

Lacy waited, the challenge hanging between them. Abigail's lips were rigid, not in fury, but in misguided righteousness.

Although, in Lacy's experience, Abigail Quire Phalen had never been a woman who turned the other cheek, her refusal to engage in verbal combat did not disturb Lacy. The sweet, unexpectedly short verbal skirmish and resulting triumph over her detested chaperone blinded Lacy to the inconsistency of Abigail's behavior.

Regally, Lacy nodded to her adversary as she rose from Harry's chair and swept out of the room past the strangely silent woman.

Celia Hancock Clary surveyed her friend's thoughtful face with satisfaction. "You finally did it, didn't you, Lacy! You finally got Mr. Innes to ask for your hand. Oh, I'm so happy for you! He's perfect for you! I told you that our first season."

Lacy waited patiently for Celia's enthusiasm to subside. The weeks had crawled by while her father and his crew had taken the *Paramour* to New York harbor and back. After the episode with Abigail, Lacy had spent as many hours as possible with her newly married friend. It was only natural that the glowingly happy Celia would decide that matchmaking was a worthy occupation.

"No, you didn't," Lacy corrected her when her companion paused for breath. "You thought I should engage Mr. Latimer's interest the year we were presented. You, if I remember correctly, languished over Jason Cook."

"I never languished," Celia insisted. "Don't change the subject. Did Mr. Innes propose last night?"

Lacy glanced briefly toward the store fronts their open carriage passed before facing young Mrs. Clary. "Actually, no, he didn't." There were times when she wondered if she were really trying to secure a proposal from Caleb. Moments when a certain woodsy scent, a particular song, or even the feel of her ivory gown swaying as she waltzed, brought back memories of a different man's face. Then she would recall much too clearly a pair of laughing blue eyes and a man who had taunted her with a reckless air of danger. She wondered where Ben Paradise was and if he ever thought of her.

Lacy pushed the thought away. Caleb was the man with whom she wanted to spend the rest of her life. She would be his helpmate, making a home for him aboard one of the many Puritan ships. Together, they would sail the world, filling the holds of their vessel with marvelous trinkets for the New England marketplace. And she would finally have her dearest wish—second, of course, to a life with Caleb—of going to sea.

Celia's shining brown sausage curls bounced at the sides of her heart-shaped face. Her rosebud lips pursed in irritation. Her China-doll blue eyes narrowed. "That man is exasperating. Did you do as I suggested? It worked wonders on Edward."

Lacy's lips curved in amusement. There was no stopping Celia's campaign. She wondered what her friend's reaction would be if she confessed to dreams of a different man. "Yes, I did everything you told me. Short of asking Caleb to marry me, I

have made it very clear that I would accept him."
And when Caleb proposed, she would accept him.
It was a logical decision. They had so much in
common: a love of the sea; the Puritan Line; their
memories. Caleb would fit into her plans. When
she thought of Ben Paradise, she knew he would
always be an alien in her world. She would stop
thinking of him. Surely it was that simple.

Based on her firm belief that all contact between
men and women could be staged as if life were one
large-scale game of chess, Celia put a gloved hand
to her mouth as she considered the next move.
"Mmm. You've seen Mr. Innes daily, haven't you?"

Lacy nodded. "Yes. Either at the warehouse or
in the evenings at various entertainments."

Celia's dark curls moved in acceptance of the
campaign. "You've invited his sister, Jessica, to
attend with you, too. He ought to realize you are
trying to get to know his family." She leaned back
once more against the plush cushions of the carriage, and retilted her parasol to protect her fair
skin from the sun. "I dare say I wouldn't have gone
that far myself. Actually, I can't *bear* Edward's
sister."

"I like Jessie," Lacy said. "The truth is, I could
not *bear* to be in Abigail's company anymore.
Jessie was a buffer."

Celia practiced her pout. "I don't see why you
couldn't have stayed with Edward and me while
the *Paramour* was gone. I'm sure I could have
coaxed a proposal from Mr. Innes for you." She
brightened as a possibility occurred to her. "Perhaps he's just waiting for the captain to return."

Lacy shook her head, sorry to disappoint her

determined friend. "Papa's been back from New York a week now."

Celia considered her mental playing board, concocting a new strategy. "Will you be at the Cooks' musical this evening?"

Lacy nodded.

"Then wear your watered silk. Didn't Mr. Innes liken you to a mermaid the last time you wore it?"

"The compliment was from Harrison," Lacy amended. "You're sure the turquoise color is right?"

Having reviewed her players, Celia grinned. The dimple in her cheek made her look more like an impish child than a matrimonial general. "It should bring him to his knees," she promised.

Caleb was surprised to receive orders to report to Captain Phalen's office two days before the *Temptress* was due to sail. Vaguely, he wondered if Lacy requested that he escort her to the Cook home. Close attendance to her desires of late was wearing at his resolve. Yet in his mind his decision to see her wed to another held.

There was a quiet dignity about the captain's office. Sparely decorated, it was reminiscent of a ship's cabin. A large desk sat in the center of the room, and at one side was a cabinet that contained various decanters and crystal. Two large, comfortable armchairs faced the desk and were duplicated in the captain's own chair.

Sean glanced up from the papers in his hand to the handsome young officer at attention before his desk. "Take a seat, Innes. Help yourself to some whiskey. You might need it for this interview."

A twinge of unease settled in the young man's stomach at the offer. He refused politely and sat down, steeling himself for the captain's next statement.

Phalen set the sheets in a neat pile on his desk. "These," he said softly, "are complaints against you, Caleb."

The fact that the captain used his first name rang warning bells in Caleb's mind. "Complaints, sir? Concerning my abilities with the ship or crew?"

"On your moral conduct, lad."

Caleb paled beneath his tan. "In what way, sir?"

Sean's hand waved over the pages. "Trumped up charges, Caleb. Yet they come from enough sources that I must deal with them."

The first mate straightened in his chair. "If it will make it easier, sir, I'll resign my post rather than cause the Line an injury."

"Commendable but foolish, lad." Sean stroked his beard. The allegations referred to a young woman being led astray. Only an imbecile would fail to recognize Lacy in the complaint. Perhaps he should have insisted she learn the spiritless constraints of society, demand she forego the freedom he had always allowed her. Had he failed her as a father and as a result ruined her reputation? Phalen sat forward, piercing the young man across the desk with a glance. "You can tell me what your intentions are toward my daughter, lad. Do you plan to wed her?"

Caleb was far from easy at the change of subject. It could only mean Lacy was involved in the charges. "Lacy's a wonderful young woman, Captain—"

"Do ye love the colleen, Caleb?"

Innes considered his statement. "Aye, I do," he said softly. "Very much, sir."

Phalen relaxed. "Then the solution is for a quiet wedding, lad. I knew you were fond of my little hoyden—"

"I am," Caleb interrupted. "That's why I can never do as you ask, sir. I couldn't bear to hurt her."

The captain's intense look bore into the young man a moment before Phalen nodded in acceptance. He played with an edge of the top paper on his stack. "You know she's set her mind on marrying you, lad," he said quietly. "You'll break her heart."

Caleb's back was rigid as he forced himself to meet the captain's eyes. "Far better to do so once, sir, than repeatedly."

"I doubt she'll agree."

Caleb swallowed. His hands were damp, his throat dry. The starched fabric of his collar seemed too tight, cutting into his skin. Did his whole career hang on his answer?

"What do you intend to do about the complaints, Captain?" Caleb's voice was a strained croak.

Phalen stood and moved to the liquor cabinet. He poured two fingers of whiskey into a glass and handed it to Innes before fixing a second for himself. The lad needed the drink now. Yet he was pleased when Caleb accepted it absentmindedly, his thoughts obviously on what came next.

Sean took a swig of his drink. He hoped the fiery taste would help him through the next step. "I'll not lose a good officer over the gossip of a bunch of biddies, Caleb. I would prefer to remove you from their wagging tongues, however, for Lacy's sake." He allowed the whiskey another chance to bolster his decision. Logic had failed to convince him it was the right move.

"Are you willing to accept a transfer to the Liverpool office?" Sean asked.

Caleb's glass halted halfway to his lips. Submitting to reassignment meant confinement to land, losing the freedom of the sea. As ridiculous as it sounded, marrying the girl he loved would be a greater disaster. Caleb knew it in his bones, had realized it as an unchangeable fact every time he put to sea and consigned her to a back compartment of his mind. Knew it was not meant to be when he put into a port and succumbed to the lure of a plump breast or knowing smile.

He could resign his commission with the Puritan Line, could move into a similar position with one of Phalen's competitors.

Caleb closed his eyes as his hand tightened around the glass in his hand. His father had been one of Sean Phalen's earliest recruits. The captain had given Caleb's father a ship of his own and, when the elder Innes had been lost at sea, Phalen had insured that the man's family was taken care of out of his own pocket. No, leaving the Puritan Line was no answer. Caleb owed Phalen too much. He would have to accept the transfer to Liverpool. What other option was there?

"T'will be temporary only, lad. I know how you feel." Sean could see the pain in the boy's face. No, he corrected himself. Caleb had proven he was a man, a man worthy of trust in refusing Lacy's hand. It would have been the easiest solution, yet Innes had shown he was a man of principles, a man who cared for Lacy's welfare and future happiness.

Caleb finished his whiskey in one gulp. His broad shoulders squared beneath the deep blue wool of his uniform. "It's for the best, sir. Yes, I'll accept the post. I expect it is effective immediately?"

Sean sighed softly, relieved that he wouldn't lose Caleb entirely. He wouldn't have blamed the young man if he had refused, if he had resigned. "Aye," he answered sadly. "Ye'll sail as a passenger this trip, lad. Sweeney'll assume first mate."

The demotion was official. There was no turning back, even if he wished to do so. Slowly, Caleb stood and placed his empty tumbler on the captain's desk. At the door he paused, his hand on the knob. "Does Lacy know?"

Phalen looked down at the nearly empty glass in his hand. "No."

"I'd like to tell her, sir. In my own way."

Sean raised his whiskey in a salute to the young man. "I wish ye well, Caleb. Don't see this as a sentence."

His hand still on the door handle, Caleb turned. "Isn't it, sir?"

Sean hated to see the pain in Caleb's eyes. He knew that pain. Hadn't he told himself it was best to stay landlocked while Lacy grew to adulthood? Hadn't he been chafing to return to the helm of his own ship for too many long years already? To sentence another man to the same existence. . . .

"Aye, lad," he agreed quietly. "That it is and I'm that sorry about it."

The door closed softly behind the former first officer. Sean listened to his footsteps echo through the warehouse.

Caleb's smile was strained when he claimed the chair next to Lacy's at the Cook home later that evening. The soft gaslight gave her skin a luminescent glow. In the shadows her hair was nearly a reflection of silver moonlight. The deep turquoise color of her gown turned her eyes to a sealike intensity that he found disturbing, considering the afternoon's events. He smiled at her sadly, the glint of humor no longer present in his golden brown eyes.

Caleb stared down into Lacy's face wistfully and with a touch of sadness. "Would you mind taking a turn in the garden?"

She agreed eagerly, her mind on Celia's instructions. "Of course, Caleb. I'd adore it."

His reserve unsettled her. Caleb had always been so buoyant. Was Celia right? Lacy wondered: Could Caleb merely be nervous about proposing to her? It would explain his preoccupied expression.

Caleb led her far from the house, along twisting paths where tall hedges hid them from view. When he stopped, they were in shadow. He turned, taking her slender hands in his.

Lacy's eyes were dark emeralds shimmering with excitement as she anticipated hearing her heart's desire from his lips.

Caleb didn't see the girl before him. Nightmare images of ships sailing away, abandoning him, filled his mind. He had spent the remainder of the day at the docks staring out to sea, watching the ships dance gracefully among the gentle waves as they lay at anchor. It would be hell watching the *Temptress* pull out to sea without him, stranding him in a foreign country far from the family he had taken for granted. Tomorrow would be spent packing, gathering his belongings from the cabin that would now belong to Sweeney, enduring the tearful farewells from his sisters and mother. Tonight he had a more difficult task ahead of him.

"Lacy," he said without preamble, "I'm leaving soon. I've accepted a transfer to the Liverpool office."

She stared, her eyes wide in shock. "Leaving?" Her voice was a disbelieving whisper. "But *why*, Caleb?"

He smiled thinly, pretending he looked forward to exile. "Everything gets me closer to commanding a ship of my own, little puritan. If I do an A-number-one job, perhaps I'll even get the *Paramour*. Wouldn't that . . . Lacy, are you listening to me?"

She had turned away, pulling her hands from his in her agitation. "Yes, I heard you. I just don't believe it," she murmured.

Caleb took a deep breath, hardening his resolve. "Believe it, Lacy. It's for the best," he said, his voice harsh.

She whirled, her eyes swimming with unshed tears. "For the best, Caleb? For whom? Not for you. I won't accept it. I'll make Papa change his mind. You don't have to know shore procedures to captain a ship. I can run that side of the Line." She paused and moved closer to him, her love apparent in her upturned face. "For you, Caleb. It could all be yours."

God, it was worse than he'd anticipated. "Lacy, don't," he pleaded. "I know what you want of me but I can't offer you a future."

"Not the future, but today, the present, Caleb. You could outfit your own ship with my dowry."

He gripped her upper arms painfully. "No. Do you hear me, Lacy? It is my decision to take the Liverpool post. No other offer can sway that decision. I want to go."

Hurt surfaced in her eyes, skimming across the trembling waters of green. How could she make it any clearer that she loved him, that she wanted to spend her life with him? "Then take me with you," she whispered. Her arms encircled his waist and she pressed against his stiff body. "Take me with you, love. If not as wife, as mistress."

Brutally, he set her aside. His once caressing eyes burned with fury. "As a mistress! My God, Lillian Phalen, have you sunk so low that you have to proposition a man? You, the belle of Boston. The untouchable! Damn it, Lacy, look at yourself. Any number of men grovel at your feet. Find one you can love and marry him."

"I thought I had, Caleb."

His fingers bit into her shoulders, hardening himself to resist the betrayal in her voice. "Lacy," he said, weary, "I'm not the man for you."

Her chin rose. "I can't accept that, Caleb. I've never wanted anyone but you. Surely you knew that."

He denied the knowledge. "If I had, little puritan, I would have transferred away from you long ago."

"Am I not comely enough, Caleb?" she demanded, desperate. "Do my kisses repulse you so?" She lifted wanton, parted lips to his.

He stood his ground, fighting the urge to sweep her into his arms, to love her as she asked.

"Come, Caleb," she urged. "Teach me more that I might enthrall, nay, enslave a husband."

Vaguely, he realized that anger was a cleansing emotion. She was not scarred by his rejection. Yet the words she spat were guaranteed to rile him, insult his manhood by dangling the temptation of her perfect and willing body before him.

A hard light glinted in his brown eyes. The gleam unnerved Lacy so that she faltered a moment. Caleb, her gentle loving Caleb, was a stranger.

"No man would attempt to tutor you, my lovely little puritan," he snarled, drawing her now resisting form into his arms. "Taming. Now, that is another matter. Would tenderness avail, I wonder?" His lips caressed hers softly. He could feel her melting against him and pulled back. "Or will brutality serve the purpose far better?" Again he kissed her, this time his mouth ravaging hers, tearing her breath away.

When he released her, gasping sobs tore from Lacy's throat. "Please, Caleb. Don't do this," she pleaded, beaten. "I love you."

His anger was spent as quickly as it flared. "I'm sorry, Lacy. It's because I care for you that I must let you go. I'm not worthy . . ."

"Don't degrade yourself," she said, trying to laugh but the sound stuck in her throat. "Let one of us emerge with a modicum of dignity. I've never been rejected before. It's a new experience.''

He was tired. The interview, his farewell, was draining his will power. "Don't take it like that, Lacy. Blame me, not yourself.''

Her smile was twisted. "I was the only one blind, wasn't I?" she asked, blinking back tears. Her jaw had squared and lifted as she gathered her pride to buffer the hurt. "If William knew, he'd be puffed up with self-conceit," she said. "Do you know he told me you didn't want me weeks ago? I just refused to believe him.''

It gnawed at Caleb to witness her self-castigation. Yet if he relented, she would foolishly wait for his return, one that could only bring them both more pain.

His hand stroked her now tumbling hair. Part of his memory of her would be of these white-gold tresses spilling in gamine disarray, of her green eyes luring him from beneath lush dark lashes, of her tempting parted lips.

Perhaps one day he would find a woman very like Lacy to entice him from the arms of Neptune's daughter. Either that or he would go eagerly to his death beneath the verdant waves likening the waters to Lacy's eyes as he sank peacefully.

"I must go, Lacy," he whispered against her hair.

Her arms tightened around him. "Will I see you before you leave?" she asked, the tightness in her voice hurting him.

"No, little puritan. This is good-bye."

"A temporary one? You won't be in Liverpool forever?"

He shook his head. He knew he would not return until she was safely wed and with a child in a cradle to bind her to her husband.

"Promise me you'll be happy?" he asked foolishly.

"No," she said then smiled up at him. "I will promise you command of the *Paramour* though."

He grinned at the rash promise. "I doubt the captain will relinquish his clipper for many years, little puritan."

"She's our fastest ship. And she will be yours," she avowed, determined, serious. "Will you write to me?"

"I'm not much of a correspondent." Letters would not make the break he wished to accomplish. No, he would not write. He would search his mother's letters for news of Lacy, devouring every tidbit, savoring her successes as if they were his. Funny. He'd never have pictured himself as a martyr and here he was sacrificing his own happiness to insure hers.

Moonlight reflected in her eyes, outlined every detail of her oval face, highlighted the full parted lips that whispered his name. Her arms stole around his neck, and Caleb could find no reason to resist her any longer. His lips crushed hers, memorizing the feel of her, the taste of her mouth. "Good-bye, Lacy," he whispered against her lips. Gently, he removed her hands from their locked position at his nape.

"Caleb . . ." she cried.

He held her hands to his chest a moment. "Be happy, Lacy. For me." He walked quickly away, back to the house and, he hoped, out of her life.

Even from his place at the rail of the *Puritan Temptress* two days later, he could see her forlorn figure standing in the tiny lookout station on the roof of the Puritan Warehouse watching him sail away. He knew she would be there long after the full sails were out of sight. Just as he would stand at this rail, staring back toward the harbor.

The days lengthened as spring gave way to the glories of summer. The Boston Common was a deep, lush green despite the rising temperature. But health conditions in the city worsened. It was a problem shared by every busy metropolitan area. And as in other cities, the upper echelons of society began packing their households for removal to the cleaner, cooler environment of the country or untrafficked seaside locales.

Daily the Phalen household was visited by acquaintances who gushed about the inconvenience of these seasonal moves. Then the guests would say their farewells and bid Lacy to write, telling them of all they missed by leaving the city.

It wasn't merely friends and acquaintances who readied to leave. Sean Phalen was overseeing the final loading of the *Puritan Paramour*. Staying busy with the ship kept his mind from his daughter's failing health for a few hours each day.

The *Temptress* had been gone a month and, still, Lacy had not recovered from the depression Innes's departure had evoked. He had delayed his own sailing, hoping to see her spirits revive, to see a return to her usually healthy appetite and the disappearance of the dark circles that hollowed her eyes.

Would he ever know if he had done both young people a disservice in separating them? It was all very well to remind himself that Caleb had rejected his daughter's hand. He'd seen the young man's face the day he left. It was the face of a man being torn from something he held dear and precious. The same look he himself had worn during Amelia's illness and after her death.

The captain couldn't continue to place Lacy before the Line, as much as he wished to do so. The expense of the clipper alone made contracts with the Far East imperative. The longer he delayed, the less his chances of securing contracts for a packet to Hong Kong became.

Harry would watch over the colleen, Sean told himself. Time would heal her heart. Perhaps Lacy would find a man to cherish during his absence. Sean prayed nightly that she would. He had given Harry the details of Lacy's dowry in the event that she chose to marry before his return. He could trust Lacy's judgment in choosing a husband.

He should stop fretting where Lacy was concerned. The girl was a survivor. She was spiritless today but tomorrow she would be arguing fiercely over a contract for the Line or over a particular frock her chaperone felt was improper.

Sean's conscience was almost at rest when he and Lacy joined Harry and Abigail for a farewell dinner at their home. He was a bit surprised that William Quire was also a guest. It wasn't that he had anything against the man. Phalen hardly knew him. Although he was the dour Abigail's brother, Quire seemed a pleasant enough fellow.

The captain welcomed the determined bonhomie that Quire exuded at the otherwise dismal dinner. "A toast to the success of your voyage, Captain," William proposed as Abigail led a morose Lacy to the parlor, leaving the three men alone with their brandy.

Sean idly filled his pipe. "Thank you, Quire. I'm sure it will be a success. If I didn't have Lacy to worry about, I'd go with an easier heart, of course."

"I quite understand your dilemma," Quire murmured with a sad shake of his head. "It is a difficult decision to make for a man with a business as widespread as yours."

Quire's attitude didn't reflect well on his brother-in-law, who would be left in joint control of the Puritan Warehouse with Lacy, Sean thought. He nodded politely and drew on his pipe. The fragrant cherry-scented tobacco was soothing.

"A change of scene may keep the colleen from being maudlin because of my absence," Phalen said. He turned to his nephew. The man was a pale reflection of Sean's older brother. Mick had been so vital. Harry was a quiet, reserved man by comparison. Sean thought Harry had shown more interest in his glass than his dinner. He drew on his pipe, glad that the tobacco chased the last memories of the tasteless meal away. He didn't blame Harry, now that he thought about it.

"What do you think, nephew? Do you think a shopping trip to New York would brighten Lacy's spirits? We should have a ship going that way soon. I expect Abigail would be willing."

Harry Phalen looked into his port, hoping for an answer. His nose glowed with the false courage he gained from his glass. When had he found more pleasure in the bottom of a bottle than he did in his wife's bed? A man's wife was supposed to comfort him, yet it seemed to Harry's befuddled mind that his life had been much more comfortable before he married. He did know she would be soundly against a trip to New York. He searched for a reason to explain her aversion to what was surely any woman's delight, a shopping expedition.

"Little Harold," he said. "No, I don't think she'd want to leave the baby."

"Take him along," Sean suggested. "They'll have the comfort of the ship after all."

Harry felt cornered.

His brother-in-law came to his rescue. "Abigail has always been a poor sailor." Quire sighed. "A shame, yet I'm afraid she would find the trip torturous. Might I offer a suggestion?" At the captain's nod, he continued, "I couldn't help noticing Miss Phalen's loss of looks, sir."

Sean bristled. Even with sadness haunting her, his daughter was still the best-looking woman in the city.

Quire appeared not to notice. "A sojourn in the countryside might avail her recovery faster than a voyage."

Thinking sea air far more restorative, Sean's brows drew together accentuating his scowl. "In what way?" he demanded.

Quire leaned back in his chair, a full glass of brandy in his hand. He looked more the master of the house than Harry did. "I had planned to invite Abigail and Harry to my farm for a respite from the heat of the city. If it appeals to Lacy, I'd be very

happy to open the house for her for an indetermi-
nate time. As you know, I spend most of my time in
town with other business affairs. She and Abigail
would be free to pursue their own interests."

The idea appealed to Sean. As much as he hated
to admit it, getting Lacy away from the sight of
ships could be just what she needed. They would
just remind her of his absence and Caleb's.

Sean took his pipe from between his teeth and
blew an aromatic cloud over the table. "Thank
you, Quire. It sounds just the ticket," he said, and
raised his glass to the man. "To a return of Lacy's
health."

"Here, here," Quire said, and drank deeply.

CHAPTER IV

The farmhouse had been built to accommodate a large family. It was two-storied with a large attic under a sharply slanted roof. Additions had been added until the house now sprawled in the shape of a misshapen *L*. A small but ancient orchard encroached upon the kitchen wing, shading a small weed-grown herb garden. Untended roses, now wild, stretched beyond the trellises at the sides of the house, finding niches in which to cling to the upper story. In a way they added charm to the building and pleased Lacy.

She hadn't been happy with her father's acceptance of the invitation to visit Quire Farm. Yet with his departure even work at the warehouse could not hold her interest. Perhaps he had been right. A stay in the country during the hot month of July might help her sleep.

Elizabeth Daniels

The room allotted to her was on a corner of the house, its windows overlooking a view of rolling hills that ended in uncleared forest land. A large bed of dark wood, piled high with soft feather mattresses, dwarfed the room, leaving small space for other furnishings. The colors of the worn patchwork quilt were picked up in a bouquet of fresh flowers in a bowl on the single highboy dresser.

Becky, Lacy's maid, stirred up dust shaking out her mistress's creased dresses. She hung them on pegs along the inner wall, clucking at the inadequate furnishings. "You'd think they'd have a wardrobe somewhere, Miss Lacy. I don't know what your gowns are going to be like! I ask you! Pegs! And the dust! I don't think those maids did more than turn the mattress for our coming!"

"Mmm?" Lacy murmured. She stood at the window, her head cocked to one side, pensive. Her blond curls rested against the sash as she gazed out at the arrangement of field and wood. Distance disguised the neglect. It turned ragged weeds into splashes of color, irregular planting rows into variegated tones of green on the landscape. "Isn't this a peaceful setting, Becky? Beautifully peaceful. I can't imagine it ever being as turbulent or as changeable as the sea."

The maid sighed. She hardly knew her mistress anymore. Imagine her even thinking a farm preferable to the sea! Becky hadn't been that keen on coming to Quire Farm, but it seemed to be doing Miss Lacy a world of good already. "I declare, miss, I ain't seen you so interested in anything in months. Other than that musty old warehouse,

84

that is. And that ain't natural, if you don't mind my saying so, miss."

Lacy turned and smiled at the dark-haired girl. Becky was her own age, yet she fretted like a mother hen. "It *is* pretty here," Lacy insisted. "If you don't look at the dust, that is. I'm sure that Mr. Quire's maids have quite enough to do taking care of the animals, making butter and cheese, and their other chores without worrying over a bit of dust."

Becky's eyes grew large. "You mean all he's got is *dairy* maids?"

Lacy nodded. "The two maids and three farm workers."

"*Them* I've seen," Becky said of the men. "Didn't have two nice words to put together, they didn't. More like walking skeletons or preachers with those hangdog faces of theirs. I'm glad we ain't staying here more 'n two nights, Miss Lacy, and that's a fact."

Lacy sat down on the bed and tucked her legs beneath her. Her pale blue muslin skirt hung to the floor, collecting a coating of dust. "I suppose we'll be sharing this bed, Becky. I don't see a cot for you. I don't even see where one would fit!" A thought struck her. "Oh, I suppose Mr. Quire forgot I would have you with me. I'll speak to him about giving you one of the vacant rooms next door."

Becky shook her head and straightened out the folds in a deep lavender silk evening dress. "No, ma'am, he didn't forget me. I'm to share a room with that Hester."

"Hester?"

"The saucy red-haired girl. Personally, Miss Lacy, I don't care for that one a bit. She's a mite too forward, if you ask me."

Lacy could guess the services the maid named Hester performed at the farm. She had caught a glance of the woman earlier. Hester was an overblown female. She dressed more like a woman who worked the waterfront than a dairy maid. She wore the same plain gown as the other maid, but on Hester it was pulled tightly across her breasts, emphasizing her generous curves. Becky's next words confirmed her suspicions.

"That Hester seems to think she can twist Mr. Quire around her finger. The other girl looks like she does most of the work. Sort of tired, if you know what I mean, Miss Lacy. Hester, though, she's always fussing with her hair and worrying that she'll get her dress mussed."

"Well, I hope you aren't too unhappy during our stay," Lacy said earnestly. "If you want, I could still speak to Mr. Quire about a different room."

Becky shook her head, pushing back loose locks of dark hair. "No, miss. I can manage," she said, adamant. "I'd rather you didn't owe that Mr. Quire any favors."

Lacy smiled warmly at her. "Thank you, Becky. I'd prefer not to ask any favors of Mr. Quire myself."

To avoid Abigail and William, Lacy chose to stay in her room until it was time to go down to dinner. The dining room was simply furnished and smelled strongly of beeswax. William set a lavish table and proved to be an excellent host. He kept Harry's glass filled with port. He pressed Lacy to sample the wide variety of dishes on the groaning sideboard and complimented his sister on her infant son.

He and Abigail carried the conversation that evening, conversing quietly of different events in Boston. Harry drank heavily at William's instigation. It relieved Lacy that Quire did not press his attentions on her. If she chose to remain silent, he appeared content, pleased merely that she shared his table. His eyes lingered on her frequently in a caress that disturbed her.

Lacy had no intention of remaining below stairs, tempting fate. When the meal ended, she pleaded weariness and returned to her room, escaping William's warm regard.

The night was close, balmy. Sounds appeared hushed, the silence heavy.

Dismissing a fretful Becky, Lacy slid into a light nightdress with a wide, scooped neckline. She spent a long time brushing her hair until it hung like a golden veil on her shoulders. The even strokes were soothing, yet, when she climbed beneath the light sheet, sleep evaded her grasp once more. Even the romantic novel Celia had pressed upon her could not keep her thoughts from straying to contemplation of a future without Caleb.

Wearily, Lacy put the book aside and blew out the candle. Her mind whirled. Would William resume his unwanted attentions? She felt sure he would. Abigail would arrange a *tete-a-tete*. To thwart their schemes, she would have to stay close to Harry.

Still restless, Lacy climbed out of bed to stand by

the open window. The countryside was bathed in moonlight, and had a ghostly enchantment. A few clouds flitted across the sky, obscuring the moon, blanketing the meadows in darkness before the moon reappeared. Night sounds reached her. The noises of crickets and the croaking of frogs on a nearby pond soothed her. She forgot her troubles as she enjoyed the beauty of the scene. Thoughts of Caleb and similar summer nights during their childhood flitted through her mind. How carefree they had been then. How proud Caleb had been to be a sailor. A man, he had called himself.

Lacy smiled sadly in remembrance.

The moonlight outlined the soft curves of her body boldly through the thin fabric of her gown. A gentle breeze stirred the worn curtains, caressing her, teasing her breasts as they pressed against the muslin.

It was difficult to accept Caleb's defection. Would she find another man to love? To father her children? She would marry, she knew, if for no other reason than to insure the future of the Line. She would conceive strong sons to sail the world on the Puritans. She no longer dreamed of Ben Paradise's lazy smiles. She had forsaken her dreams.

From his position in the doorway, William Quire admired the intimate silhouette Lacy presented. The sight of her thinly clad form was merely titillating. Soon he would know every inch of the girl as he claimed her, making her undeniably his. Once he had balked at Abigail's insistence that he force his way into Lacy's bed. Her vivid description of the girl's eager response to Caleb Innes had irritated him, then intrigued him. Now that the moment had arrived, he wished to savor it fully.

"Waiting for me, Lacy?" William asked, closing the door.

Lacy went rigid with fear. Why had she not realized he would come to her room? Why had she thought he needed Abigail's assistance in his plans? She was a dozen times a fool. Harry was sleeping soundly, his senses dulled with alcohol. Abigail's room was at the far end of the house. She could easily say she had not heard a struggle or cries if Lacy were rash enough to make them. Becky had been carefully removed to a room where Hester could keep a watch on her and prevent any interference on her part.

For all intents and purposes, she was alone in the house with William Quire.

William came to her. He kissed her ear as his hands skimmed over her body. "You have no need to hide yourself from my gaze, Lacy."

She pulled back but could not escape his touch. Trapped. But with that knowledge came a resurgence of spirit. Warm tentacles of anger moved through her. Her eyes flashed in the moonlight. She had been disillusioned, blinding herself to danger from William and his sister through a surfeit of self-pity. Her father was at sea. Caleb was lost to her. And in William Quire's home there would be no dashing stranger to rescue her. How she fared depended entirely upon her own wiles.

His fingers slid across her shoulders, pushing her night rail from her shoulders.

"Please, William." Lacy touched his rough hands. Her voice was husky. "Not quite yet. Later."

He turned her quickly so that the moonlight illuminated her oval face. She forced a smile, hoping he would not see her terror or hear it in her voice.

She was incredibly lovely with her hair spilling over her shoulders and over his hands in a gossamer cloud. Quire feared to read deception in her perfect features. It seemed incredible that she would accept him now. Was Innes's departure the event that would change his life? Would she accept him as a lover eagerly? Welcome him as a husband?

"God, you're beautiful, Lacy." He crushed her slim form against the length of his body, devouring her with his lips.

Lacy was stiff, unable to relax as she played the complacent maid. William did not seem to notice. His tongue invaded her mouth, exploring with thick, repulsive thrusts. She turned her head and felt his teeth nipping at her earlobes on down to her shoulder. Despite her futile efforts, he pushed the gown away so that moonlight fell on her naked skin, exposing the swell of her breasts. His mouth continued to caress, to feast, unaware of the loathing his touch inspired.

"You were right, William," she said. "Caleb never truly loved me."

"You were always meant to be mine," Quire whispered, pleased with her final acceptance. He swept her up into his arms and carried her to the bed, gently placing her on the mound of soft mattresses. His mouth claimed hers once more as his fingers freed her creamy breasts from the neckline of her gown.

Lacy pushed at him, panicked by his actions. William's hands moved lower, pulling the gown up over her thighs.

"No!" she ordered sharply, relieved that her voice hadn't betrayed her fear.

"Come now, Lacy. This is not the time to turn virtuous on me." His hand moved up along her leg.

She retreated from his touch, backing up against the headboard until there was no further escape.

"William, please, I . . ."

Quire halted, his eyes narrowed as he read the disgust and horror in her face. The bitch hadn't changed. She'd tried to trick him, to lure him to relax his vigilance so that she could elude him once more.

She quailed at the smirk on his face.

"Lacy, I'm very upset with you. You've been leading me on. You never were going to give yourself to me, were you?"

The movements of his fingers on her leg were painful now. "No, William, don't . . ."

"Don't?" He withdrew his hand and stood up. "My dear Lacy, are you sure you know what you are saying?" he cajoled harshly. "I'll give you one more chance. Do you want me for your lover?"

She clutched the nightgown to her breast, and pulled the hemline down to cover her legs.

"Lacy?" There was no gentleness in his voice now. He dragged her head back by her hair, delighting in her gasp of pain. "I've asked you if you want me. I wish to hear you say it. Say it, Lacy. Tell me you want me to take you. Say it!"

Hatred lashed at him from her eyes, but Lacy's lips remained tightly shut.

"No? I'm not worthy, is that it?" he persisted. "Are you still weeping nightly over that sea dog Innes?"

Her steady gaze refuted his right to question her.

Quire's eyes narrowed suspiciously. "You sheathed him, didn't you, you little whore?" he ground out. "And willingly. What did he have to do for you to wrap your long legs around him?"

He tugged his neckcloth until it was loose in his hand. Before she realized his intention, he had pulled both her hands above her head and bound them to the headboard.

"William." Her voice was tight with suppressed emotion. "Don't do this. Please, don't do this. You don't know. It isn't true. I never . . ."

He turned, snatching up a neatly folded petticoat, and ripped it. He stuffed a section of the mangled garment in her mouth. "I should have done this from the beginning. I should have known a bitch like you would play games," he spat.

Lacy twisted her hands in their bonds in a vain effort to escape as he disrobed, dropping his clothes on the floor in his hurry. When he stood naked before her, William smiled. "Comparing me to your other lovers, Lacy? Or don't you believe your good fortune?"

Her mouth worked uselessly at the gag. She prayed for the comfort of unconsciousness. Must he rape her mind as well as her body?

Quire's hands pulled her down in the bed and spread her legs. Lacy twisted and screamed impotently against the gag.

He laughed and slowly ran a hand up under her gown, playing with her as a cat would a mouse.

Lacy struggled again which excited him. He gloated at her helplessness. She was a prisoner, her legs extended. Soon her body would be forced to accept him against her will. Tears rolled down her face as her body strained against the bonds.

"Still no, Lacy? Or are you willing to admit you want me now? I'd like to hear it from your own lips. Like to hear you plead."

She made a last effort to free herself.

"What a stubborn woman you are, Lacy Phalen."

His hands pushed her legs wider until she feared she would split in two. Shadows painted his body grotesquely as he hovered over her. He reached for the neckline of her gown, intent on rending it from her.

"That's enough, William," ordered a voice. "I believe we have made our point." Abigail stood in the doorway, a small pistol in her hand. "The wedding will be quiet but quite soon."

Quire stared at his sister, his expression malevolent. "Get the hell out of here!"

Abigail stepped farther into the room, aiming the gun in his direction. "I was afraid you would need convincing." She sighed as if she were loath to interfere but was resigned to do what she saw as her duty. "I would prefer not to shoot you, dear brother. But if necessary you will have a slight hunting accident during our visit. It would give you an interesting . . . limp, shall we say?"

Lacy's eyes widened. Would Abigail actually carry through her cold-blooded threat?

William apparently believed his sister very capable of maiming him. He moved off the bed and scooped up his clothing. "Damn you to hell!" he snarled.

Abigail nodded coolly and moved aside as he pushed past her, out the door.

Lacy waited, doubting that Abigail was satisfied yet. Her cousin's wife had planned and executed her plot carefully. But the game was far from finished.

Abigail's head cocked, listening. When the sound of the main door slamming shut was heard, she gave a slight smile of satisfaction. "I believe Hester is about to receive a visit from my brother," she said. "Or perhaps your girl will accommodate his baser instincts."

Frightened for Becky, Lacy renewed her struggles to free herself.

Abigail laughed softly. "So eager to go to her rescue, cousin?" she mocked. "William's appetites have always been voracious. When you are his wife, you may feel grateful that he shares his favors with your maid. But I will leave you to think on the matter." She surveyed Lacy huddled against the headboard. The young woman's eyes burned with verdant hatred above the crude gag.

Abigail smiled, her face twisted in malicious joy. "I do hope you are comfortable, Lillian. I would hate for you to have ill memories of your first night in what will soon be your home."

Lacy watched the shadows grow and recede in the corners of the room. Her ears hurt from the strain of listening for William's return. Not long after Abigail's departure she had thought she had heard a scream. It had been quickly cut off. Now Lacy wondered if it had been her imagination or a night bird. Whatever it had been, the peril to Becky and herself was real.

Slowly, she inched upward toward the headboard. Her wrists were still tightly bound but her fingers were free. She picked at the gag until it loosened and dropped to the floor.

Her tongue was like cotton in her dry mouth. She ignored it and the tightness in her throat. Forward she moved, straining to reach the bonds with her teeth. Minutes ticked by as she tugged with slow deliberation at the knots at her wrists. The first streaks of dawn aided her progress.

Pain shot across Lacy's shoulders and up her neck as she continued to work. When the first knot fell away, she maneuvered her hands, sliding first one free, then the other.

Where she expected to go once she left the room she did not know. Nor did she know where Becky was, or if Abigail was correct in her estimation that William was now with the maid.

Lacy's bare feet were silent on the rag rug. Forcing herself to move slowly, she ripped the torn nightgown off, deciding to burn the repugnant remains later. Now it was imperative that she leave Quire Farm. Lacy took down the blue day dress from its peg on the wall and slipped it over her head. She struggled with the back fastenings.

The enormity of the situation was nearly overwhelming. But Lacy had no intention of bowing to fate. She would not become William Quire's wife.

She kicked at the torn nightgown, the evidence

of her vulnerability. She had prided herself on her ability to control her own life, yet Abigail had shown her how false that assumption was. It was a man's world she had tried to enter, naively unaware that it was not men but women such as Abigail Quire Phalen who actually manipulated things.

The captain had placed her in Harry's care unaware of Abigail's control of her weak husband. Lacy was very aware of her cousin's failings, and knew she could not look to him for help.

She moved to the open window, hoping to clear her thoughts in the early-morning breeze.

She was miles from Boston with no way to return. She hadn't the glimmer of an idea in which direction to head once she left the farmhouse. Without the smell of the sea to guide her, Lacy realized she was lost.

CHAPTER V

Abigail waited a full week before announcing her charge's engagement to William Quire. Lacy could see the woman reveled in the culmination of her plan. Abigail enjoyed the younger woman's subjugation and gloated over Lacy's inability to control her own life.

It amused Abigail that Lacy had tried to thwart her plans. The young woman didn't realize that it had been Abigail who had dropped hints in the right ears to ensure the removal of Caleb Innes. And the suggestion of bringing Lacy to the farm, relayed through her brother to the captain, had come from her also. The days at the farm had taken Lacy far from the hope of outside help. Soon Lillian Phalen's generous dowry would be in Quire hands, Abigail assured herself. It was just the beginning.

Reeling with success, Abigail failed to note the gradual return of Lacy's health. Her appetite returned and her days now ended in exhausted, healing sleep.

Outwardly, Lacy was compliant. Inwardly, she seethed. Abigail and William had used her, degraded her. But they would not conquer her. It was a small satisfaction, but Lacy had removed Becky from danger. The maid had joined Celia Clary's staff at Lacy's request. Now it was time to remove the Phalen fortune from the Quires' grasp as well. And to accomplish that, Lacy knew she needed an accomplice, preferably someone Abigail would never suspect.

Polly MacGuire's cottage was in a quiet lane, not quite in the Beacon Hill district, but not far removed. As a widow, Polly enjoyed a freedom that Lacy had long envied. Polly's late husband had left her a modest, but comfortable, income, and Sean Phalen watched over her investments. The captain had managed unobtrusively to shower gifts upon his lady love so that no breath of scandal attached itself to Polly's name. But Lacy had discovered his secret liaison with the vibrant widow. Fortunately for the captain's state of mind, his daughter had adored Polly from the moment she met the petite woman.

The admiration and affection had been reciprocated, leaving Lacy with an open invitation to visit Polly whenever she wished. Between her diligence at the Puritan Warehouse and social obligations, Lacy had rarely been able to take Polly up on her hospitality. Now she visited her friend on a pretext involving Polly's investments with the Puritan Line.

Polly was pleasantly astonished to find Lacy on her doorstep. She greeted the girl with a fond hug. "Lacy! Don't tell me you have word from your father already?" She drew her guest into the front parlor. When Lacy admitted that she had come on quite a different matter, Polly's eyes widened. "I must say I was surprised to read of your engagement," she said, guessing at what disturbed the girl. "It seemed decidedly odd with Sean gone."

Lacy smiled warmly at her father's mistress and settled in a large armchair, her feet curled cozily beneath her full gray-and-silver striped skirts. The bodice of her gown was trimmed with black cord, accenting her narrow waist. Lacy removed her hat and picked at the tight fingers of her gloves, stripping them off.

Polly vibrated with a special *élan* despite her modest appearance. The skirts of her peach-colored silk dress were of a moderate width, the neckline high and rather prim. Her dark hair with its silver highlights was dressed simply and gathered into a snood. Yet there was a vitality that shone from her gray eyes, an animation that had attracted both Sean and his daughter.

"I'd never marry in Papa's absence," Lacy assured her hostess. "I intend to be miles away when the guests are gathered in Abigail's home."

The girl's self-confidence worried Polly. "I've heard rumors," she allowed carefully, and bent forward, pouring tea into delicate china cups. She didn't like the aura of suppressed excitement that radiated from Lacy. Without Sean to temper his daughter's high spirits, Polly decided she would now have to guide the girl. Lord knew that Phalen woman had no control over Lacy, she thought in exasperation. Abigail aggravated the poor child to new bursts of folly.

"There have always been rumors about me, Polly," Lacy said matter of factly. "Falsehoods started by my dear cousin-in-law, Abigail."

Polly ignored the venom in the girl's statement and passed a cup to Lacy. "These rumors had a strange ring of truth to them," she said, offering a plate of biscuits.

Lacy accepted a pastry and sank sullenly back in her chair. She hadn't wanted to recall the Quires' latest ploy.

"Naturally, I could hardly credit it, Lacy," Polly persisted. "No one who knows you would believe that you would allow your fiancé to—how can I say this?—anticipate the wedding night?"

Lacy blushed yet could not admit the degrading events at Quire Farm. "They want my money."

Polly nodded, thinking only that the child was embarrassed by the crudity of the rumor. "The Quires have always had their eye on the riches of others." In an effort to comfort, Polly reached to pat Lacy's arm. "If you don't wish to marry the man, no one can force you to, Lacy."

The girl clasped Polly's hand urgently, her eyes reflecting the terror that haunted her. "But they can, Polly. Believe me," she murmured.

The elder woman sat back, unnerved by the look in Lacy's eyes.

"They'd take great pleasure in breaking me to

their will," Lacy continued. "And who's to stop them? Certainly not Harry. He's their puppet." She paused. "I need your help to escape."

Common sense had righted Polly's placidity. What Lacy was asking was impossible! Still, she had never believed William Quire was the right man for Lacy. "I'm not very adept at holding ladders. Isn't there some young man with whom you'd rather elope?" she asked flippantly, hoping the incident was just a result of Lacy's contention with her chaperone.

Lacy accepted Polly's skepticism. It *was* inconceivable that this horror was happening. When she was away from Abigail and William, her terror subsided and she was inclined to think she had dreamt the nightmarish attack, that her dislike of the Quires made her see things out of proportion. Once she returned from the warehouse to Abigail's home, however, the horror came rushing back.

"There used to be someone."

"Caleb," Polly identified.

Lacy didn't correct her, although it hadn't been Caleb's handsome face she had seen momentarily in her mind's eye. It had been a dark man with unforgettable light blue eyes.

"I believe Abigail was behind the accusations against Caleb," Lacy continued. "Harry told me of them yesterday. And Celia Clary discovered Abigail has been dropping hints that I have been promised to William since my presentation. Only Caleb remained a threat so she had him removed." Lacy sipped at her tea, her turbulent eyes demanding Polly's help. "If I'm to escape, I will do it on my own, but I would appreciate your assistance, Polly."

The controlled hatred and determination in her voice convinced the older woman. Whether she agreed to help or not, Polly realized Lacy was going to evade the Quires' trap. "I take it you have a plan in mind already."

Assured by Polly's tone, Lacy smiled at her. "Well, yes, I rather did," she said, her mood light once more. "I think I can get out of the house all right. I've managed to convince them that I am a broken woman without spirit left to fight."

"I can see that is far from the truth of the matter." *Ah, the resilience of youth,* Polly thought. At least as a conspirator she would be able to assure Sean of his child's safety.

The girl nodded. "But a few weeks ago it was the truth."

The set line of Lacy's jaw reminded Polly strongly of Sean. In a surge of affection, Polly squeezed Lacy's hand. "I'm glad to see you are beginning to recover, dear."

"Aye." Lacy grinned ruefully. "I'm recovering. I can not stay in Boston and let the Quires control me as they do Harry. Think what would happen to the Line in their hands. I have to escape before it is too late."

"What is the rest of your plan, Lacy? And what part do I play?" Polly pressed.

Lacy breathed easier. She had been right in coming to Polly for guidance and support. "It would have to be late at night, of course, to avoid any chance of being apprehended. But if I took a hired coach out of Boston and caught the old stage line to New York, I doubt if they would be able to determine where I had gone."

Polly got up from the sofa to walk up and down the room. The house was that of a woman alone. All the furnishings were delicate. The furniture did not seem sturdy enough to support a man. Fragile porcelain figurines and Chinese vases decorated the room. Even the soft colors of her Oriental rugs were feminine. Lacy wondered if her father ever felt comfortable in this dainty parlor. If he did not, he could always do away with Polly's separate residence by marrying her. Perhaps that was the reason Polly had furnished her rooms as she had. Polly MacGuire was a very subtle woman. And Sean Phalen, his daughter thought, was a damn fool.

"Why not the train?" Polly asked.

"I'd be seen."

"But they could reach New York before you."

Lacy chose another pastry from the platter. "How are they to know I am headed for New York?"

"It's only logical, child."

"No, it isn't. What would they think I would be doing in New York, Polly? All my acquaintances are in New England." She nibbled at a biscuit.

Polly considered how few people she herself knew outside of Boston. They lived in a very narrow world, bound by family connections. It was possible to count on one hand the people she knew outside of that charmed circle. But those few were very special. Polly thought about one particular friend. A very resourceful one.

Polly's eyes began to glow. "No, no. You must

make them believe you have run off with another man!"

Lacy frowned. She would prefer to avoid aid from any man. She still felt far too vulnerable. "What other man?" she asked suspiciously.

Polly chuckled. "That's the charm of it, you goose. There is no other man! But you have got to leave a false trail or they will track you to New York. What will you do there, if I may ask?"

Lacy finished the pastry and picked at the crumbs that had fallen on her lap. "Go to the employment agencies. I hope to find a position as a governess or a schoolmistress until Papa returns. I just want to be far enough away that they don't find me and force me to return before I'm ready. I'll need a letter of reference, Polly."

"Absolutely. More than one, I believe, dearest," the tiny woman observed.

"They must be convincing, assuring my employer I'm not about to run off with the family silver, Polly," Lacy insisted.

The older woman picked up one of the delicate figurines, a sheperdess, and seemed to be intent upon admiring the detailed work of the statuette's gown. "I have a far better idea, Lacy. I have a friend I'd like you to meet."

"Not a mysterious man, I trust," Lacy demanded, now leery of the gleam in her friend's eye.

Polly smiled. "No, a very discerning woman."

CHAPTER VI

Harry and Abigail Phalen hosted a private party on the eve of Lacy's wedding to William Quire. Just a few close friends, Abigail insisted. Yet Lacy was not well acquainted with any of the guests. Abigail was not taking chances.

William, in an exquisite black suit with long tails, stayed at Lacy's side, his fingers brushing possessively against the curve of her breast when he took her arm. His face was flushed, his eyes ravenous as they flickered over her, lingering on the deep neckline of her mint-green gown. The brandy fumes on his breath suffocated her. His offer to fetch her a glass of wine was refused. Belatedly, remembering she was a complacent bride, Lacy tempered the statement. "Possibly tomorrow, William," she said.

Quire looked at her demurely lowered lashes, so

long and dark against her ashen cheeks. He was proud that she'd soon be his wife. Proud of the fact he'd tamed the wild fey creature and created the perfect helpmate. William's arm went around her slender shoulders as he hugged her quickly, a jovial glow coloring his face. "I wouldn't want you inebriated on our wedding night, Lacy." His voice was slightly slurred, the result of too many toasts to his good fortune.

"But I would prefer to be so, William." Lacy felt reckless as she smiled for the benefit of the guests. Soon she would be free. The thought made her almost lightheaded. "Shouldn't you grant a lady her last wish?"

Stung by the retort, William scowled at her. Had he heard correctly? Lacy appeared to accept his attentions, yet her tongue contained a viper's sting. "I don't see why you can't accept this marriage," he said.

It was hard to maintain her meek act as the wedding day drew near. Lacy forced herself to lift her eyes to his, to touch his arm in a false show of tenderness. Her voice was schooled to a husky monotone, stripped of emotion. "I thought I had, William."

His temper turned foul. "Damn it, Lacy. I'm not a bad fellow. A lot of women would envy your getting a husband such as I."

She opened her fan and played with it. "Really, William," she said, looking away from his flushed face, "this is hardly the place to discuss it. We have guests."

He grabbed the fragile fan and snapped it in two. "Yes, my dear, we will discuss it. In our bed."

Anger flared in her eyes. "We aren't sharing one yet, William," she reminded him crisply.

His fingers played along the creamy expanse of her neck, lifting the rope of pearls that lay at her throat. "The night is still young, Lacy. Who knows what may yet happen?"

She shivered in the warm room. If he came to her, the plans she had made to escape would come to nothing and tomorrow she would find herself his wife. Pride alone would force her to accept him if she found herself at the altar.

William smiled humorlessly, pleased to see fear replace anger in her face. "Who knows what it will bring, indeed," he murmured.

The hours crept by as Lacy waited for the house to settle for the night. The guests stayed on drinking her health and William's until quite a late hour. When she retired, it had been amid a number of good-natured comments about a bride's needing her beauty sleep.

Her door was locked, a weak and futile precaution against William's threat. As footsteps passed her door, Lacy mentally identified them. Abigail's steps were a quick tatoo on the uncarpeted section of the hall. Harry's had been slow and dragging. William was the last to stumble up the stairs. She watched in horror in the dim, moonlit room as the door latch turned soundlessly. He gave the door a slight push but the lock held. Softly, he called her name. Lacy didn't move. She hardly dared breathe. When there was no answer, William seemed satisfied that he had made an effort. His footsteps continued down the hall.

The hall clock struck three before Lacy felt safe enough to leave her bed. She packed a serviceable dark gray dress in an old portmanteau along with extra undergarments and a nightgown. Dressed in a black suit and a crisp white shirt, she perched a plain bonnet on her carefully controlled blond curls and tied her favorite shawl around her shoulders.

The reflection in the mirror showed the smooth curve of her cheek and the startling contrast of her sooty lashes and green eyes. The pinched, scared look had disappeared from her face along with the dark circles. Her cheeks blossomed with health again. She wished she had a veil to disguise her features more. If only she'd been born plain, Lacy thought and laughed. If only she were *poor*, none of the nightmarish events would have happened.

Before placing the key in the lock, she stood close to the door, listening for any sound of movement in the household. Slowly, she turned it until she heard the tiny catch of the lock opening.

The air in the hall was suffocating, tainted with the party odors of stale cigars and alcohol. There was a path of brandy spills on the hall carpet. A large one stood before her own door, evidence that William had not gone to bed empty-handed.

Cautious, she lifted her skirts and stepped over the wet carpet, and pulled the bedroom door closed. By relocking it, she hoped to gain precious time. It would be midmorning before anyone thought to disturb her and by then she would be miles away, enroute to the teaching post Polly's friend, Martha Haskell, had secured for her in Missouri.

Lacy strained to hear over the whisper of her skirts on the stairs as she descended to Harry's study. Her actual flight from the house had presented a problem. Abigail herself checked all doors and windows on the ground floor every night. Only the terrace doors of the study were bolted rather than locked.

No glint of gaslight found its way through the wide windows of the study. Thick rhododendron challenged even a faint beam of moonlight, keeping the room in a hushed, inky shroud.

She had rehearsed her route frequently in preparation. Flawlessly, her feet found the path past Harry's desk. Careful not to make a sound, Lacy slid the first bolt back. Her feeling of elation began to build. Within minutes she would be free. Yet she would be bound by her fear of the Quires. Would it follow her, haunt her even on the frontier?

She reached for the second bolt and barely stiffled a scream as she brushed against a human hand.

"Lacy?" a slurred voice asked.

"Harry?" She sighed in relief. "What are you doing here?"

"Couldn't sleep," he mumbled. His breath smelt strongly of port. "Let the cap'n down 'lowin' Ab'gail push you. Don't like Will, do you, Lacy? Me either." He brightened and raised the bottle. "A little more wine, huh? Care to join me?" Lacy doubted he knew she was there at all. Harry looked disoriented.

She declined. "I understand, cousin. I couldn't sleep either. I thought perhaps some fresh air would help me."

"Wine's much better," he said. Lacy saw him raise the bottle to his lips and drink fully.

"Maybe for you, Harry. But I believe fresh air would be of benefit to me. It is so stuffy in the house after the party. Could you open that last bolt for me? It's just a little out of my reach."

He was beginning to weave on his feet. "Ab'gail won't like it. Night air bad f' you."

"I won't tell her," Lacy soothed. "Will you?"

"No."

"Then how is she to find out?" she whispered brightly. "Just open the door very quietly. We don't want to wake Abigail or William."

Lacy was surprised he did as instructed. A wave of affection for the gentle man constricted her throat. Swiftly, she kissed his flushed cheek. "Thank you, Harry. I'll never forget this." Lacy stepped into the garden. "And neither will the captain."

But her cousin did not hear. He sprawled against the open door already fast asleep.

CHAPTER VII

The young woman was about as calm as a cyclone, the spare little man behind the hotel desk decided. She had breezed in with the afternoon stage, bent on disturbing his peace.

She paced before his desk, her heavy dust-stained skirts sweeping the freshly scrubbed floor boards. Her boots kept a steady beat as she moved. The sound reminded him that, despite his wife's wishes, he had imbibed a little too much rotgut whiskey at the saloon the night before. His brain throbbed, taking great exception to the impatient visitor.

Two strides to the left, two strides to the right. She never slowed.

"Are you positive there is no one to meet me?" Lacy Phalen demanded without slowing her pace.

"Pos'tive," the man said then brightened momentarily as inspiration struck. "Might check down at the sheriff's office. Might know somethin'." *Foist her on another poor soul,* he thought. Anything to get this whirlwind out of his hair.

Lacy sighed and paused pushing a loose curl back under her hat. She had been traveling nonstop since leaving Boston. Basking in her independence, she had sailed to New Orleans and booked passage up the Mississippi on a keel boat upriver to Saint Louis. From there, the trip inland had continued via the stage bound for Hopkins Bend.

Since beginning the final leg of her journey, Lacy had traveled over rut-infested roads in a carriage that rocked even more than the ship from New York. The close quarters of the stage and the unwashed bodies of the passengers added to her nausea. It receded as the coach careened ever nearer the mountains. She was convinced she owned relief to the fact that she now smelled as badly as her fellow travelers. When the stage deposited her in Hopkins Bend, Lacy was covered in dust and grime and bone-weary.

Facing the now cringing man behind the counter, Lacy felt at the end of her endurance. "But I'm sure someone is to meet me," she insisted. "Haven't you heard from anyone? I know a letter was sent. I was *told* I would be met!"

With a superhuman effort, Jed Schmidt drew his thin shoulders straighter and looked her right in the eye. "Well, you ain't, miss, and that's a fact."

Exasperated, Lacy returned to the hotel porch and stared at the town. She wouldn't let the situation get the best of her. She wasn't desperate. Not yet, at any rate. She still had enough of the money she had borrowed from Polly to survive for a month or more if necessary. A breath or two of air and a respite from the uncooperative hotel clerk would help her think clearly.

Hopkins Bend, Missouri, was her first real taste of the frontier. It consisted of two main thoroughfares, both very dusty and uncobbled. One street ran approximately north and south. The other crossed it midway and ran east and west. Neither was glorified with a name.

The stage had deposited her in front of the only hotel in town. Directly across the street was a general store. Next to that was a saloon, a bank, and another saloon. Next to the hotel Lacy caught sight of a small dressmaker's shop sandwiched between a second dry-goods store and a third saloon. All the buildings were built of wood. Few had ever known a coat of paint.

The hotel, however, was in good condition. Its freshly painted exterior instilled Lacy with confidence. The ground-floor windows had neat muslin curtains, and the sign stated that bed and board for ladies and gentlemen were available.

The stage had barely paused long enough for Lacy to leave its stuffy, well-worn confines before rolling on down the street, leaving her gasping in the cloud of dust its wheels churned up in the dry, dirt roadway. She was not only tired, she was lonely and disgusted.

The new schoolteacher for the town of Paradise *had* to be expected and met. Martha Haskell had been very sure, had assured Polly repeatedly that

113

life on the frontier was not hazardous, that the residents were respectable citizens.

Lacy turned and went back inside the hotel, away from the heat of the day.

"Just how far is it to Paradise?" she asked.

"Farther than I'd care ta walk," Jed Schmidt mused, irritated that the cyclone had returned to disturb his slumber.

She studied the weathered face of the gaunt man behind the counter. His eyes were an incredible pale violet beneath sun-bleached bushy eyebrows. His face was lined with creases. His thinning hair was carefully combed to cover a bald spot.

"I don't suppose there is a stage to Paradise, is there?" Lacy demanded.

"Nope."

His calm infuriated her. "Well, what do you suggest I do? Just sit here and wait for someone to show up and claim me?"

Schmidt pulled on his upper lip thoughtfully. The attempt to send her off to the sheriff's had failed but he still had another card up his sleeve with which to stump her. "Tell ya what, miss. There's a gent staying here from Paradise."

"Then he must be here to meet me."

He shook his head slowly from side to side. "The gals he meets up with ain't exactly yer style, miss. Ask him when he comes in though."

"And when might that be?"

"Be here fer his dinner this evenin'."

"This evening! What am I to do till then?"

He slid his guest register around to face her. "Happen ya'd like ta freshen up a bit?"

Lacy looked at the coating of dust on her once

114

immaculate clothing. "Might there be a bathtub for hire?"

The creases in his face deepened unhappily. More trouble! "Best in town."

She pulled the book forward and dipped the pen in the bottle of ink at his elbow. "I'll take it and your softest bed," she said decisively, and scrawled her name in his register.

The hotel keeper turned the book around and nodded over her signature. "Whatever ya say, Miss Phalen."

"And the man from Paradise will be in for dinner, you say? Would you be sure to call me then?"

The room was spartan in furnishings. Just a bed and a stand with a washbowl and pitcher. Faded wallpaper clung to the walls, and neatly mended curtains waved gently in a breeze from the window. Lacy thought it looked marvelous.

Luxuriating in her first bath in over a week, Lacy lathered the dust from her hair. The black suit took a little more time but she managed to make it presentable once more. She hoped the citizens of Paradise would conceivably recognize her as a respectable member of the teaching profession.

The featherbed felt luxurious after the cramped quarters both on the stage and aboard the river keel boat. Lacy stretched and smiled at the ceiling. Her father would be appalled at her current surroundings, but she felt he would applaud her flight to a quiet, respectable life in Missouri rather than her accepting a loveless marriage with William Quire. It was bizarre that the town carried the

same misnomer as Colonel Webber's attractive
grandson. A coincidence. Perhaps a good omen.

Lacy sighed contentedly and pulled the worn
patchwork quilt over her head.

The short rest replaced the sparkle in her eyes
and color in her cheeks. She spent long moments
considering her image in the speckled mirror over
the washstand. The irritable manager downstairs
had said the man from Paradise did not usually
associate with respectable women. At least, that
was the impression she had received, and Lacy was
afraid some of her respectability had washed off
with the soap. Her skin glowed with health. Her
hair, despite the severe knot she now affected,
glowed with a quiet radiance of its own. She found
the refurbished suit fit snuggly, accentuating her
figure, highlighting her breasts and small waist.
Perhaps there were advantages to looking tired
and dusty, she thought as she prepared to head for
the dining room.

The hotel's appearance and comforts were the
province of Helena Schmidt, the proprietor's robust wife. A tall woman with broad shoulders, her
brown hair was streaked with gray and her face
beamed with health. She wore a neat calico dress
covered by a fresh white apron.

Mrs. Schmidt served an enormous plate of stew
to the mysterious young woman, then hovered
with motherly concern while Lacy finished it with
unladylike haste.

Back in her kitchen, the landlady shook her
head sadly. "Poor mite," Mrs. Schmidt told her
cringing husband without a merciful thought to

his still-pounding head. She filled his plate, adding an extra serving. She had been trying to fatten him up since the day he'd walked her to the altar. "This Miz Phalen is too skinny and too young to be alone. A sight too pretty to stay out of trouble, too. There'll be fights aplenty over her if she heads out to Paradise. Those farm boys ain't never seen a lady like her before." She held a plate of buttermilk biscuits in her hand as she considered. "Elegant, that's the word for her."

"Do fine," Schmidt insisted. "Damn feisty little thing. 'Minds me of you, sweet."

His spouse ignored his attempted compliment. "Humph. The Lord does work in mysterious ways though. Maybe He's sent Miz Phalen to tame those great oafs out in the back country."

With this thought in mind, Mrs. Schmidt hustled back to the dining room, determined to bolster the young lady's reserves with an additional helping of stew. "Let me get ya a bit more, Miz Phalen."

Lacy smiled gently at her eager hostess. "I couldn't possibly eat anymore. But if you have a pot of tea brewing, I wouldn't refuse a cup."

Mrs. Schmidt returned with a full pot and a slice of hot apple pie. She brushed Lacy's objections aside. "Nonsense. Yer much ta thin," the older woman stated with a warm-hearted smile and settled cozily in the vacant chair across from her guest. "Besides, I know the way schoolteachers are treated. The ladies fall all over themselves fer a schoolmaster but rarely lift a finger fer a schoolmarm. Jest find yerself a husband and settle down. We lose more teachers that way, but it's a good way." Helena Schmidt winked.

Lacy laughed and savored a bite of her pie. "I'm beginning to wonder if I'll ever get to Paradise, you know. There hasn't been any word of a welcoming committee and the man your husband mentioned hasn't returned."

Mrs. Schmidt got slowly to her feet and wiped her hands on her snowy apron. "Ya mean Ben. He'll be along any minute now."

The man's name sent a shiver along Lacy's spine. It couldn't be the same man!

As if drawn, she glanced up at a new arrival as he closed the street door. Had he been conjured by Mrs. Schmidt's words? Or perhaps her own thoughts?

He was a tall man, athletically built with broad shoulders and well-manicured hands. He wore a well-tailored black suit, and his silk vest gleamed with silver threads. His white shirt was dazzling, its modest ruffles crisp and rather flamboyant. His dark cravat was tied loosely about his collar. She caught the glint of gold at his cuffs. His ebony boots shone as brightly as a looking glass. His skin was deeply tanned by the sun so that his teeth seemed to flash when he smiled as he greeted a few of the diners. He moved easily among the other guests, calling many by name. As Lacy watched, one forward lady ran a hand through his thick brown hair. He smiled good-naturedly and slapped her rump.

Then he saw the housekeeper standing complacently at the table. "Helena," he crooned, his voice a pleasant drawling baritone. "I'm starved." He swung her into his arms and kissed her cheek.

"Now, ya ought ta know I'm proof against yer

wooin'," she cried, delighted. "Besides, I've got somebody here who's been waitin' ta see ya."

His clear blue eyes barely registered surprise at Lacy's unexpected appearance so far from Boston. "I don't believe I was expecting anyone," Ben Paradise said. "Certainly not anyone as delightful as this." His eyes twinkled, reminding Lacy of her father's merry eyes.

She felt herself blush but, remembering Mr. Schmidt's comment about Benjamin Paradise and women, *and* the shameless behavior of the girl three tables away, Lacy reminded herself of the reason for her presence in Missouri.

It certainly would have been easy to fall under the spell of Ben Paradise, a thing she could not afford to allow.

Surely, she was more beautiful than he had remembered, Ben mused. It hadn't been easy for him to act like a stranger and not rush across the room to her side, and sweep her into his arms. Her lips were parted in shock, luring him with their softness. Her tongue licked nervously at her upper lip. Her teeth worried the full lower lip. Her deep emerald eyes pleaded that he not reveal he knew her.

"The poor thing was supposed ta be met, Ben. She's yer new schoolmarm. Schmidt and I thought ya might be able ta help her," Mrs. Schmidt informed him then hurried off, deserting the couple.

Ben swung his leg over the back of the recently vacated chair and seated himself across the table from Lacy without invitation. "Can't say I'm familiar with the education needs of the town, ma'am,

119

but I'll be glad to be of what help I can."

"What are you doing here?" Lacy hissed.

He took her hand in a strong grip as if she had merely introduced herself and smiled. "I live here. At least I do in Paradise."

Lacy was surprised at the thrill she experienced as his hand imprisoned hers. No other man had made her as acutely aware of her own feminine attractions as did Benjamin Paradise. And no other man had sent chills racing pleasantly along her spine with such a casual touch. Not even Caleb.

Charm eminated from the man and Lacy knew only too well she was falling under its spell. "I take it you are the founder of the town."

"To be more precise, Miss Phalen, my father was. Rather egotistical perhaps to name a town after yourself but folks around here seemed to fancy the name." He appraised her intently. "You know, I can't help wondering why you are planning to teach school in Paradise, Miss Phalen."

Mrs. Schmidt returned and placed a steaming plate of her stew before him. "Jest never ya mind why she does, Ben."

"Are you jealous, Helena?" he teased.

Lacy sipped her tea, considering her answer. Should she confess the circumstances that had lead to her flight or convince him she had needed to keep occupied during the captain's voyage?

The housekeeper's next statement drew her full attention. "This young lady is respectable and ya see ya keep her that way," Helena admonished.

Lacy choked.

"Mercy! Are ya all right, miss?"

The girl nodded, a napkin pressed tightly to her

lips as she coughed, gasping for breath. Ben Paradise smiled wickedly across the table at her.

"Crumb?" he offered.

Lacy nodded vigorously.

"Perhaps some water, Helena."

"Of course, Ben," the housekeeper said, and hurried away.

Paradise's smile grew wider. "First time I ever saw anyone choke on the word respectable," he mused, and dug into his stew. "I think it would be best to stick to the crumb story though."

Her face flushed, Lacy swallowed quickly in an effort to control her breathing once more. "I assure you, Mr. Paradise, I am very respectable," she rasped.

He admired the quick rise and fall of her tight bodice before dragging his gaze to meet the impotent fury in her eyes. "Oh, I know you are, Miss Phalen," he said, buttering one of Mrs. Schmidt's muffins. "It's the good ladies of Paradise you will have to convince. You're a darn sight too attractive not to have a sordid past. Especially since you've decided to hide out in a remote place like Paradise. Too suspicious by half. And those fine ladies have a penchant for airing other folks' dirty laundry."

The anxious housekeeper arrived with the water. "Are you all right, miss?"

Pleased with the woman's interruption, the frown faded from Lacy's brow as she reassured her hostess.

"I hope it weren't my cookin'." Helena Schmidt twisted a corner of her apron nervously.

Embarrassed now at the big woman's concern,

Lacy smiled and sipped at the glass of water. "Not in the least," she insisted. "It's just as Mr. Paradise said. I choked on a crumb."

"Could happen to anyone," Ben said. The studied look of amused innocence on his bronzed face caused Lacy's eyes to narrow with contained fury.

Mrs. Schmidt sighed in thanksgiving, her heavy breast heaving with the effort. "Well, if there's anything more I can get ya, jest let me know," she said, and answered a call from another customer.

Lacy's companion gave a low chuckle. "If I weren't busy eating, Miss Phalen, I'd applaud. You haven't tried your hand at the acting profession since we last met, have you?"

Her eyes snapped, incensed that he found her predicament amusing. "Really, Mr. Paradise. If you are an example of the town leaders, I believe I'll go back to Boston."

"Where's your sense of humor, Miss Phalen?" he cajoled. "You don't have to worry though. You see, I'm more in the line of the black sheep of the town. Your employers are the salt of the earth and respectable as Job."

Lacy mulled over his statement before answering. "I'm glad to hear that." Her anger cooled somewhat, replaced by concern. "I am beginning to wonder if they know of my existence. A letter was sent telling them of my arrival."

He finished off the last bit of stew. "You have to remember that the frontier has a convoluted postal service, Miss Phalen. All of Paradise's mail comes here to Hopkins Bend. It is picked up when someone happens to come this way. I myself picked up the accumulation of mail for the last month just today. Ten to one the letter announcing your arrival is in the batch."

"But that's terrible!" she cried. "No one knows I've arrived."

"Well, I know," he said.

"You also said you knew nothing of the matter."

"True. The children of Paradise aren't mine." He paused. "That I know of."

Lacy sent him an icy glare.

His teeth flashed again. "Are you going to finish that pie?"

"No!" she said tersely.

"Then I'll help myself," he said, and reached across the table.

"What am I going to do?" Unconsciously, Lacy pulled tendrils of hair loose which curled softly to frame her face.

Across the table Benjamin Paradise paused in his eating, struck by the charming affect. "Come home with me, of course," he said.

She sat straight up in her chair. "Come home with you!"

"To Paradise." He grinned. The last of her pie disappeared. "How else are you going to get there?"

"I hadn't thought of that," she admitted.

He wondered if the bemused expression on her pretty face foretold pleasure or merely consideration of his offer. "Like some coffee?"

Absently, Lacy glanced up. "No, thank you. It keeps me awake."

"I'll remember that." He grinned, one corner of his mouth quirking attractively.

Lacy's cheeks turned crimson. "Really, Mr. Paradise!" She stood, dropping her napkin to the floor. The man was insufferable! How could she ever have spent hours mentally reviewing—and enjoying!—the time she had spent with him in Boston?

Paradise admired the naturally sensuous sway of her heavy black skirts as she left the room. "We start early, Miss Phalen," he called loudly after her departing figure only to be met with a renewed stiffening of her back.

Lacy was quite sure a number of heads turned to stare at her. Fighting the impulse to turn back to the table, she walked up the stairs, devoutly wishing she could wipe that infernal smile off Ben Paradise's face. But it was still in evidence the next morning.

"You're looking lovely this morning, Miss Phalen," Ben said as Mrs. Schmidt ushered Lacy to his table for breakfast.

Lacy looked around for a vacant table. There were none.

Ben saw her hesitation and his smile widened. Reluctantly, she took the chair he held for her.

"Thank you, Mr. Paradise." It was disconcerting to find he was just as vital and masculine as she had remembered last night. Imagination had not embroidered her memory.

Mrs. Schmidt filled Lacy's cup with coffee and moved off to refill the cups of other diners around the room.

A sleepless night had not provided a solution to Lacy's transportation dilemma. Much as she decried the necessity, she would have to accept

Paradise's offer to drive her to his town.

Lacy stirred her coffee, venting her anger in the tiny whirlpool.

Ben watched her surreptitiously, amused yet puzzled by her obvious reluctance to confide in him. There was something different about her. A new determination in the uncompromising line of her jaw.

She glanced away toward the window, yet he noted the fleeting shadow of fear haunting the depths of her eyes.

Lacy sipped her coffee and grimaced at the bitter taste.

The corner of Paradise's mouth moved infinitesimally.

She eyed the sugar bowl next to his cup, her ire growing with imagined slights.

"Will you pass the sugar, please?"

Her voice rivalled the arctic chill of a mountain blizzard.

"Sugar." His fingers brushed hers at the exchange.

Lacy's heart skipped a beat, fueling her anger that she should react so to this man.

"Thank you," she said, her jaw clenched.

"Not at all." Wolfish teeth glinted. "Could I trouble you for the cream?"

She sat the pitcher down quickly just past the center of the table. It slopped over onto the white tablecloth.

"Temper, temper," Ben said. "It's going to be a long ride. Hadn't we better call a truce? Or better still, kiss and make up?"

She glared at him. "You have a very perverted sense of humor, Mr. Paradise."

He chuckled. "I can't help it, Miss Phalen. You bring out the worst in me."

"Perhaps it would be best if I remained here at the hotel until I'm sent for," she suggested stiffly.

His brows drew together above his nose in consternation. "That is the most ridiculous statement I've heard you make yet. Helena!" he called, half rising. "Come over here and vouch for me. Miss Phalen doesn't think I'm a proper escort."

Mrs. Schmidt bustled over, the coffeepot still in her hand. "It's probably yer own fault, Ben Paradise. Ya always did have a wicked tongue."

He laughed and pushed the chair back, rising to tower over the young woman at the table. "I believe it is my wicked hands Miss Phalen doesn't trust."

"Oh, now, miss, really," the housekeeper enthused, "ya don't have ta worry about Ben Paradise. He knows the difference between a lady who's respectable and one who ain't."

Ben's eyes twinkled.

"He'll treat ya jest as ya should be treated," Helena continued.

His grin was more a leer. "That is what Miss Phalen is afraid of, Helena," he murmured softly.

Mrs. Schmidt slapped him playfully on the arm. "If that's the way ya've been carryin' on over here, I don't blame her fer worryin'."

Theatrically contrite, he placed one hand over his heart. "I swear I am the soul of discretion, Miss Phalen. I will touch you only if you wish or if your life depends upon it. I will not trade you to any Indians, no matter how much they offer me. I will—"

"Indians?" Her eyes widened. Why hadn't she recalled there were red savages on the frontier? Had she run from a threat to her sanity to one of her life?

Ben waved his hand airily. "Just a few. But you've disturbed my train of thought. Where was I, Helena?"

Mrs. Schmidt smiled at him fondly. "I think he means he'll be a perfect gentleman, Miz Phalen. More coffee?"

Ben stayed her hand. "No, my love, I want to make Paradise by dark so we must be on our way. Besides, it keeps Miss Phalen awake."

The kindly housekeeper looked startled a moment then chuckled as she noticed the distinct twinkle in his eye.

Lacy seethed.

"Did you put up the lunch?" he asked.

"Of course I did. Ya jest go settle with the Mister and I'll put it in the wagon." Helena hurried off again.

Ben looked down at the silent young woman seated stubbornly at the table. The ruffles of his blindingly white shirt were freshly starched and crisp. The early sunlight made the gold at his cuffs flash and the diamond stickpin in his cravat twinkle in a rainbow of colors.

"Well, is it yea or nay? Do we go together or do I go alone?"

Lacy touched the napkin to her lips. "I suppose

I'll have to trust you," she conceded.

"My dear Miss Phalen, even if I swore on a stack of Bibles, you wouldn't trust me. Just believe me when I say your virtue is safe in my keeping."

Lacy felt his eyes bore into hers, the spark in them warm and sincere, no longer teasing.

"I'll just get my hat," she said.

CHAPTER VIII

If there was a road to the town of Paradise, Benjamin Paradise elected not to use it. Lacy struggled to keep her seat next to him on the large wagon as they rumbled over rocks and ruts in the trail. The countryside was beautiful. The rolling green land was sprinkled with a variety of yellow, russet, and blue wildflowers. Birds called to each other in the forest areas. Twice she saw deer standing between the majestic trees.

They traveled along the northern slopes of the Ozark Mountains then turned into the hills themselves. A number of cultivated fields lay along the route but for the most part the landscape was that of forests so dense with trees and brush that Lacy could see no way to enter them.

Ben found the nearly nonexistent trail with no problem. It was quite narrow in the forests but disappeared to Lacy's untutored eyes in the open meadows.

They were silent for most of the morning. Ben hunched forward, an elbow resting on one leg, the reins dangling loosely in his hands. The horses needed encouragement only when a particularly steep grade was reached. Then he would softly coax them, calling endearments.

Lacy's time was occupied with keeping her seat. Occasionally, she looked back into the trailing cloud of dust to the lost comfort of Hopkins Bend, and wondered if she would ever return to the life she had known. Even in her wildest imaginings, she had not pictured her destination so isolated.

It was a little past noon when Ben called the team to a halt in a shaded glen. A stream bubbled from the depths of the forest and cascaded over a small formation of rocks near a fallen log. Wildflowers carpeted the ground. Even at high noon the forest afforded some shade on the fringes of the clearing. Lacy rubbed her aching neck and sighed with relief.

"Lunch?" Ben inquired.

"I thought we'd never stop," she breathed gratefully.

His lips quirked in a knowing half-smile, irritating her. "Not sore, are you, Miss Phalen?"

Her back stiffened unnaturally. She snatched her gloved hand from the corded muscles at her nape to smooth the straggling wisps of hair beneath her hat. "Certainly not, Mr. Paradise," she insisted tightly. "Perhaps a bit parched."

Beneath the brim of his low-crowned hat his brow arched satirically before he swung down from the high, supply wagon with a single fluid motion.

He had removed his jacket and vest earlier as the day grew warmer and now Lacy found herself admiring the way the fabric of his shirt stretched across his broad shoulders. She flushed when he glanced up, noting her interest.

"Need a hand down?" He carelessly cocked his hat back as he gazed up at her.

Lacy's lips thinned in anger. "No, thank you. I can manage." Determined, she pushed thoughts of tumbling to the ground in a confusion of petticoats from her mind. She was the woman who clambered aboard her father's ships with the agility of a born seaman. Surely the slight drop would do her no harm.

Ben strolled leisurely around his team, caressing damp blowing muzzles, patting glistening necks in approval. His eyes were on the slim, stubborn young woman on the wagon seat. Surreptitiously checking the harness, he admired the trim ankle and calf displayed as she lifted her skirts, and her booted foot felt for a foothold. It was a sight he had viewed in Boston as she scrambled up the rope ladders of the Puritan ships ahead of him. She had been as unconscious of the display then as she was now.

She glanced to find him smiling a lopsided grin, an arm draped casually over the back of the horse nearest her. She frowned at the secret amusement in his face and dropped her skirts quickly. If the clod wanted to stare like a fool, let it be at another woman's ankles!

Yet, at that same moment, she slipped, falling

forward only to find his hands gripping her waist, encircling it. Her hands grabbed at his shoulders and slid tightly behind his neck as she sought to steady herself.

"Easy now," his pleasant baritone purred in her ear. "You're all right."

Lacy dangled in his arms, unaware that her feet had not yet touched the ground. He regarded her with a warmth she found disconcerting. Laughter fled as passion stirred in the azure depths of his eyes. He was caught in the womanly scent and feel of her. She felt mesmerized, seduced by the desire in his face, by the strength and feel of his sinewy muscles and his soft dark brown hair beneath her hand.

His mouth drew close to her parted lips.

Hastily, Lacy turned away, surprised to find her fingers entangled in his hair. Ben's lips grazed her cheek before he reluctantly allowed her to slide down his body.

Her cheeks burned with shame at the encounter, yet she felt a tinge of regret as the comfort of his arms slid away.

"Thank you," she said, her voice a tiny, husky whisper.

Puzzled by her rejection, Ben stepped back and tugged the rim of his hat in acknowledgement. "Pleased to be of service, ma'am. I can see you haven't ridden the Puritan freight wagons. You have yet to learn the knack of getting down."

"You made it seem so easy," she murmured, careful not to look at him. What was the matter with her? It was imperative she maintain an inflexible guard on her actions. Even a solitary kiss could be her downfall with the rigid moral attitude of her employers. Martha Haskell had warned her in particular that her personal life would be up for censure. Schoolmarms were a new innovation, a necessity caused by the falling numbers of schoolmasters. Respectability was valued higher than actual academic qualifications in a schoolmistress.

Ben reached under the tarpaulin for the basket Helena Schmidt had packed. She had provided an enormous repast of chicken, ham, biscuits, and apple pie. He unearthed a bottle of wine from one of the boxes in the back of the wagon, and placed it in the stream to cool. Then he leaned back against the log and stretched his long legs out, his arms folded across his chest, his hat tilted easily over his eyes.

"Be a little while before that's ready." He gestured toward the bottle of wine in the creek. "If you are thirsty now, the water is nice and cold."

Lacy followed his example, seating herself against the log, her legs curled safely out of sight beneath her full skirts. "Tell me about Paradise," she urged, curiosity winning out over her embarrassment. "Do you run a general store, Mr. Paradise?" The large freight wagon was filled with barrels and various wooden boxes which were covered with a heavy canvas cinched tightly to the tall sides.

His voice was muffled by the hat covering his face. "No. My business is a little more important than that, Miss Phalen. I supply the citizens of Paradise with a much more valuable commodity."

Lacy was puzzled. "I thought general stores supplied all the necessities."

She could hear the smile in his voice. "Not quite. True you can get flour, seed, cloth, farming implements, and gossip at the general store, but not fun." He tipped the hat and peered at her from beneath the shadowed brim. "That is the commodity I deal in."

"Fun!" Her eyes grew wide in astonishment and belated understanding. "You mean you own a . . ."

She caught the glint of startling white teeth. "Dance hall," he completed. "Not just a dance hall, but *the* dance hall. Only one for miles around."

She gestured wildly toward the wagon. "And those kegs are . . ."

"Whiskey. And a couple cases of wine for the more discerning customers."

Lacy put a shaking hand to her brow. "I really am ruined. I should have stayed in Hopkins Bend."

His hat hid his face again, leaving only the strong line of his jaw visible. "Nonsense. It would have been weeks before anyone came to fetch you. They might even have sent me."

"What kind of a reputation do you think I'll have left, arriving in a wagon loaded with whiskey in the company of a libertine and rake?"

"You really shouldn't flatter me, Miss Phalen."

"I never should have left Boston."

"Ah, yes, I have been wondering why you suddenly appeared in Missouri. The captain sailed, didn't he?"

Lacy glared at him, fury kindling in her eyes. "Yes. I just prefer to choose my own bridegroom."

From the blind of his hat, Ben watched the shadow of indecision flit across her lovely face. A breeze stirred the golden wisps of hair that straggled to frame her newly sun-kissed cheek. The nearness of her soft body drew the knot in the pit of his stomach taut. After months of determinedly squashing all dreams of her, she had walked back into his life, upsetting the careful balance he'd built.

"A wicked stepmother? Not a cruel father," he murmured, keeping his voice devoid of expression.

"You've seen too many melodramas," she said curtly. "I haven't a stepmother and, as you know, my father is the kindest man in the world."

"But he still forced you to accept a husband you didn't care to bed."

She missed the bitterness that crept into his voice. "Really, Mr. Paradise!" She blushed anew at his phraseology. "Papa hadn't anything to do with it. He *is* on his way to China."

Ben sat up and reached for the basket of food on the ground between them. "You might as well confess, Miss Phalen. People are bound to ask me what the new schoolmarm is like after spending a day in her company."

She scowled, her face still a vivid pink. "And you would paint the worst picture."

The smile she was beginning to believe was perpetually in his eyes was now absent. "Not in the least. I will be the first to say that Lacy Phalen is a lady with proper upbringing and strict morals. You will be a credit to our town."

She lowered her eyes penitently. "I apologize, Mr. Paradise. I have not behaved as if I had any refinement. I'm sorry."

"Maybe if you got it off your chest, Miss Phalen, you'd feel better. It will go no further."

She played with a tiny yellow wildflower, twisting and twirling it between her fingers. "I talk too much."

"Miss Phalen," he murmured.

She glanced at him. His eyes reflected friendship and concern. She recalled the impression of strength and security she had felt in his arms. She desperately needed a friend. Should Benjamin Paradise be the one in whom she confided?

He smiled at her, a magic smile which soothed her troubled mind and coaxed a reluctant grin from her. "Perhaps you're right," she said. She would make herself respectable and maintain that attitude even if, after the events in Boston, she felt it was a fiction.

Lacy centered her tale about Abigail and her fear that the woman would eventually succeed in bending Lacy to her will. Abigail and her brother would have destroyed her in time. The fright and hatred she felt for Abigail made Lacy's voice waver as she told of the flight from Boston. Lacy knew it sounded like one of the melodramatic stories she had accused him of enjoying. Something straight from the stage. She wondered if he would believe any part of it.

She need not have worried. When she had finished, his face had a grim look. He made no comment at first but merely nodded.

"It all sounds impossible, doesn't it?" Lacy said, accepting a crockery cup of wine from him.

Ben considered. "Improbable maybe. But unless you are a very talented actress, Miss Phalen, I find it hard to accept it as anything but the truth."

Lacy looked down at her hands. She had twisted the fringe of her shawl into knots as she recounted her terror. "Thank you, Mr. Paradise. You don't know what that means to me. I didn't think you would believe me. That anyone would believe me. But it did happen."

"And it is part of the past," he said. "For the residents of Paradise I believe we should simplify your story. Oversimplify. The facts are trimmed to a single desire to spend the long wait for your father's return in teaching. Since his voyage may extend to a number of years, they won't feel they will lose you in the near future. I think we would be best advised to stress the fact that your father will be in the Orient quite awhile, in fact."

Lacy sipped at the now ice-cold wine. "Oh, but he won't. He thought perhaps two years at the most."

He smiled. "That is something else we will keep to ourselves, Miss Phalen."

The way he kept repeating "we will" gave her a nice feeling. His confidence in her abilities bolstered her own flagging spirits. A single nagging doubt remained. She had neglected to mention William Quire's visit to her room. Would Ben have been willing to help if he knew the whole truth?

Lacy smiled at him. "I can see why Mrs. Schmidt thinks so much of you."

Ben got to his feet lazily and reached down to give her a hand. "If you keep smiling at me that way, Miss Phalen"—he smiled, the twinkle back in his eyes—"we'll never get to Paradise before dark."

Compared to the frontier town of Paradise, Hopkins Bend had been a metropolis. One narrow, dirt street comprised the whole of Paradise's business section. A general store, a livery stable, and a tiny dressmakers' shop lined one side of the street while the other side boasted the long narrow length of the Paradise Saloon. The church was situated just past the saloon, and at the opposite end of town a rather small shack had been designated as the schoolhouse. The saloon seemed to be the largest, sturdiest building in the hamlet.

Few of the residents lived in town; the majority of them had homesteads that dotted the surrounding countryside. Their homes were little more than large one-room shacks. The barns were more substantial.

Lacy did not learn this until the following day for it was dusk when Ben pulled his team up before the dry-goods store. Despite the fact that he had stopped the wagon before reaching town so that she could shake some of the dust from her skirts and set her bonnet straight, Lacy still felt she would not make a very good first impression on her employers.

"Stay here," Ben instructed as he pulled the horses to a standstill before the dry-goods porch. "I'll find out where to put you."

Lacy smiled, totally at ease in his company once more. "Mr. Paradise, I understand what you mean, but must you phrase it as though I were a sack of flour?"

He laughed and jumped down from the wagon. Lacy watched his tall form stride across the raised wooden porch, his footsteps echoing down the quiet street and into the store's lighted interior. A number of male voices greeted him, but at first only Ben's voice rose clearly above the din demanding to know who the devil had requested a schoolteacher.

"A schoolteacher? Well, I reckon we all did, Ben," one man said. "Why ya wantta know?"

Ben growled in a theatrical show of irritation. "Because I got saddled with her in Hopkins Bend and would like to get her off my hands. I've had more than my share of lectures on geography today. And believe you me, Charlie Delaney, you owe me a number of drinks to make me forget you foisted her on me. It's only fair. What do you say, boys?"

A number of other voices chuckled and agreed with him.

"The least you could have done is warn me, Charlie," Ben continued. "I was never so surprised in my life when this female insists she is bound for Paradise and demands that I escort her."

"Poor Ben," someone said. "She must be a real hag."

"Just take her off my hands," he pleaded. "Where does she go?"

"Suppose I get her right now," a voice said sadly. Lacy recognized it as the first speaker, presumably a man named Charlie Delaney. "A real dragon is she?"

"A tyrant," Ben declared.

Another of the unseen men chuckled. "Sounds jest what we need ta get our brats in line."

"Where is she?"

Lacy could almost picture the smile on Ben's face. "Right outside listening to every word you've said, Charlie."

"Jeez. Why didn't ya say so!"

Lacy schooled her countenance to a prim expression. Yet when she faced the townsmen she was hard pressed not to smile.

Ben had his hand firmly on the shoulder of a stout little man with rapidly thinning dark hair. A merchant's apron was wrapped around the man's wide girth nearly covering his trousers. His collar was opened and his sleeves rolled up.

"Miss Phalen, allow me to present Mr. Charles Delaney, mayor of this fine town. Charlie, this is Miss Lillian Phalen, your new schoolteacher," Ben said.

Delaney's mouth dropped open, his jaw slackened as he stared up at her. The men around him succumbed to a similar malady.

"I'm pleased to meet you, Mr. Delaney," Lacy said, hoping she sounded authoritative rather than scared.

The men seemed paralyzed as they gawked at her. She had often been the recipient of masculine stares but they had always been admiring. These men appeared to be struck dumb in her presence.

Uneasy at their continued silence, Lacy glanced at Ben.

He took her cue. Quickly stepping forward, he placed his hands on her waist and swung her to the ground.

The mayor still appeared disinclined to welcome her.

Lacy's stomach fluttered nervously. She had never considered that the citizens of Paradise would reject her. Were her credentials in question? Was she too young?

Ben's firm hand on her elbow urged her toward Delaney. Lacy took a deep breath and stepped up to the mayor. She pumped his near lifeless hand energetically.

"I'm very glad to finally be here, Mr. Delaney. It's been quite a long journey from Boston. I do trust you were expecting me?"

The rotund little man seemed to come to life. "Oh, yes . . . er, I mean, welcome ta Paradise, Miz Phalen. We . . . er . . . we were expectin' ya but didn't know right when . . . This is a bit of a surprise . . . and, er, I'm sure we're very glad ya've arrived."

Relieved, Lacy smiled at him. "Thank you, Mr. Delaney."

The spell broken at last, Lacy saw one of the men dig an elbow in Ben's side. "Hag, my ass. Ya lucky bastard, drivin' all this way with the likes o' her."

Ben wasn't to be drawn in. "Oh, you partial to lectures, Frank? 'Spect we'll be seein' you enterin' the schoolhouse quite regular now," he drawled.

Another man laughed. "What I wouldn't give ta hear what yer missus might say ta that, Frank boy."

Lacy tensed at the teasing comment. "If you will just escort me to my . . ." she began.

"Hell, yes, Charlie," someone said. "Take the little lady home. We'll help ya."

Charlie Delaney looked pained, and the other

men grinned widely. Lacy was leery. What would happen when the new schoolmarm was presented to the hapless mayor's wife?

It was an effort not to appeal to Ben as she faced the jovial men. Their intent was not vicious, she was sure. Yet the results could be just as destructive.

Under the cover of her lowered lashes, Lacy darted a glance at Ben. He stood back from the crowd, an impartial figure. "Don't count me in, boys," he recommended. "I just want to get rid of Miss Phalen's trunk and settle down with a bottle of whiskey."

"Ah, come along, Ben. Sadie Delaney's sure ta put on a right proper show of shriekin' at Charlie here."

Ben shrugged noncommittally. "Seems to me you went to a lot of trouble and expense"—he stressed the word "expense" lightly—"just to bring Miss Phalen here for a tongue-lashing."

Lacy breathed easier as the men's attention swung to Ben's tall figure.

"Didn't bring her here fer that, Ben," Frank protested. "Hell, why should Sadie be mad at Miz Phalen? She ain't done nuthin'."

"Nuthin' 'cept look purty," one man added.

Ben settled on one of the porch chairs and tipped his hat over his eyes. "Up to you," he said nonchalantly. "But I'm not taking her back to Hopkins Bend when your women refuse to have anything to do with her."

The man named Frank rounded on the gambler. "Now, why in the samhill should they do that?"

"You ask me that?" Ben snorted in derision. "You're the ones with wives. You ought to know better than I how they are once they get a bee in their bonnet about something."

Next to Lacy the round little mayor came to life. "Ben's right, boys," he declared. "If ya'll come home with me, ya'll have the womenfolk down on Miz Phalen like a hawk on a junebug. And 'fore long we won't have us a schoolteacher again. Ya want that?"

"Hell, no. Been long enough without one as it is, Charlie."

"I still don't see why they'd be down on her," Frank insisted.

"Cause she's purtier, ya damn fool," someone growled, and swatted Frank a cuff with his hat.

Frank laughed good-naturedly and glanced at the new schoolmarm. "Ah, now ya done made her blush," he observed.

The respite had given Lacy a chance to study her employers. They were errant schoolboys out for a good time, at her expense perhaps, although their intent was far from malicious. She did not relish offending the wives of this small community by having their husbands trailing her skirts like infatuated puppies.

"Gentlemen," she said sternly, her speech as stilted as Abigail's. "I thank you for your compliments. But I did come here to teach school. It has been a very long day. And I would like to rest before I meet your children. If they are anything like you, I am sure I shall have my hands full." She smiled to soften the retort.

They grinned foolishly at her but only Ben's smile warmed Lacy. His eyes applauded her handling of the situation.

"Are you buying me a drink or not, Charlie?" he asked, quarrelsome. "I haven't got all night, you know. There's a wagon full of whiskey to unload."

Delaney bustled toward the shop door, removing his apron as he moved. "Yes, damn ya, Ben, I'll buy ya a drink after I've taken Miz Phalen back ta the house," the mayor growled. In the doorway he turned, his voice softened as he assured Lacy. "If ya'll excuse me just a moment, ma'am, I'll just close the store and bring the buggy around."

She nodded. "Of course, Mr. Delaney."

He started into the store then turned to the still-staring men. "And ya boys go on back ta yer own homes. Leave the lady alone," he advised.

They chuckled and threw some outrageous suggestions to him on how to handle his wife. But they did move off down the dusty street, tipping their hats to the new schoolmarm and grinning foolishly.

Behind her, Lacy heard Delaney locking up. He rejoined her on the wooden-planked porch, buttoning his jacket. "Won't be a minute hitching the buggy up, miss. Oh, ya still here, Ben?"

Ben unfolded his long legs and rose from the chair in the shadows. "I still have Miss Phalen's trunk, if you recall, Charlie."

"Oh, yeah. 'Course, Ben."

Lacy watched the mayor's round figure disappear down the street and into the livery stable.

Ben moved silently across the porch to his own

wagon and began pulling her travel-worn trunk from its nest among the whiskey barrels.

She hoped the meager wardrobe she'd purchased in New York would survive the duration of her exile. The trunk that housed the serviceable gowns was already deteriorating under the abuse of travel.

"I appreciate you turning the tide, Mr. Paradise," she said softly. "I don't know what would have resulted if I was given such a mass escort."

He smiled. "Other than you being tarred and feathered by the good ladies of Paradise? I did warn you that you were far too beautiful not to raise comment, Miss Phalen." He swung the trunk down from the wagon. She was so defenseless, so fragile. She'd never last the winter under the stern eyes of the women. At the first show of spirit, they'd hound her out of town. "If things become too uncomfortable for you, just let me know."

Amusement colored the seductively husky sound of her voice. "You also have a way with the ladies, Mr. Paradise?"

He chuckled. "Miss Phalen, wasn't it you who termed me a rake and libertine? Yes, I will modestly admit, I do have a way with the ladies."

She felt her color rise. "That isn't what I meant, Mr. Paradise. I meant . . ."

"Could I dissuade the hanging party," he finished. "No, but I could be of assistance to you if you ever need me."

His sincerity unnerved her. "Thank you, Mr. Paradise. That is very kind, but I hardly think I shall ever need to call upon you." It would be so easy to throw herself against that broad chest, to melt into his embrace, welcoming the hunger of his kiss.

Delaney arrived with his rig, and Ben swung the trunk into the buggy and helped Lacy onto her seat.

Afraid Delaney would sense the tangible attraction between them, she moved away from the touch of Ben's hand quickly, still feeling the fire where he'd held her so briefly, burning her with even a casual touch.

In the dim light she caught the flash of his wolfish grin. "Good night, Miss Phalen," he purred, caressing her name. "I'm sure you and Sadie will get along. Charlie, I'll see you later," he called, and climbed back up to the box of his own wagon. The last Lacy heard, he was coaxing his tired horses in his quiet drawl.

CHAPTER IX

The days ran into a monotonous stream broken only by a change in schedule on the Sabbath. Lacy fretted under the restrictions, dutifully spending her daylight hours in the schoolhouse and her evenings in near servitude to the numerous families who boarded her. The length of her stays varied with the men's interest in her. Fiercely protective of their husbands, the women passed her around. Yet there was only one man in Paradise who drew her, who understood the hardship of stiffling her effervescent personality beneath the threatened shroud of community disapproval.

Often after the children had left the schoolroom for the day, Lacy found herself staring out at the distant forest wistfully. It was beautiful in its multicolored cloak of fall. The brilliant orange, reds, and yellows turned to brown all too soon. The children brought bouquets of the pretty leaves, and she showed them how to press the leaves between the worn pages of the few books the school boasted. Yet when the children had returned to the fields, Lacy would stare unseeing at the woods, her mind back in Boston treading a graceful waltz.

Not long before the harvest was completed, Lacy was seated at her makeshift desk, staring out the window thinking of Celia Hancock Clary. She wished she could see Celia or even write to her friend. She could not chance a letter going astray, however, or Celia's tongue for that matter. Lacy was lonely for company. Only Sadie Delaney was friendly. The other women were standoffish and she had seen looks of distrust on their dour faces.

Last year in Boston she had danced until dawn with Caleb and a multitude of other men. She had scandalized Abigail with the low-cut necklines of her ball gowns. Her golden curls had clustered around her ears, just brushing her bare shoulders. In her imagination Lacy could almost hear the musicians beginning a waltz.

"Why the sigh, dearest heart?" asked a familiar deep voice.

Her heart caught in her throat, the pulse pounding against the high tight neckline of her gray woolen dress. It was the suddenness of his appearance, she argued, not the man that flustered her so. Where was the cool woman who held court among the dandies of New England, careless of their hearts? "Oh, Mr. Paradise. You startled me.

I'm afraid I was woolgathering. Is there something you wanted?"

He smiled and closed the schoolhouse door behind him. "Not a very prepossessing place, is it?" he asked.

It was impossible not to answer the warmth in his eyes. She grinned at him, her pleasure in his company causing her eyes to glow radiantly. "No, I'm afraid the decor leaves much to be desired."

The schoolhouse had once been used as a storage shed for grain. It had received far more attention in that capacity than it did as a school. The desks were little more than rough tables and benches with deeply carved initials decorating the surfaces. When Lacy had first arrived, the floor had supported an accumulation of dirt that rose in choking clouds when a breeze found its way through the open door. She had swept like a woman possessed and had made little headway against the accumulation.

Ben looked toward the ceiling. "I'll bet the roof leaks."

"It does. Believe me, when it rains, it's almost drier outside the building than inside."

He laughed. "I'm here, by the way, as a representative of Joey Baker who sends you these."

From behind his back, Ben brought forth a handful of multicolored leaves, some well on their way to deterioration.

Shyly, she accepted them.

"A sad lot, I will agree, but I understand from Master Joey that Miz Lillian adores brightly colored leaves. In my day we brought apples to our teachers," he added, and dipped a hand into the pocket of his black suit coat to produce a brightly shined example. "Of course, we had schoolmasters then as well. I'd ask if you mind me taking a seat but I'm afraid I do not see one I would trust to hold me."

Lacy looked at the apple and smiled happily. "Are you a mind reader, Mr. Paradise?"

"That, I'm afraid, depends upon the lady." He made a tour of the room, inspecting the furnishings and few fittings. "Don't know if I'd trust this fireplace. Probably burn the building to the ground if you lit a fire. Why, were you thinking about me? I'm touched, Miss Phalen. I thought you'd forgotten me completely."

Lacy blushed beet-red. "I meant the apple, Mr. Paradise."

"I am devastated," he said. "Here I thought you were wondering if I would dance with you at the harvest shindy and you were merely hungry. Will you, by the way?"

"Will I what? You really are going too fast for me, Mr. Paradise."

His tour ended at her desk. He grinned. "Will you honor me with a dance this Saturday night, Miss Phalen?" He bowed low over her hand.

"Really," she said, flustered at the rush of excitement his touch elicited. "I have no idea if there will be dancing. It is a church social, Mr. Paradise. And if you have ever heard one of those sermons . . ."

He grimaced. "I've had the pleasure, Miss Phalen."

"Then do you really believe there will be dancing at this . . . er, what did you call it?"

"Shindy. And, yes, there will be."

Lacy realized he was still holding her hand and pulled away. "I hardly think that . . ."

"That you can refuse. I absolutely agree. It is the least you can do under the circumstances."

She blinked, staring at him dumbly. "Under what circumstances? Did I miss part of this conversation, Mr. Paradise? I know I was daydreaming but I was under the impression I had been following you thus far."

He picked up the apple and reshined one side of it against his jacket. "Why the dangers I risked stealing this apple for you out of Harper's orchard."

"You stole it!"

"Tradition. I always stole apples for my teacher."

"Mr. Paradise, I must insist . . ."

He perched carefully on the edge of the desk and picked up the slate laying there. "I know. I have to write "I must not steal apples for teacher" one hundred times." He scribbled on the slate.

Lacy found she was tempted to smooth back the dark lock of hair that fell forward on his brow. "Mr. Paradise . . ."

He handed her the slate. On it he had written: "Have dinner with me."

Sadly, she shook her head in denial. "Mr. Paradise, you know I can't accept. I shouldn't even be seen talking to you." She stood up and walked quickly over to the window. "And you know I shouldn't."

He admired the pert profile she presented. A few unruly curls had escaped from the tight knot at her nape. Even the stark lines of her gown couldn't disguise the fluid movements of her body. "But you're tempted."

She glanced back at him. "Yes, I'll admit I'm tempted. You are the only person in this town who isn't . . . well, stuffy. So, please don't tease me."

Ben grinned, pleased with her comment. "Dearest heart, I'll endeavor to keep my distance if you'll promise me that one dance."

Lacy eyed him. "I'm not sure I'll know how to dance here. And you wouldn't want me for a partner if I developed two left feet."

"Stop trying to get out of it," he recommended. "I can guarantee a waltz."

"A waltz! You really are trying to ruin my reputation." She was pleased though. With the idea of the dance or with Ben Paradise? Lacy wasn't sure she wanted an answer to that question.

He moved off the desk. "Then it's settled. You're mine for the first waltz."

"If there is a waltz," she temporized.

His smile was warm. Far too warm for her peace of mind.

"Until then, Miss Phalen." He pulled the door open. A biting breeze swept the bouquet of leaves to the floor. "Oh, damn, I almost forgot. Joey Baker wishes to know if you return his love. I left the poor fellow in a quandary."

Since Joey Baker was nine years old, Lacy readily agreed that she returned his affection.

"And what about me, dearest heart?" Ben asked.

"You?"

"No tender feelings in your heart you wish to impart?"

"Mr. Paradise . . ."

"The name is Ben."

"Mr. Paradise." She grinned warmly. "Good-bye."

He sighed. "I never thought leaves would have it over apples."

"Out!"

He shut the door, but she heard his laughter through the thin partition. Lacy walked back to her desk to pick up the scattered leaves and smiled. She was glad Ben Paradise had come by the schoolhouse. Very glad indeed.

In answer to the children's prayers, Saturday dawned bright and brisk. Lacy's own enthusiasm went unnoticed amidst the excitement of the Harper family, her current hosts.

In record time the children completed their chores. Mrs. Harper accepted Lacy's offer to help in the kitchen with a modicum of friendliness. The woman was effusive on one subject alone: the box-lunch auction. The young unmarried women of the town would be selling their lunches to the highest bidder to benefit the building of a larger church. Repairs on the school were to be passed over another season as unnecessary.

Not expecting to compete in the auction, Lacy was surprised when Esther Harper presented her with a beribboned basket and advised her tersely to stock it well.

"Men 'round herebouts eat a powerful amount, Miz Lillian. Keep that in mind," lectured the stern woman.

Flustered and fearing she was overstepping the

bounds set for her behavior, Lacy protested. "Oh, but Mrs. Harper, I hadn't planned . . ."

Esther Harper frowned, her worn face drawn in lines of impatience. "Miz Delaney gave me this basket special fer ya," she insisted. "Said there was a lot 'o the young men would be mighty unhappy if ya wasn't one o' the ladies they could bid fer taday."

Lacy warmed with the thought of Sadie Delaney's kindness. "I thought it was the lunch they bid for, Mrs. Harper." She laughed.

"Meals they can get anywhere," Mrs. Harper said shortly, then turned almost gregarious. "But a purdy gal ta eat with is somethin' else. That's how I met Harper. He outbid all the other men ta get ma basket. And I've never regretted it. Not one day."

Lacy found it difficult to picture her hostess as a happy woman at all. Nor could she see the woman's straight-faced husband as a determined young man out to win the girl of his choice.

Was she about to plunge out of her depth in frontier customs? "I hope that outbidding another man for a girl's basket is not tantamount to announcing their engagement," Lacy said carefully.

Mrs. Harper's tightly bound, dull brown-haired head gave a short shake. "No. Many's the gal don't cotton ta the man that's bought her basket. There's the undesirables."

Now amused, Lacy assured her. "I hadn't thought of that."

"Yes," Mrs. Harper enlarged, quickly packing a large basket for the younger members of her family. "I always pity the poor gal who has ta set with that Benjamin Paradise. But he always gets the bid up ta a tidy amount. That's nice fer the church even if he ain't a churchgoer."

Lacy smarted under the harsh judgment of Ben and sprang to defend him. "Mr. Paradise can be a very gentlemanly . . . er, gentleman, Mrs. Harper. I doubt if you need pity the girl who's basket he, er, buys."

"Oh, the gals don't seem ta mind none either," the woman agreed, unaware of the anger burning behind the young woman's carefully lowered lashes. "It's disgustin' the way they all make eyes at him. I'm just glad ma Betsy's not that age yet. I hope ta beat more sense inta her 'fore she's ready fer courtin'."

Lacy had a moment of pity for young Betsy Harper. Silently, she stuffed the basket with the plain, but delicious, tidbits Mrs. Harper had prepared.

When the Harper wagon reached the church, Lacy found long tables had been erected outdoors. A number of tidy baskets and cloth-wrapped bundles were already laying on the table in anticipation of the auction. She deposited her own basket among them and strolled off with young Betsy to greet other families as they arrived.

The auction was to begin at eleven o'clock followed by a church service later in the afternoon also held outside to accommodate the large gathering. Following a sermon, there would be a potluck dinner to which the ladies brought their own specialties. Since it was late in the fall, Betsy explained, there would be dancing in the Gablers' barn. It was the largest building in the church's vicinity. They would have a large bonfire outside, but it was the fiddler and the dancing that kept everyone tapping their foot in the cold barn.

Sadie Delaney chuckled when Lacy thanked her for her thoughtful offer of the basket, insisting it had been Charlie's idea. However, when Lacy sought Delaney, he refused to take credit as well.

The day was quite different compared to the stately affairs she had attended in Boston. The casual, neighborly atmosphere pleased Lacy though. She discovered the church social was one of the rare occasions when many of the families actually saw their neighbors. They were kept busy scratching a living from the ground during the rest of the year, or in some cases, were snowbound.

There were numerous arguments concerning the first snowfall. It was in the air, some groups insisted, while others laughed at the idea, declaring that the snow was weeks away.

Bemused by the weather topic, she moved into the pleasant warmth of the sun. The air was crisp, yet it was impossible to feel winter's kiss in the beauty of the bright fall day.

There were few clouds in the sky, yet Lacy heard a sound reminiscent of distant thunder. Puzzled but unconcerned, she moved further into the sunlight.

It wasn't an incoming storm that threatened the day. Lost in her reverie, Lacy wasn't aware of the danger until she heard Sadie Delaney scream her name, her voice shrill with terror.

The runaway team of horses was almost upon her. Their galloping hooves flashed, thundered over the beaten earth. A boy and girl clung to the box of the wagon, bouncing with each jolt. The boy dragged ineffectively at the reins, fighting the stampeding horses.

Mesmerized by the danger, Lacy stood waiting to be struck down. The sound of pounding hooves came closer and yet she could not move. Her limbs had frozen with fear.

The team was almost upon her. She could see foam about the horses' mouths, see it flick away in tiny beads as they thundered closer.

A second missile hurled itself at her from the forest, blurring as it rushed forward to intercept fate. Bodily, Lacy was lifted and swept from the path of danger. The arm around her was strong, a steel band that crushed her ribs. The fluid motion of a horse's muscles against her side registered before she was dropped in the dust by the side of the road.

Lacy lay winded, stunned by the swift brush with death. Slowly, she realized that a man lay in the dirt beside her, his bay horse gently nuzzling his dark hair.

"Damn," Ben swore, sitting up to push the blowing wet muzzle away. "I must be out of practice. My apologies for dropping you, Miss Phalen. But I hadn't planned on falling out of the saddle myself. I hope you're not hurt."

Lacy sat up, raising a hand to her head. "Yes, I am all right." Her voice trembled, her hand shook. Carefully, she gained her feet with the aid of young Betsy Harper's arm. "Thank you, Mr. Paradise. You saved my life."

He shrugged off her statement and got up, brushing at his dust-covered suit.

"By gum, but that was a fancy piece o' ridin',"

one of the men congratulated Ben as the crowd converged on them.

"Even fancier piece o' fallin'," another added with a laugh. "How long ya been practicin' that, Ben?"

Ben wasn't in the mood for joking. He'd thought Lacy would be trampled before his eyes. His lovely, delicate Lacy.

"Who the hell owns that damn team!" he demanded, angry. "Someone could have been killed." His eyes blazed at the men surrounding him.

They looked shamefaced. "Don't get mad. Hell, it was the Furrier kid tryin' ta show off fer Baker's eldest gal. He didn't mean no harm. Got 'em under control now, Ben."

Cold fury from arctic eyes licked at the speaker, causing the man to fall back a step in fear. "If Furrier can't teach his kid to handle his horses—" Ben began only to find a slim hand on his arm.

Her eyes were enormous, her face pasty white. Yet the hand on his arm was steady. "Please, Mr. Paradise. No one was hurt. Let the matter drop," Lacy pleaded softly.

He covered her hand protectively. It quivered, fluttering like a captive bird within his grasp. The movement convinced him that her control was merely on the surface, that she realized exactly what would have happened but for his intervention. "Miss Phalen, if nothing is said . . ."

"The excitement will die down. Please, Mr. Paradise." Fear shadowed her eyes, yet the squared tip of her jaw was thrust upward, determined to put the incident behind her. Only her voice betrayed her as it now wavered. "For my sake."

He looked down at her hand, so pale against the black cloth of his sleeve, so small beneath his. "All right. If you wish it. But . . ."

Lacy smiled up at him, dazzling Ben with her resilience. "Thank you, Mr. Paradise," she said, and allowed Betsy Harper to draw her to safety beneath the large elms.

CHAPTER X

The preacher was a pious little man who leveled fire and brimstone at his parishioners on Sundays. He had strong lungs and, Lacy discovered, a keen sense of wit. During the auction he answered the sometimes ribald comments of the bidding men with quips that redirected the laughter. He urged each young man to bid and outbid each other for lunch with a lovely partner. The ownership of each basket was supposedly secret, but courting couples had no trouble exchanging signals, enabling each young beau to win the girl of his choice.

"Oh, look, Lillian," cried Sadie Delaney bouncing with excitement. Sadie was determined to withstand maturity. Neither her often staid, but fond, husband nor her children could contain Sadie's enthusiasm. Prevented from participating in the auction by her married status, Sadie

Delaney had chosen the lovely new schoolmarm as her protégé. "Isn't that your basket he's holding up now?"

Lacy had joined a group of ladies eager to discuss the progress of their children in the classroom. "Yes, I believe so." She glanced at the group of single men gathered near the proceedings, and wondered which of them she would soon be forced to sit with for the remainder of the afternoon. What could she possibly talk about with them? What did she know of crops or cattle? She could talk easily about the sea, but it was doubtful if any of the young men had ever seen the Gulf of Mexico much less the Atlantic Ocean.

The minister held Lacy's basket high. "What am I bid for this delightful basket? I'm sure the contents are as delicious as the basket looks."

"What about the lady who owns it?" one of the men asked, digging his neighbor in the ribs with a sharp elbow.

The minister smiled and shook his finger. "Now, that, as you well know, is a secret."

"That one sure is," someone shouted, earning a laugh from his friends.

"What am I bid?" demanded the auctioneer. "Do I hear one dollar?"

"Mighty steep, ain't it, preacher?"

The minister was nonplused by the heckling. His smile was complacent. "Ah, but the cause is worthy, my son."

"One dollar!" the shout went up.

"I have one dollar. Do I hear two?"

"One twenty-five."

Lacy sat at Sadie's feet, wondering when the

bidding would end. Very few of the baskets had gone for more than a couple dollars, which was quite exorbitant for these hard-working people. The time element depended upon the comments and roasting that went on between the auctioneer and the bidders.

"Ten dollars!" cried the preacher in a carrying voice. "I have ten dollars for this basket."

"My heavens, Lillian. You must have an admirer or two who saw you bring that lunch," Sadie Delaney commented, a gleam in her eye.

Lacy laughed. "I doubt that. They probably think it is Lisa Hartack's basket. Hers is very similar."

"True," Sadie admitted. "I wonder who is running the bidding so high?"

The minister beamed at his flock. The bidding was going better than he'd dare hope. He noted the silent signal and shouted anew. "Fifteen dollars! Do I hear twenty? Come now, gentlemen, only fifteen dollars for this fine lunch?"

"Who the hell is biddin', Preacher? I ain't heard nobody callin' out but me," Judd Thompkins demanded angrily. "Ya tryin' ta pull somethin' on me?"

The other young men laughed.

"Not at all, Mr. Thompkins," the auctioneer assured him, his face angelic in its innocence. "Your rival is leaning on that tree yonder." He pointed with his gavel.

The crowd turned of one accord to look at the tall man taking his ease in the shade.

Thompkins's eyes narrowed as he recognized his opponent. "Why can't ya sing out like the rest of us, Paradise?" he shouted.

163

Ben was unperturbed by the man's glare. "Didn't you hear me, Thompkins?" he answered. "Maybe you're going deaf. The bid is fifteen dollars. Do you raise it? I don't know about you but, personally, I am getting hungry. I don't think I care to wait for the next lunch to be auctioned off," Ben said, moving away from the tree, and walking nonchalantly toward the group.

Thompkins grumbled under his breath. "Too high for me. Take it."

"Gladly," Ben said. Lacy heard the clink of coins as he paid for the basket.

"Now, if the young lady will just come forward," the minister instructed, and looked around.

Sadie nudged Lacy with her foot. "Go on, Lillian."

"Oh, but should I? I mean, Mr. Paradise!" she stuttered, flustered. Would her hard-won veneer of respectability withstand an afternoon in Ben Paradise's company?

Her mentor laughed. "The man can't eat you. Go on."

Uneasy, Lacy slowly got to her feet.

"Ah, there you are, Mr. Paradise. You've just bought Miss Phalen's basket," the auctioneer said above the buzz of the crowd. "Now, what am I bid for this next basket?"

Lacy felt the eyes of the crowd on her as she moved to where Ben stood. With a smile, he handed her the basket and offered her his arm. When she accepted, albeit reluctantly, he led her toward the tree he had recently left.

"I certainly hope this lunch is worth fifteen dollars," he said.

Acutely aware of the eyes that followed them, Lacy answered, "I couldn't tell you. It's all Mrs. Harper's cooking."

He seated her beneath the tree and settled down next to her, one leg drawn up. "The company alone is worth fifteen dollars." He smiled. "And it was the only way I could have that dinner with you. Now no one will look askance when you sit with me later."

Lacy looked at him in wonder. She realized he had chosen a setting that was removed from the rest of the gathering yet kept them in full view of all interested parties. She could relax and be herself without censure for a few hours thanks to Ben's thoughtfulness. "You knew that was my basket," she accused.

His smile widened, warming her with a flash of mischief.

"Wait!" Her eyes narrowed with suspicion. "Isn't that the same basket we brought from Hopkins Bend?"

He chuckled. "I'm afraid you've found me out. Yes, this is Helena's basket. I borrowed the ribbons from my girls at the Paradise and in a roundabout way arranged for you to receive it this morning."

"Very clever," she conceded.

"Naturally," he said. God! How could he resist the temptation of her gently curving lips? The sun played games in the gilt curls that escaped in attractive disarray about her face.

"What if someone else had outbid you?" she pursued.

"Ridiculous," he scoffed. "Who would do a thing like that?"

Her long dark lashes swept down for a fraction of a second. "Mr. Thompkins for instance," she teased.

Ben considered the pert thrust of her nose, the tilted angle of her chin. How often had his memory painted a flawless portrait of this woman in his dreams? "You'd rather have him win you?"

"No." She grimaced. "Must you phrase it that way?"

He grinned. "Perhaps I should say you've won me. I come with my heart in my hand," he added lightly.

Lacy laughed. It felt wonderful to relax her vigilance, to indulge in flirtatious repartee once more.

"If you will unpack this delightful lunch," Ben said, "I'll bring you a glass of whatever it is they are serving."

She wrinkled her nose. "I happen to know it is very weak tea."

Ben got to his feet. "I'll see if I can't do better," he promised, and left.

The afternoon sped by in a pleasurable blur. Lacy blossomed under Ben's attentive eye and appreciative smile. Her beauty overshadowed the prim character she endeavored to portray as a schoolteacher. The town was stifling her, Ben knew, yet she strove diligently to maintain a facade the townsfolk considered proper. Her act forgotten in the pleasure of his company, Lacy's deep-throated laugh rang true and clear across the clearing.

He maintained his distance, courting her boldly with words, caressing her with his eyes. Every fleeting change of expression on her face was familiar to him. In Boston he had committed every nuance to memory. If his eyes lingered overlong on the tempting contours of her lips or caressed the graceful line of her throat down over the stiff dull fabric of her gown, no one knew. Family groups and courting couples scattered in their own intimate groups, listening with varying degrees of attention as the auctioneer turned preacher once more. If glances turned frequently toward the radiant young woman and tall attentive man beneath the tree, perhaps it was to envy the pair's tranquility.

The intimate atmosphere of the afternoon soon gave way to a boisterous jostling of elbows and good-natured comments concerning the mountain of food prepared by the ladies.

Sadie Delaney took Lacy in hand, placing her amidst the Delaney children at the long makeshift trestle table. Immediately, four separate versions of the children's afternoon assaulted the young teacher's ears, distracting her from the busy adults.

Charlie Delaney was amused at the children's enthusiasm and affection for Miz Lillian. His youngest son was fervent in his assurances that the frog in his hand would not give her warts. The lovely woman laughed softly, the low husky quality stirring Delaney so that he glanced toward his wife in embarrassment.

Lacy reached out to stroke the tiny creature. It jumped, startling her and causing a squealing hue and cry after the frog. Restraining a panicked Betsy Harper while Brian Delaney dove beneath the table in hot pursuit, Lacy's eyes sought Ben Paradise to share her amusement.

Delaney was floored at the mischievous yet tender expression that passed between the couple, and he lost track of the conversation.

"Kids! 'Spect the table ta go over with Brian hoppin' about," Delaney mumbled. "What was that, Ben?"

Ben surveyed his friend over his tankard before taking a sip. "I said," he repeated, "I'd be glad to bring back merchandise for you, Charlie. Just give me a list of items and I'll visit your supply house. It'd be no trouble. I've been planning a final trip before the first snow."

"It better be soon," Delaney remarked, glancing heavenward. A few soft billowing clouds marred the peaceful blue sky, defying a forecast of snow.

"Piffle," Sadie snorted, coming up between the men. With the ease of long acquaintance, she linked arms with Ben rather than her husband and lifted her face for an expected peck on the cheek. "It won't snow for over a month yet, or longer. How was your luncheon, darlin'?" she inquired saucily of Ben. "Everything to your satisfaction?"

Ben thrust his empty tankard into Charlie's hands, and swept Sadie into his arms. "When are you going to run away with me, sweetheart?" he drawled. "Let's sneak away to Hopkins Bend. I'm much more fun than this sour old cuss of a husband of yours."

Sadie gurgled with laughter and cast sly glances at her husband, insuring that she had his full attention. "It has to be Saint Louie, not Hopkins Bend," she insisted. "I'll have you know I expect the very best. And," she added with a twinkle in her eye, "I'm expensive, darlin'."

Charlie sighed. "She is that, Ben. Ya'd be doin' me a favor takin' the woman off my hands."

"Don't you listen to him," Sadie purred, and pulled free of Ben's arms. "Come with me. You'll need to keep up your strength to please me. I can't abide a man who's wastin' away."

Ben eyed the mayor's extended waistline. "I can see that, Sadie."

Sadie gripped his arm, turning him toward the table. "I'll be gentle, darlin'. Just sit and enjoy." With a slight push, she forced Ben down on the bench between Betsy Harper and Lacy Phalen.

The meal passed in a pleasant haze of contentment for Lacy. She listened to the conversation, her concentration wandering. She was very conscious of Ben's leg pressed close to hers beneath the table and the feel of his shoulder bumping hers on the overcrowded bench.

Sadie Delaney glowed with satisfaction whenever she glanced at the handsome couple. The rest of the town had to be blind not to see a romance blossoming between those two, she thought. It was a shame the majority of the women chose to look down on Ben Paradise, remembering only that he was Elisha's son, never recognizing that he was a different breed, a man of whom to be proud. Sadie was sure the exploits abhorred at the Paradise Saloon were far more vivid in the women's closed minds than in truth. Perhaps it was right to decry the three women who offered more than mere libation at the Paradise. Her Charlie never strayed and if the other women's husbands did, it was their own damned fault!

Sadie had set her mind on finding a wife for Ben the first time she met him. She and Charlie had come to town as newlyweds, tempted by Elisha Paradise's claims of easy wealth. Elisha had been a randy old man, but Sadie had been attracted to his two motherless sons, Ben and David, immediately. Rough, wiry lads, both eager for a fight, they'd been anxious to meet life rather than stagnate in the backwoods of Missouri. David's attempt to break free had ended in tragedy. The town still rang with the sound of that years-old scandal.

Sadie pushed it from her mind. Both Elisha and David were dead. The past should be forgotten, not dredged up to destroy those who had their lives still ahead of them.

Lacy was relieved when the meal was over and the men left. Pleasant as his company was, she feared continued contact with Ben would be her downfall. She had gathered from hints dropped that many town residents preferred to forget Paradise's founding family. Only the Delaneys sought Ben out, taking obvious pleasure in his company. It wasn't an old scandal about Ben's family that motivated Lacy to renew her silent vow to keep him at a distance but her own position which called for impeccable behavior. She feared the madness that crept into her blood at the casual touch of his hand, tempting her to throw caution to the wind.

"Now comes the best part," young Betsy Harper stated excitedly, pulling Lacy toward the barn.

"Jack Reeves can fiddle like mad so as yer feet just can't help but start dancin'."

Lacy laughed and allowed Betsy to lead her toward the music. The best part of her day was past. She no longer had an excuse to spend time with Ben. Once more she was Lillian Phalen, a respectable schoolmarm. Her guard was back up. Oh, but how she had enjoyed dropping it for those few hours.

The dancing was similar to that of Boston ballrooms, though far less stiff and formal. There were a dozen variations her partners insisted upon teaching her. Much sought after, Lacy was whirled on to the dirt dance floor by one man after another. Some were married but for the most part her partners were the young, unwed farm workers and cowboys from the surrounding area.

She was standing by Betsy Harper, catching her breath when the fiddler slowed down his tempo and began coaxing a stately waltz from his instrument. Betsy had appointed herself Lacy's shadow, rarely leaving her teacher's side, her eyes worshipping Lacy's every move.

"My dance, I believe," a lazy baritone drawled.

Despite her vow, Lacy felt a resurgence of pleasure at his appearance. "I'm not sure I dare dance with you."

"Don't trust yourself, Miss Phalen?" His eyes twinkled merrily. "What do you think, Betsy? Your teacher promised me the first waltz and now she's trying to back down."

Betsy's big eyes glowed rapturously as she stared up at him. "Oh, Miz Lillian, if ya promised, ya have ta dance with him," she insisted breathlessly.

"You see?" Ben said. "You can't get out of it."
Allowing Lacy no chance to refuse, he led her out
to the floor and into his arms.

"Confess," he urged near her ear. "You were
afraid I'd become clumsy after my exhibition of
horsemanship earlier."

Far too aware of his hand at her waist, she stiffly
forced distance between them. "You know that
wasn't the reason. You aren't exactly the typical
country bumpkin, Mr. Paradise."

He sighed. "Then I'm damned if I know the
reason, dearest heart."

Her brow furrowed in irritation. "I wish you
would stop calling me that. It makes me feel like
one of your horses."

Ben grinned. "Oh, you needn't feel that way,
Miss Phalen. Only you are my dearest heart."

"Mr. Paradise, you'll make me blush."

"I sincerely hope so," he said. "I do have a
reputation to uphold."

She fought back a smile. "Yes, you do," she
declared. "I hope you'll not break Betsy's heart as
well."

Ben's grin widened. "As well, Miss Phalen?
Don't tell me your own heart is in danger?"

Her chin came up. "Absolutely not. I was speaking of the young women of this community in
general. I have been led to believe that they all lose
their hearts to you."

Still, he smiled, amused at her attempt to scold
him. "I've heard the same rumor."

"Rumor, Mr. Paradise?"

"And, believe me, I had the devil's own time
starting it."

Lacy laughed, feeling thoroughly trounced in the battle. "Have you no modesty at all, Mr. Paradise?"

"I have never found the need for it, Miss Phalen. Now, as the music is about to finish, would you care to take a walk in the moonlight with me?"

He admired the sweep of lashes against her cheek, wondering at her game.

"That sounds far too romantic. I fear I'll be tempted to lose my heart to you." She glanced up, the complete coquette.

A half-smile played about his lips, yet his eyes were serious blue slates, devoid of amusement. "Believe me, Miss Phalen, I sincerely hope you do," he said as the music ended.

Uneasy at the unexpected turn of conversation, Lacy stepped out of his arms. "Will you take me back to Betsy, please?"

He nodded. "I see I've offended you."

She was equally serious as she faced him once more. "No, Mr. Paradise, you've only made me realize I cannot allow myself the pleasure of flirting with you. I'll only get in much too deep."

"You seem to be an excellent swimmer, Miss Phalen."

"Still, I prefer to know I can still touch bottom if I wish," Lacy said.

Ben bowed, acknowledging defeat.

"Oh, ya both danced so beautiful," Betsy breathed reverently. "Ain't no one else done as good."

"Did as well," Lacy corrected absently. "There was not anyone else who did as well. Oh, dear, that doesn't sound right either."

173

Ben smiled. "Either way, I thank you, Miss Harper. I believe another waltz is beginning. Might I have this dance?"

Betsy's eyes grew larger. "Oh, Mr. Ben, sir, I don't know how!"

"Come and learn," he urged. Betsy followed him as if in a trance.

"First love," a voice quipped behind Lacy.

"I'm afraid you're right, Mrs. Delaney," she said. "Her mother will be beside herself."

Sadie chuckled. "Oh, yes. Don't I know it. Ben's a nice lad. I like him." She looked closely at the young woman. "And if I'm not mistaken, you do, too. Take a warning, Lillian. Don't lose your heart to him . . . yet."

"I had no intention—"

"You don't need an intention, dear," Sadie said.

Lacy looked at her solemnly. "Aye, I know that only too well."

Sadie squeezed Lacy's hand. "Just a hint, dear. Just a friendly hint. You are so young."

"Not really. I'm nineteen," Lacy insisted.

"Such a great age."

Lacy smiled. "Yes, it does sound terribly ancient, doesn't it?"

"Well, I for one need a breath of air," Sadie declared. "Would you care to accompany me?"

Readily, Lacy agreed and left the barn. She needed to escape from the memory of a caressing warmth in laughing blue eyes.

Their walk was cut short when Charlie Delaney called his wife to join him. Lacy continued alone toward the grounds where they had picnicked earlier in the day.

The bonfire burned brightly, but many couples wandered arm in arm away from its illumination. In the barn the fiddler continued to saw his way through tune after tune, stopping only to quench his thirst.

It was cold under the trees, and Lacy wrapped her shawl closer to fight its chill. The cold seemed to grip her heart.

What was she doing in Missouri? Loneliness crushed the lingering pleasure of her easy flirtation with Ben earlier. The pangs of envy were sharp, painful, as she watched the couples stroll in the moonlight.

Sadie was right. Ben was not the man for her. She had named him right as a libertine. He would only break her heart if she were foolish enough to let him. She must be strong and fight the way she felt about him.

"All alone out here, Miz Lillian? Or ya waitin' fer someone?"

Startled, Lacy turned toward the unknown male voice. At first she saw no one. Then a man stepped forward from the shadows. He was broad in the shoulders with a barrel chest and just a stump of a neck.

Rather than relax as she recognized the Thompkins' eldest son, Lacy grew uneasy. His sudden apperance from the shadows brought the realization that she had wandered too far from the party.

"Oh, Mr. Thompkins," she twittered nervously.

"I didn't hear you come up. No, I'm not waiting for anyone. I just felt the need for some fresh air. It's such a lovely night. And party. This is the first of its kind for me."

"Shouldn't be the last," he said. "Purdy gal like ya shouldn't have ta walk alone on a night like this here."

Looking anxiously back through the trees, Lacy missed the leer and thought his statement mere gallantry. "No, I suppose not. I'd best be getting back. They'll be wondering what has happened to me."

Thompkins barred her way. "Ya ain't very friendly, Miz Lillian."

Lacy clutched the shawl tightly, her chin lifting in challenge. "I beg your pardon?"

Thompkins let his eyes travel suggestively down her body. "Feller meets a gal in the moonlight he figures she ought ta be a little more friendly-like," he said.

Fury flickered in her eyes, her shoulders squared as Lacy faced him haughtily. "Was there something you wanted to discuss with me, Mr. Thompkins?" Her voice was cold, flat. "I'm afraid I am at a loss. You will have to enlighten me."

He came closer. The moonlight shone on his face. Fear licked at the foundations of her courage. The expression in his eyes was the same look William Quire had worn that night at the farm.

Thompkins lifted one large hand toward her hair. "Why, I'd think that somebody with such nice yaller curls and such a friendly smile would want ta get ta know a feller better."

She stepped away from his touch. "I'm not

smiling, Mr. Thompkins. I really must get back. If you will excuse me."

His arm shot out, pulling her back into the shadows beneath the tree, pinning her to the trunk. Lacy could feel the bark bite into her shoulders through her dress and shawl.

Green fire lashed at him from her cold, hard eyes. "Leave me alone," she growled.

Thompkins's gaze dropped to the pulse leaping in the slim column of her throat. "Now, I was hopin' fer a real friendly-like kiss," he insisted.

Lacy was repulsed by the mere suggestion. How dare he! To think that she, Lacy Phalen of the Puritan Line, would demean herself with this . . . this bumpkin! William, at least, had possessed some claim to being a gentleman. Judd Thompkins would not have been termed civilized by Boston standards.

Throwing caution to the winds, she tried to push past him.

Judd snapped her back against the trunk. The violence of his move loosened the tight knot of her hair, spilling it over her shoulders. His hand grabbed the moon-kissed gold tresses cruelly, imprisoning her. "Guess I'll just have ta take one," he said.

The pain as he pulled back on her hair forced her lips open. His tongue thrust into her mouth, savage in its questing. Lacy twisted, fighting panic.

"Fight all ya want, Miz Lillian," he said thickly against her lips. "I like a little fight in ma women."

Lacy avoided his kiss. "You're drunk," she spat. "Leave me alone now and I'll forget this whole sordid episode."

Elizabeth Daniels

"Little licker never dulled me yet with the ladies," Thompkins boasted, as his free hand
roamed over her rounded hip.

Terrified, Lacy clawed at his face, as her mind
dredged up all the horror of the night at Quire
Farm.

"Come on, schoolteacher," he taunted. "I
knows an experienced woman when I sees one."

Lacy stared at him in terror, unable to separate
this man from William Quire. To her, they had
become one and she was back at the farmhouse in
Massachusetts.

"No, please," she pleaded, tears spilling down
her cheeks unheeded. "Please, not again."

"Again?" Judd released her hair and pulled her
sharply by the arm so that Lacy dropped to her
knees. "Come on."

A darker shadow loomed. A grip of iron pulled
Thompkins back from the cringing woman.

"I don't think the lady is willing, Thompkins,"
Ben said.

Thompkins's eyes narrowed in anger. "That so,"
he ground out, eyeing his opponent.

"That's so," Ben said, his voice hard, deadly.

Judd heard the threat and backed down. He
straightened and shrugged. "Guess I got what I
came fer. Fer the moment. Ya ain't always goin' be
'round, Paradise."

"I wouldn't count on that, Judd," Ben said
quietly.

Thompkins stormed away, disappearing in the
woods. Ben bent and gathered the hysterical woman in his arms.

She sobbed uncontrollably, her cheek pressed to

178

the cool silk of his waistcoat. Ben held her tight, stroking her tousled curls gently. "There, there. It's all right," he soothed. "Go ahead and cry your eyes out. You'll feel much better."

Lacy hiccuped. "But g–g–gentlemen hate getting their c–c–coats wet," she insisted, her arms locked about his waist.

Ben smiled against her hair, pressing a kiss to the golden veil. "Thank goodness I'm no gentleman," he said.

Lacy sobbed against his lapel. "It was s–so much l–l–like—"

"Hush. It's all over." Again his lips brushed her hair.

Lacy pulled back from his arms and glanced up, her eyes still swimming with tears. "I'm sorry. I've completely soaked your jacket."

Ben's smile was tender. "It needed washing after that tumble in the dust earlier today."

Lacy tried to answer his smile, her lips trembling, twitching with the effort. Moonlight bathed her glistening face, highlighting the damp path of her tears. Ben drank in the sight. "You're really quite beautiful, Lacy," he said reverently, his voice fervent, caressing her name.

Her eyes shone in the aftermath of tears as she raised her face to his. "Ben . . ." she whispered.

His lips found hers eagerly parted, as hungry and insistent as his. The past and future forgotten, Lacy lived only in the present, in his embrace. Her arms tightened, holding him closer. He answered her urgency, crushing her against his chest.

They parted, breathless, stunned by the naked passion of the moment.

179

"Lacy . . ." He tasted her name, savoring it.

She stared at him, her eyes wide as the enormity of what she had done washed over her, overwhelming in its implications.

Lacy pulled from the safety of his arms. One slender hand to her mouth, she stared at him in horror. "No," she whispered in painful realization. "Dear God, no!"

Passion clouded his mind. He moved to embrace her once more, not comprehending the new terror that haunted her. "Lacy!"

"No!" she cried. With a strength born of anguish and fear, she pushed him away. Blindly, she turned and ran back toward the barn, the bonfire, and sanctuary among the townspeople.

CHAPTER XI

December came and Lacy moved to the Baker homestead.

At school the children's excitement grew as Christmas drew near. They talked excitedly of the gifts they were making for their families, and their enthusiasm increased Lacy's depression. She had no family with whom to spend the holiday season. She was an outsider.

Her father would have reached China months ago and would be celebrating with his crew in Hong Kong or Canton. In Boston, Abigail and Harry would have attended Christmas services and Harry would spend the day playing with his son. Little Harold was probably walking now. Perhaps he had even said his first word.

Lacy tried to act as excited as her students. She

asked about the Christmas traditions on the frontier. She even joined in their sledding adventure after the first snowfall. But her heart was not in it.

In the end she wrote Polly MacGuire a long letter about her new life, wishing her a happy holiday season, although Polly would also be alone. The letter would not arrive until after the New Year, but Lacy felt she had shared the season with Polly.

Carefully locking the schoolhouse, Lacy walked into town to give her letter to Charlie Delaney at the dry-goods store for posting. In front of the Paradise Saloon, Ben's large freight wagon stood. His horses were patient as they awaited the signal to move. Ben checked the harness and glanced toward the saloon door. Praying he would not see her, Lacy slipped into the cozy interior of the Delaney store.

Charlie looked up as the door closed behind her.

"Good afternoon, Miz Lillian," he greeted, coming from behind his long counter. "Come fer more handkerchief goods, have ya?"

Lacy laughed, the sound seeming halfhearted even to her. "No, Mr. Delaney, not this time. I've almost completed the children's presents. I'd like you to post this letter for me, if you will."

"A letter! Well, ya certainly came at the right time. Ben's jest about ta leave. Goin' as far as Saint Louie this time fer supplies 'fore the winter gets too bad. Folks might even get yer letter by the holidays if the river don't freeze up."

He bustled over to the door and dashed across the road, sidestepping the larger mudholes from habit.

"Glad I caught ya," he called to Ben. "Got a letter fer ya ta take."

Lacy remained just inside the open doorway of the store. She had not seen Ben since the church social but had not been able to stop thinking of him and of the kiss they had shared.

She watched as Ben took the letter without glancing at it and placed it inside the bulky, fur-lined jacket he wore. He was dressed in buckskin breeches, which were stuffed into the tops of his tall, burnished brown riding boots. A black hat with a wide-curved brim and flat crown was pushed back on his head.

"Gettin' kind of a late start, ain't ya, Ben?" Charlie asked.

"Hell, yes. Sara is as slow as molasses in January." He turned toward the door of the saloon and bellowed, "Sara, if you aren't out in two seconds, I'm leaving without you!"

There was a flurry of activity inside the saloon and much giggling before a slim girl of medium height ran out the door.

"Ya can't leave without me, Ben!" Her voice was high-pitched but playful. "Ya promised me!" She gave her head a coquettish toss. The hood that covered her hair slid to her shoulders. "And, besides, if ya leave me, who'll keep ya warm?"

Ben jumped to the saloon porch, and pulled the hood back up over her shining dark curls. He laughed and swung her up on the high box seat.

A buxom blonde moved sensuously out on the porch into Lacy's line of sight. "Ya sure ya got enough blankets, honey? I'd hate like hell fer ya ta catch yer death out there."

The girl giggled and clutched Ben's arm as he settled himself next to her. "Oh, I'm sure we'll be warm enough."

Ben patted the tiny hand on his arm. "In any case, I still hope to make Hopkins Bend tonight, Rose. We should be able to make better time without a loaded wagon. Sara will be as cozy as if she were in her own bed tonight," he called.

"Hurry back," the blonde urged. "Place is duller than a doornail when ya ain't around, honey."

"It's just a week, Rose. We'll bring you a new dress," he promised, and slapped the reins.

Lacy stepped back quickly as Charlie Delaney remounted the wooden steps. "What a pretty girl," she commented, moving back into the store to hide her interest. There was a lump in her throat that made her voice tight.

"Who? Sara? Yeah, she's gonna make a right pretty bride, too," Delaney agreed.

Blood drained from Lacy's pinched features.

Charlie studied her. "Somethin' the matter, Miz Lillian? Ya don't look so good."

Lacy's chest felt constricted. "No, I'm fine," she insisted with a weak smile.

"Ya look awful pale," Delaney noted. "Probably spendin' too much time in that drafty school-house. Don't know why ya insist on goin' down there when there ain't classes. Best ya go back ta Baker's and take some tonic. Can't have ya sick fer Sadie's little party Christmas Eve, can we?" He chuckled.

Lacy agreed and left the store, her footsteps dragging as she walked back to the Bakers' cabin.

The memory of Ben smiling down into the up-turned face of the beautiful girl named Sara hurt unbearably. Charlie had rubbed salt in the wound with his casual comment that Sara was to be a bride. Ben's bride.

Blindly, Lacy ran straight into the woods, un-aware of the path her feet flew along. Tears spilled down her cheeks. She tripped, caught herself on a tree and moved on, stumbling more often as exhaustion took its toll. Still, she ran on until an exposed root sent her sprawling on the snow-covered ground and she sobbed hysterically.

At last the sobs changed to dry-eyed calm. Lacy sat in the cold biting air, chilled to the bone, her cloak wrapped tightly around her ankles, chafing numb hands, warming them.

She could not stay in Paradise. Not while Ben Paradise and his bride lived there. She could not bear seeing him again, seeing them together, laughing, happy and in love. She had to leave.

Perhaps Martha Haskell could provide another position. She enjoyed being with the children, yet she missed the sound of the sea and the smell of salt air. The last time she had seen a ship had been in New Orleans before boarding the keel boat for the trip upriver.

Caleb. His face flickered through her mind. Caleb could make her feel alive again. He could make her forget her fascination for Benjamin Paradise, make her forget everything.

Slowly, Lacy got to her feet and brushed the clinging snow from her cloak and skirt. She would write to Caleb. Caleb couldn't fail her this time.

Until his arrival, she would stay out of Ben Paradise's way.

The Delaney home was decorated with holly and fir branches gathered in the forest. Sadie set the children to stringing berries and making paper ornaments to decorate the tree, while she and Charlie attached tiny candles to the tips of the branches to be lit later in the evening. Bringing an evergreen into the house and bedecking it with trinkets was a German custom that Sadie had brought with her from Saint Louis when she married Charlie. Lacy found it was a delightful, beautiful tradition.

In the classroom Lacy had thrown herself into the holiday spirit by drilling the children in Christmas carols more diligently than she'd ever concentrated on teaching them to cipher or to form letters.

She had embroidered and hemmed handkerchieves for all the students. Bound in paper and colorful scraps of yarn, they were bright and gaudy beneath the Delaneys' tree.

"The children will be thrilled," Sadie insisted, arranging gifts under the evergreen boughs. "I just wish I had seen your needlework before you tied these up. It must be excellent with your upbringing."

"Upbringing has absolutely nothing to do with it, Mrs. Delaney," Lacy said. "It is a talent. One that I am lacking as you will see when the children open these packages."

Sadie snorted in disbelief. "You are being far too

modest, Lillian. I'm sure of that. However, speaking of packages, Ben found one waiting for you in Hopkins Bend and brought it over when he returned yesterday."

Lacy was silent. He was back. With his bride. And she was still working on the letter to Caleb. She found it difficult to write convincingly of her desire to leave the frontier.

"I'm dying to see what it is," Sadie rattled on. "My guess is a Christmas gift from your family. Isn't it fortunate that Ben took that last trip for supplies? I know Charlie was overjoyed with the goods he got from Saint Louie. I am in ecstacy over some of the fabric we got. You must come see it, Lillian. I'm sure they don't have any prettier in Boston or New York.

"Of course," Sadie continued blissfully, "you know that you and I are the only respectable ladies who will appreciate it. I wouldn't be surprised if those women at the Paradise don't end up with it on their backs. That little minx Charlie calls Sara apparently went with Ben and picked the stuff out herself from our suppliers. Not that I mind, you realize. Charlie still gets the profit. It is a shame we'll never get a chance to see it made up though."

Sadie rambled on as she dragged Lacy up the stairs to the glorified loft that served as her daughter's bedroom.

Under the sloping eaves was a large bed with straw-filled mattresses and a mountain of quilts. At the highest point sat a large wardrobe. A washstand topped with a large mirror was placed next to the bed in the opposite corner.

Sadie moved across the bare wood floor to the wardrobe and took out a package the size of a bandbox.

"Do open it now, Lillian. Charlie says I've not been fit to live with since Ben dropped it by yesterday. Just the fact that it's come all the way from Boston gives me goose bumps," she said.

Lacy sat on the side of the bed and began unwrapping the string-bound package. When the paper dropped away, she recognized the name of one of Boston's leading merchants.

Inside was a letter and smaller wrapped packages. Sadie breathed over the young woman's shoulder in anticipation. Lacy opened the letter.

"Dear Lacy,

"Before he left, Sean insisted that I not forget you during this holiday season. Of course he had no way of knowing you would be so far away, my dear, and that his package would mean even more to you now when you have no family near. I have included a small token of my own love for you.

"Martha coerced me into teaching classes at the girls school. It makes the time go by much faster, of course, but my heart is somewhere in China with your father.

"I have not written him where you are, just that you are safe and well. I'm sure we both look forward to his return.

"Yours truly,
"Polly"

Lacy wiped away a single tear and refolded the letter.

"How sweet," Sadie said, unashamed to pry. "Didn't you tell me your mother was dead? Is this package from your aunt?"

"My . . . stepmother," Lacy said. "A woman I admire very much."

"That's nice," Sadie allowed. "What has she sent, do you think?"

Lacy smiled at the eager woman. "You are far worse than the children, you know," she said, and began opening the first package.

Sadie laughed. "If you had never been to a larger place than Saint Louie, Lillian, you would be just as eager to feast your eyes on treasures from the East."

"But Saint Louis is a good-sized town."

"It isn't Boston or New York," Sadie said, closing the subject. "Oh, how beautiful!"

Lacy pushed the paper away to display a gown of dark blue silk bound in silver cord. The neckline was modestly cut, the sleeves were long and cut for a snug fit. The skirt billowed in a succession of tiers.

The next package held matching slippers. A shawl of Norwich silk embellished with silver embroidery cascaded from the final package.

"You will look lovely in it." Sadie sighed. "I wish I had something as lovely to wear."

Lacy smiled. "But where can I wear a dress like this? Certainly not to Sunday services. I'd bring fire and brimstone down on myself."

Sadie stroked the fabric, her touch reverent.

"There's no reason you can't wear it to my party tonight, Lillian. No, didn't your stepmother call you something else in her letter?" She snatched the scraps of paper up from the bed. "Yes, she called you Lacy."

Lacy smoothed the silk shawl, carefully refolding it. "Aye, it's my father's pet name for me."

"I like it."

"Isn't it rather frivolous for a schoolteacher?"

"Piffle," Sadie said. "We still have time to press this dress for this evening. I'll hear no arguments, I warn you. I intend to make my party a great success and this dress will do it."

Lacy's protests were overruled in the matter of the dress. Sadie insisted her party deserved the latest hairdo from civilization. She stood by enthralled as Lacy arranged her golden locks. Soon curls spilled from a high knot to brush her shoulders. Smaller curls clustered at her ears and framed her face.

"Everyone will think I'm absolutely decadent," Lacy insisted as she stood before the mirror.

Sadie sighed in envy. "If I could look as beautiful, Lacy, I wouldn't give you that"—she snapped her fingers in the air—"for their opinions."

"Mrs. Harper will . . ."

"Don't think about Esther Harper or any of the other women. You are my present to the men. You outshine us all."

"Which is why I should change back into my gray gown and tame these curls," Lacy said.

"If you do, I will personally tar and feather you, Lillian Phalen, I promise you." Sadie linked arms with the young woman, drawing her toward the

190

staircase. "I can't wait to see Ben's face."

Lacy jerked away from her friend sharply. "He's going to be here?"

"Of course," Sadie said, complacent. "No party is a success without Ben. For one thing, he always brings the whiskey to keep the men entertained. And he's the only man in town who knows how to compliment a woman so she knows it. These others . . . Where are you going, Lacy?"

"I'm changing and leaving."

Sadie followed her back into the bedroom. "So that's the way of it," she said in awe.

Lacy frowned, her eyes narrowing in anger. "Aye, that's the way of it."

Sadie was nonplused. "I did warn you, Lacy."

The young woman whirled, a tempest of billowing blue skirts and gilt curls. "Do you pity me?"

Sadie plunked down on the bed content to ride the storm. "Definitely not, my dear. I adore the man myself."

"But you do see that I can't meet him," Lacy insisted, her anger cooling in the face of Sadie's calm acceptance.

Sadie shook her head, tossing her own carefully cultivated curls. "No, I think you're being a coward. I think you should brazen it out. Show him you don't care."

"Well, I don't care," Lacy said unconvincingly.

"In that case, why hide and lead him to believe you do?"

Lacy paused, half the buttons of her dress undone. Sadie was right. She would not give Ben the pleasure of knowing . . . no, thinking that she cared. She could brazen it out just this once in a room full of people. It wasn't as if she would be alone with him.

Her stubborn, squared little chin came up. Her green eyes brightened with the light of battle. "I've changed my mind. I am going to your party and dazzle all the men. Ben Paradise notwithstanding."

Sadie applauded. "Now that's what I wanted to hear. Here, let me rehook you or we'll never make it to my party."

Although the Delaney home was the largest in the neighborhood, it was still inadequate for the size party Sadie had planned. She had invited everyone in town with the exception of the dance hall girls.

True to Sadie's prediction, Lacy's gown and curls caused a sensation. The men clustered about her while the women either asked to finger the cloth or ignored her presence.

She was acutely aware that Ben's eyes followed her movements. He waited for a waltz before advancing to where Sadie and Lacy stood conversing.

"Hello, Sadie. Miss Phalen. I believe they are striking up a waltz." He smiled warmly at both. "I'm sure you won't mind if I make off with your beautiful guest, Sadie."

Sadie chuckled. "She is making quite an impression. How dull my party would have been if you hadn't brought that package back for her. The latest from Boston, you know."

Lacy's brow creased in irritation. "I doubt Mr. Paradise is interested in our wardrobes. Won't you waltz with him, Mrs. Delaney? I'm afraid I'm promised to your husband for this dance."

Sadie looked surprised at the blatant lie but she smiled, willing to play matchmaker. "Charlie is a terrible dancer. You sure you wouldn't rather change places with me?"

Lacy favored them with a brilliant smile. "Don't be shy, Sadie," she urged the older woman. "You told me yourself you have a *tendre* for this rogue. Dance with him."

Recognizing a trump, Sadie laughed gaily. "You little minx. I told you in the strictest confidence!"

"Have fun," Lacy advised, and walked away from them.

Up at the house later, the children stared in admiration at the tree as Sadie completed lighting the tiny candles. She had the men turn down the oil lamps so that the tree glittered in all its glory.

Few adults had elected to join the children, preferring to stay in the barn where liquor still flowed and the dancing continued unabated.

Sadie had gone around the barn, haranguing different couples to join the small party. Lacy had caught her friend's eye across the room as Sadie approached Ben. The plump brunette was smiling mischievously when she took Ben's arm. The frequent glances she tossed in the schoolteacher's direction infuriated Lacy.

Now he stood behind her chair, his broad shoulders propped against the doorjamb as if attending children's parties was an everyday affair for him.

The gifts were distributed with many sighs from

the girls and wide grins from the boys as they pointed out the initials Lacy had stitched in a corner of each handkerchief.

They in turn bombarded her with their own tokens. She opened pen wipers, bookmarks, and samplers with crooked stitches. Joey Baker proudly presented a rock the size of her fist, describing it as a paperweight. He boasted that the thin vein that sparkled with a warm glow in the candlelight was gold.

"Ain't no gold in Missoura," one of the older boys informed him.

Joey took exception to the remark and was only deterred from instant battle by the large hand on his shoulder.

"Best not to fight in front of the womenfolk," Lacy heard Ben's soothing baritone say. "They get squeamish at the sight of blood."

Joey was quite sure that the blood would be Josh Arnold's rather than his own, but he nodded sagely and contented himself with an angry glare across the room at his opponent.

Betsy Harper had strung a necklace of seeds for her teacher, and Lacy pleased her by immediately putting them on. Her curls caused some trouble, getting in the way as she tried to tie the necklace. Betsy's attempt to help was just as futile. Once again Ben stepped into the breach. Betsy held Lacy's golden wealth of curls aside while he tied the necklace behind Lacy's neck. Tingling from the touch of his fingers at her nape, Lacy hoped that in the dim light no one else would notice her embarrassment.

She needn't have worried. Betsy was drawing all the stares.

"Mr. Ben," she said, her childish voice ringing out, "I sure did like yer learnin' me that there dance. Would ya mind practicin' it with me some? I'm mighty partial to it."

The tall man was very gallant. "Not at all, Miss Harper. I'm mighty partial to it myself." There was a smile in his voice, one of appreciation. "There aren't many women in these parts who dance it as well as you do. But I doubt if Mrs. Delaney's party is quite finished. I promise you more lessons as soon as it is."

Sadie had already turned the light back up and was snuffing candles on the tree. "I'm quite longing to get back to the dancing myself," she said. "You and Betsy lead the way, Ben. We'll follow as soon as Miss Phalen has gathered all her gifts together. Lacy, I do believe you've dropped one of your pen wipes."

Betsy needed no more encouragement. She dragged Ben out of the room. He smiled down at her, offering her his arm. "Oh," her voice carried back to the gathering, "you mean the way Miz Lillian does? Ya really think I can dance like her, Mr. Ben? Floatin' like? I want ta be jest like her. She's beautiful."

Sadie helped Lacy gather her gifts. "I'm afraid Betsy is doomed to disappointment." She sighed.

"In what way?" Lacy asked. "She really is a marvelous dancer, you know, Mrs. Delaney. She catches on fast."

Sadie chuckled. "You mean in starting up a

flirtation with Ben? Well, I'm sure you were flirting long before you were eleven, Lacy. And didn't you call me by my first name earlier this evening? I thought we were friends and now I'm back to being *Mrs. Delaney*."

Lacy threw a smile back over her shoulder. "Oh, I was getting even with you."

Sadie chuckled. "I know you were, you wicked girl. That's why I invited him up to the house." She deposited Lacy's treasures in an empty bandbox. "It's very entertaining having you around, Lacy. I swear, I'm ready to tell Charlie to forget his silly boarding system and have you stay here. We do have the room."

Lacy began smoothing her discarded gray dress on the bed.

"Whatever are you doing?" Sadie demanded.

Lacy folded the dress and fit it into the waiting box. "I'll be leaving early with the Bakers. The children can't stay up much later, you know. I thought I'd better be ready when they are."

"Well, you can't go," Sadie said. "You're indispensible to me."

Lacy laughed. "In what way? No, I will leave with the Bakers, Sadie. It's best that way."

Sadie checked her hair in the mirror. "Best for who . . . or is it whom? No matter. I won't let you go and that's final."

Lacy's head cocked to one side. "Just what are you planning, Sadie? I'll stay if you want, but only on the condition you'll stop playing matchmaker."

"Piffle. I'm not doing a thing. Now, I must run and find Mrs. Baker and give her the good news."

"Joey will be heartbroken," Lacy warned.

"Oh, yes, which reminds me of Betsy Harper. I'd best see to her before she convinces Ben to elope." She gave a sidelong glance. "I wouldn't put it past her but I have different plans for him."

"As long as they don't include me," Lacy said.

"I do wish you'd stop being a stick in the mud, Lacy," Sadie advised, and vanished out the door.

CHAPTER XII

Judd Thompkins sat hunched over in the saddle, his short neck tucked down in the heavy folds of his jacket, his hat low over his eyes as he rode alongside the wagon. His younger brothers and sisters were huddled beneath furs in the back while his parents braved the biting cold on the box. The youngsters were still wiggling with excitement, their shrill giggles piercing the night, hurting their elders' drink-befuddled heads. Mr. Thompkins growled as he slapped the reins. Mrs. Thompkins, her back ramrod straight, shushed the children angrily.

"I don't see why ya had ta act that way ta Josey Hodge, Judd," his mother whined. "She's a decent gal who'd make ya a good wife."

"Don't want no wife," Judd muttered. " 'Specially not Josey Hodge."

"She's a good girl . . ."

"Horse-faced," he said, and received a grunt of agreement from his father.

"Judd's got his sights set on a different filly," Thompkins senior explained. "Ain't ya, boy?"

Mrs. Thompkins sniffed. "That schoolmarm. Don't think I haven't seen ya lookin' at her. Them ain't healthy thoughts, Judd. She's not fer the likes o' us. Now Josey Hodge—"

"Quit yer harpin', woman. Leave the boy alone," Mr. Thompkins insisted with another frustrated slap of his reins.

"I'm only pointin' out what's good fer the boy, Ezra," Mrs. Thompkins declared.

Judd listened in silence to their argument. In his mind's eye, there floated an image in blue silk and golden curls. As delectable as taffy and just as sweet to the taste, she was. He'd shucked off all thoughts of wedding Josey Hodge the first time he'd laid eyes on Miz Lillian. She always seemed so far above his touch until he saw the way she looked at Ben Paradise. He had known she was no better than those other fancy women up at the saloon then. Flaunting those fancy clothes, flirting with her eyes like a jezebel. Acting so pure and innocent, too, making him think she was above mating with the likes of him.

An angry gleam flashed in Judd's eyes as he pulled his horse up, turned and rode off into the woods. The schoolmarm was staying at the Delaneys' tonight. He'd heard Baker say so. Paradise was a friend of Delaney's. Could be Paradise was planning on staying as well, getting cozy with the schoolmarm.

"Judd, Judd! Ya come back here!" Mrs. Thompkins called.

"Ah, leave the boy be, Emma," Judd's father snorted. "Hell, he's a man now. Prob'ly off ta the saloon ta scratch his itch."

"Ezra! The children!" screeched the woman.

Thompkins chuckled. "Got an itch maself, Emmy."

From the porch, Sadie waved the last of her guests farewell.

"It was a perfect party," she breathed.

Lacy grinned at her. "Yes, it was lovely. The equal of many I've attended in Boston."

Sadie glowed. "I know it's a lie," she declared, linking arms with her young friend. "But I think I'll consider it a compliment all the same. Oh, Lacy, you've lost your beautiful shawl somewhere."

"No, I believe I left it in the barn." Lacy sighed. It had been a lovely party despite Sadie's attempts at matchmaking. Didn't the woman know of Ben's attachment to the beautiful Sara? It seemed common knowledge among the men.

Sadie turned toward her large kitchen. "I'll get Charlie to get it. The cats are sure to find it and ruin it."

"Don't bother him, Sadie," Lacy insisted. "It won't take me a minute to get it."

Sadie waved the suggestion away. "Oh, it's no bother. He's talking to somebody, though goodness knows who is left! I quite lost count of who went and when."

"Nonsense. Don't disturb him." Lacy reached

for her cloak on a peg near the door. "There's a lantern on the porch. It won't take me long to find. Just go up to bed. I'll be in shortly."

Sadie hesitated. Still, what harm could befall the girl? The last of the drunken young men had gone. She'd be safe. "If you're sure . . ."

"Of course I am." Lacy swung the cloak around her shoulders and reopened the door. "Sleep tight."

Relieved at Lacy's insistence, Sadie smiled. "Believe me, I'm exhausted. I'll sleep like a log!"

Lacy returned her smile fondly and went back out to the porch.

She lit the lantern Charlie kept outside the door. It cast a very feeble beam. The amount of illumination didn't really matter. Lacy knew her way.

Above the sky was cloudless. Stars too numerous to count winked in the velvet of the heavens. Lacy stood gazing up at the moonlit sky.

Christmas Eve. Or perhaps it was Christmas Day already. On board the *Puritan Paramour*, her father and his crew would be celebrating with roast goose and toasts to their loved ones back in Boston. Caleb would have shipped gifts to his mother and sisters from England, and Polly would probably spend the day with Martha Haskell at the girls school.

She should feel fortunate Sadie Delaney had rescued her from the prospect of Christmas with the Bakers. Sadie's household was a buoyant, cheerful one, unlike the depression-bound homes of many of the farmers. Sadie offered a respite that in itself was a gift Lacy treasured.

She took a deep breath of the crisp, chilling air

and moved into the darker area of the barn.

The lantern cast shadows that danced grotesquely on the stable walls. Charlie Delaney was fortunate in having two large barns in which to store his grain and animals. The larger one usually housed the horses, but he had moved them to the smaller one prior to the party. The quiet unearthly atmosphere urged Lacy to move swiftly across to where she had dropped Polly's gift across a stall door earlier. The silver embroidery gleamed in the lantern glare.

From the cover of the trees, Judd watched the wraithlike figure float across the snowy yard toward the barn. Was she sneaking off to meet Paradise?

He tied his horse out of sight and followed the young woman inside the dark confines of the barn.

"What's the big hurry, Miz Lillian?"

Startled, Lacy turned the lantern so that the light fell on the speaker. "Oh, Mr. Thompkins. I thought you had gone with the others."

He stood in the doorway, blocking the exit. "Had. Thought I might come back."

"Well, as you can see, the party is over." Lacy retrieved the shawl and moved to pass him.

His large hand shot out, gripping her arm. "Like I said, Miz Lillian, what's yer hurry?" Her fingers were numb as he took the lantern from her hand and hung it on a hook. "We kin have ourselves a real nice *private* party now, can't we?"

Lacy felt a tinge of fear. "Mr. Thompkins, please. I thought you understood. I'm not interested in starting a . . . a romance with you."

He grinned, his lips pulling back to show uneven teeth. No sign of Paradise. But he wasn't about to pass up this opportunity. "Maybe I can change yer mind. That one kiss jest weren't enough fer me. If ya know what I mean."

Her eyes narrowed in irritation. She could smell the whiskey fumes on his breath. "Mr. Thompkins," she said, endeavoring to keep her voice calm and free of emotion, "will you please let go of my arm? I'm expected at the house."

"No," he mused as if she had never spoken, "no, jest made me want more."

Lacy pulled away from him sharply. "If you will excuse me," she said, her voice icy. "I don't believe this is the place or the time for a discussion. It is late. It's cold and I'm tired. Good night, Mr. Thompkins."

Judd jerked her back, his hands cruel, tight on her arms. "Ya don't seem ta smart, Miz Lillian," he muttered dangerously. "Ya ain't goin' nowhere. Not 'til I'd ma fill o' ya."

There was no mistaking his meaning. Lacy's facade of courage disappeared. Wrenching herself from his grasp, she made a frightened dash for the door.

Judd was faster. He swung her around, knocking her off her feet into the loose hay on the floor of the nearest stall. He dropped down beside her and tried to take her into his arms.

Lacy clawed wildly at his face, raking his cheek with her nails.

"Fight all ya want, Miz Lillian," he said thickly. "Like I tol' ya before, I like ma women ta fight."

Lacy's nails made contact with his face, drawing

blood. Judd snickered and grabbed both of her hands. He pulled them over her head and moved his body to straddle hers. Lacy twisted furiously under him.

Judd's leering face was grotesquely shadowed in the meager lantern light. Her strength was waning, making Lacy aware of her own helplessness. She was at his mercy and Judd Thompkins did not know the meaning of the word.

His breathing was labored as his free hand loosened the cloak from around her neck, pushing it aside. At long last he touched the silken texture of her pale skin. His fingers explored the neckline of the blue gown.

Lacy heard the sound of rending silk, felt the pull of the dress at her shoulders before the fabric gave under his hand. "Please, don't," she pleaded.

Judd paused, tearing his gaze away from her naked flesh. Would she weep? He disliked wet-eyed women. If she did, would he be able to stop the raging need he had for her?

She was faintly flushed but dry-eyed, he noted with pleasure. Her breast heaved in indignation rather than terror. Almost gently, he ran a callused hand down the delicate curve of her throat, past her pale shoulders to the quivering fullness of her breasts.

Her eyes spit hatred, hardening rather than softening as he'd seen them do for the gambler. "Did ya fight this much against Ben Paradise?" His voice was harsh, angry.

"You're hurting me."

Judd's hand continued its exploration, tearing her clothing with excruciating slow movements.

205

"Did he please ya, Miz Lillian?"

Lacy's courage snapped as his mouth descended, sucking at her exposed flesh. "Let me go!"

Judd was deaf to her cries. He heard them as whimpers of ecstasy and renewed his attack. Still, the picture of her writhing in Paradise's arms haunted his mind. Had she moaned his name, wrapped her shapely limbs around the gambler? "Did he pleasure ya like this?" he persisted harshly.

Lacy twisted violently beneath him, panicked, nearly blind with fear. "Ben never touched me!" she sobbed.

He halted in his movements as if stunned. Lacy hardly dared breathe.

"Ben, is it! Don't lie ta me." His whiskey-soaked breath scorched her cheek. "I've seen the way ya look at him." He released her arms to fumble with his belt.

Lacy's outthrown hand contacted with an empty bottle, a memory of the laughter and Christmas good will. She swung it, catching Thompkins a blow on his ear. He reeled back. She put all her strength into a last heave, throwing him off balance.

Judd wrenched the bottle from her grip and swung, backhanding Lacy as she lunged from the stall. The blow knocked her sideways. She fell, her head hitting the side of the wooden barrier, and slumped down into the straw, unconscious.

Judd rolled her limp body over. He bent close, assuring himself that she still breathed. Damn her!

He wasn't missing his pleasure just because the bitch was. . . .

He stopped, listening. Voices were approaching the barn. He recognized Charlie Delaney's chuckle.

Judd put the lamp out. There'd be another time. Soon, he promised. He eased out of the stall, out the back door, disappearing back into the night, leaving Lacy's unconscious form sprawled in the straw.

Lacy regained her senses slowly. She shivered. Judd Thompkins had gone. The barn door yawned wide, admitting a biting wind. She barely felt its sting against her bruised and battered body. The new dress was torn and gaping, offering no protection from the weather or the sharp, brittle hay upon which she lay.

Would he return? Was he somewhere near, in the dark?

She lay staring blindly at the small section of loft she could discern in the moonlight.

If she remained where she was, unprotected from the elements, perhaps she would die. At the moment it was all she asked. Thompkins had crushed any desire to survive. Even William Quire had not behaved like the rabid animal Thompkins had become. She shrank away from the memory of what his hands had done. Terror, a blinding, all-consuming terror, left her numb and apathetic as to whether she lived or died.

Slowly, her instinct to survive swelled inside her, and Lacy managed to pull herself up with the help of the stable partition. She was tired, exhausted. Her head throbbed. If she could just go to sleep. . . .

A small voice inside her head would not allow it. She had to survive. Return to Boston. Return to the captain and Polly. She was going to meet Caleb and. . . .

No. Lacy retreated from that thought. How could she ever allow another man to touch her after what she had just experienced? No, she would not think of Caleb. Would not think or plan any further than dragging herself to the Delaney home.

Her legs were liquid. Sheer will power made them support her. She stumbled often, falling to her knees in the snow and mud, no longer cognizant of the pain each movement, each fall, renewed.

When at last she reached the porch, Lacy was reduced to crawling on her hands and knees. Her mind as well as her body was numb with fatigue. She had reached the sanctuary and was content to lie there, half-naked, oblivious to the dropping temperatures.

Lacy dreamed she heard the startled snort of a horse, that a hand touched her. Faceless men surrounded her. She shied away, whimpering, afraid she would feel the cruel hands and see the leering, lusting face of her attacker once more.

The two men exchanged a look. One turned into the house, shouting for his wife. Lacy was not sorry to see him leave. She only wished the other man would too. Instead, he gathered her in his arms. Gentle, tender arms. A deep, quiet voice whispered meaningless words meant to soothe. She struggled, barely stirring in his arms. Then a sense of contentment settled over her, as if she had come home. She never wished to stir from those strong, comforting arms. She wished the voice would go on forever. A voice that called her "dearest heart."

CHAPTER XIII

January 1849

Lacy awoke in a dream world. Was it a continuation of that same dream, the nightmare? She was not sure.

Above her floated a cloud of pink calico. Winter sunlight poured through lace curtains onto a quilt of the same print. She blinked and looked again expecting to see the stark timbers of the Delaneys' barn roof over her head. The pink canopy remained.

"How ya feelin', honey?" asked a hoarse female voice.

She was alive! Slowly, expecting a surge of pain, Lacy turned toward the woman. Her throat hurt. "Where am I?" she croaked.

The woman's voice was near. "Don't ya remember?"

Lacy closed her eyes, remembering Judd

Elizabeth Daniels

Thompkins's angry face. "I . . . I don't want to . . . yet."

"Don't blame ya, honey." The chair creaked as the woman got to her feet and moved to the bedside. She was a large woman, inclined to be plump, more so than was considered modish. Her generous attributes were displayed to advantage in a beribboned corset, short petticoat, black stockings, and high-heeled slippers. A frilly pink wrap was draped over one arm. Blond hair fell down her back in a cascade of curls. Her lashes were darkened with cosmetics, and the bloom in her cheeks had originated in a paint box. The expression on her faded, pretty face was one of concern.

"I'm Rose," she said. "This here is my room."

Lacy glanced from the calico of the bed to the lace curtains and dainty chairs. They did not seem to fit the blowsy woman hovering over her. "It's very pretty."

Rose beamed with pleasure. "Ben thought ya might like it."

"Ben!" As Lacy struggled to sit up in bed, the sheet slid away, revealing a thin nightgown. Modestly, she pulled the quilt up to her neck.

"I'll go tell him yer awake. He's been figgetin' like a skittish colt," Rose said.

Lacy clutched the quilt even closer. "I can't see him like this!"

Rose chuckled. "Oh, he won't mind, honey. But if ya want, one of the girls left ya a robe ta slip inta. She figured ya wasn't gonna feel comfortable in the nightgown I borrowed. She's a sight more yer size." Her hips swayed as she went over and pulled the door open. "Oh, anythin' ya need, jest help

212

yerself, honey. I'll hold him off fer ten minutes 'er so." She winked and closed the door gently behind her.

Bewildered, Lacy climbed out of the bed and was immediately sorry. The room swam before her. She clutched at the bedpost until the room steadied. Her whole body ached. When she moved, it was impossible to keep back the groan that escaped her lips. Her body rebelled with every movement.

From the sounds in the street and the bright sunlight, Lacy realized she had lost more than a few hours. It must be late in the day. Although what day it was, she could not recall. Had Sadie's party been held last night? Lacy's forehead wrinkled in thought. There seemed to be some memory of a woman forcing broth into her mouth, of a gray-haired man examining her. How long had she been unconscious?

She swayed to the dressing table mirror and gasped at her reflection. The gown was similar to one Celia Hancock had purchased as part of her trousseau. The wispy white cloth did nothing to hide her blushing flesh. The deeply scooped neckline nearly exposed her breasts while the fabric clung tantalizingly to the slim curve of her waist, the fullness of her hips. It highlighted her shapely long legs.

Lacy cautiously made her way to the wardrobe and found the robe among Rose's spangled collection. It, at least, was made of sturdy quilted calico in a pale green shade. Obviously made for warmth, Lacy was pleased it would cover the highly indecent nightgown. She wrapped it and cinched the belt. The robe stubbornly refused to lend itself to propriety, however, leaving an amazing amount of breast still exposed. With a sigh, Lacy resigned herself to a display of charms and borrowed Rose's hairbrush.

The door swung open at Ben's tentative knock. "Miss Phalen?" he called cautiously. Her voice was soft yet carried no hint of her illness. It was strong, determined, as she invited him in.

He pushed the door open and smiled. "Rose says I must leave the door open while I visit. How are you feeling?"

She was seated on one of Rose's dainty chairs, the robe arranged to cover her bare feet. Her hair spilled in burnished glory over her breasts almost to her waist.

He was not wearing his coat or cravat and his ruffled shirt was open at the neck. On his right hand was a rough bandage that looked suspiciously like the torn flounce of a petticoat.

Lacy was overcome with shyness. Events at the Delaneys' had intruded once more on her memory, leaving her with a feeling that she was indebted to Ben.

The sweep of her long lashes shielded the uncertainty in her eyes as she played with the belt of the borrowed robe.

"I'm all right," she answered softly. "How did I get here? I take it I'm at the Paradise Saloon."

He settled in the second chair. "You are, and putting a real dent in Rose's business, believe me."

His attempt at humor earned him a timid smile. Yet she turned away, embarrassed to meet the tender expression in his eyes. "I hope she doesn't mind," she said softly.

Ben crossed his legs, one booted ankle resting on a black-trousered knee. "She says it gives her a chance to rest."

Lacy abandoned the belt and pleated a fold in the skirt of the robe. "How did I get here, Mr. Paradise? The last I remember . . ."

As the shadow passed over her face, Ben frowned. "Don't think about it. You weren't in very good shape when Charlie and I found you."

Lacy kept her gaze fixed on her lap. She had begun to remember far too much about that night. The sound of rending silk, the stiff straw of the stall, the bitter cold. Thompkins's face. She shuddered slightly.

Ben untangled his long legs and leaned forward. "I wish we could have . . . well, done more. You were half frozen, bruised. If only we had known what you were going through . . ."

Her lashes fluttered against the bruised shadows beneath her eyes. "Please, Mr. Paradise."

He nodded in silent affirmation that the subject of her ordeal would no longer be mentioned.

"Sadie wrapped you in blankets and doused you with laudanum. She never left your side the whole night. Charlie and I could not make sense of anything you said before you fell asleep. But the next day the whole story was all over town."

Lacy flinched. In her lap her hands began to sweat.

"Seems Judd Thompkins couldn't wait to brag about what he'd done. I'm sorry, Lacy, but that is the only way to describe it."

"I understand," she whispered.

Ben's injured hand clenched in fury. "Hell, I saw how you looked when he'd finished with you." Unable to stay seated, he strode to the window and gazed out in silence. "The bastard deserves to be strung up."

Lacy continued to contemplate her hands. They lay calmly in her lap, belying the turbulence of her emotions. "He made comments . . . about you and me," she murmured.

Ben nodded, staring unseeing at the afternoon traffic in the street below. "I'm afraid the whole town or rather the majority believed him, too." He flexed his bandaged hand. The satisfaction he'd felt disabusing Thompkins of his accusations had been faint and short-lived. "I wish Charlie had let me kill him."

Lacy glanced up to meet a wry smile on his face.

"Or at least try to," he added, his lips turning up in a crooked mirthless grimace.

"Oh, but you—"

"No, no." He shook his head. A lock of dark hair fell over his forehead. "Charlie allowed me the pleasure of blacking his eye, no more."

Her gaze dropped once more to her lap as she again played with the belt. "I . . ."

"Don't think about it," he urged. "It's past. You have to make a new start now."

A new start. Hadn't that been the reason she'd run from Boston? Not just to escape but to find a new, albeit temporary, life as one of Martha Haskell's schoolmarms?

Lacy glanced up in agitation to meet Ben's eyes. "The school!"

"No, I'm afraid you can't go back there."

"But—"

"The town council has voted to apply for a new schoolteacher."

"You mean I've been dismissed."

"Yes."

"I see." The belt was quite mangled. She smoothed it out on her thigh almost absentmindedly. "I should return to the Bakers' and . . ."

His voice was very quiet. "They won't take you, Lacy."

She stared at him, a blank expression in her eyes that scared him with its desolation. "No one will now, is that it?" Her voice hardened.

"Sadie would but with the community against you . . ."

Sadie was her friend but Lacy would never do anything to hurt Sadie's standing in the community. "So no one will take me in."

Ben made a helpless movement.

"No one except Ben Paradise," she said.

He grinned at that, but his eyes remained solemn. Her chin had come up in the determined stance he was learning to appreciate.

"I don't suppose you know of any other towns in need of a teacher?" she asked, her voice strengthening with resolve.

Ben regained the chair and leaned back. She was going to be all right. The ordeal had merely dented her spirit. "I do know someone who needs a housekeeper." The teasing quality crept back into his deep voice. "I don't suppose you have any training in that position though."

A flare of temper flashed in the murky green depths of her eyes. "Oh, no," she said, her tone carrying a sarcastic sting. "I wasn't the one who looked after my father's home after Mama died."

Ben's eyes warmed as he watched her. "I didn't think you could have been. Most likely the evil cousin."

"Abigail Phalen doesn't know a feather duster from a rag mop," Lacy spat before she realized his tone had been teasing. Her burst of temper died as quickly as it had flared, but she felt better for it. More alive. Once more in control of her destiny.

Ben's smile touched his eyes. "I think you'll make it, dearest heart."

Lacy tossed her hair back as a wayward curl tickled her nose.

Ben's eyes dipped appreciatively to her exposed breast. "Yes"—his voice was a soft drawl—"yes, I think you'll be fine now."

Lacy wished she had not disturbed the once careful arrangement of her hair after all. "Is there a shawl I could borrow from one of the girls? It's rather cool in here."

"Is it? I was feeling rather warm myself."

She frowned at him but could not help the slight flutter of her heart in response to his smile. "You mentioned a housekeeping post, I believe. It can't possibly be here in Paradise."

"Why not here in Paradise?" His smile was growing far too warm for her comfort. "Why not here *at* the Paradise?"

"Here?"

"Sure. Even a dance hall needs someone to keep it running smoothly."

She flushed at the thought. "Oh, but I couldn't. What would people say?"

He brushed a nonexistent thread from the immaculate black trouser leg, preferring not to see the pain surface in her face once more. "I hate to remind you, Lacy, but after what Thompkins said, no one will be surprised."

Her color heightened.

Ben opened and clenched his hand again, studying the snowy-white bandage. "Beautiful young women from big cities are flirts and willing participants." He glanced up to meet the rekindled fury in her eyes. "*Everyone* knows that, Lacy. Just ask Esther Harper if you have any doubts on that score."

"From Boston?" she sputtered.

"Especially from Boston," he said. "Want the job?"

Her anger receded in the face of his calm statement. "Your offer is very kind," she said, and contemplated her lap again. "But I know you're only trying to help me. Rose probably handles everything very well." She had no intention of mentioning the beautiful Sara who would soon be mistress of the saloon as well as of its owner.

The fluctuation in her moods from fury to timid acceptance irritated him. "Damn it!"

Startled, Lacy looked up to find Ben striding to the open door. His bellow was followed by a scampering of high-heeled shoes from rooms down the corridor to the accompaniment of giggles. Coming through the door, Rose gave Ben a playful shove on the arm that would have sent a giant reeling. She swept into the room and took the chair he had vacated. Behind her, two other women not much older than Lacy entered. They were both in various stages of cultivated undress. One favored virginal white, the other pale blue. Both were slim, well-proportioned young women of medium height. Their skin was fresh and smooth, their faces decorated with a minimum of makeup.

Lacy recognized the young woman in white immediately. She was even lovelier close up. A thick mane of dark hair hung past her waist and over her creamy white shoulders to curl provocatively on her breasts. There was an etheral quality about her that brought out a latent desire to protect. Lacy could easily understand why Ben had fallen in love with her.

The young woman in blue had hair the color of wheat piled in an artful arrangement on her head. Her eyes slanted slightly, giving her a feline quality.

"This is Sara," Ben said, placing one hand on the brunette's shoulder. "And this is Lily." Lily got a familiar slap on the seat. She squeeled and looked at him coquettishly. "This, girls, is Lacy Phalen, whom I hope will be joining us soon."

Lacy smiled at the new arrivals uncertainly. Although she had seen Sara from a distance, she had expected her and the other dance-hall girls to look hard. But they differed from her friends back in Boston only in their dress. Rose, overflowing the dainty chair, had not the hard, worn look of a prostitute. Her smile was warm and generous. In fact, more so than the so-called good women of Paradise whom Lacy had accompanied to church meetings and who had now branded her an outcast.

Rose smiled in welcome. "We'll be right glad ta have ya, honey."

Sara and Lily enthusiastically agreed with her.

Lacy's eyes widened. They couldn't mean that she. . . .

"But I can't . . . I mean, I . . ." Lacy sputtered, her eyes going from one woman to another searching for an answer.

Unaware of the girl's horror, the younger women sought to assure her they would not resent her.

"Phoo!" Sara said, giving her long dark hair a toss. "I'm glad yer here."

"Men and ta spare," Lily declared, and curled up on the bed with the grace of a cat.

Lacy's eyes widened in disbelief. "Oh, but I wouldn't . . . couldn't . . ." she stammered.

Rose leaned forward in her chair and patted Lacy's knee. "Course not, honey. Not unless ya want ta. But that time will come."

Lacy looked at the older woman as if she were out of her mind. Didn't any of them realize what she had gone through? Could they really believe she would ever want another man even to touch her?

Sara moved gracefully toward the bed, her movements dainty and feminine. Lacy found it hard to believe that this delicate woman was a saloon inmate. But it was very easy to picture her as a bride. The thought alone was a knife twisting in Lacy's heart.

"Oh, Ben ain't like the others," Sara said in a soft voice.

Elizabeth Daniels

Lacy was startled enough to glance at his tall figure towering over Rose in her chair. Could the girl actually mean what Lacy thought she meant?

He met Lacy's eyes and laughed. "What the girls are trying to say, dearest heart," he said, "is that you only . . . ah, entertain if you want to entertain."

Still, she looked at him stunned.

"None of us came here with the intention of . . . of, well, ya know," Sara said.

"Well, almost no intention." Lily giggled.

Sara joined in Lily's laughter. They sounded like schoolgirls.

"The rule around here is that ya are hired ta push drinks and dance with the men," Rose continued the explanation. "Nothin' else. Course if ya want a little extra, the rooms are here and we jest charge a little rent when we have guests."

"Right," Lily put in. "Now, I can't help myself. I like men. But Sara here, she's a one-man type. Even got herself engaged."

Sara blushed. Lacy turned a shade whiter and gripped the arms of the dainty chair until her knuckles ached.

"Weddin's gonna be in the spring, ain't that right, Sary?" Rose beamed.

Sara nodded, an angelic smile lighting her face. "Oh, yes. And Hank ain't a bit nervous. I sure am though."

"Hank?" Lacy's voice vibrated with hope.

Sara's head bobbed again. "My . . . my . . . What was that fancy word, Ben?"

"Fiancé," he supplied.

"Yeah. Fee–an–cee. He works fer Charlie Delaney tendin' cattle. We're gonna have a little cabin all our own and everythin'." Her smile was angelic, lighting her face and making her even more beautiful. "Got me a fancy weddin' dress ordered in Saint Louie. Ben took me along special his last trip jest ta get it."

"Enough about the wedding for now," Ben said, his voice soft and low in comparison to the shriller tones of the women. "Since it's the only topic of discussion around here anymore, I'm sure you'll, er, gander all the details later, Lacy."

She smiled at him almost timidly. "Oh, yes, of course," she said although she hadn't really heard what he said. Her heart was singing. He was free. Free!

Ben grinned. "What we really need is someone to look after the housekeeping here at the Paradise. Right, girls?"

Rose leaned forward in her chair again. "Ya know about those sorts of things, honey?"

"A little," Lacy admitted.

"That's more'n any of us." She chuckled.

"Oh, but this room and your clothes," Lacy cried. "Everything is so clean and neat."

"There's a woman comes in," Rose said. "But she needs ta be watched and told what ta do."

Sara curled her legs beneath herself and leaned forward eagerly. "Can ya cook, Lacy?"

"A little," the young woman admitted.

"Then ya've jest gotta join us. I don't even know how ta boil water and I gotta learn before I go ta Hank."

Lacy could not picture the ethereal Sara slaving over a stove in a rundown cabin. She deserved a wealthy man. At the same time, Lacy was very glad Sara had found her cowboy. She wanted the other woman to be very happy because she was quite ecstatic.

"Well?" Ben's deep tone was more caressing than questioning.

"We really could use ya, honey," Rose said.

"Please," Sara pleaded.

"Be fun havin' another around," Lily sanctioned.

"And, besides"—Ben's teeth flashed—"you can't leave Paradise until spring when the snow melts."

Lacy looked at each of them in turn. Sara with her halo of shining dark hair. Lily with her feline grace and fashionable air. Rose with her blowsy looks and gentle smiles. And Ben.

She remembered the many times he had teased her. His concern. His championship of her in the Thompkins affair. And the light in his eyes when they met hers. It was dancing in them now, reminding Lacy of the passionate kiss in the woods. She wished her heart would not beat so quickly. Or that her blood would not hum as it rushed madly through her body, leaving her tingling and oh, so alive. Rose was quite right. The time would come when she would welcome a man in her life, in her bed. It was still too soon. But the time would come.

"You've got a housekeeper," Lacy said. "When do I start?"

"Sooner the better," Ben said.

Lily wiggled off the bed. "First she'll need some clothes."

"And a room of her own," Sara added.

Rose rose majestically from her chair. "The first ain't no problem. We got yer things from the Bakers and Lily can go off ta the dry-goods store with ya fer a few extras. Heard tell Delaney's got some right fancy stuff there right now. Lily's got the best sense about clothes."

"And we'll stop by ta see Miz Schiller, the seamstress," Lily put in.

"But about a room now." Rose put her hands on her hips and turned to where Ben lounged in the open doorway. "Lily and me use ours fer business and Sary's got her Hank comin' every evenin' so I don't think Lacy will want ta share with us. Ya know what that means?"

He nodded sagely. "Yes, I know what that means."

"I don't think she's ready ta share with ya either, honey."

"There's a cot in my office, Rose."

"Jes hope ya remember that, Ben honey. I'd hate ta get waked up with Lacy screamin' her head off."

He took her hand in a courtly gesture. "Rose, my love. If I find the cot uncomfortable, I'll come to you."

"Ya!" she cried delightedly, and gave him a shove.

Ben flashed his mischievous smile.

In her stomach Lacy felt a knot of unease. When would that spark between them flare again as it had the night of the church social? How long would it take for the terror of the night in the

Delaney barn to cede? She knew she had ceased to be the girl she'd been scant months before in Boston. If Ben Paradise made the smallest overture, Lacy realized she would yield to him. Willingly. She only hoped he did not recognize her weakness. For weakness it was.

CHAPTER XIV

Few strangers passed through the town of Paradise. It was the local men, landowners, and laborers, who filled the Paradise Saloon with boisterous laughter each evening.

Lacy found she was fascinated with the colorful spectacle that unrolled on the wooden floor of the saloon once the sun set. As the housekeeper, she was not involved in the nightly gala. The saloon girls were kept busy running from table to bar with mugs of beer and tumblers of whiskey, their gaudy dresses the only spot of color among the bearded customers. Their shrill laughter and saucy comments blended with the men's, drawing Lacy from the comfort of her room. She stood at the ballustrade watching, her dark gown blending into the shadows of the landing.

Ben watched as well. He was always aware of Lacy's ghostly appearances on the balcony. Her expression was wistful as she watched a young man in buckskins swing Sara around the small dance floor until the young woman was breathless. A boisterous request coaxed still another spritely tune from the piano, and Sara was swung back into the dance.

Did Lacy dream of her life in Boston or of a particular man? The memory of her lips, warm and eager beneath his, haunted Ben. Many a night he had tossed on the narrow cot, unable to get the vision of her out of his mind: her scent, her smile, the promise he'd read in her eyes the first night they'd met. He remembered the pale silky sheen of her skin rising from the daringly low neckline of a ball gown and the feel of her in his arms as they danced. Some nights he was sure he would go mad thinking of her, upstairs, alone, in his bed.

A week had passed since Lacy had taken up the keys to his household, and there was a different feel to the place. Nothing really noticeable other than a few changes in the evening meals. Mrs. Mackley hummed while she worked, polishing until every wooden surface gleamed and the air was cloying with the scent of beeswax. Somehow, the saloon seemed warm and welcoming now, not just a false-fronted frontier building where men gathered each evening. It was a home as well.

Lacy leaned contentedly on the rail above the saloon floor, engrossed in a card game at the table beneath her. The soft glow of the oil lamps reflected the angelic halo of her hair yet kept her face in shadow. He had no need of bright lights to refresh his memory. Every delicately hued feature from her turned-up nose and gypsy eyes to the graceful promising curves of her body haunted Ben nightly.

He relaxed back against the bar, drinking in the serenity of the young woman and her absorption in the game.

As if she felt his eyes on her, Lacy glanced up, finding Ben easily in the dim light. A shy smile lit her face as he raised his glass in salute.

There was something about Benjamin Paradise that drew her to him, and it wasn't just his magnetism. Every woman he met responded to the pull. Was it the unwarranted affection in his eyes, the way one brow rose questioningly, or just the way he moved that attracted her so? The attraction was ill-fated. She was doomed to be drawn to a man she could never have. His life was the frontier, a poker table, and few responsibilities. She belonged in Boston, running the Puritan Line.

A swirl of wintry wind announced a new arrival to the convivial warmth of the saloon. The man stood silently in the doorway, patient for once to study the gathering. He noted the relaxed stance of Paradise at the bar and the direction of his glance. So, she was here. The man grinned to himself, aware that a hush had fallen over the room as his presence was noted.

He was a big man. In the fur-lined buckskin coat, homespun trousers and shirt, he blocked the doorway of the saloon, his bulk and stance alone threatening. He wore his hat pulled low over his eyes, yet there was no doubting he stared directly at Paradise.

The men around the bar eased away, sensing a confrontation.

Ben chose to ignore the newcomer. Outwardly calm, he moved behind the counter and opened a fresh bottle of whiskey.

"Understan' ya think I'm not good 'nuff fer this here saloon," the man in the doorway said.

A cold chill ran down Lacy's spine. The last time she had heard that voice was in Delaney's barn.

Ben poured two fingers of amber liquid into his tumbler. "You heard right, Thompkins."

"Didn't care fer me cuttin' maself in on some of yer action, did ya, Paradise?"

Ben took a sip of his drink.

"Wanted her all fer yerself."

Ben set his whiskey down. "You never were good enough for this saloon, Thompkins. Get out."

"Well," Judd leered, "I hear Miz Lillian works here now. Thought I might give her some more business." He smiled mirthlessly and looked over the gathering, sizing up each man before his attention returned to Paradise.

On the balcony rail, Lacy's hands were wet with sweat. Whether she feared for herself or Ben, she didn't know. She knew Thompkins was a danger to them both.

"You heard wrong," Ben's voice drawled.

Thompkins took another step inside the saloon and tilted his hat back on his head. "Where is the purdy little lady bird? Don't ya think she'd like ta see her ol' friend Judd?" he taunted.

Lacy stepped back from the rail lest Thompkins

see her. Her attention never left the two men on the floor below.

"You can leave walking or flying, Thompkins," Ben said.

"Ya plannin' ta make me, Paradise?"

On the top of the bar Ben flexed the fingers of his now unbandaged right hand. "If I have to."

Thompkins brushed the leather strapped to his upper thigh. The heel of a hand gun protruded within his reach.

The men at tables around the floor began moving to the sides of the room.

Ben appeared unconcerned as he uncorked the whiskey bottle and poured another portion into his glass.

"Let's see ya try," Thompkins said.

Ben sipped at the whiskey. "You never were much of a man, Judd. First you force yourself on an unwilling woman . . ."

"None of yer women are unwillin', Paradise," Thompkins snarled.

". . . on an *unwilling* woman," Ben repeated, "and now you'd shoot an unarmed man."

"I'm not afraid of ya, Ben Paradise. Go ahead and git yer gun."

Ben surveyed the liquor in his glass. "Sorry. I won't kill an unarmed man."

Thompkins's teeth bared. "I ain't unarmed," he spat, but it seemed the word "kill" had shaken his confidence.

"Same as," Ben said, and sipped at his drink again. "I'm a better shot."

A murmur of agreement came from the crowd.

"He's right, Judd," one of them said. "But yer better with yer fists."

Another man laughed. "That eye don't look it, Judd."

Thompkins rubbed his jaw thoughtfully. "I do owe ya one, Paradise."

Ben replaced the whiskey bottle on the shelf behind the bar. "Since you insist upon being thrown out, Thompkins, I guess I'll just have to accommodate you."

A murmur of excited anticipation rose as Judd tore his gun belt off and threw it aside. "Come on, Paradise. Gonna hide behind that bar all night?"

Ben vaulted over the counter. "Mind if I take my coat off?"

Thompkins's hat sailed into a corner. "Not at all," he said, and charged into Ben.

They both hit the floor. Ben, temporarily tangled in the folds of his jacket, managed to roll away from Thompkins's attack and get to his feet. Lily ran forward to take his coat while the crowd of men growled their displeasure at Thompkins.

Ben circled Judd, his arms slightly spread before him, his knees bent as he balanced for his opponent's next move. Judd took a wild swing which Ben parried with his left and followed with an uppercut that sent Thompkins reeling back against the bar. The women cheered.

Their cries made Judd see red. He launched himself from the bar and drove Ben back against the tables beneath the balcony. He did not let up but fell on Ben with a vengeance, his large hands encircling the other's neck. A couple of men in the crowd objected but dared not interfere with the fight.

Stars blurred Ben's sight. His fingers tightened on Thompkins's hands, steadily forcing them back until the strangle hold was broken. His bent knee thrust the heavier man back, stumbling into the chairs, his weight splintering a table beneath him. Barely stunned, Judd snatched up a sturdy table leg, and swung it at Ben's head. Ben ducked the blow and plowed his fist into Thompkins's soft, unprotected stomach. A chopping blow knocked the makeshift weapon from the man's hand.

Thompkins was far from finished. His foot lashed out, catching Ben off balance, sending him skidding into another table.

Judd's lips curled in a cruel smirk. His attention briefly diverted to the tense young woman on the landing as Ben slowly got to his feet. "Just be a minute till I finish off yer lover, Miz Lillian. Then I'll be up fer ma reward."

Ben felled him with the rickety remains of a chair.

The two men were unevenly matched. A black bear and a stag: Judd was slow and ponderous in his movements; Ben was quick and agile. They were the same height but Thompkins carried more weight. Ben's blows infuriated his opponent, goading Judd on.

Ben gasped for breath, as a trickle of blood ran from the corner of his mouth.

Judd was winded but he managed to dodge Ben's next punch and get in one of his own. A sadistic grin twisted his lips.

Lacy turned away sharply in reflected pain as Thompkins's meaty fist made contact once more, driving Ben back. The feathery fronds of the potted fern on the table outside her room brushed against her arm, their touch ghostly. Without thinking, she grabbed the plant.

Ben and Judd were locked in a crushing embrace. A gasp came from the watching men as Thompkins's knee came up to break the hold, catching Ben in the groin.

He dropped to the floor, doubled over, rolling with the kick. Feigning a more serious injury, Ben watched for an opening.

Judd staggered back, his eyes glowing in triumph. Then he stepped forward, preparing to kick the downed man as he lay curled defensively.

Ben's leg shot out. With a quick twist, his foot caught and pulled Judd's ankle, sending him crashing heavily to the floor, shaking the building. The sound of crockery breaking followed a scant second later as Lacy added her missile to the melee. Judd sprawled unconscious amid the wreckage of furniture, a drooping plume of fern adorning his head.

A cheer rose as the men rushed forward. Ben waved congratulatory hands away and got to his feet, leaning heavily on a chair.

"Is he all right?" Lacy demanded, calling down to Rose who hovered over Ben's prone body. Her face was pale in the lamp light as she paused undecided at the rail.

Rose nodded. "After a while. Don't think he's much damaged."

"Wouldn't you like to find out?" Ben said

through gritted teeth. Damn, now that the fight was finished, he hurt all over.

Rose laughed. "Ain't nothin' wrong with him."

Unable to believe the statement, Lacy ran along the balcony and down the stairs, pushing her way through the crowd of men.

Ben was supported on either side by Rose and Sara. Their concern irritated him. A man ought to be able to crawl away and tend to his wounds in private. He flinched away from Sara's tentative touch to his broken lip. "I'm all right," he snapped. "Just get a doctor for Thompkins."

Lacy pushed to the front of the crowd and surveyed his bruised and bleeding face. "I don't think he should be up, Rose."

The older woman snorted. "'Course not, honey. But he won't listen."

"I'm all right," Ben repeated.

"See if ya can convince him, honey," Rose said, and stepped back. "Man's as stubborn as his pa."

Ben grinned down at Lacy's concern and swore as the grimace brought new pain. "We make a hell of a team. Thank you."

She put her hand on his arm. "There's nothing to thank me for, Ben," she murmured.

He touched her hair tenderly.

"He could have killed you," she said.

He shrugged the suggestion off and turned to greet the doctor, afraid that he'd forget who she was and sweep her into his arms.

Doc Brent was more horse doctor than physician. Despite the women's concern, he looked at Ben and laughed. "What this boy needs, Rosie, is a good stiff drink. Make him good as new."

"Damn," Ben said. "I do need a drink. In fact, we all need a drink. Rose! Drinks on the house!" He wiped at his swollen lip with the back of his hand and grinned. "We'll drink to the little lady of the hour. Lacy Phalen!"

The men cheered and crowded around the bar. Lily and Sara joined Rose in dispensing bottles and tumblers while one of the men passed a bottle to Ben.

He took a long swig and handed the bottle back. "Enjoy the entertainment, Frank? You've been arguing that we needed some around here."

Frank chuckled. "Sure did, Ben."

Rose arrived with a drink for the doctor, now bent over Judd's inert form. "He'll live. What happened?" Brent asked.

"He had a run in with a wildcat," Ben said, and winked at Lacy.

She touched his arm gently. "Are you sure you are all right?"

"Perfectly." He took a healthy drink of whiskey from the bottle in his hand and passed it to one of the men. His hands found her waist and swung Lacy up on top of a table. "Gentlemen! I give you Lacy Phalen!"

Everyone cheered and drank to her health. Lacy blushed, her eyes shining with pleasure at the accolade.

Another cheer and another toast followed before Ben reached up and helped her down, his hands lingering slightly on her waist. At his touch, Lacy grew confused and moved away, afraid of the longing the contact evoked.

"What should we do with the trash?" Lily asked, pointing to Judd.

Puzzled by Lacy's sudden coldness, Ben surveyed his fallen opponent. "I suppose someone should get him home."

Minutes ticked by before two men stepped forward and reluctantly picked up the unconscious Thompkins.

The doctor dragged Ben and a bottle off to the tiny office in the back to attend to his injuries. Rose, Lily, and Sara were kept filling empty glasses as the men refought the fight verbally.

With the antagonists gone and the other women busy, Lacy felt a little left out. The debris of furniture, soil, and pottery shards littered the saloon, leaving it in dire need of a housekeeper. Strangely depressed, she went in search of a broom.

CHAPTER XV

Things ran smoothly at the Paradise Saloon in the following weeks, leaving Lacy with time on her hands. Mrs. Mackley, the widow who came in to "do" for the saloon, was a hard worker and did not seem to mind Lacy's few suggestions. Lacy had met Sara's betrothed, a quiet man who could not look at Sara without adoration lighting his face. Hank insisted his Sara did not need to cook, that he could handle that as long as she always looked pretty. Lacy found them very romantic if a bit unrealistic.

It was impossible to vary menus much since the town of Paradise subsisted on its own produce and local game. Lacy missed the smell of the sea and the lack of seafood. The day Ben brought back fish from one of the local mountain streams, she could have kissed him.

But she did not. He had returned to the bantering manner that always seemed to infuriate her and make her lose her temper. He also appeared to be avoiding her. Lacy saw him at dinner and in the saloon in the evening. Ben usually joined a card game early in the evening and let it run until after closing time. He himself locked up. During the day he was absent, riding into the forest early in the morning before the rest of the house awoke.

Occupying his room, Lacy surprised herself by being disappointed that Ben had not stumbled into his old room by mistake. Not that she wanted him to, but she was haunted by fantasies of him in the room.

It was decidedly masculine, furnished in heavy, dark-stained wood and lacking the frills found in the three women's rooms. The large wardrobe had been filled with dark suits, rough but durable riding trousers, and soft linen shirts. Rose had come in and taken them away to accommodate Lacy's own clothing. She knew they were now scattered in the wardrobes of the other three women and felt excluded in not being allowed the privilege of giving up some of her own closet space.

The bed was large and comfortable, but she did not sleep well within its confines. The nightmare episode with Judd Thompkins had begun to fade from memory as William Quire's had. And as the terror receded, the image of Ben Paradise taunted her. She recalled how his arms had felt around her. How his eyes danced with mischief and laughter, the caressing sound of his voice, and worst of all, the touch of his lips that night in the forest. The thoughts caused her many a sleepless night.

Ben's present apathy troubled Lacy. He had found her desirable once. He had arranged the box lunch, had sought her out at Sadie Delaney's party. But since her arrival at the saloon, he had ignored her existence.

Piqued, Lacy was little more than civil to him when they did meet. Once more she began planning to leave Paradise in the spring.

She never tired of hearing the women talk of Ben. Rose had known him the longest and succumbed to flights of fancy when she spoke of him. He could be both prince and ogre it seemed. The ogre showed itself only when Rose tried to buy a share of the Paradise. Otherwise, she thought him a paragon. It was Rose who told Lacy of Ben's family and past. She had drifted into the town of Paradise fifteen years before and fallen in love with Elisha Paradise, Ben's father. Elisha had recently lost his wife and was determined to raise his two sons alone. Ben had been thirteen, on the threshold of manhood. His elder brother, David, had been sixteen, a tall cocky frontiersman.

"Where is David Paradise now?" Lacy asked, curled on the bed while Rose painted her pretty face.

"I'm comin' ta that, Lacy. Ya see, Miz Paradise was a religious woman, but Elisha liked his women and his drinkin'."

"And gambling?" Lacy inserted.

"That specially, Lacy honey. But as I was sayin', Elisha was hard put ta raise those boys as his missus woulda liked. He had come out here and cleared the land and started a settlement of his own. But she wasn't strong and died the first year they were here. I heard tell she had family back in Virginny. Proper folks like ya, honey. But I can't swear ta it.

"It was lucky them boys was old enough ta get along without a ma. None of them was exactly happy workin' the land. So they sold it and opened this here saloon. I was one of their first girls."

Lacy tried to picture Rose as she had been fifteen years ago. She was still pretty. Without the wrinkles and extra flesh, she must have been quite beautiful.

"I even had hopes back then that Elisha would marry me," Rose said. "He was right fond of me but he never seemed ta want ta replace his first missus. We had good times though. This place was a success from day one. It weren't too good a place ta bring up young boys though. They took after their pa, and there wasn't a gal in the place that wasn't willin' ta show 'em the ropes, so ta speak."

Lacy propped her chin in her hands and watched the careful strokes of Rose's brush around her lips. "Well?" she prompted the woman.

"Well, David and Ben both fell in love with this one gal, and she started playin' one against the other. Ben was about seventeen then, I'd say, cause David was twenty."

"What was she like, Rose?"

"Belle? Oh, let's see. As I recall, she had a forward way 'bout her. She was from New Orleans and had a Frenchified accent. She had dark eyes that could look right through a person. Both them boys was mad fer her."

Lacy stared past Rose into the mirror, trying to picture the fatal Belle. Her own eyes looked dark in the mirror with their thick lashes. "What happened?"

Rose finished her face and walked over to the wardrobe with the sway of hips that brought a light to the men's eyes every night. She considered each dress a moment or so before going on to the next.

"David talked Belle inta runnin' off with him," she continued.

"Oh, poor Ben. Where'd they go?"

Rose chose a spangled dress of crimson. "Didn't get far. Guess ya could say they went nowhere. Headed west inta Injun country and that's where they stayed."

"You mean they settled down on a piece of land?" Lacy persisted.

"Sorta, but under is more how I'd put it."

Lacy scrambled off the bed to assist Rose with her corset. "You can't mean . . ."

The older woman took a stance by the bed, offering Lacy the strings of her lacing. "Ben went after 'em," she said. "He's the one found 'em. Injuns had got the whole train. He buried 'em and sent word back ta his pa. Then he traveled, I guess ya'd call it. Joined some mountain men and made a fair amount on furs. Late last spring he came back here. Elisha'd been dead couple years, leavin' everythin' ta Ben. We was a little surprised when Ben stayed on. Guess he thought he had ta take care of things here. I've tried ta buy him out but he jest keeps sayin' no." She chuckled. "Never thought he'd be a man fer sayin' no, neither."

Lacy tugged on the lacing, drawing it tight.

"Funny, though," Rose mused, "the way he keeps away from ya, honey. I'd a thought he'd be around ya like a bee on a flower."

"Ben's a man of his word," Lacy said. "He once promised not to touch me."

"That right." Amusement crept into Rose's voice.

"Yes, last fall when I first arrived." Lacy gave the lacing on the corset a slight tug.

Rose watched the other woman in the mirror. "Well, he sure ain't touched ya. 'Cept ta help ya outta wagons and that time he put ya on the table fer the toast. Ya'd a thought he'd burned his hands each time."

Lacy frowned at the stubborn corset. "I appreciate his thoughtfulness. It hasn't been easy for me since I was forced by the community to accept his hospitality."

"Yer a strang gal, Lacy. Sometimes I could swear ya was in love with the man. Hey, not so tight there. A gal's gotta breathe."

In love with him? Impossible. She was attracted to him certainly. But love? "You just hold on to the bedpost, Rose," Lacy said, and eased the corset stays. "You were saying?"

Rose twisted to look over her shoulder. "I ain't sayin' no more 'till yer finished, honey. Maybe not even then."

"I'm finished. What's so strange about me, Rose?" Lacy curled up on the bed.

Rose took a few test breaths to see if the corset was comfortable, then picked up her dress. "Well, ya ain't really strange, Lacy. But one minute yer worryin' about Ben and the next minute ya act like

244

ya'd like ta scratch his eyes out."

"He does make me mad," Lacy admitted. "When have I ever worried about him?"

Rose stepped into her gown and wiggled it up over her hips. "When he took that lickin' from Judd Thompkins."

"He was hurt, Rose. Everyone was worried about him," Lacy countered.

Rose shrugged her plump shoulders. "Maybe," she said, busy arranging her deep-cut neckline to show her breasts to advantage.

Lacy's eyes narrowed. "What are you suggesting?"

Rose stared critically at her reflection in the mirror and tugged the neckline lower. "Not supposed ta mean anythin', honey," she said, sidestepping the issue. The gal was testier than a rattlesnake! "Ya ready ta join the fun downstairs?"

After that conversation with Rose, Lacy found herself thinking of Ben often. As a result she snubbed him when they did meet. He responded by returning to the saloon long after the women had finished eating.

His absence made Lacy fretful. She wished she had someone with whom to unburden her mind, a friend with whom she could talk.

Sadie often sent letters by way of her husband. She regretted that she and Lacy could no longer see each other in person. Their friendship had just begun when the will of the community had swung against the schoolmarm. In her notes, Sadie apologized frequently for her lack of courage in not standing up to the "good ladies" of Paradise and championing Lacy. The young woman had no ill feelings toward her. Sadie would continue to live in the town. Lacy would be leaving.

Lacy could tell from the bulk of the envelope that Sadie's latest note was lengthy and she was anxious to read it. Since the dry-goods store was directly across from the saloon, she had not bothered to wear sturdy boots but had dashed across the road in light slippers. Thus, when she returned, her ascent on the stairs was silent.

"Well, I don't know about ya, Rose," she heard Lily's voice say angrily, "but I'm worried about him."

Lacy froze outside the door of Sara's room. There was only one man the women of the Paradise Saloon cared about: Benjamin Paradise.

All three women were gathered. Lacy could see them through the crack of the partially opened door. Rose sat in a chair near the window. Lily and Sara were both curled up on the counterpane.

"Me, too," Sara declared. "There must be somethin' we can do."

The captain had often told Lacy eavesdroppers heard nothing to their gain. Yet she could not move. She stood rooted outside the door, straining to hear.

"It ain't like Ben ta stay away. 'Course when he does come home he ain't in a very good mood. Why, I even heard him snap at Mrs. Mackley yesterday," Sara continued.

Rose sighed. "Honey, I know. He jest ain't the sweet-tempered fella he was. And ya know why as well as I do."

Sara nodded. "Her."

Lacy felt a sick feeling in her stomach. She touched her dry lips with the tip of her tongue.

Rose inspected her hand, admiring the highly buffed nails. "It ain't jest Lacy, Sary, and ya know it."

"He ain't visited any of us since the church social last fall. Leastwise that I know," Lily said.

"No, he's not been with me since Hank asked fer me," Sara declared. "I thought it was jest ya, Lily."

Lily shook her head in denial.

"It jest ain't natural," Rose said. "A man like Ben needs a woman. Trouble is he's got some maggot in his head and he only wants her."

"Grouchier than an old bear about it, too," Lily agreed.

"Oh, but she's no better," Sara declared. "Bit ma head off yesterday when I asked her somethin' about ma weddin'."

Rose chuckled. "Jest about killed me with ma own corset the other day when I said she was in love with him."

"Speakin' of that," Lily said, "I'd be pushin' up daisies if looks could kill. And all 'cause he put his arm 'round me."

"Too bad that's all he did." Rose sighed. "He'd be feelin' much better if he jest let one of us take care of him."

They were silent a moment, staring unhappily at each other.

Sara broke the silence. "I think she's holdin' out fer marriage."

Rose snorted. "Well, 'course she is. She's brought up proper."

"Ben ain't a marryin' man though," Lily said.

"Hell, honey, all men are that till they're catched."

"Didn't Judd Thompkins say . . ."

Rose cocked her head to one side. "What? Ya gonna believe that weasle? We don't know nothin' 'bout her past."

Lily was thoughtful. "That's right. She might be no better 'n us."

Rose laughed. "If ya think that, honey, ya musta been born yesterday."

Sara giggled. "Or she's just plain jealous."

Lily threw a pillow at her.

Lacy stole back down the stairs and made a commotion as she remounted them.

Rose's blond head, still in curling papers, poked out of Sara's open bedroom door. "Have a nice visit with Charlie, honey?"

Lacy summoned a smile as she reached the landing. "Oh, yes. He had a letter from Sadie. It's so thick I can't wait to read what she has to say." She moved past Rose to her own room.

"Ya do that, honey," Rose called. "See ya at supper."

"All right," Lacy said, and opened the door. Once inside the room, the letter lay forgotten in her hand. She stared unseeing at the walls. What was she going to do? The women were right. Her own temper flared easily these days. Why was she so aloof to Benjamin Paradise?

Lacy could not sleep again that night. The women's conversation echoed in her mind. Why was she distant? Because of a promise she had made herself? She had been willing to join Caleb only two months ago, before the disasterous Christmas Eve at the Delaneys'. She hadn't thought of marriage, had she? Was Sara right? Was she waiting for a wedding ring?

Her thoughts locked on Rose's comment that she was in love with Ben. Was she? No, Lacy decided, she definitely was not. She liked him very much. He had given her a refuge at the Paradise Saloon until such time as the captain returned from China. He had made it very clear to the other men in town that she was not for sale. She liked the way he looked, walked, talked. She liked the way her heart pounded when they brushed hands at the dinner table.

Angrily, Lacy punched the pillow—his pillow—into a more comfortable shape.

All right. She did not love him. The truth of the matter was she wanted him. She wanted to experience physical love. She was no different than the other female occupants of the saloon. She had need of a man just as they did.

But they were still wrong. Marriage? No. She had no desire to bind herself to a husband.

Lacy sighed and smiled at the ceiling, content that she had come to a decision. She would accept Ben as a lover. It was still more than a year before the *Paramour* was due to return from China. Rather than leave Missouri in the spring, she would remain at the saloon.

Still, sleep eluded her. A small voice within demanded yet another answer. It was all very well for Lacy to decide to welcome Ben into her bed. But she had only the women's word that he was interested. And the memory of a single kiss. He had not approached her in the six weeks since she had joined the saloon's staff. Perhaps he no longer wanted her. Had Judd Thompkins's attack made him adverse to her?

Lacy tossed in the bed until the sheets were a tangled mass.

Ben had not returned when Rose sent the men home earlier. Was he still in the woods?

Lacy climbed out of bed, oblivious to the cold, unheated room. Outside the moon shone brightly on new-fallen snow. Its virgin white disguised the harsh details of the street. The frozen mud was hidden beneath the clean, unblemished blanket. Charlie Delaney's dry-goods store had accumulated a small drift against the door. The few chairs on the porch sported snowy dust covers molded to their contours.

She stood staring at the street without really seeing it. When a heavily clothed man moved wearily from the livery stable in the direction of the saloon, Lacy came to life.

He had come home.

Quickly, she lit a candle and checked her reflection. Her pale gold hair was escaping from the long braid hanging down her back. She loosened it, brushing fiercely until her hair was a glittering cloud around her shoulders, then pulled on a robe.

When Lacy entered the kitchen, Ben was making up the fire, his back to the door. His heavy jacket was flung negligently over one of the chairs. His damp, snow-encrusted boots were placed near the fireplace.

Lacy set her candle down on the table softly.

Ben hadn't sensed her presence. He fumbled with the flint.

"Damn," he mumbled under his breath.

Silent on bare feet, Lacy moved toward him. "Let me."

He started. "Oh, Lacy. I'm sorry. I didn't hear you. I didn't disturb you, did I?"

"No. I wasn't asleep. I was waiting for you." She realized it was true. She *had* been waiting for him. "You're cold."

He smiled wearily. "Much too cold. I think my fingers are half frozen."

She took the flint from him and bent over the fire. The tinder caught, bathing them in light, igniting the larger logs in a few moments. Ben held his hands out to the welcome warmth.

"Have you eaten?"

He shrugged.

"Stay by the fire," Lacy ordered. "I'll fix you something."

Raiding Mrs. Mackley's pantry, she found bacon, fresh laid eggs, and a loaf of bread.

"There isn't much." Lacy brought the few supplies to the table. "It won't take me long to get a fire started in the stove though."

Ben moved away from the comfort of the now raging fire, taking her hand in his. His fingers were warm, and Lacy's pulse beat faster.

"Go back to bed, Lacy. I can manage. I'll cook something over the fire. No need to start the stove for this."

She smiled. "Do as you are told, Mr. Paradise. I swear, I never met a more stubborn man."

He laughed softly. "All right, I yield. Do your worst, Miss Phalen. I am hungry enough to eat anything."

Reluctantly, Lacy drew her hand from his and took the skillet to the fireplace. The smell of frying bacon soon filled the room. "I don't guarantee the quality of my cooking," she said. "I've never cooked over an open fire before."

"I wouldn't mind even if you burn it." His voice was tired, but his inflection still held a hint of humor.

When the eggs were finished, she set a plate before him and busied herself brewing coffee. Neither spoke during his quick meal.

Ben pushed back his plate.

"Coffee?"

He nodded. She could feel his eyes following her as she moved around the kitchen collecting cups, cream, and sugar. She poured two cups and placed the pot near the fire to keep hot.

Ben caught her hand. "You needn't have stayed up, Lacy."

"I know." She tried to draw her hand away, suddenly afraid of her decision.

He drew her closer. His arm went around her waist, pulling her down to sit on his lap. Lacy did so without a struggle, unable to resist. Her limbs had begun to tremble at his touch.

The firelight danced in the blue depths of his eyes. How could she ever have thought them cold or icy? They warmed her, flickering with a fire of their own. She traced the stubble of beard on his chin, the hint of a mustache that had grown since she had seen him last. Her hand moved to smooth back his tousled hair.

"You'd better return to your bed, dearest heart," he said at length.

"But the coffee . . ."

"Cold. And it's too cold for you to stay down here in that flimsy outfit."

Lacy glanced down at her heavy nightgown and robe. "I've worn flimsier ones, I assure you." She grinned.

A smile flickered in his eyes. "Nevertheless, it's back to bed for you."

Lacy got to her feet and moved toward the door. She looked back at him, questioning. "Aren't you coming?"

The fire in his eyes seared her, but he remained seated at the table, toying with the cup of coffee. "No, Lacy. Not tonight." He grinned ruefully. "To tell you the truth, I'm in no shape to accommodate you. I'm just too damn tired."

Lacy smiled, happy just to know they had shared these moments. "Good night, Ben."

"Good night, my heart," he whispered.

CHAPTER XVI

Lacy slept late the next day, coming down only in time for the noon meal. The women were already assembled at the table, nibbling at meat pies.

"Good morning," Lacy greeted brightly.

"Good afternoon," Lily said. "Thought maybe ya weren't puttin' in an appearance today."

Lacy beamed at her. "Better late than never."

Rose and Sara exchanged puzzled looks. Their bewilderment deepened when Ben ambled through the door, resplendent in black suit and ruffled shirt.

"Miss me?" he asked, bending over Rose to plant a kiss on the side of her neck.

"If yer gonna act like that, honey, ya bet I missed ya," she declared.

Lily eyed him from his cravat to polished boots. "Stayin' in today, Ben? Thought ya'd taken quite a shine ta them woods lately."

He pulled back the chair at the head of the table and leaned back in it. "They are quite beautiful at this time of year," he agreed.

"Ya been settin' traps?" Sara asked.

"No, just admiring nature."

"But not taday," Lily commented.

"No, not today. It's quite inclement out today."

"Inclement?" Sara looked bewildered.

"He means it's snowing," Lacy said.

"Never stopped him runnin' out on us afore," Lily noted.

"That's right!" Sara declared. She glanced at Ben suspiciously. "And he's usin' those big words again. After he promised not ta!"

"Tsk, tsk. Did I indeed? How obtrusive of me."

Sara giggled. "How are we supposed ta know if yer sayin' anythin', well, improper if we can't understan' what yer sayin'?" she demanded.

"Oh, that's easy," he replied, reaching for the plate of meat pies. "Lacy will blush."

Which she then did.

Ben smiled at her affectionately, and she turned an even deeper red.

The other women all exchanged wondering glances.

"What time did ya get back last night?" Rose asked. "It had ta be pretty late cause Mrs. Mackley was complainin' this mornin' 'bout a fire in the grate and havin' her coffeepot sittin' in the middle of it almost boiled dry."

Lacy knew she looked guilty. She had forgotten

the coffee. She hadn't cleared the remains of the meal or the telltale coffee cups.

Ben shrugged. "I was very tired when I got in. And hungry. Didn't she complain about a pan as well?"

Rose looked shrewdly at him. "Yeah, she did, honey. And she mentioned *two* cups of cold coffee on the table. Now, I wonder how that coulda happened?"

Sara and Lily leaned forward in their chairs.

Ben reached for the freshly made pot of coffee. "*Now* you know how tired I was. Couldn't stay awake to drink it and couldn't remember I already had one cup."

"Sure ya made it ta yer own bed?" Rose pursued.

He grinned at her. "Oh, I was sorely tempted, Rose, but couldn't crawl any further than my lonely cot. Would I have disturbed you?" The smile accompanying the statement was innocent and yet reminded Lacy of a satyr.

Rose laughed and accepted his offer to refill her coffee cup. He turned, offering the coffee to Lacy. She declined, holding a hand over her cup.

"Delicious meal, Lacy," he said. "Don't think we've ever had better, have we, girls?"

"Mrs. Mackley deserves your praise," Lacy declared.

"So she does," he said with another maddening grin that warmed her all over.

"The place seems to run very smoothly in your hands," he continued.

Emboldened by the smooth way he had dismissed all the women's suspicions, Lacy decided to broach another subject. "I've been meaning to ask why you have never asked to see the household accounts."

"I haven't run out of money to meet them yet, Lacy. Why? Should I want to see them?"

"Yes," she declared. "How do you know I haven't overspent?"

He grinned at her. "If you have, I'll bill your father when he gets back from China."

"He might not have a successful journey. What if he can't afford to pay my debts?"

His smile widened. "Oh, I'm sure we could work something out."

The saloon girls' interest was rekindled. Lacy blushed. Her mind flashed over the evening before, of what her father would think of her actions. Although she knew the fortune she stood to inherit with the Puritan Line was more than sufficient to cover her expenses on the frontier for a lifetime, Ben's teasing sent her babbling. "B–but I . . . Papa could . . . The Puritans are . . . You p–promised!" she stammered incoherently, her thoughts at last centering on Ben's unctuous remarks months before in Hopkins Bend.

"Such a glib tongue," he said. "Is that what you Irish call a bit of the blarney?"

Rose laughed. "No, honey. Blarney is what rolls off yer tongue right regular-like."

Ben chuckled. "If it will make you feel better, Lacy, I will take a look at your household accounts. You *do* have some, I take it?"

She drew her slim frame up. "Of course I have!"

"Then let us get this over with quickly. Ladies, if

you will excuse us?" His chair scratched over the wooden floor as he stood up.

Meekly, Lacy allowed him to guide her from the room but not before she caught the glances Rose and the two other women exchanged.

The office was small with a desk pushed against one wall and a safe next to it. The cot that Ben had been sleeping on since her arrival was against the other wall under a window. A few books and a half-empty bottle of whiskey sat on the desk.

He waited until she had entered the room and then closed the door.

"Now, did you really want me to look at your accounts?" he demanded, taking her in his arms. "Or was that just an excuse to be alone?"

"Of course I want you to see the accounts," Lacy said, her cheek against his lapel. "It's only businesslike. I don't know what your expenses are. I could easily bankrupt you. And I don't want that to happen. It would be a terrible way to repay your kindness to me."

He sighed. "You're set on my seeing them, are you?"

She pulled back in his arms. "Yes, I am."

He let her go. "Well, since I've only room for one chair, would you care to take it, Lacy?"

"No, no. I'll stand." Just from the short contact with him, her nerves would not have allowed her to sit still. She got the ledger from the little-used desk and handed it to him.

Ben looked at her closely. He was sure he hadn't misread her invitation the evening before. Had she suffered a change of heart? He settled back in the chair and opened the household accounts.

Lacy paced behind him. He could hear the whisper of her skirts, the firm click of her heels on the wood flooring.

"Is there something the matter, Lacy?"

"No." She would not admit to being nervous.

Amusement colored his deep voice. "Just thought I'd ask. You pace a lot, I take it?"

"Everyone needs exercise," she told him curtly.

Ben continued to pursue the list of expenses. "Everything looks to be in order. I knew I need not fear leaving things in your hands."

"Don't you even want to question anything?" she demanded, her pacing arrested.

Ben's brow rose. "Such as?"

She looked over his shoulder. "Well, such as the expenditure for bacon."

"I like bacon," he said simply.

Exasperated with his calm, Lacy was insistent. "Look how much has been spent on soap."

"I like things clean."

"But the scented soap costs . . ."

"It makes the girls smell nice." He smiled and his voice took on a serious tone. "You smell nice."

She wasn't ready to abandon her hedge. Time was racing past too quickly. Daylight made her doubt the hard-won decision she'd made. "Did you see what it cost to replace the broken table and chairs?"

He was patient, watching her, waiting for an opening. "No, I must have missed that."

"I don't see how you could," she said. "It's right here."

"Where?" He sat forward to peer at the ledger, his attention centered on her every motion.

"Here." Lacy leaned over his shoulder, pointing to the figures in the book. So close were they that her breast brushed his shoulder. The next thing she knew she was seated once again on his lap.

Startled at the swiftness of his move, she squirmed in his arms. "What do you think you are doing, Benjamin Paradise?"

Ben settled her firmly. "I thought it was obvious, dearest heart." He grinned.

The endearment quieted Lacy. "I wish you would stop calling me that." Her lashes swept down to shield her eyes from him. "Besides, I . . ."

"You what?"

"What if someone should see us?" Her arms stole around his neck, belying the timidity of her question.

Ben laughed. "Can this possibly be the same woman who propositioned me last night?"

Her chin snapped up. "That's a terrible thing to say. Anyway, I did no such thing. Please let me go."

Ben was pleased to note her arms remained intimately about his shoulders.

The light that reminded Lacy so strongly of her father came into his eyes. "All right," he said. "Ransom yourself."

Lacy pulled back, surprise registering on her face. "Ransom myself?"

"If you really want to escape," he added.

"And the ransom?" she inquired, her lashes shielding the excitement building in her eyes.

His glance dipped to her lips fleetingly. "I'm

sure you'll think of something."

Lacy kissed him quickly and wiggled free of his arms.

"That wasn't a proper ransom," Ben declared, getting to his feet then moving toward her. Lacy moved a step or two away. "It was just a sample."

"It seemed perfectly acceptable to me," she insisted.

He took another step, stalking her boldly. "A mere tidbit, dearest heart."

Lacy retreated another couple steps and bumped back against the cot. "I am not your dearest heart and . . . and can't we get back to business?"

"I do mean business." The look in his eyes certainly brooked no refusal. "Now, Lacy, my love, my heart, my own. I was under the distinct impression last evening that you had made a decision."

Her cheeks colored brightly, but she did not refute his statement. "I wish you would stop calling me endearments. I'm not anything to you!"

Ben took another step. "You are my housekeeper, aren't you?"

It was ludicrous. He was playing with her. Yet she thrilled at the idea that she was his quarry. "That has nothing to do with this conversation," she insisted, a hint of her prim schoolmarm role intruding. "However, since you remind me, I do have things to see to. If you will excuse me." She made to move past him.

Ben's arm prevented her exit. "But I have a complaint about things around here," he drawled. "And you did want to discuss business. Shouldn't you stay and hear what it is?"

Lacy eyed him, suspicious. "You didn't have any complaints earlier. What is it?"

"It's this cot," he said, and gave her a slight push. Lacy fell back against the pillow and rolled off quickly. "It's lumpy, uncomfortable and"—he caught her hand—"lonely."

Lacy tried to pull away. "I'll order a new one."

His grip tightened. His eyes had turned serious. "This isn't a game, Lacy."

She stared up into his face, a flicker of anxiety rippling in her green eyes. "Oh, but, Ben . . ."

He drew her closer. "There's nothing to fear."

The look on his face took her breath away. Could he actually care for her? "I—I—" she stammered.

"A kiss between friends isn't much, Lacy." His hand touched her cheek, lightly caressing the delicate curve, tracing it to the now softened line of her jaw.

Mesmerized, Lacy moved nearer. Her lips parted. "No, I . . ."

He tilted her head, his touch tender though insistent and then he kissed her. Just as in the woods that night, his lips were on fire. Lacy was caught up in his touch, burning with desire, never wishing the embrace to end. She clung to him, molding her body to his.

When they parted, her sanity returned. Decisions reached in the dead of night when her imagination led her down blind alleys of desire were no longer binding in the bright light of day. "No!" She pushed him away so that he fell on the cot. "Leave me alone."

Running to the desk, she picked up the ledger. Ben laughed. Lacy looked at him warily. Mischief mingled with the passion in his eyes. "You can't run away from it, Lacy. My heart's delight."

She threw the ledger at him.

He ducked the household accounts and tried to reach for her. Lacy threw the books, the ink bottle, the whiskey bottle, then headed for the door. He caught her and slammed it shut.

"I hate you," she said, fearing the madness that had her in its grip. Why should she admit any man to her bed? She would be firm. Distant. But in his arms, reason retreated as it had when she had made the decision to accept him, and now she knew she would stand by it.

He loomed over her, his stance holding her imprisoned against the door. "Tell me again," he urged softly.

"No, Ben, I . . ." she began, but his lips stopped her.

"Tell me, Lacy," he murmured. His lips forged a burning trail across her face, her eyes, and along the column of her throat.

"Ben." Her voice sounded strange, husky. Her arms were around him, one hand entangled in his thick dark hair. Her lips found his again, telling him of her need with their eagerness. She was swept up in a wave of longing, her emotions a raging tempest.

When they parted, his eyes were smouldering. "I think we'd better adjourn to your room as you suggested last night."

"Ben," she said again wonderously. "It can't last. I'll be returning to Papa."

He ignored the speech. "Your dress is ripped," he said. "I've always hated these dresses of yours.

Now the one you wore at Sadie's was more to my liking."

Lacy frowned. "Did you have to remind me of that horrible night?"

He touched her cheek with a forefinger. "I will wipe that memory from your mind, my heart."

Lacy could not help but smile. "Do you think you can?"

He grinned. "Do you doubt my proficiency?"

"Oh, no," she said, knowing her face had reddened again. "Never."

Ben bent his head to hers, searing her lips with his. "Lacy," he whispered. "My dearest heart."

She stirred in his arms. "Am I really?"

"Really what?"

"Your dearest heart? Or do you call all your women that?"

His smile was tender. "Don't you already know?"

Lacy looked into the blue of his eyes, knowing the fire burning there was for her alone. Hunger was in her own blood. She experienced a thirst that only he could now quench.

He was waiting, fearing her rejection. The question hung between them.

Lacy met his eyes squarely. "Yes, Ben," she whispered throatily, all indecision vanquished by the warm glow he evoked. "Oh, yes."

He pulled her into his arms for a long kiss that left her panting and disoriented.

A timid knock on the door interrupted them. Reluctantly, Ben left the intoxicating nectar of her lips. His arms held Lacy closer as if she might escape now that the spell was broken. He needn't have worried. She snuggled against him content-edly.

Rose's carefully curled blond head peered around the door. "Thought maybe ya two had killed each other," she said.

"Not yet." Ben looked down at the flushed woman in his arms. "Rosie, would you tell Frank and the boys I can't make the game tonight? Oh, and, Rose, have dinner sent up. To *our* room. We won't be coming down until tomorrow."

Lacy blushed a deeper shade.

Rose smiled warmly. "It's about time. Now maybe things will settle down ta normal around here again!"

"Normal?" Ben demanded. "Normal? Nothing will ever be normal again!" he breathed joyfully. He bent swiftly catching Lacy up in his arms.

Lacy wrapped her arms around his neck. "Ben! What are you doing? Put me down!"

He ignored her request. "Rosie, isn't there something you ought to be doing?"

She grinned broadly. "Come ta think of it, there is," she agreed, and hurried out of his way.

"You know, I can walk of my own accord," Lacy said as he mounted the stairs.

"Don't deprive me," he told her.

"I'm too heavy."

"Extremely. But I'll bear up under the strain."

She smiled sweetly. "I'm sure you will."

He reached the bedroom door and leaned so that she could open it. When it was closed again, he lay her on the bed.

"Sorry you agreed to this?" he asked as he

stripped off his jacket and cravat, tossing them over a chair.

Lacy smiled as he dropped down next to her. "No, I've wanted you for a long time," she admitted shyly.

Ben rolled over and stared at the ceiling, his hands clasped behind his neck, savoring the moment yet to come. "Tell me more. When did you first discover you felt this way?"

Lacy leaned on her elbow to look down into his face. "When? I don't know. I only realized I did last night."

"And you waited up for me," he said wonderingly.

Disconcerted by his emotion, she looked away. "Yes."

"And bastard that I am, I disappointed you." He put one hand to her hair. "I liked your hair down last night."

"Did you?" She sat up and pulled the pins from the tightly bound locks until they spilled free to her waist.

His hands stroked the gilt glory. "It's such a pale, silvery-gold."

Lacy lay back down, supporting herself on her arm. "Tell me more," she urged in turn.

His smile was tender. "Hasn't any man ever told you you were beautiful? I find that hard to believe."

"Oh, yes, but they never enumerated." She paused. There really should be no secrets between them. Secrets between lovers led to pain, and Lacy wished for happiness. She had experienced enough pain this last year. She could not tell him everything but there was one event in her past she thought he should know.

"Ben."

He could tell by the change in her tone that she was done with banter.

She stared at a button on his shirt rather than meet his eyes. "There was a man in Boston . . ." she began.

Playing with a lock of her hair, he brushed it casually down her arm. "Did you love him?"

Her chin came up. "I hated him. It was—."

His finger on her lips silenced further confidences. "I understand, Lacy."

"It's just that—"

He kissed her lightly. "It won't be like that. I promise." His arms encircled her and he moved to lay Lacy back, her hair spreading out over the pillows. His hands moved to explore her body through her clothing, and Lacy's fingertips slid under his shirt to trace the muscles along his back.

One by one, she felt the tiny buttons down the back of her dress release at his touch. When they were undone, she slid from his arms and stood up. She let the dress slip to the floor and stood before him in her camisole and petticoats. Gently, she pulled at the ribbons across her breasts, teasing, displaying their fullness by tantalizing degrees.

His eyes were blazing in intensity. "Come over here." He sat up and swung his legs over the side of the bed.

Lacy stood before him, between his trousered knees. She smiled tenderly, her skin feverish from the look in his eyes alone.

Ben's hand dipped under her petticoats and up her leg to her garter and further up her thigh. Lacy gasped in delight as he touched her briefly. He removed her garters and silk stockings, the skillful caresses he imparted making her weak.

Lacy leaned against him for support. "Hurry," she whispered.

"Dearest heart"—he chuckled, his voice hoarse with emotion—"how plebian. We have the rest of the day, the evening, and the night. Hurry? Never!" It was a shout of joy.

They tumbled back on the bed. Wantonly, she moved above him, tempting and taunting him as her breasts spilled from the loosened bodice, gently touching his chest. Her hands peeled his ruffled shirt away so that the fevered crests of her breast were caressed by the dark, curling hair on his chest.

He groaned deep in his throat. "Sweet torturer, you tempt me sorely."

Lacy looked down at him, her lips wet and parted. She smiled. "Is the pain too dear, my love?" She made to move away, knowing full well he would not allow her to do so.

"You are a sorceress and I am but a slave to your beauty," he murmured.

"Sweet words indeed," Lacy cooed. "But must I wait much longer?"

"Don't pout." He rolled over so that she was imprisoned beneath him. His lips traced a molten path across her shoulders, smouldering kisses that brought her to a fever pitch. Lacy panted, gasping, clinging to him, responding to each touch, each caress, and still hungered for more, returning his ardor a hundredfold.

He freed her of the sweat-dampened camisole, tossing her petticoats after it. Lacy tugged impatiently at his belt with fingers that trembled and would not obey her command. The few moments it took him to rid himself of his own clothing stretched into an eternity.

"Lacy," Ben whispered tenderly. She reached for him, enfolding him in her arms, naturally arching her body to meet his. She moaned against his lips as he slid within her, crying out in pain and elation. He halted in his movements, fearful that he had hurt her. But Lacy's body moved under him, duplicating his motion. She was possessed not only by him but with him. His own actions became more demanding. She matched his passion, oblivious to everything but the man who was one with her and the ever-rising tide of excitement he wrought.

CHAPTER XVII

Lacy noted her final tally of barrels with a sigh of relief. With the end of winter in sight, Ben would soon be making another trip for supplies into Hopkins Bend or perhaps Saint Louis. This time there would be no Sara to envy. She smiled in remembrance of the turmoil Ben's trip in the fall had caused. It seemed incredible that now she, Lacy Phalen, would be the fortunate woman to share the seat on the wagon next to him.

She was happy. Aye, very happy and content. For the past month she had shared a bed with Ben and the hours she spent in his arms sped by far too quickly. She had learned to hate the dawn that drew them apart, and every day that passed meant spring crept ever nearer, forcing her to make a decision once more. Should she stay or return to Boston?

Lacy closed her ledger and surveyed her domain with a pleased half-smile. Now was not the time to fret about her future. She thought with satisfaction how much the saloon had changed due to some of her own suggestions. Mrs. Mackley had been in accord with her wishes to combat the stale smells of tobacco and whiskey that clung to the main room of the saloon. The bustling little woman had scrubbed floors, polished rails, and begun waxing the scratched table surfaces with a vengeance.

Though it was a brisk March day, although not overly cold, Mrs. Mackley had thrown open the doors, declaring she could taste spring in the air.

Lacy grinned happily to herself, hugging the ledger. Despite Mrs. Mackley's prophesy, it had snowed which meant that spring was still weeks away. Long weeks of long nights to share with Ben.

Oliver, the barkeep, halfheartedly swept the light dusting of snow from the wooden walk outside the double doors, idling away the time until the saloon came alive once more.

Most of the men in town were busy on their farms. Only the occasional sound of wagon wheels rolling into town to stop across at Charlie Delaney's store disturbed the sleeping town.

Small brown birds hopped about, nibbling daintily at bread crumbs Sara had scattered earlier.

Not expecting to see any customers until dark, Lacy was disconcerted when a giant ambled through the open door.

The stranger stopped just within the threshold and stared at the young woman behind the bar. She wasn't exactly the type of gal he'd expected.

Her gold hair was pulled back in a severe knot, although it straggled about her pretty face. Her dress was dark, high-necked, and down right unattractive.

Acutely aware of her dress, a sturdy remnant of her teaching days, Lacy eyed the newcomer. "May I help you?"

He looked her up and down slowly as if he were considering her points as he would a horse.

A vivid blush rose to her cheeks, pleasing him. "Is there something I can do for you?" she demanded sharply, and immediately regretted her choice of words.

A smile broke his stern face. It said he found her desirable and that it had been a long time since a woman had eased his needs.

"Might be," he said carefully.

Angry, Lacy studied the man in turn. His hair was long and dust-colored. From the wrinkles on his bronzed face, she judged his age to be near fifty. He wore buckskin trousers and moccasins and beneath a heavy jacket his homespun shirt was opened almost to the waist, revealing a chest covered with thick hair.

The stranger took stock of his surroundings before ambling to the bar. "There wouldn't by any chance be a fella name a Benjamin Paradise 'round here, would there, little lady?" he asked lazily.

"There might," she hedged, on the defensive.

His grin widened. "And there might not, that it?"

"Possibly," Lacy said, her head held high.

He leaned across the bar, his face an inch or so from hers. He smelled of horses, and Lacy stepped back, her nose wrinkling.

"Well, if there might be a Ben Paradise 'roundabouts here," he said, "would ya tell him George Travis 'ud like ta see him?"

Oliver stepped back into the saloon, his broom trailing behind him, dragging a feathering of snow inside. "Not *the* George Travis," he said.

The giant turned around slowly. "Might be," he drawled. Somehow he made those simple words sound like a challenge. Or a threat.

Oliver did not seem to notice. He propped the broom up against the wall and came over eagerly, his hand stretched out in greeting. "Damn! George Travis! Heard a lot about you, Mr. Travis."

"Not all good, I hope," Travis said, and grinned evilly at Lacy.

She frowned. The man was an obnoxious bore, a frontiersman with an inflated opinion of himself and his prowess with women. "If you wouldn't mind taking care of Mr. Travis, Oliver," she instructed, "I have to see Mrs. Mackley about dinner."

"Ya go on, Miss Lacy," Oliver said, still pumping the stranger's hand. "Wait till Ben hears yer here. Damn! George Travis!"

With a suspicious glance at their guest, Lacy slipped from behind the bar and into the office. Ben had his feet on the desk and was balancing his chair on its two back legs. As she turned to close the door, he let the chair drop on all fours.

"How did you know I was thinking about you?" he said, taking her in his arms.

"I didn't." She smiled, pleased. "There is a stranger in the saloon asking about you."

Ben's lips hovered near hers. "Hmm?"

Lacy's heart raced as she slid her arms about his neck. She watched his lips part slightly, his head dip toward her. "He said his name is George Travis," she murmured, and closed her eyes in anticipation of his kiss.

It never came.

"George Travis!" Ben gripped Lacy's shoulders and looked into her face. "You're sure he said George Travis?"

"Yes, I'm sure," she said, disappointed.

"George Travis!" He gave her a quick kiss and was out the door.

Lacy followed more slowly. In the saloon Ben and the stranger were slapping each other on the back and exchanging bear hugs.

"Damn! It's been a long time," Ben said.

"Hell, it ain't been that long, yer young bear cub." The giant laughed. "Got yerself a nice place here, Ben."

"Have a drink," Ben urged. "Oliver, I'd like you to meet George Travis, the man I told you about." Ben kept an arm around the man's shoulders.

"George Travis," Oliver breathed again reverently. "*The* George Travis."

The big man looked amused.

"Lacy! I'd like you to meet an old friend of mine, George Travis." Ben let go of the giant to pull Lacy forward, his arm now around her shoulders. Whether to denote possession she was not sure.

The stranger grinned wickedly again.

"Travis, this is Lacy Phalen."

"Pleased to make your acquaintance, Mr. Travis," Lacy said carefully, no longer sure how to treat the big man.

The trapper nodded stiffly in a semblance of courtesy. "Miz Phalen. Right careful gal ya got there, Ben. Wouldn't admit ta a yea or a nay ta yer bein' here."

"Lace," Ben said, "this man saved my life many times. He taught me how to trap and how to stay alive in Indian country."

Ben grabbed two whiskey bottles from behind the counter. "What have you been up to, you old grizzly? Last I heard you were headed for California."

Oliver perked up. Even the winter snows had not kept news of the gold discoveries at a place called Sutter's Mill from reaching Paradise.

Travis ignored the reference. For the moment. "I know what ya've been up ta," Travis told Ben as his eyes roamed over Lacy again.

Ben laughed and, swinging his leg over the back of a chair, sat down. "And if you remember, Travis, I've never been one to share. Look all you want, but hands off."

Travis settled his bulk across the table from Ben and stared at Lacy. "Well," he said, "I do prefer more of an armful. Rosie still here?"

Feeling slightly insulted, Lacy left them to their whiskey.

Ben came into the bedroom that evening while Lacy was putting the finishing touches to her hair. He dropped his black coat on the bed and stood behind her, admiration for her appearance clear in his face. They did make a very handsome couple, Lacy admitted, meeting his eyes in the reflection. His tanned complexion and dark hair were such a contrast to her own pale skin and golden curls. The candlelight picked up the gleam of satin threads in his vest and the flames danced in his eyes.

"You're looking especially delectable tonight, dearest heart," he said.

"No more so than usual," she assured him.

Ben's hand slid to her shoulder, pushing the dress off and down her arm. He stooped to kiss her nape.

Lacy's head moved sensuously in response. "This close to dinner?"

Ben's eyes met hers in the mirror. "And why not?"

"You have a guest."

"We have a guest," he corrected. "One who would understand."

"Even though he prefers more of an armful?"

Ben laughed. "Travis hasn't the taste for wild-cats that I have." He blazed a trail of kisses from her ear down the delicate curve of her neck and on toward her gently sloping shoulder. In the mirror, Lacy saw mischief play in his eyes as he watched her reactions. "What's for dinner?" he asked.

She growled in mock anger and gave him a push.

Ben fell backwards against the bed and slid to the floor. "Disappointed, my heart?" he asked innocently.

Lacy got up from the vanity stool and stepped

over his sprawling form. He caught her skirt and pulled her down to his level.

"I'm going to look a sad sight," she said, pulling the gown back into place on her shoulders.

Ben pushed the sleeves back down and let his fingers play around the loosened neckline of the bodice, his eyes on the swelling mounds of her breasts.

"Do you ever think of leaving Paradise, Lacy?"

"Well, of course I do."

"I mean before the captain returns," he said. His fingers followed the trail his eyes blazed across her skin. "Possibly meet him at a different port and sail back to Boston with him," he suggested.

Since they had become lovers, she had wanted time to stand still. Spring had been a distant milestone. While the idea had often occupied her at idle moments the previous fall, she had thought about returning to Boston very little of late. The intoxication of life with Ben held the time of decision at bay. But it was fast approaching. Lacy recognized it in the ever-shortening nights.

"Meet Papa? I hadn't thought of that possibility," she said, her voice husky with desire. Her lips parted, tasting his briefly.

His hands went to the tiny buttons down the back of her dress. One by one, Lacy felt him release them.

"What ports do you think he might put into on his way back?" he continued conversationally.

"I don't know," Lacy said, and caught her breath as his fingers found their way inside her corset, loosening it. "I'd have to think about it."

"Perhaps California," he said, pausing to see if she refuted the suggestion. "San Francisco." Content with her lack of reaction, Ben's lips caressed her neck, the arch of her throat. "Do think about it, Lacy," he murmured before claiming her lips hungrily. "Later. Much later."

CHAPTER XVIII

The city of Saint Joseph on the plains of northwest Missouri bustled with activity. Groups of travelers and canvas-covered wagons dotted the frontier as far as the eye could see. May had brought temperate weather and an end to the road-miring showers of April. As the byways cleared, men from every echelon of society succumbed to the lure of adventure and turned their eyes and wagons to the west.

They gathered at what they considered the edge of civilization in communities that catered to travelers. Towns like Saint Joe and Independence. The "jumping off" points.

A fair atmosphere dominated. Men in dust-covered homespuns shouldered rifles as they lounged against their waiting wagons. Women, dressed in simple calico dresses and sunbonnets, their feet shod in durable boots, shrilled at the children dragging at their skirts for attention.

Lillian Phalen, late of Boston, Massachusetts, and Paradise, Missouri, sat on the hard seat of the large freight wagon, her full calico skirts spread demurely to hide her new moccasins. She was dubious about the suitability of the comfortable fringed buckskin leggings as well as the trip ahead. It was by far easier to concentrate on the moccasins than the trail or Ben's assurances that the *Puritan Paramour* would drop anchor in San Francisco harbor enroute to Boston. His glib tongue had convinced her no merchantman could pass up the opportunity gold-rich San Francisco offered. She still wondered if she believed him or just could not bear to leave him yet.

Despite the cool May morning, Lacy was in a nervous sweat. Her printed cotton gown, with its simple gathered skirts, long sleeves, and high collar, was similar to those worn by the other women on the plain, and already hot. Ben had run a tanned index finger down the row of tiny buttons from collar to the tightly nipped waist earlier, and prophesied an uncomfortable journey.

Ben himself had changed his mode of dress drastically. In place of the gentleman gambler there stood a backwoodsman in pale form-fitting buckskin breeches, tall fringed moccasins and a dark cotton open-necked shirt. A gun belt was buckled around his slim hips, the dangling holster bound to his right thigh with strips of rawhide. His Colt .44 revolver was similar to those issued to enlistees during the recent war with Mexico. Ben's nestled comfortably in the leather, and could be aimed with a swift and deadly accuracy. Lacy had hurled bottle targets in the air and watched Ben pick them off with amazing speed. In addition, he had spent two months teaching Lacy to handle a rifle and hand gun. She had surprised him by developing into a fair shot, and carried a tiny single-shot pistol strapped to her thigh. Recently invented by Henry Deringer, it fit easily into her hand and was lightweight though of a heavy calibre.

The early-morning breeze stirred the golden curls escaping from her print sunbonnet. Lacy looked back into their wagon at the carefully lashed wheels of chance, monte table covers, cartons of cards, dice, and other implements that would give birth to the Paradise Palace, the saloon Ben and George Travis planned to open in San Francisco.

There had been no room for a bed, just the necessary supplies. One of the things considered indispensable had been her wardrobe. Directly behind her perch, the new trunk was packed full of silk dresses to dazzle the male residents of California. She only hoped that after six months in the trunk she would be able to remove the wrinkles from the elegant gowns.

A wagon rumbled past kicking up a cloud of dust. The woman on the seat waved cheerfully. "Beautiful day," she called.

"Isn't it though," Lacy answered with an eager smile. "California?"

The woman leaned out of the wagon to look back as it passed. "Where else?"

Lacy grinned after her.

Ben waved his low-crowned hat in an effort to

clear the air of the dust cloud raised by the iron-rimmed wheels. "Damn, I'll never get used to eating all this dust and it's bound to get worse."

Lacy looked down at him as he rechecked the harness on their three yoke of oxen.

"You should be used to it, shouldn't you? After all, you've been out this way before."

He grimaced. "But I wasn't hampered by cursed wagons. I was a trapper then. The only dust I ate was when I lost a damn fight."

"We could always go by the sea routes," Lacy suggested, reviving the argument they'd had since Travis's departure.

"Not that again." His pained expression was belied by the twinkle in his eye. "You know what the shipping costs on this equipment would be, Lace? I'd be broke before we were around the Cape."

His head ducked under the lead oxen as he surveyed the harness. Satisfied, he straightened and looked around at the crowd of strolling pioneer travelers. Two teenaged girls walked by surveying his robust appearance appreciatively. Ben flashed them a smile, all dazzling white teeth in a sun-browned face. They giggled and hurried away, their hips twitching seductively.

Ben gathered the reins and climbed aboard the wagon. "You look respectable enough for a prayer meeting this morning," he commented.

"I know your opinion of my dress," she said. "But it's better than your suggestion that I wear trousers." Her eyes followed the girls. "*I* am worried about the affect you are having on these Sweet Sues."

"Jealous, my heart?"

"I would hate to have you worn out, my love," she countered, her husky voice thick with sarcasm.

His hand dropped on Lacy's thigh. "Unless it's by you, that is." He smiled wickedly.

Lacy removed his hand. "Which is the train we join?"

The reins slapped gently on the oxen's backs as he urged them forward into the stream of traffic. "It's over by that clump of trees. I met the leader last night in the saloon."

"But which saloon of the many you visited would be hard to say."

"I wasn't that mellow." He looked at her with the hint of passion in his eyes that never ceased to make Lacy's heart beat faster.

"Watch where you are going," she advised.

Ben grinned, again that flash of white teeth. "As with most of the trains this year, the majority are of men headed for the gold fields. This train has three family groups already signed up. Thought you'd feel comfortable having other women in the train."

Lacy agreed and silently offered a prayer that it was never discovered that she was not Ben's wife. The attitude of the ladies of Paradise had hurt considerably. They had labeled her his mistress long before she had welcomed him to her bed. In the smaller and closer-knit society of the wagon train, it would be unbearable to be an outcast. At least in Paradise she had enjoyed the company of the three women at the saloon.

"Will they be leaving soon?" she asked of the wagon train.

"That's another reason I signed on with this particular group. We pull out at dawn tomorrow."

Now, after all the weeks of planning and waiting, Lacy looked toward the small cluster of wagons near an oasis of trees on the prairie, and felt a renewal of apprehension. Perhaps she should have returned to Boston. She should have contacted Miss Haskell about another teaching post and hoped rumors of events in Paradise had not preceded her arrival. She no longer thought of Caleb Innes, for if mistress she must be, Lacy preferred to be Ben Paradise's. He was the whole reason she now sat on the rough seat of the conestoga.

She would never admit such a weakness to Ben though. She feared that the euphoria they shared was temporary. Something to be enjoyed, savored. But she had no future with Ben. She had always known her fate lay with the Puritan Line. Ben's was with a deck of cards.

For now Lacy lived in the present only. She basked in the warmth of Ben's smile, his company, his embrace. They were joys she was not ready to foreswear yet. Thus the suggestion he had made that her father would make San Francisco one of his ports of call was sensible. It was a sound business move. And, more important, claiming a desire to meet the captain in California gave Lacy an excuse to stay with Ben a while longer.

The wagon rumbled through the dust, through the crowds of people and wagons. Lacy clutched at Ben's arm as they lurched over a rut on the plain. "Did you tell them anything about me?" she asked, her thoughts on the wagon train.

Ben gave the reins another snap. "Not a thing."

"Will they think I'm your wife or sister, do you think?"

"Certainly not my sister, dearest heart."

"You don't mind if they think we're wed?"

"Can you act like a sweet, little self-effacing bride, Lace?" She could hear the amusement in his voice.

"If you can perfect a performance close to that of a besotted husband," she countered.

"It would be difficult."

"Don't put yourself out, Benjamin Paradise."

He laughed and taking her hand kissed it. "Things will be fine, Lace. Don't worry."

She glanced down at her ringless left hand, then at the intricate ring Ben had given her for her twentieth birthday. The ring had made a white mark on the finger of her right hand as the sun had darkened her skin.

Ben noticed her nervously turning his gift on her finger. Her furrowed brow was easy to read. "Why not, Lace? If it makes you feel better."

"You wouldn't mind?"

"What's one finger among friends?"

Pleased with his answer, Lacy leaned over and kissed his freshly shaven cheek. A thin middle-aged lady in a wagon nearby looked shocked.

"Now would a self-effacing wife act like that?" Ben laughed.

"No," she agreed, "but a besotted one would."

"Best hurry with the exchange if you want to be proper when we join the train. We're almost up to them."

She worked the elegant little ring off her finger and slid it on the third finger of her left hand.

Ben pulled back slowly on the reins to slow the wagon until it rolled gently to a stop.

"Paradise?" called a spare leather-skinned man in well-worn breeches. The top of a pair of red long-johns showed at the open neck of his patched shirt.

Ben secured the reins and jumped down to pump the stranger's hand. He towered over the man.

"Glad ya made it. We're jest about ta vote on regulations fer this company." The stranger glanced up at Lacy. His eyes were such a clear blue they seemed a continuation of the sky overhead. "This yer missus?" he asked.

Ben reached up to help Lacy down. "This is my Lacy," he said. Hands on his shoulders, Lacy landed lightly in the dust beside him.

"Glad ta have ya join us, ma'am. Name's Clancy. Buck Clancy," the man said, tipping his head rather than his hat.

Lacy put her hand out to shake his. Buck Clancy looked surprised then gripped her hand so tightly Lacy thought her fingers would be black and blue.

"Care fer a cup o' coffee, ma'am?"

She smiled brightly. "I'd love some, Mr. Clancy."

He led the way to a moderate-sized campfire in the circle of wagons. Three women in calico dresses were busy preparing a meal near the fire. They looked up as the group approached.

Again Clancy nodded, his hand moving toward

his hat yet never quite touching it. "Ladies, this is Mr. and Miz Paradise. Jest signed on with us. Told Miz Paradise she could get a cup o' coffee while her Mister an' I go ta the meetin'."

The youngest of the women came forward with a smile of welcome. Her dark hair was parted severely in the center and bound in a tight bun at her nape. Like so many of the women on the frontier, she was thin, almost gaunt.

"Welcome to our little group, Mrs. Paradise. Of course you can have a cup, if the men left any."

Lacy looked uncertainly at Ben. It was one thing, she felt, for him to sanction moving her ring to her left hand, but entirely different for her to answer to the title "Mrs." especially when it was coupled with his name.

"Don't be shy, dearest heart." He laughed and dropped an arm around her shoulders for a quick hug. "Get acquainted."

The woman smiled warmly at him. "She's in safe hands, Mr. Paradise."

Ben's lips curved into what Lacy recognized as the smile he reserved for pretty women. "Ben, ma'am. The name's Ben," he insisted, and went off with Clancy.

"You have a very charming husband, Mrs. Paradise," the woman said.

Lacy glared after Ben's departing back. "Yes, don't I."

"I'm Amy Smithson." The other woman held out her hand.

"I'm very happy to meet you, Mrs. Smithson," Lacy said, taking the proffered hand. "But if my . . ." She just could not call Ben "husband." "If my . . . beloved is going to be so agreeable, I feel you should call me Lacy."

"And I'm Amy. Come meet the others," she urged.

Amy had a quick, friendly smile that smoothed the harsh lines a life of early hardships had etched upon her face. She had once been very pretty, Lacy realized. Yet Amy's real beauty was in her sweet open personality. Lacy was drawn to her immediately, confident a deep friendship would develop between them.

The other women were older and more reserved in their acceptance of a newcomer. Amy introduced them as Mrs. Pritchard and Mrs. Court. They both impressed Lacy as women with rigid religious views and unbending ideals. They would certainly disapprove of the supplies in the wagon. She dare not consider their reaction should they learn of her true relationship to Ben Paradise.

They were austere women, their cheekbones standing out in plain faces, their eyes almost sunken in hollows. However, they both were very strong personalities, judging others by their own morals and finding fault with the rest of the world.

"Yer husband would seem ta have a roamin' eye," Mrs. Court said as she sat ramrod stiff on a small camp stool mixing a flour concoction.

"He's the type young women run after," Mrs. Pritchard commented.

Lacy sipped at her coffee. It tasted like weak mud. "I believe he favors his father," she said, and perched on the edge of a crate with Amy Smithson. "Are all of you bound for California?"

Two gray-streaked heads nodded in unison.

"They've all gone mad over this gold strike," Mrs. Pritchard said.

"Mr. Court gave up a very prosperous farm," her crony informed Lacy. "He won't listen ta reason. Jest uprooted the family."

Lacy could imagine the scenes that raged in the Court farmhouse before Mrs. Court had loaded children and belongings on the wagon.

"Pritchard were the same," his mate said sadly. "I hope he comes ta his senses by the time we reach the cutoffs. Better if we was ta head fer Oregon. They say there's land ta spare fer farms out there. Where ya bound, Miz Paradise?"

Lacy untied her bonnet and ran a hand through her curls. "We hope to make San Francisco," she said. "Ben owns some land there. He isn't interested in the gold fields per se."

Mrs. Pritchard frowned at the golden tresses. "He will be," she assured Lacy.

Amy Smithson laughed softly. "I'd say he has all the gold he needs right now in his beautiful wife's hair."

"It's a terrible nuisance, really," Lacy complained. "I wish it were straight and more manageable. It's always working out of the pins."

"A little grease, perhaps," Mrs. Court said. "I've heard the Injun women wear bear grease in their hair."

Lacy's nose wrinkled. "I don't think Ben would care for that exactly."

"Another cup of coffee, Miz Paradise? There's just a bit left."

Lacy looked down at the near full tin cup and

wondered how she was ever going to get rid of it. "No, I believe I've had enough. Is there something I can do to help you?"

They assured her that her services were not required. Mrs. Court whispered to Mrs. Pritchard that she doubted the girl could cook.

"Have ya any children, Miz Paradise?"

Amy Smithson chuckled. "I doubt they've been married long, Mrs. Pritchard. Just newlyweds."

Sharp eyes demanded confirmation.

Lacy blushed and nodded. "I hadn't thought of children yet," she murmured.

"It's never too soon ta start a family, Miz Paradise," the older woman lectured. "If there's one thing keeps a man from strayin', it's havin' a son of his own. They feel obliged ta ya when there's a son ta follow 'em."

A vigorous nod of agreement was given by Mrs. Court. "Yes, the sooner the better, Miz Paradise. That husband of yers is too handsome fer his own good. Ya've got ta make sure of him."

Lacy recalled the married patrons of the Paradise Saloon and the girls upstairs. Their activities certainly gave lie to the women's statements. "I don't know if I'm ready for a family," she temporized.

"Ya married."

"It's yer wifely duty."

"Large families, Miz Paradise, that's what this country needs."

"Bind him ta ya, gal. It's the only way."

Lacy squirmed uneasily. "How many children do you have?" she asked Amy, hoping to turn the conversation.

Amy's face glowed with pride at mention of her offspring. She was the mother of a boy six and girls aged five and three. The other women had borne their husbands a total of fifteen of which only ten survived. Mrs. Court was the mother of six. Mrs. Pritchard sadly admitted her brood numbered but four.

"My health jest ain't been what I'd like," she said.

They questioned Lacy about her origins and how she had come to meet her "husband."

The coffee mug turned in her hands nervously. "I was a schoolteacher in his town," she said tentatively.

"Educated," they cooed. "Yer parents must be well off."

"I was an only child."

Mrs. Court and Mrs. Pritchard looked at each other, their faces clearly declaring an only child to be the root of all evil.

Angered, Lacy's voice became cloyingly sweet. "Mother's health." She smiled sadly at Mrs. Pritchard. "You understand."

The woman unbent to pat her shoulder. "I doubt ya have much ta worry about, ma dear. Ya seem ta be a strong gal and yer husband is very manly. I predict a very large family."

Fortunately for Lacy's peace of mind the men's meeting broke up and they began to drift near the fire. Ben joined her and took the cup of coffee from her hand. He took a drink and tried to control his features. Lacy caught the grimace and smiled mischievously at him.

"Delicious, isn't it, darling?"

Ben put the cup down on a makeshift table. "Wish you'd get the recipe, Lace. How about a walk? I'm sure these lovely ladies won't mind if I tear you away for a short while." He put his arm around her waist, holding her at his side.

Mrs. Court frowned yet urged her. "Ya go ahead, ma dear."

"We can handle things jest this once, Miz Paradise," Mrs. Pritchard allowed.

Amy waved Lacy away with a genuine smile.

"Newlyweds!" Mrs. Pritchard hissed after the couple.

"Cain't keep his hands off her!" Mrs. Court agreed with repugnance.

Ben led the way toward a small patch of woods, his arm possessively around Lacy. She could feel the eyes of the men and women following them. A couple of the younger men nudged each other.

"Thought I'd better put my mark on you, *Mrs. Paradise*," he said with a satanic grin. "You've made quite an impression with the men already."

"And you with the ladies," she insisted. "They kept bringing the conversation back to you. Mrs. Pritchard and Mrs. Court have warned me that you have a roving eye and that you are too handsome for your own good."

"Didn't I hear some talk about a large family?"

Lacy felt the blood rush to her face. "They think I should provide a son to make you beholden to me."

"Do they now." He laughed. "We'll just have to discuss that someday."

As they passed out of sight among the trees, he swung her into his arms. "See how much trouble you've gotten yourself into, *Mrs. Paradise?*"

Lacy grimaced. "I should have been your sister."

"Never," he said, and kissed her softly, desire stirring in his eyes.

"How was the meeting?"

He played with her loose curls. "We voted on a route, worked out wagon rotation . . ."

"Wagon rotation?"

"To ensure the same people don't eat all the dust," he explained. "We won the number-three spot for tomorrow. You'll be able to shake the dust from your curls in two days' time."

"You *won* the place?"

He smiled down at her. "Of course. Didn't I tell you I'm lucky? Lucky at cards. Lucky at love."

Gently, he pushed her down on a bed of wild-flowers.

"Ben!" she cried as he stretched out beside her. "Not here! Not with all these people around!"

"Tell them we're working on that large family," he said.

"Ben!"

His fingers strayed to the buttons of her bodice.

Lacy caught his hand. He moved, cupping her breast. Lights danced in his eyes.

"We really shouldn't," she said.

"My prim and proper Lacy." He smiled.

She welcomed his kiss but continued to catch his exploring hands.

Sunlight filtered softly through the canopy of newly leafed branches, flickering as a gentle breeze stirred the trees. The noises of the train were muffled by distance and easily forgotten. The squeal of excited children, of jangling harness, and impatient men did intrude, however.

Lacy pulled away reluctantly. "Behave," she said, then laughed at Ben's assumed expression of innocence. "Ben, please. What if someone comes along? What would they think?"

Neither had noticed the silent approach of the watching man. Now he stepped from the cover of brush, a sneer on his broad face.

"Why, Miz Lillian," drawled a voice she remembered with fear, "they'd think Ben Paradise had brought his whore along fer the ride."

Ben rolled to his feet in an instant, his right hand poised near the handle of his gun.

From her bed of wildflowers, Lacy stared at the hate-filled face of Judd Thompkins.

Thompkins's eyes were leveled on the dangerously alert man crouched over the girl. "That's what she is, ain't she?" he demanded.

Ben growled deep in his throat. It was a savage sound. The sound of a cornered animal protecting its own.

Judd was amused. He leered openly. For once he held all the aces. Weren't no way Ben Paradise was gonna win this hand, he thought with satisfaction.

He glanced at the pale-faced girl sprawled attractively on her side in the grass. Her eyes were wide with fear. Her hair tumbled in golden waves about her shoulders and curled entrancingly over her quickly heaving breasts. His eyes roamed boldly over her then he turned. "Jest a common whore," Judd said, and walked out of the glade.

CHAPTER XIX

The first days on the trail were apprehensive for Lacy. She expected Judd Thompkins to reveal her real relationship to Ben and was uneasy when he did not.

Thompkins had joined the train late, a member of a group of single men bound for the gold fields. Lacy knew the older women of the train would no longer accept her once they learned she was a mistress rather than a wife. At present it was only in Judd Thompkins's eyes that she was a harlot. Soon he would expect to buy her favors in exchange for his silence.

Ben spent the evening insisting there was a vast difference between being a prostitute and a beloved mistress. But Lacy knew the women would fail to see the distinction.

It was agonizing waiting for Thompkins to make

his move. She began carrying her small derringer in the top of her moccasin. When she did fall into exhausted sleep, she was disturbed by chilling nightmares that combined elements of both Thompkins's and William Quire's attacks. When she cried out, Ben was there immediately, rocking her tenderly in his arms, attempting to soothe her fears. But Lacy saw the hunted look remained in his eyes.

When the other men of the train discovered Ben had traveled the country they were covering, he was drafted for scouting duty. This left Lacy prey to Thompkins's unwanted attentions. They had been on the trail over a week, working their way toward the South Platte River. Thompkins had not yet attempted to lay claim to her. At least once a day, however, he would ride alongside the wagon as she urged the oxen team in the dust-ridden path of the lead wagon. His detailed descriptions of what he intended to do to her rubbed her nerves raw.

Daily the tension built.

When he returned late each evening, Ben found renewed pain in Lacy's haggard face. The trail, though grueling, could not be blamed for the drawn expression and total exhaustion that haunted her. He cursed the necessity of his scouting expeditions.

Still covered in dust, he sat watching Lacy prepare the twice daily meal of oatmeal mush, bacon, and pilot bread. She deserved better. He should have listened to her and sailed to California. If he hadn't preferred the laborious land journey over a cramped ship's cabin around the

Cape, she would not be in danger.

"Do you have your gun near, Lacy?" he asked as she passed him a cup of the now familiar weak coffee.

"I'm never without it," she answered.

He grimaced ruefully. "I never thought you'd need it for protection in the camp. Let me see it."

Lacy turned her back on the camp and pulled her skirt up to retrieve the derringer. Ben checked the chamber and the hammer movement, then handed it back.

"Keep it near," he instructed. "I have the watch tonight."

She nodded. "Would it be possible for us to join another train? Even if it means dropping back a day?"

Ben ran a weary hand through his hair. Despite the dangers, it was tempting. Shadows hollowed her eyes and she'd lost weight worrying about Thompkins's next move. The trail was difficult enough when one was healthy. It was fatal for the ill and Lacy was wasting away. No, he couldn't chance it. "Not until we reach the fort, Lace. It would be too dangerous to stay out here alone. We've got to stay with the train."

After a quick meal, they sat silently watching the sky darken. Ben's arm dropped around Lacy's shoulders. Her head rested against his chest. When the first stars began to twinkle above, he kissed the top of her head lightly. "I have to leave now. Remember. Keep the gun within reach."

She nodded, solemn. "I will," she promised.

She was so frail. How could he live with himself if anything happened to her? The glib reasons he'd used to persuade her to attempt the journey haunted him. Was it really logical to think Captain Phalen would land in San Francisco? From Lacy's calm acceptance of the idea, it appeared very probable that Phalen would drop anchor there. She knew her father and the workings of the Puritan Line far better than Ben could ever second guess.

Would he be able to let her leave when the *Paramour* arrived though? Lacy Phalen had captured his heart—hell, his soul—long ago. If only she hadn't agreed to accompany him because she believed the *Puritan Paramour* would visit the gold region.

Her eyes glowed when she spoke of sailing back to Boston on the clipper. Her continued reminder that she would not be staying kept Ben from ever telling her of his love. He could only hope she would grow to love him as well and change her mind.

Ben pulled Lacy close for a lingering kiss, unconcerned that they were seen by the silent watchers around the campfires. Then, rifle in hand, he moved out of the circle of wagons.

Other members of the train cast giant wavering shadows as they moved about the fire, preparing to retire for the night. Lacy unrolled her bed of blankets beneath the wagon. Mindful of Ben's warning, she placed the tiny gun under the pillow, and kept her hand on it as she settled for the night.

The evening was still. Only the soft rustlings of night creatures stirred out on the prairie. A buffalo lowed to her calf, the once eerie sound now comforting Lacy, lulling her. The gruelling hardship of the trail took its toll. Lacy gazed out at the dying flames of the campfire, her mind cognizant only of fatigue.

Was it possible she had once danced until dawn? Had been courted, pampered, perhaps even spoiled? How foreign her memories of Boston were.

Ahead stretched nearly six months of constant bone-jarring travel. After the plains they would encounter the deserts then the mountains before they reached the new land of milk and honey, the verdant gold-laden hills of California.

Often she had questioned her decision to follow Ben Paradise. Would the *Paramour* dock in San Francisco? It hardly mattered. It was the excuse she had embraced to remain with Ben.

The leaden weight of her eyelids fluttered closed, her face softening as awareness slipped away.

The sound awakened her, a stealthy sound that jarred her nerves.

Her eyes closed, Lacy listened, straining to identify the creature that stalked her. Something— *someone*—was very close. Could Ben's watch be over? The men split their watch nightly, rotating at one o'clock.

A hand brushed against her arm, slipping toward her breast. A touch that was not Ben's, Lacy realized. Carefully, she slid her hand under the pillow. The comforting feel of the derringer was no longer there.

"Lookin' fer this?" Thompkins's harsh voice said in her ear.

Lacy's eyes flew open. The tiny gun was in his hand. She heard the catch of the hammer as he brought it back.

"Now, Miz Lillian, yer goin' ta do exactly as I say an' not make a sound. Understan'?" Thompkins was intoxicated. His eyes reflected a wildness that belied the firm yet slurred threat in his voice.

Lacy looked down the barrel of the small gun and nodded.

"Get outta that dress."

Barely daring to breath under the Cyclopean stare of the derringer, she reached toward the buttons. Her hands shook as she loosened them one by one. When they were all undone, she lay passive.

"Off," Thompkins growled, gesturing with the gun.

Lacy's glance never wavered from the threat of steel dwarfed in his large hand. "I can't," she said, hoping she sounded reasonable rather than frightened. "Not under the wagon. There isn't enough room."

Impatient, Judd's free hand pulled the bodice away from her breasts and ripped at the camisole. He smiled, sure of himself. His lips pulled back from his teeth in an evil leer. The bitch was cowed already, he smirked to himself. She remembered the last time just as he did. Memories of unfulfilled pleasure made him hard and eager to take the Phalen woman. He eased the hammer of the gun and threw it into a clump of brush on the far side of the wagon.

"Reckon I can make do," he said, and pulled at her skirts, hiking them up to her waist.

"No!" Lacy choked. With the threat of her gun removed, she acted quickly, rolling from beneath the wagon.

Judd swore and caught her as Lacy stumbled to her feet. The back of his hand caught her cheek in a savage blow that sent her reeling. He dragged her back on her feet.

"Listen, Miz Lillian," he hissed, "or da ya like ta be called *Miz Paradise* now?"

Lacy tore from his grasp. Her pale hair swirled with a life of its own, shielding her from his leering eyes.

Unaware that the moonlight reflected the glory of her mane, calling attention to their struggle, Thompkins dragged her back. Spinning Lacy to face him, he twisted her left arm, forcing it up behind her back so that she curved her body toward him to ease the pain.

"Either ya give me what I want, when I want it," he growled, "or I'll kill that fancy man o' yers."

Fear for Ben more than her own distress stilled Lacy's struggles. "You wouldn't dare," she whispered, horrified.

Thompkins sneered as his threat bore fruit. "Wouldn't I?"

He was no better than a hungry wolf, ready to turn on his own kind. His eyes were wild, glowing with a rabid satisfaction that made Lacy's blood run cold.

"I'll do anything you say," she whispered.

Judd was pleased by the terror in her voice. "That's more like it." His eyes lingered on the creamy white mounds of her breasts, thrust forward by her supplicating stance. The fast rise and

fall of her breathing seduced, beckoned his touch.
The taste of her lingered in his mind until he
buried his face in the enticing exposed valley. He
crushed her against his hard manhood, gyrating
against her.

Lacy twisted away in revulsion. Judd forced her
arm higher, pleased to hear her gasp in pain.

"I ain't in a mood fer wrestlin' tonight, sweetheart," he said, his stale liquored breath against
her cheek. "Let's go somewhere where we ain't
likely ta be disturbed."

He pushed her forward, keeping her arm in a
painful lock. They moved out of the safety of the
wagons into the prairie night. But even Judd was
afraid to leave the train far behind. When they
were a wagon's length from the camp, he shoved
Lacy to the dirt. He was on her immediately,
forcing her down, dragging at her skirts.

The specter of his previous attack did not raise
its head to distract her. The months of tender
loving in Ben's arms had somehow laid the shade
to rest, freeing her to fight Thompkins as she had
been unable to do before.

Lacy twisted from side to side to avoid
Thompkins's touch. Irritated, he grabbed a handful of her hair, determined to force her into
compliancy. He buried his face against her throat
and fumbled with his belt.

Her strength was fading quickly. Lacy prayed as
she had on Christmas Eve, asking for deliverance,
asking for the sanctuary of unconsciousness.

Thompkins pushed her tightly clamped legs
apart. His mouth and hands were cruel on her

exposed breasts. She cringed in anticipation of his entry.

Then suddenly he was no longer a weight on her limbs. Five men stood over her. Thompkins dangled in the hands of one of them. Hastily, Lacy pushed her skirts down and tried to draw the ragged pieces of her bodice together.

"Put him down, Paradise," one of the men said.

"Ya all right, Miz Paradise?" another inquired.

Lacy nodded. "Yes, I'm all right now."

"Parkins, ya take Thompkins back ta the train. I don't want Paradise ta kill him. Ya see ta yer missus, Paradise," Buck Clancy's authoritative voice rang out. A rifle was raised in Judd's direction while another man pried her attacker from Ben's grip.

Ben had no memory of grabbing Thompkins, of dragging him from Lacy's struggling body. Sanity returned with the men's interference. "Lacy," he whispered hoarsely as Judd was led away. "If he hurt you, I'll kill him. I swear I'll kill him."

The deadly calm of his voice frightened her as much as Thompkins's assault. Judd had promised he would kill Ben. The determination in his voice had sealed the gambler's fate. She couldn't let Ben go after Judd. Shakily, Lacy got to her feet with the aid of Ben's arm. "I'm all right, Ben," she insisted, and plunged into the lie. "He didn't hurt me."

One of the men had thrown fresh tinder on the fire at the campsite. It flared back to life, making the men's shadows dance grotesquely on the wagons' canvas. The camp was coming alive. Men scrambled from their blankets, women peered cautiously from the depths of their wagons.

Lacy rebuttoned her dress and held the torn section in place.

At their arrival Clancy sent two men back out on watch. He stared woodenly at Thompkins. "Takin' another man's woman is a serious matter," he said.

Judd snorted in derision. "She ain't his woman. She's a whore from his saloon."

Ben made a move toward Thompkins. Lacy gripped his arm, holding him back with the strength of her fear for him.

"She's his wife," Clancy continued.

Thompkins gave a shout of laughter. "Ha! She come with me willin', Paradise. Couldn't wait ta have another go round with ol' Judd Thompkins."

Ben stiffened. "Liar," he snarled.

Thompkins leer was confident. "Ask her."

Lacy preferred not to wait to see if Ben had his doubts. She could not have borne seeing any uncertainty in his eyes. "He threatened me with a gun," she said. "He said he would kill you if I didn't do as he said."

Ben frowned. He had no reason to doubt Lacy. Why was Judd Thompkins so cocky then? "What happened to your gun?"

Lacy's calm did not falter. "He threw it in the bushes."

Clancy looked at Thompkins. "That right?"

Judd shrugged his shoulders. "Sometimes they need a little tamin'."

"So ya forced Miz Paradise."

"I'da paid handsome. Whatever her regular price happens ta be." Thompkins grinned evilly across the fire. "Like I said, she's a whore."

"She is his wife," Clancy maintained.

Disgust was written on Thompkins's face as he answered the wagon master. "Did he tell ya so? Or did ya jest take it fer granted? What man would marry a woman when she's givin' it away?"

Lacy felt chilled. He had made a point with them. She read the doubts in the faces of the men and women alike.

"Don't much matter. She was introduced ta this train as Mr. Paradise's wife. She will continue ta be treated as such and respected," Clancy declared. He turned to Lacy. "And ya, miss, will refrain from conductin' yer profession while a member o' this train."

Ben stiffened. "She has never been for sale."

Clancy's expression was stony. "See that it stays that way, Paradise."

Ben's eyes hardened. "We will be leaving this train at Fort Laramie, in any case."

Clancy nodded. "It'd be fer the best." He tucked his rifle under his arm and turned away.

"Just a minute, Clancy," Ben said. "I'd like to know what you intend to do with Thompkins."

Clancy turned back, his leathery face stern. "He's been warned off."

Paradise's voice lashed out. "It isn't enough. He attacked a member of this train."

The train master surveyed the tall man. Feller was right riled, he decided. Good reason, though. His wife was a right fetching gal. They wouldn't be the first couple to set up together without a preacher's blessing. A lot of folks couldn't wait for a man of the cloth, since there were so few ministers available on the frontier.

One side of Clancy's mouth curved in derision. "Then teach him a lesson," he suggested.

Judd laughed. "Didn't larn yer lesson the last time, did ya, Ben?" He rubbed his hands together in anticipation.

Slowly, Ben unbuckled his gun belt, and dropped it near the wagon. His eyes never left Thompkins's face.

"Be careful," Lacy warned. Her face had blanched in fear but Ben did not see it. His eyes were trained on Thompkins.

"I've got his measure," he said.

The other members of the train moved back, allowing the two men plenty of room. A confident smile played on Judd's harsh face. He dropped his gun belt and circled Ben.

Ben dropped into a wary stance, awaiting his opponent's first move. Judd's foot came up, aimed for the groin. Ben sidestepped, caught Thompkins's ankle and threw the man off his feet. Surprised, but still confident, Thompkins rolled to his feet. He got in under Ben's guard and sent him reeling with a right to the jaw. Ben's head snapped back but he stayed on his feet. A blow to Thompkins's stomach almost toppled him, but he managed to rush Ben, butting him to the ground. Before Ben could catch his wind, Judd had fallen on top of him. His hands went for Ben's throat.

Sweat broke out on Lacy's forehead. She gulped at the night air as if she was the one being strangled. Forgetful of the state of her dress, she wrung her hands. No one noticed the pale glow of her shoulders. All eyes were trained on the fight.

Ben's teeth gritted in the effort to break Thompkins's hold. His hands were locked around Judd's wrists, straining to break his enemy's grip.

"Please!" Lacy screamed at the watching men. "Do something! He's trying to kill Ben!"

"Wouldn't do that, ma'am," one of them said, but he did step forward and gave Judd a blow with the butt of his rifle.

The strangle hold released, and Ben managed to knock his opponent off. He gasped for breath, his face deathly white. The ice-blue of his eyes gleamed in the light of the fire with hate. He launched himself in a flying leap at Judd.

Both men crashed to the ground near the fire. Ben, on top, pushed the side of Judd's face into the dirt, his hand spread over the other man's ugly features. Thompkins gave a shove that nearly threw Ben off balance into the flames. He staggered and regained his balance.

"Down, Lacy," Ben yelled.

Lacy looked toward the group of men. One was sprawled on the ground. His Kentucky rifle was in Thompkins's hand, pointed straight at Ben.

She stood hypnotized as the rifle exploded. The dirt where Ben had been standing spit. Ben dived to the ground and rolled away. He was on his feet in a split second.

Thompkins threw the discharged rifle from him, and grabbed the gun from his holster on the ground. Ben was running toward Lacy, shouting. He gave her a push that sent Lacy sprawling beneath the wagon's wheels.

She heard the impact of a bullet hit the side of the wagon. Another followed it.

Ben dove to the ground again, rolled and was on his feet, his Colt revolver deadly in his hand.

Another shot rang out from Thompkins's gun. Ben's answered in the same instant. The antagonists stood as statues, staring at each other across the fire, their pistols smoking faintly. Then Judd Thompkins slumped to the ground.

The members of the train stood, stunned at the turn events had taken. A number of the smaller children cried in their wagons.

Ben's gun dropped to the ground.

The soft sound seemed to animate everyone at once. Clancy bent over Judd's fallen body. Lacy rushed to Ben's side. His arm went around her waist, holding her close.

Clancy's stern face raised, his eyes meeting Ben's steady regard. "He's dead," he announced.

Ben's arm tightened. Lacy put a hand up to his shoulder and felt something warm and sticky.

"You're hit!" Her voice broke as she looked at the blood on her fingers.

Ben was silent. He continued to stare across the clearing at Buck Clancy bent over Judd's body.

Clancy got to his feet, using his rifle as a crutch. He motioned to the watching men to remove the body, and moved toward the still couple. Funny, he mused. The gambler protected his woman with the ferocity of a wild beast. He had the impression that the lady was just as protective of her man. They'd always been a self-sufficient unit. If the old seer woman had been right, this would be his last trip to the Rockies. Those God-fearing fools would have to put their faith in Paradise to bring them through. It wouldn't do those Friday-faced women

any harm to look to Miz Paradise—or whatever
her name was—for the courage to face the hardships ahead. The young lady wasn't one to bow to
fate.

"Right through the heart," Clancy said to a
stern-faced Ben. "I'd hate ta be up agin' ya in a
showdown."

"I expect you want us to leave now," Ben said.

"'Cause ya killed a man in self-defense?" Clancy
asked. "Not likely. Glad ta have ya with us.
Comfortin' ta know there's at least one man knows
how ta handle hisself if'n we get in a tight spot."

"Thanks," Ben commented, his voice flat.

"Best see ta that arm," Clancy said, and walked
away.

CHAPTER XX

Lacy stood on the bank of the South Platte in the midst of chaos. Men swore at bellowing animals, driving them across the riverbed in a rush, trying to avoid the quicksand bottom, trying to beat the setting sun. Each wagon was harnessed with ten to fifteen yoke of oxen. In an effort to keep water out, the wagon beds had been raised by driving blocks between the bed and the bolster. Now the teams were being driven off the four-foot drop into the river.

As she watched, the lead animals sank, held under until the whole team was submerged. Bovine heads thrust from the water, eyes rolling in terror as the men herded them across.

It was a desolate area. The muddy water tasted of alkali and was full of microscopic animal life.

Even boiled, the bitter water did not improve.

Cottonwood, willow, and wild plum struggled to survive on the plain between the forked branches of the river. Buffalo grass grew in abundance, the short tufts decorating the flat land, offering grazing for gigantic buffalo herds.

Ben tread water alongside his team, urging the oxen on, soothing them with softly spoken encouragement interlaced with a generous supply of endearments.

She held her breath every time he took a team across.

He scrambled onto dry land, dragging the team and the Smithson wagon up the slope. His bare chest glistened in the sun, the dark curls matted and gleaming. His broadcloth breeches clung like a second skin. Beside Ben, Sam Smithson was a pale, dripping shadow.

"Disgusting," Mrs. Pritchard declared, staring at the men.

Lacy ignored her. Despite Buck Clancy's assurance that she would be treated as Ben's wife by members of the train, the older ladies proved to be a law unto themselves. Once more Lacy was an outcast. Amy Smithson occasionally braved disapproval. She was unhappy about the treatment Lacy received but she dared not make a show of friendship. Amy's situation reminded Lacy strongly of Sadie Delaney in Paradise. How many other friends would she lose, Lacy wondered, because she had given herself to Ben without a preacher's sanction?

The men unhitched the wagon and led the

animals back into the river. There were still a number of wagons to cross.

Lacy added a small measure of coffee to the steaming pot. She wondered if it would last. They had lost some of the precious supply in the river crossing but at least they had not lost everything. One wagon had been swept away, its traces breaking as the animals panicked.

They were still months away from California. How many other losses would be incurred along the trail? Would she ever become immune to the hardships, to the weariness?

Ben dropped down next to her. His hair was still damp and curling, his dry clothing already dusty from the plain.

"Everyone's across." He sighed.

"Safely?"

"Yes." He stared at the campfire, watching the coals. Buffalo chips had replaced wood weeks ago. Because his duties as a scout took him away from the train most days, gathering them had fallen to Lacy. His beautiful, delicate Lacy. God, what had he done to her, dragging her so far from civilization? She should be dancing, enjoying life. She should never have left Boston. He loved her but all he'd given her was a life of hardship, drawing her with him across the brutal wilderness.

He watched her as she put together the daily meal of sowbelly and biscuits, fried bacon with bread dipped in the grease. Even around an open campfire her movements were graceful, her face serene. She smiled as she passed him a plate.

God, he loved her.

"I'll be back late," he said. By rights, they should lay over a day, resting both men and animals. But Clancy had insisted they push on, that Ben scout the trail ahead.

"Be careful," she said.

He wished he could stay, wished he could take her to bed and make her love him.

He pushed to his feet. "Have you seen Amy Smithson, Lace? She didn't look well when we brought her wagon across."

Lacy agreed with him when she visited her friend a little later. Amy did look ill. Her already-thin face was gaunt and pinched. Her eyes were sunk in deep dark pools. Her youngest child clung to Amy's skirts, smiling shyly at Lacy.

"I think you should lie down, Amy," Lacy urged. She knelt down and held her arms out, grinning at the child and was rewarded with an eager hug.

"It's nothing," Amy answered, her voice little more than a whisper. "Just so thirsty. It's the heat."

Lacy made the woman sit down and took the little girl up on her own lap. "How long have you been feeling this way, Amy?"

"An hour, maybe two."

Lacy frowned. She forced Amy to lie down on the feather mattress in the back of the Smithson wagon. Then, taking a bucket and the child, she went down to the river for cold water to bathe Amy's brow.

She was trying to hold on to the child and climb

the slope with the bucket of water when Clancy arrived.

"Mrs. Smithson ill?" he asked, taking the water bucket. Lacy swung the little girl up in her arms. The child giggled delightedly and put her thin little arms around Lacy's neck.

"She says it's the heat," Lacy answered. "I thought fresh water might help."

"I'd better take a look at her." His leathery face was set in sterner lines than usual.

Amy welcomed the water when Lacy wet a piece of cloth and bathed her face. Buck Clancy asked a few pointed questions.

"Ya ferget about fixin' yer family any supper," he advised her. "Miss here can fix 'em somethin'. Ya rest."

Amy smiled weakly.

"Don't worry." Lacy smiled. "I won't poison them."

"Take care of them," Amy whispered.

Clancy climbed down from the wagon and motioned to Lacy to follow him. They walked a little away from the wagon.

"What is it, Mr. Clancy?"

He shook his head. "Cholera. Most likely be dead by mornin'."

Lacy paled. "It can't be," she insisted.

"Happens along this stretch," he said. "Seen it too much. I'm sorry, miss."

Why Amy? The gentle woman had maintained a cheerful demeanor no matter how back-breaking the trail was. Lacy had come to count on Amy's smile to lighten her day. She gripped Clancy's arm.

"If you're right, we can't let the children near her."

"Cain't let anyone near her," he said.

Lacy's chin raised defiantly. "Someone has to look after her, Mr. Clancy. People do recover from cholera."

"Very few, miss. 'Specially out here."

"Someone had better tell her husband. I'll do what I can for her." Lacy turned back to the wagon.

"Better not, miss," he warned.

A defiant look came into her eyes. "She's my friend, Mr. Clancy."

He shrugged his shoulders and walked off toward the other men. From the heads turned in the direction of the Smithson wagon, Lacy knew that word of the disease would soon be rampant in the camp.

Amy was fretful, insisting she would be fine in a few moments. Lacy rebathed her face. To keep them occupied, she sent the children to play with Mrs. Pritchard's offspring.

At last, Amy slept while Lacy kept vigil. She administered laudanum to ease Amy's discomfort, and she prayed.

It hurt to watch her friend worsen, hurt to be so helpless. When Amy began gagging with the effort to keep what food she had eaten down, Lacy's eyes filled with tears. She blinked them away. Amy would not see pity, she vowed. She would remain cheerful for Amy's sake.

The bucket was refilled with water often. Amy's skin turned a bluish tint, and her fingers appeared to shrivel before Lacy's eyes. She was beginning to believe Clancy's prophesy.

Amy woke fretting about the children.

"They are playing," Lacy soothed, placing a fresh compress on her friend's brow. "I told them it was a holiday since we aren't on the move."

But Amy would not be appeased. She gripped Lacy's hand with a strength that belied her shrunken frame. "Promise me you'll look after them, Lacy. Promise!"

"Nothing is going to happen, Amy. You're a little under the weather today. Who wouldn't be? Tomorrow you'll be wishing you had the time to relax."

Amy's pressure on Lacy's fingers increased. "Promise me."

Lacy patted the young woman's hand. "Of course, I'll look after them, Amy. Don't get yourself upset. Would you like a drink?"

Amy sank back on her pillow. "If anything should happen to me, Lacy . . . and Sam . . . promise you'll send the children back to our family."

Her eyes glistening with unshed tears, Lacy nodded. "I will, Amy. I won't fail you," she vowed.

News of the cholera spread throughout the camp. An ominous silence hung over the regrouped wagons. Men looked at each other for signs of the disease. The other families forbade their offspring from playing with the Smithson children. Sam Smithson spent his time staring into the fire. Occasionally he would mutter, "She's so young."

The children were affected by the atmosphere. They huddled together near their father. The two girls held rag dolls tightly against their chests, and Amy's son manfully tried to hold back his tears.

Lacy stayed with Amy, easing her discomfort, afraid to leave her side. Clancy had been right. Amy was dying.

Ben swung down from his horse, bone-weary. The sky was beginning to darken with storm clouds. With luck, it would storm and clear the air. Tomorrow's trail might be laborious in the mud, but he thought it preferable for once to the dusty, rut-filled trail they had been following for weeks.

He saw Lacy returning from the river with a bucket of water. Unaware of his return, she headed for the Smithson wagon.

He unsaddled his horse and turned it loose in the rope corral. Strange. The camp was usually ringing with sounds even after the most grueling days. Tonight it was like a morgue.

Sam Smithson had unearthed a whiskey bottle during her absence, Lacy noticed, and was attempting to drown his sorrows. She glared at him, disgusted with his acceptance of Amy's fate. The children were sleeping, at least. She checked on them, tucking blankets around their tiny forms, kissing them lightly for their mother. Then she returned to the wagon to care for Amy.

She dipped a cloth into the fresh bucket of water and reached to wipe the sleeping woman's face. A rough hand caught her arm and dragged her back.

"What are you doing?" Ben snarled.

Lacy looked at him in surprise. "Caring for a friend."

Ben glanced at Amy's wasting body. "Clancy

says it's cholera. He ought to know. He's seen it enough."

"Yes, I know." She turned back to her task.

"Get out of that wagon." Ben's voice was harsh.

Lacy's brow rose in reproof. "I can't leave her. There's no one else to take care of her."

"Get out of that wagon," he repeated. He was no longer merely angry, he was scared.

Amy stirred fretfully. Lacy glanced at her patient then put the cloth down and gathered her skirts to descend.

Ben's hand was like a vise on her arm. "Get back to our wagon."

She brushed back a lank curl from her forehead. "I told you. I can't leave."

"You can and will leave," he ordered.

Her jaw jutted out. Hands on hips, she stared into his frightened eyes. "No, I will not."

Sam Smithson took another pull at his bottle.

"You will," Paradise said.

"No!" she cried.

His fist caught her jaw, jerking her head back in surprise. Her vision blurred, and she crumpled. Ben caught her as she fell. He'd never struck a woman before but, by God, it was better than watching her flirt with death! Damn! He'd even asked her to check on Amy!

"You understand," he said to Sam Smithson.

The man nodded sadly and took another drink of whiskey as Ben walked off with the unconscious Lacy.

That night Amy Smithson died.

321

CHAPTER XXI

In New England they would have called it Indian summer. In California they called the temperate weather normal for November. Clouds were gathered just off the coast, but, directly above, the skys of San Francisco were as blue as the wing of a jay.

"Took yer time gettin' here," Travis welcomed, slapping Ben on the back. He swept Lacy into a bear hug.

Ben surveyed the busy square. On all sides, tents, lean-tos and wooden-frame buildings crowded, jostling for attention. The majority were gambling halls, yet none lacked for business. "Looks like a good location, Travis."

The big man swept a hand above his head in a flourish to denote the legend painted on a rough board above the open doorway of a moderate-sized tent. *The Paradise Palace* it proclaimed in bold, lopsided letters. "Figured we might as well open up soon as possible. Been doin' pretty well 'spite the tables. Been usin' barrels."

Lacy turned hungrily to the bay, lifting her face to breathe deeply as a breeze rolled in off the water. It was so good to smell the sea once again. It invigorated her, chasing away the vivid memories of hardships on the long march from Missouri.

They had made excellent time. Six long months she had dreamed of the salty taste of the sea. Now it caressed her sun-darkened face. Six months she had endured the plains, the deserts, and the mountains, had lived with alkali-tainted water, few supplies, and bone-jarring travel. Yet she had made it to California. Amy Smithson had not. She had been the first of many cholera victims. Clancy had succumbed as well, causing the immigrants to look toward Ben for leadership. They had pushed on, driving their wagons over the freshly dug graves, packing down the earth, eradicating the site to discourage animal and human scavengers alike. Ever onward they moved, slowly inching toward the promise of El Dorado.

It was behind her now. Only the ravages of the trip remained.

Untying her sun-bleached bonnet, Lacy shook her hair loose, lifting the now straw-textured strands off her neck to spill in golden glory over her shoulders.

A hush fell over the area, as if the budding town of San Francisco held its breath.

Ben and Travis were unaware, continuing their discussion of furnishings for the Paradise Palace.

Lacy moved closer to Ben, seeking security in his presence.

"Something the matter, Lace?" he inquired.

From one makeshift saloon to another, men were pouring out into the square. They were all silent, bearded, wearing rough, well-worn clothing and clutching dilapidated hats in their hands.

"Why are they staring at us?" she asked.

"Not us, Lace. You," Ben insisted.

Travis laughed. "Cause women 'er scarce out here, Lacy. Worth two, three times their weight in gold."

"And you, dearest heart, are a beauty even in your calico." Ben's arm went around her tiny waist, clearly marking his own claim for the watching men. He hoped he hadn't made a mistake in bringing her. He glanced at Travis to communicate his concern only to find his friend staring foolishly at Lacy.

"I do believe ya've took the persimmon, Lacy." Travis grinned. It amused him to see the frown on Paradise's face. Fool should have known a gal with Lacy Phalen's looks would cause a stampede in this womanless herd. She'd be safe enough with both of them watching over her. A show of gun play wouldn't hurt, of course.

Ben scowled. "I believe *that* was a compliment, Lace," he said. Damn, if it wasn't out of character for Travis to make one. What was the bastard up to now?

Lacy's eyes widened. "How very strange," she murmured.

* * *

During her first days in the boom city, Lacy found many strange yet exhilarating things in San Francisco.

It was a rather dismal-looking town by daylight. The multitude of canvas tents, shacks, and lean-tos were slapped together with little thought of longevity. Yet at night, the town the miners lovingly called Frisco was transformed. Light from the tents crisscrossed the dirt streets like beacons tempting the passerby into the interior of each of the gambling halls. The canvas Paradise Palace was no exception. The laughter and noise of young men, freed from the constricting conventions of the East, flowed from its confines. The air was smoke-filled and reeking of whiskey fumes, and the miners loved every breath they breathed.

Ben watched uneasily as Lacy blossomed under the adoration and respect the grisly young miners bestowed. She reveled in the freedom she was allowed in the male-dominated society. Evenings she danced with one bewhiskered gentleman after another.

The population consisted largely of single men in their twenties. They were a jolly group who preferred athletic gallops around the small dance floor over a sedate waltz. None overstepped the boundaries of self-imposed propriety. Miss Phalen was recognized as a lady. They told her of their sweethearts back East, even flirted lightly with her, cherishing the throaty sound of her laughter. Yet no one forgot the existence of the steel-eyed man who guarded her, or the very visible presence of the Colt strapped to his thigh.

By late December a more substantial building of

lumber replaced the tent Paradise Palace. Walls, covered in a deep red paper with scroll designs, were outlined in a dark wood trim. The bar was made of beautifully polished oak and ran the length of the two-storied main room. The wall behind it was mirrored to the ceiling to reflect the guests and brilliant light from a large, central coal-oil chandelier. A wide staircase led to the living quarters above and the rooms reserved for dealers.

While the building progressed, Lacy did not lose sight of her reason for journeying to San Francisco. Repeatedly during the long trip to California, she had declared her father would make San Francisco one of his ports of call. The more she spoke of it, the more she believed in the logic of the statement herself. When he had left Boston in '48, rumors of the strike in California were filtering into town. The captain would have heard of the soaring prices from the merchants in Canton and Hong Kong. He couldn't help but hear. Everyone from the grubstake miners to the well-to-do saloon owners sent their laundry to China. It was logical to assume the *Paramour* would follow the winds of profit into San Francisco Bay.

While she waited, Lacy was quite content to reign over the evening revels at the Paradise Palace.

The four women arrived with the new year, before the sound of workmen's hammers had stilled: two winsome Spaniards, a roguish American, and a cool-eyed Frenchwoman.

Lacy was disconcerted when the door of her

sitting room was thrown open to admit the unknown beauties and a beaming Ben. He oozed
charm as he saw that each of his finds was comfortably settled, explaining to her rather vaguely that
they were new employees at the Paradise Palace.
He was so intent on playing host that Ben failed to
notice the slight stiffening of Lacy's shoulders or
the suspicious narrowing of her eyes.

Confident that everyone was at their ease, he
moved from one woman to another, introducing
each. As a man used to intimacy with women, his
actions were too casual and familiar for Lacy's
peace of mind.

His hand rested on the shoulder of the most
aristocratic of the new arrivals. The woman's
intricately arranged dark hair gleamed with auburn highlights. Her carriage was just shy of regal
and, although she barely reached Ben's shoulder,
her bearing gave the impression that she was tall.
The severe cut of her loden green suit emphasized
her petite, boyish figure. As slim as she was, there
was no doubting she was a sensual woman. Her
movements were erotically orchestrated to draw a
man's attention. When she looked up at Ben, her
dark eyes smouldered.

Lacy took immediate exception to the woman.

Ben didn't seem to notice either Jeanne's come
hither glance or Lacy's animosity. He was boyishly
pleased with himself.

"Lace, this is Jeanne," he introduced. "She is
from Paris, France."

The Frenchwoman's gaze shifted, appraising
Lacy's quietly elegant amber day dress and the
simple arrangement of her white-gold curls. A

slow smile of contempt curved Jeanne's delicately shaped lips.

"Jeanne," Ben continued, unaware of the tension between the two women, "this is Miss Lacy Phalen. If there is anything you need, just let her know." He smiled fondly at Lacy. "We'd be lost without her around here."

Jeanne cast Ben a warm look. "I'm sure I will be *tres heureuse* here, *cheri*," she murmured, her voice with its slight-lisping accent sounding erotic.

Ben completed the introductions quickly, eager to return to the saloon proper and spread the word of his discoveries.

The Spaniards, Rita and Consuelo, were both full-breasted women with thick blue-black hair, olive complexions, and flashing dark eyes. They spoke very softly and eyed the newly furnished Paradise Palace with admiration.

Pearl, the American woman, was a fresh-faced farm girl from New York. In answer to Lacy's soft questioning, she freely told of how she and her brother had shipped around the Cape in the spring of '49 in search of their fortune. Her brother had lost his life in a fight in a mining camp, and Pearl had been making her way to San Francisco, selling herself in one camp after another. An attractive sprinkling of freckles ran across the bridge of her nose. Her hair was a pale, soft shade of brown and was arranged in braids that coiled over her ears. When she smiled, an elfish dimple appeared near her mouth. Her honey-colored eyes crinkled at the corners. Lacy was drawn to her immediately, as sure that Pearl would be a friend as she was sure Jeanne was an enemy.

Lacy settled each of the women and went in search of Ben.

She found him stretched full length on his bed, his arms behind his head, totally relaxed, a pleased expression on his face. Even the abrupt slamming of his door did not jar the serenity of his smile.

Finding four totally different yet lovely women to fill the vacant rooms had eased the tension of constantly guarding Lacy. The girls would be token dealers only, their main purpose that of catering to the miners' baser needs.

"Why didn't you tell me you were hiring women?" Lacy stormed, her emerald eyes flashing behind the dark sweep of her lashes.

Ben straightened with a grin of welcome. "I hadn't planned it myself," he drawled. "My lucky day, I guess. Found them at the docks. Think they'll be a profitable addition to the Paradise?" He cocked his head in the direction of the women's rooms.

The wind taken from her sails, Lacy quieted, perching on the edge of the bed. "They're all very beautiful women."

"And very different."

"Very," she agreed. "Do you want them at the tables tonight?"

Ben reached out to entwine one of her loose curls around his finger. "You're beginning to sound like a governess," he teased.

His breath tickled her nape. "What do you expect from a schoolteacher?"

"But such a delectable schoolteacher." His arms encircled her waist, pulling her back against his chest. "Tomorrow is early enough."

Lacy's head lolled back against his shoulder, contentment replacing her anger. "We rarely manage to spend time together," she murmured. "There's so much to do."

Ben breathed in the delicate scent of her perfume. "Building is complete. The rest of the tables and chairs have arrived, and the artist Travis found has completed some highly improper paintings."

Gilt tendrils brushed his cheek in a feathery caress as she turned, her lips near his. "I can just imagine," she said. "Shall I be put to the blush?"

His eyes danced with mischief. "Most definitely."

Blood rushed to her face. "Oh!" She pulled out of his arms. "My imagination is probably much worse than the paintings."

"I doubt it. Travis was in charge of that detail."

"I don't see why you couldn't have just let me faint dead away at the sight of them."

"Come now." He grinned. "My Lacy do something so proper? Don't tell me you're reverting to a society miss. I rather like the frontier wildcat myself."

"Oh, I hate you, Benjamin Paradise."

His arm shot out, pulling her down on the bed, his own body hovering above hers. "Show me how much you hate me, dearest heart," he whispered, his lips close to hers.

The tip of her tongue touched her lips in anticipation, and she closed her eyes.

"Oh, *pardon,*" a lilting voice said from the doorway. "I did not realize you were occupied, *m'sieur. Mademoiselle.*"

Ben rolled from the bed, coming to his feet

quickly. "Not at all, Jeanne. What did you want?" he asked politely. He took hold of the door, hoping to send the Frenchwoman on her way.

Jeanne looked at him invitingly, her dark eyes promising delights never before imagined. *La* Phalen obviously did not have a hold over the man for him to abandon her so, the Frenchwoman mused. "I wished to know at what time I should appear at the tables this evening," she purred.

The hall lights outlined her slim form. Her dark red hair fell in heavy waves about her face. The ivory silk of her loosely tied robe clung seductively to soft curves, spilling open nearly to her waist. The fabric whispered suggestively against her bare skin as she moved.

Jeanne glanced past Ben's shoulder at the young woman sprawled on the coverlet. The whiskey-colored fabric of Lacy's dress was crushed and disheveled. The Frenchwoman's lips sneered ever so slightly. *"M'sieur* Paradise has consented to a table for lasquenet," she said.

Lacy frowned at Ben. His eyes had begun to flame in a way she remembered only too well. "Isn't that rather dangerous?" she asked. Many a man had already lost his fortune and his life over the banking game.

"I'm sure Jeanne can handle things. One smile from her should have the men thinking of better things than a fight," Ben answered.

Jeanne almost lowered her eyes. The coy gesture was implied, although she continued to regard him invitingly. "You are too kind, *M'sieur* Paradise."

"The name's Ben," he insisted, and immediately

cursed himself as Lacy's eyes narrowed.

She got to her feet and smoothed her rumpled skirt, indignation clear in her every movement. "In any case, Jeanne, you are not expected in the Paradise tonight. If you wish, I can have dinner brought up to your room," she suggested briskly.

The Frenchwoman smiled, smug. "That won't be *nécessaire*. I will come down. Tonight we all become acquainted, yes?" Her dark eyes assessed the tall man patiently holding the door.

Lacy fought an uncontrollable urge to scratch Jeanne's eyes out. "I'll see you then," she said, and swept past the couple in the doorway, her head held high.

The arrival of a ship in the harbor often meant mail had arrived from the East. Lacy watched eagerly for the flags to go up announcing the arrival of the mail packet. Polly corresponded infrequently, but letters from Rose in Missouri arrived with each packet. She and Lily were doing well and had found another girl to replace the newlywed Sara. "Miss ya both, honey," Rose wrote. "Hope business is good fer ya."

The saloon was doing very well with the addition of the four women. They all headed tables for a few hours each night. Pearl had proved a master of monte, the most popular game in California. Rita and Consuelo were likewise engaged and Jeanne had her lasquenet table. She had handled all situations very well, quelling hotheaded players with a word of promised pleasures upstairs.

Other halls in San Francisco employed twenty to thirty girls. The Paradise Palace kept only the four.

Unlike other saloon owners, Ben did not depend on a percentage from the courtesans but on what he made at the tables every night. He was, as he had once pointed out, very lucky at cards. At any rate, he was a very skilled player.

Weeks of working and living in close association with Jeanne had not improved Lacy's opinion of the Frenchwoman. She could neither like nor trust Jeanne. Yet she watched as Ben appeared to grow more fascinated with the woman daily. Was Jeanne anything like the women he had loved in the past? Lacy agonized. Rose had mentioned dark eyes and French airs, hadn't she? Jeanne possessed both and an abundance of wiles.

Lacy realized she had no hold over Ben. The day was fast approaching when her father would arrive and she would return to Boston and the life she had always planned. For too long she had told herself Ben did not and could not fit into that future. She was fond of him, but she refused to give the depth of her feeling a name. Instead, she clung to the ruse she had used to follow him to California, convincing herself that it was in truth the real reason she had come—to meet her father.

From the very beginning of their relationship, Ben had known she would be leaving when the *Paramour* pulled anchor for the trip around the Horn back to Boston. If he cast his eyes in Jeanne's direction now, there was absolutely nothing she could do to stop him. She had set the rules, and, if he chose to take her at her word, she would just have to accept it.

Still Lacy could not vanquish her vehement

hatred of Jeanne. The sooner the *Puritan Paramour* made harbor the better. She was having difficulty concealing her jealousy, which did not diminish as time passed but in fact grew. The separate rooms she and Ben maintained no longer pleased her. They had shared a bed for almost a year and her large four-poster was very empty without him. He still visited, calling her special endearments, but too often his eyes followed Jeanne as she mingled with the guests.

With the arrival of the women, Lacy's duties had been reduced. Customers were far more interested in buying a female's favors for the evening. Lacy had long been on the list of untouchables. It was only the newcomers who approached her now and they were soon warned off by the others. In an effort to keep busy, she turned more to her responsibilities as housekeeper.

Ben braced a shoulder against the window molding and stared remorsefully across Portsmouth Square toward the bay. His second-story perch made it possible to see the multitude of deserted ships that nearly clogged the harbor. Fleetingly, he wished the *Puritan Paramour* was among the abandoned ships, her crew having fled to the gold fields like all the others. Perhaps then he could resolve his relationship with Lacy.

He knew he would never be able to let her walk out of his life. He'd been a fool to think a temporary arrangement would suffice. The months of shared labor, hardship, and passion only made him want her more at his side. Him! The man who had loved many women and forgotten them. The man who craved freedom to roam, to discover what lay over the next mountain.

She was just so damn busy all the time. The saloon ran smoothly, effortlessly, with little involvement on his part. Lacy handled staff, supplies, menus, balanced his books, and still looked radiant each evening. Daily he saw evidence of her organization and supervision. She kept him informed on all her activities yet rarely spent any time alone with him. How could he ask such a self-sufficient woman to give up her dreams and remain with him in San Francisco?

Outside a light rain added to his depression. It had been a very damp winter. The streets of the city were a muddy mire. In many places, signs had been posted warning that the area was unsafe for man or beast.

Shopkeepers and merchants had sunk any staple they possessed in quantity into the mud in an effort to make the path somewhat stable to walk on.

The rain only served as a reminder that Lacy planned to rectify a similar dilemma at their door. Her work party had been collecting everything they could find to fill the sea of mud.

It was ridiculous to hope that he could lure her away for an afternoon of love. Lacy would never shirk what she saw as her duty. Would things be any different if she stayed, or was she trying to avoid him, to break their relationship off before her father arrived?

The thought stirred him to action. He'd received word of the *Puritan Paramour* at the docks. It had cost a pretty penny, but he'd managed to convince the captains to withhold the information should Lacy seek them out. Captain Phalen definitely was sailing for San Francisco and would put into port late in the spring. He had to know how he stood with Lacy long before Phalen docked.

Ben shrugged into his frock coat and left the room, hoping Pearl or one of the other girls had been the recipient of Lacy's confidences.

Lacy gave her hair a last pat and smoothed the crisp apron that covered her calico gown. The stack of empty cases and bottles were sure to stabilize one's footing in the street. Perhaps even cut down on the quantities of mud tracked into the saloon twenty-four hours a day. She hadn't realized that the upkeep of the saloon would involve so much time.

It had been nearly two years since she had first met Ben, and had never expected to see him again after he left Boston, much less ever dream that she would share his bed, or travel with him on the difficult road to California. Since that first dance with him at the Forsythes' ball, her life had been as turbulent as a frigate's deck in a storm. The view from the crests of passion was blindingly beautiful, but she'd also seen and experienced the hellish depths to which men sank to gain their own ends.

What would this new decade bring? Lacy wondered. Around her every evening men were already declaring that 1850 would see statehood for California. San Francisco spread out and up the hills daily. Perched on the steep angle of Portsmouth Square, the Paradise Palace Saloon and

Gambling Hall had an excellent view of the frantic construction. The town thrived on excitement, whether it was the arrival of a new ship, a new gold find, or a lucky run of cards. She would be sad to leave it.

But leave it she must. She had aspired to be an active partner in the Puritan Shipping Line all her life. Nothing could replace that dream, not a galvanic new city, nor an intoxicating man.

The lengthening days of spring measured the short period left before the *Puritan Paramour* could be expected to drop anchor. She expected word of her father daily. His arrival would spell the end of her Iliad with Ben Paradise.

But the *Paramour* hadn't arrived yet, and at times Lacy wondered if she had misjudged the mercantile bent of her father's mind. Lacy had written to Polly before leaving Missouri, explaining that she was going to California. In the event that the captain made for the Horn and home, her days with Ben could be savored for a while longer. Lacy doubted her father would bypass San Francisco though. When he arrived, she would be ready to leave with a clear conscience. To Lacy, that meant that the staff at the Paradise ran smoothly without constant supervision. Organizing and training the housekeeping force was the least she could do to show her appreciation to Ben for his protection this past year, she decided and left her room to join the waiting work crew.

As she passed his closed door she paused, wondering if he still slept. Often he spent the night at the tables rather than in her bed. She missed the tenderness, the insistence with which he claimed her body.

Still, she had been fortunate in not becoming pregnant thus far, but she would have to be very careful not to surrender to him often. Her carefully hoarded supply of Rose's elixir to prevent conception was nearly gone.

Silently, Lacy continued on down the hall, turning into the corridor where the other women were housed.

Her step faltered, and Lacy stood frozen, mesmerized by the couple in Jeanne's open doorway.

Seemingly unaware, Jeanne and Ben were locked in a warm embrace. His back was to Lacy. Jeanne, however, saw her and pressed closer against him.

Hurt and anger flooded through Lacy. Despite her suspicions, she had not believed Ben would really turn to the Frenchwoman. Now the pain was a knife cleaving her heart. She had thought she meant something to him. More than just another conquest. How often had she evoked a special light in those blue eyes? One that burned for her alone. Had the caresses, the smiles, the endearments been a facade? He had even killed a man defending her honor. Now it seemed he had replaced her with the sultry Jeanne. Did he now call the redhead his "dearest heart"?

The embrace ended. Ben stepped back into the corridor, still unaware he was observed. Jeanne wore only an ivory robe. It hung open to the floor, boldly revealing her pale body.

Ben hesitated. Jeanne was very desirable, and

her invitation was very clear. Yet neither her sudden warm embrace nor the flagrant display of her slim form stirred him as did Lacy's smile.

A faint tick of irritation twisted Jeanne's lips as Ben refused her yet again. Still, she had succeeded in the first step on her plan to claim him for herself. With cool deliberation, she stared past his shoulder to the immobile Lacy.

Ben turned, following the direction of Jeanne's smile only to meet a furious green glare.

Lacy's face was white yet her chin was up, challenging him to explain.

Jeanne's smug expression burned behind Lacy's closed eyelids as she blinked back tears of shame. What a fool she had been to love Benjamin Paradise, to give herself up to pleasure in his arms.

Puzzled, Ben glanced from Jeanne to Lacy before it dawned on him that Lacy had witnessed Jeanne's attempt at seduction.

Lacy's shoulders squared determinedly as she attempted to pass the couple.

"Lacy." Ben grabbed her arm. "Let me explain."

She stopped and looked coldly at his hand. "If you will excuse me." Supressed rage gave her voice an arctic edge.

Slowly, his fingers released their grip. It was futile even to attempt an explanation right now, he realized.

"Thank you." Her words lashed him before she swept past and down the staircase to the group of waiting workmen.

CHAPTER XXII

An afternoon nursing her wounded feelings left Lacy determined to show Ben she was apathetic toward him. If he wanted the French bitch, he was welcome to her. If any noticed she dressed with particular care that evening, no one dared comment on her beauty. The hard gleam in her eyes warned of a short fuse and an imminent explosion.

She passed through the main room quickly, bound for a smaller side room reserved for those who preferred a quiet friendly game of cards, checkers, chess, or dominoes. Looking strangely out of place among the scruffy miners, a grand piano sat squarely in the center of the floor. Since its arrival Lacy often made it a practice to entertain the men with lighthearted songs. As soon as Lacy entered the room, she was beseeched to sing a song. Regally, she spread her rich skirts over the chair and made selections from the sheet music on the stand.

"Could you use some assistance?" a pleasing masculine voice inquired. There was a quality to his soft, clipped tenor not unlike that of New England.

Lacy glanced up to find humor dancing in a pair of wide-set, smoky gray eyes. He had a strong face. The prominent cheekbones, hawk nose, and neatly trimmed beard and mustache made an attractive arrangement. Fair hair waved back from his brow and curled faintly against the stiffness of his collar. Unlike most men of the Mother Lode, he was impeccably dressed. His dark suit was of excellent cut.

She smiled politely.

"I am much applauded for my dexterity in turning the pages of a lady's music," he persisted.

His was a pleasant smile, and she liked the way it crinkled the corners of his eyes.

The stranger admired the way her pale gold curls lay along the creamy length of her neck. They drew his gaze lower to her naked shoulders and the gentle upper curves of her breasts rising from the cool indigo silk gown.

"Your assistance would be greatly appreciated, sir," Lacy acceded, and turned back to her music.

Her husky voice seduced him. He stood near her, apparently engrossed in the music, turning the pages mechanically, his senses atuned to the woman at the piano.

After a dozen ballads, Lacy thanked the stranger and retired to a quiet corner table. Few guests intruded on her privacy, yet she was not surprised when the stranger accompanied her.

"May I compliment you on a lovely performance?" he asked, drawing out her chair.

It was amusing and, yes, easy to fall back into polite platitudes with the man. "You are too kind," she said. "I know I am a mediocre performer. There are many in San Francisco who are far more accomplished."

He signalled a waiter before leaning toward her confidingly, one hand braced on the back of her chair. "But none so beautiful, Miss Lacy."

One brow arched defensively at his use of her name. "I'm sorry that I don't know your name, sir. You seem familiar with mine."

He grinned. Lacy could barely make out the curving of his lips beneath the soft fullness of his beard.

He straightened and remained patiently awaiting an invitation to join her. Smile lines deepened at the corner of his eyes. "Ian Hawthorne," he replied, "of Somerset, England."

She put out her hand. "Lacy Phalen, Boston, Massachusetts."

Rather than shake the proffered hand, Ian Hawthorne kissed it.

Confused but pleased, Lacy blushed slightly and withdrew her hand from his bold clasp. "Won't you join me, Mr. Hawthorne?"

He pulled out a companion chair, moving it near hers. "I'd enjoy that, Miss Phalen. I hope you don't mind, but I've requested a bottle of champagne. Might I press you to join me in a glass?" As if on cue, the waiter arrived with a bottle and two delicately stemmed goblets. "I must warn you, I won't take no for an answer," he chided.

Lacy smiled, genuinely amused. "I can hardly refuse, can I, Mr. Hawthorne?"

Hawthorne chuckled. "I'm a persistent fellow, Miss Phalen. I don't rest until I have what I want."

Despite the lightheartedness of his reply, Lacy sensed he had issued a warning, one that concerned her. "Have you been in San Francisco long, Mr. Hawthorne?"

He poured the champagne and handed her a glass before answering. "San Francisco, no. I've been touring the mining camps." He made it sound like a picnic expedition. "I arrived in your fair city a few days ago and one of the first things of wonder with which I was regaled was the legendary beauty of the fair Miss Lacy of the Paradise Palace."

There had been so many compliments on her looks in the time since her arrival that she felt jaded by the repetition. "I'd hardly term myself legendary, Mr. Hawthorne. I've only been in California a few months myself."

"Please, call me Ian," he urged.

She was about to decline and take her leave when she noticed Ben standing in the archway.

Hawthorne was momentarily nonpulsed as her champagne glass halted halfway to her parted lips. He watched her eyes harden before she settled back in her chair behind the shielding shelter of a large potted palm.

Ben surveyed the room as if he were a king and it his domain, Lacy thought testily. Well, she certainly was not going to be one of his obedient subjects!

He'd learn soon enough that Lacy Phalen was not a woman with whom to trifle! Angrily, she took a healthy drink of the champagne and gave Hawthorne a provocative smile.

"Ian," she purred. "I've always liked that name."

Hawthorne approved the change in her demeanor. He had thought his informant wrong in describing Lacy Phalen as a complete lady. No lady would ever consent to live within the confines of a saloon much less appear each evening to mingle with the customers.

Yet he recognized that her manner was not assumed. She was a woman born to polite society. Her responses had not been contrived or forced but natural. Her every movement was graceful. He could easily see her seated at his mother's tea table at Hawthorne Hall.

The thought of his parent brought the unwelcome memory of her last stricture before he sailed. It was time he took a wife, she insisted. Time he followed his brother's example and began to fill the nursery with sons and daughters. Time he stopped this incessant wandering in search of adventure. Rebelliously, he had pointed to his nephews. Two sons were more than sufficient to carry on the Hawthorne traditions. As a younger son, Ian had not been burdened with the responsibilities of the estate, and he was quite comfortable with the inheritance from his godmother. It allowed him the freedom to follow his muse.

However, Lacy Phalen was just the sort of woman he would choose for a wife. Her exceptional beauty and the fact that she lived under a gambler's protection gave her an additional mystery, an allure.

If he read the invitation in her gemlike eyes correctly, she was ready for a change of protector.

Under the table, Hawthorne's hand found Lacy's knee.

The contact made her uneasy. Or was it the enormity of her behavior toward Ian that frightened her?

Lacy's hand rested on his and plucked it from her leg. "Let's not rush into things, Ian," she said.

From her secluded position, Lacy saw Ben stop George Travis in the doorway. Travis shrugged in reply to Ben's question, causing the gambler's brow to wrinkle in a frown.

"That makes my next suggestion rather premature then," Hawthorne said. He glanced toward the archway and back to Lacy who was finishing off the last of her champagne. Without asking, he refilled the glass.

"And what might that be, Ian?" The champagne helped dull the ache of betrayal, dulled her mind to thought much beyond proving to Ben that she did not care.

"Dinner," he offered. "At my hotel." Before she could refuse, he rushed on. "I'm thinking of writing a book on my travels and would be very interested in hearing of your own journey across the plains."

Her head cocked to one side, as she considered his request. He was an attractive man and obviously attracted to her. She hadn't missed the way his gaze dropped often to her breasts and paused, lingering there. She knew the tale of her own journey was merely a blind to lure her into dropping her defenses, such as they were.

Lacy sipped at the champagne, gathering courage for the path she'd already chosen. What difference did it make if she took Ian as a lover? She had been Ben's mistress for the past year. After the bruising her ego had suffered, perhaps she needed to heal the ache in someone else's arms. Someone to make her feel special, needed, desired.

She finished the second glass of champagne, not noticing Ian's had barely been touched. "I'd enjoy dinner with you, Ian," she said softly. "I'll just get my cloak."

The lines near his eyes deepened. "I'll be waiting."

She was mad. Certainly she was not responsible for her actions. It was the champagne that ruled, not reason, as Lacy hurried toward the staircase. Reason quailed before the urgency that filled her mind. Ben must be avoided. No one must distract her from her purpose, although the exact details were growing hazy.

She paused, one hand to her head as it swam, her thoughts swirling, blending with facts, clouding her perception.

Ben saw the grimace of pain on her lovely face as she faltered. Quickly, he crossed the room, taking the steps two at a time.

"Lacy, are you all right?"

His concern didn't register in her mind. The

touch of his hand on hers did, however, fueling her waning anger.

"Perfectly!" she snapped.

Her eyes were dangerously bright, her cheeks flushed unnaturally. "Listen," he coaxed, "I've been looking for you. I'd like to explain."

He stood a step or two below her, one foot a step ahead of the other. The snowy-white silk of his shirt contrasted sharply with the midnight sheen of his frock coat and trousers. One side of his coat was brushed back allowing the cool heel of his Colt to protrude from the leather holster strapped to his thigh. The lamp light picked up the twinkle of diamonds in his cravat and highlighted the deadly bit of steel at his hip.

He was no gentleman, a fact he'd often stated himself. His polish was a veneer that did little to disguise the savage beneath. How could she expect such a man to treat her any differently than he had? She'd been a toy, his plaything. Only now she saw him for what he really was.

"There's nothing to explain." She bit each word off brutally. "Neither of us is answerable for our actions."

Ben frowned at the irritation in her tone. This was going to be a hell of a lot more difficult than he'd imagined.

"Lace, you can't ignore . . ."

His determined patience and the insistent pressure of his hand sent flames of rage roaring in her ears. "I'll ignore what I wish," she growled, jerking her hand free from his grasp.

"Lacy."

The adamant set of her shoulders allowed no quarter. She sailed up the stairs, her skirts twitching provocatively with each step as she accentuated the natural sway of her hips.

Ben's knuckles whitened as he gripped the bannister. Of all the cantankerous, contrary . . . Damn it, he had to go after her, make her listen to reason.

A soft hand stole over his, caressing it lightly. *"Cheri,"* Jeanne's lisping voice said, "come and the ruling make at my table. The gentlemen threaten the fisticuffs, no?"

His jaw tightened. "No, is right. I'll take care of it, Jeanne." Absentmindedly, he patted her hand, his thoughts on Lacy, then turned back to the casino.

Ian Hawthorne was relieved when Lacy appeared in the saloon doorway. She was so fragile, huddled in the heavy folds of her cloak. His arm gathered her close, urging her toward the warmth of his coach.

The sharp slap of damp night air cleared the numbing alcoholic haze from Lacy's mind. Her step faltered but Ian, misreading her hesitation, swept her up in his arms and carried her over the mud.

Inside the coach, she huddled in a far corner as he joined her, dropping the oiled cloth curtains in place over the windows. The enveloping darkness made it easier to carry out her plan. He was just an indistinguishable shadow on the seat next to her. Her heightened senses picked up the manly smell of his soap as the jostling of the carriage threw her toward him.

"Is your hotel very far?" she asked.

"Not very. Are you cold?"

"No."

Silence fell. Lacy closed her eyes, her hands gripped tightly in her lap. She could feel his eyes on her even in the dark.

"Ian," she whispered, "kiss me. Please."

"Of course, my dear." There was a smile in his voice. "My pleasure." What a delightfully forward woman this Lacy Phalen was.

Her lips were soft and pliant beneath his, and he savored the taste of them with growing fervor.

"Hold me," she pleaded, returning his kiss timidly, almost tentatively, as if she were still considering her actions.

He crushed her to him, breathing her name over and over again as his lips lingered over each of her exquisite features before returning to her waiting mouth.

Determined to vanquish the ghost that haunted her, Lacy's lips parted. His tongue skimmed her teeth before plundering the sweet recess of her mouth. His hand found the gentle curve of her waist beneath the cloak and moved upward to cup her breast.

His touch did not excite her as Ben's had. Neither did it repulse her. Perhaps in time she would grow used to another man's touch and forget the charming gambler from Missouri.

Her cloak fell open, allowing Hawthorne a glimpse of pale satin skin. His mouth moved downward, sampling the tender hollow of her throat, moving on to caress her shoulder, her breast.

Lacy's hands found their way into his fair hair. It was so unlike Ben's in color and texture, and a bittersweet pain burned in her stomach. She recalled a dozen nights of shared wonder and mystery at Ben's hands. The glorious adventure of learning to make love had begun in his arms. For that alone, no other man could ever displace his memory. Yet, other men there must be, perhaps many men, to dispel the enchantment Ben had cast on her heart.

She pressed closer to Ian, arching against him, hoping to lose herself in him.

The sound of drumming hooves registered slowly on Ian's consciousness. He was unprepared as a harsh-voiced order slashed the night. The carriage skidded to a halt in the mud, accompanied by the coachman's curses and the nervous whinnies of his team. Cold fingers of evening gripped the entwined couple as the carriage door was wrenched open. It slammed back against the outer wall and rebounded, half-shutting before the man on horseback caught it. He took in the disarray of clothing and the couple's intimate frozen pose.

Danger emanated from his immovable form. His lips were white with fury. Blue fires of hell burned from the dark recesses of his eyes.

Despite herself, Lacy's heart turned over at the sight of him.

"Take your filthy hands off her," Ben growled in the doorway.

351

Ian drew her cloak together and pushed Lacy behind his back, protecting her. "You have no claim on this lady."

"Haven't I, though." The statement was flat, devoid of emotion.

"She stays with me," Ian said.

Lacy glanced from one man to the other. They were two dogs snapping over a bone. Was she nothing more than a piece of pretty property both coveted?

Ben's teeth were bared. "Name your seconds, Hawthorne," he snarled.

"Gladly," the other agreed, his eyes never leaving those of the man whose very presence crushed his own hopes concerning Lacy Phalen. He mentioned two names.

Paradise nodded curtly. "My friends will call upon them tomorrow afternoon."

Fear drove Lacy to grasp Ian's arm. "You can't fight," she shouted. "I won't let you!"

Ben misread her action as concern for the Englishman. The deadly gleam in his eyes hardened. No one would ever take her from him. The idea of her quivering naked in another man's arms produced a red haze which blinded him.

Ian did not miss the raw terror in Lacy's eyes as she stared at Paradise. If the man held her in thrall with cruelty, it was imperative that he free her. "I believe I have the choice of weapons," he said.

Lacy's fingers were like claws digging into Ian's arm. Blood drained from her face, leaving it chalk-white. "Please, Ian, don't meet him," she pleaded.

Slowly, it registered on Ian that she did not fear

the gambler. She feared *for* him. Still, the die was cast. He had accepted the gauntlet and honor bade him to see the duel to its conclusion.

"Let me warn you that I'm very handy with a gun," Ben said flatly.

Hawthorne met the other man's gaze squarely. "And I," he retorted.

A silent message passed between the antagonists.

Ben nodded shortly. "No harm will befall her. You have my word on it."

Assured more by the expression in Paradise's eyes than in his harsh tone, Ian turned away, lifting Lacy's hand to press a fervent kiss in her palm. For a few moments he had entertained dreams of a lifetime spent with this woman. Foolish dreams that left him feeling robbed. She had always belonged to the gambler. Fear for him was stark in her eyes, betraying an unquestionable depth of emotion.

If only she could have cared for him as deeply.

"You had better return with him, my dear. I will see you tomorrow," Hawthorne said.

"Ian, promise me you won't fight him," Lacy pleaded.

He refastened the cloak around her shoulders and moved aside. "I can make no such promise."

"Lacy." Ben sat solidly on his horse, blocking the doorway, his hand outstretched to assist her from the carriage.

Fire spit at him from her eyes, yet she accepted his arm as he deftly swung her before him into the saddle.

Ben gathered the reins, turning his mount away.

"Hawthorne," he said in dismissal.

She was rigid, trying unsuccessfully to balance on the saddle without touching him. The easy rolling gait of the bay made contact with the broad chest at her back inevitable.

Ben refrained from slipping a steadying arm about her waist, her closeness and the scent of roses tempting him to cool his anger.

"How dare you!" she demanded.

"You're mine." His tone was final, unflinching, branding her.

"I belong to no one."

"Don't you?"

"I see," she said, her voice thick with sarcasm. "You can leap into as many beds as you please, but I must deport myself like . . . like a *lady*." She spat the word. "Or ease only your desires."

"That's right."

"I hate you."

"You have informed me of that before."

"This time I mean it."

"I doubt it."

Silence fell broken only by the sucking sound of the bay's hooves in the mud. They traveled the dark back streets, passing cribs where painted women of a dozen nations comforted miners for a price.

"You have quite an opinion of your own worth, don't you, Ben?"

"And you, Lacy, have underestimated yours."

"Ah, I see. I'm a business acquisition."

"If you like."

"May I ask how you found me?" she demanded. "And so quickly?" She would never admit that she had welcomed his sudden appearance.

His breath came in visible puffs of vapor. "Travis and some information from some of your admirers. Your friend was not unknown."

"I see."

Ben guided his horse behind the saloon and dismounted. His hands reached up, grasping her waist. Slowly, he lowered her to the ground. The iron clasp of his hands held her a prisoner against him.

"Hear me, Lacy," he said. "You belong to me and me alone, until the time your father comes to claim you. I've killed one man over you already and I'll kill others if need be."

She struggled. "No! No man is master of me. I will choose my own friends. Male friends. And if I choose to be intimate with them, I will do so. You can go back to your French whore."

"I may." His voice was grim. "But I will not share my New England sea witch."

His arms tightened and he kissed her savagely.

He was a complete stranger, one who frightened her. Lacy pulled away from his touch and ran into the rear kitchen. Edith, the young maid, looked up from the mending in her lap, disconcerted to see her mistress arrive through the Paradise Palace's back door. She'd never seen Miss Lacy looking other than neat as a pin. Never a harsh word and always a sweet smile, that was Miss Lacy. This harridan with tangled golden hair and mud-splattered cloak and gown couldn't be the same woman. Why, her lovely evening slippers were quite ruined!

Edith jumped to her feet. "Miss Lacy! Here, let me take your cloak."

Lacy looked at her wild-eyed. "No!" she cried, hysterical.

Edith stepped back, startled. She had no way of knowing Lacy saw only Ben.

He entered the kitchen, tramping more mud across the once spotless floor boards.

"Give your cloak to Edith," he instructed harshly.

Edith looked at him in surprise.

Lacy turned to flee but Ben caught her arm. He ripped the cloak from her shoulders and flung it at Edith. The maid seemed paralyzed as the cloak fell at her feet unheeded.

"Don't touch me," Lacy said, her voice as hard as his. "I'm not staying here another minute."

"Aren't you?" His grip on her wrist was painful.

Lacy laughed shrilly. "Am I a prisoner now? I can just hear what San Francisco will have to say about that. Benjamin Paradise can't even keep his mistress without resorting to violence."

"Apparently you want violence, Miss Phalen," he said, his voice cold.

"Leave me alone." She managed to pull free of his restraining hand. She turned away, running toward the back stairs and the sanctuary of her room.

He was right behind her, and his shoulder caught the door as she slammed it. The force of his thrust threw her back against the bedpost. She slumped partially dazed to the floor. Ben entered, closing the door and locking it behind him.

"I believe we have something to discuss, Miss Phalen."

"Do we?"

He pulled her to her feet. "Perhaps discuss is the wrong term. Don't you think you have some explaining to do?"

"Me explain!"

"What were you doing with Hawthorne?"

Lacy laughed mirthlessly. "I thought that was obvious."

Ben released her and leaned back against the door. "So you admit it. You were selling your favors. A new profession for the hauty Miss Phalen."

Lacy turned away from him and sat down at her dressing table. She began taking the pins from her tumbling hair. "I admit nothing. I don't belong to you, Ben Paradise. You aren't my keeper, despite what you say. I am my own woman."

One dark brow flew upward evilly. "And apparently the price was right. Why else have you kept aloof from your other admirers?"

Lacy shook her hair free and reached for the brush. The candlelight made her hair a deeper, lusher gold.

She stared at his tall shadow in the mirror. "You have shown you have no use for me any longer. When I saw a man who interested me, I had no qualms about returning his affection."

"Lust, don't you mean, Lacy?"

"If you wish," she conceded.

"And your fee?"

"I hardly think that concerns you, Mr. Paradise."

"Perhaps it does. I have been offered quite a tidy sum for you, Lacy. If I had know you were so anxious to entertain, I might have considered it."

She put her brush down and moved to the wardrobe. "Really? That is very interesting. But I believe I prefer to choose my own customers."

"How much?" he reiterated.

One gown after another was pushed aside unseen. "What did you have to pay Jeanne?" she asked casually. "I would think I could command as much or possibly more."

She hadn't heard him cross the room. His breath on her shoulder was warm, reminding her of other times, happier times.

He spun her around to face him and dropped a heavy pouch of gold dust into the bodice of her gown. "Five hundred ought to buy me a night worth bragging about then," he said. "You're going to need references from satisfied customers to—"

Lacy slapped his lean cheek. "How dare you!"

His face was a mask. "Temper tantrums are not what I paid for."

"If you think—"

He smirked. "Refusing your first customer? I notice you aren't returning my money."

In blind fury, she reached for the pouch as it nestled between her breasts. Ben's hands stopped her, holding her prisoner against his body. "Keep it, sweetheart," he growled. "I'm not leaving without having what I paid for."

"Bastard!" she spat.

"Undoubtedly." His fingers found their way into the neckline of her gown and tore it. The pouch hit the floor and broke open, scattering minute particles of gold at their feet.

If he had said one kind word, had apologized for

his infidelity with Jeanne, she knew she would have yielded to his touch. She would have forgiven him and apologized for going off with Ian Hawthorne.

"Are you going to get out of those clothes or do I have to tear them off you?" he asked.

CHAPTER XXIII

Ben sat slumped in his chair, staring unseeing into the dying flames of the fire. The empty whiskey bottle at his side had failed to dull the memory of what he had done.

Irritated, he tossed the empty tumbler into the grate, gaining little pleasure from the sound of shattered glass.

He had been an animal, a savage beast, mindlessly taking the woman he loved. Damn, he did love her. Yet he had taken her brutally, expecting to meet resistance. Instead, she had opened to him like a parched flower in a spring rain, clinging to him as her need grew. Inhibitions stripped away as passion clouded the issues. And, still, he had ridden her angrily, the hate in her eyes goading him.

He recalled how the firelight enhanced the glory of her hair and lent a warm glow to her pale, soft skin. She had responded strangely to his lovemaking, driving herself until he thought them both exhausted. But Lacy had renewed her attack with subtle caresses, had brought him alive and ready to fill her once more with feather-light kisses.

Tiny flecks of gold dust had clung to her body as they lay entwined once more on the rug. Gilt sparks drew his gaze to her breasts, her flat stomach, the curve of her thigh. Her long white-gold hair had hidden, then swirled aside to display the glory of her body, driving him mad with desire for her.

The woman was a witch and had bewitched him anew, showing him that he could spend a lifetime with her and never be bored.

He wanted her again. Wanted her long, slender, silken legs to wrap around him once more.

After tonight, she would hate him in truth.

Good God! If it took a lifetime, he'd make it up to her. If she could forgive him. If he could forgive himself.

The sound of timid knocking woke Lacy. Her limbs were cramped from sleeping on the cold floor, her face ravaged by tears.

"Miss Lacy? Mr. Paradise said he thought you'd want a nice hot bath early this morning." It was Edith.

Ben. Ian. The argument. Memory flooded back with painful accuracy.

Lacy reached for her robe. Her body ached. The thought of a leisurely bath was ecstasy.

"Yes, Edith, I would enjoy that very much." Robe tied, Lacy bundled the tattered remnants of her gown and stuffed them into the wardrobe. Gold dust spilled from the cloth in a glittering waterfall. She brushed at it, clearing it from view.

A key turned in the lock and Edith came in followed by two workmen carrying the large bathing tub.

Edith busied herself, straightening the barely rumpled bed. She didn't notice the deepening frown on Lacy's face.

"Why was I locked in my room?"

The maid continued fretting with the bed. "Goodness, I don't know, Miss Lacy. Mr. Paradise gave me this key and said I was to see that you got this here bath and lock you in again. I think he's awful mad at you about somethin', miss."

Lacy walked to the window on bare feet and looked out across the village of canvas and wood that comprised the city of San Francisco. "Did he say anything else, Edith?"

"No, ma'am. He just called Miss Jeanne into his office and shut the door."

Lacy ground her teeth.

Another knock heralded the men with buckets of still-steaming water. They filled the tub in three trips. Edith brought bath oils from the bathing closet and added them to the water with a generous touch. Lacy watched the girl stick her fingers in the water cautiously.

"It's just the way you like it, Miss Lacy. There's plenty of fresh towels here on the bed. You just enjoy yerself. Would you like anything special for breakfast? I could bring it up to you. You look a bit peaked, if you don't mind my sayin' so, miss."

When she left, Lacy heard the small click of the lock turning over. She ran over to check the door. It would not budge.

She really was a captive. Ben would never allow her the chance to see Ian Hawthorne again.

Lacy retraced her steps to the bath and let the hot water envelop her.

She thought of Ian and the pleasure she had experienced in his arms. Perhaps she was not any different than Ben. She knew she had not loved Ian. She had not had time to discover if she even liked him. In his arms it had been so easy to soothe her injured ego, to abandon herself to his wishes.

Behind her, Lacy heard the catch of the lock in the door. Ben walked into the room, key in hand.

"Come to gloat over your victory?" she asked archly.

He stared down at the way the water lapped on the mounds of her naked breasts.

"No. I came to apologize."

"I don't believe it." Wantonly, Lacy stood and stepped from the tub. Her body glowed pink from the bath. He noticed she had bruises, tokens of their brutal joining the night before.

Ben's eyes smouldered. She had been incredible, insatiable. The battle begun in hate had ended in love. He doubted Lacy recognized that fact though. Her attitude was as inflexible now as it had been the night before. Why couldn't she admit that last night made it impossible for him to relinquish her? Even to her father.

He picked up a towel and threw it at her.

Lacy shook it out and let its folds caress her

glistening body in a slow sensuous display. Her eyes never left his face.

With effort, he tore his gaze away and turned to stare out the window.

"You'll catch cold," he said.

With his back to her, Lacy quickly finished drying and slipped into her robe.

"I want your promise that you won't try to see Hawthorne."

"I can't do that," she replied. "Will you try to kill him?"

"It's possible."

He turned as if watching events in the street below, his profile outlined against the gray winter sky. She had seen his face against a backdrop of wilderness forest, desert sand, by the light of a campfire, by candlelight. She had watched the ever-changing emotions in those blue eyes. Laughter, desire, fear. They had experienced all three together.

"Ben." Her voice was barely a whisper she was not even sure he had heard. He stood like a statue, framed by lace curtains and streaked windowpanes. "Ben, don't do it."

"You care about him so much, Lacy?"

"I care about you!" she wanted to say. Instead, she sat down heavily on the edge of the bed.

Silence filled the room. Lacy shivered in her light robe. Ben continued to gaze out the window. When at last he spoke, his voice was filled with pain. "Why, Lace? Why?"

Tears ran down her face and dropped unheeded on the folds of her robe. "I could ask the same question, Ben."

He half-turned to look at her. "Jeanne?" The time was past for explanations. Last night had made even the attempt ludicrous.

"I was so angry," she sniffed, and wiped at the tears with her fingers. "So hurt."

"Does it do any good to say I'm sorry?"

Lacy shook her head. It was too late now.

Edith pushed the door open cautiously. She carried a tray upon which breakfast items were neatly arranged. Ben motioned her to put it down on a small table near the bed. She did so and left the room quickly.

"You'd better eat your breakfast while it's hot," he recommended.

Lacy stared bleakly across the room at him, her heart in her eyes. But Ben didn't notice. He had turned away.

"Good-bye, dearest heart," he said softly, and locked the door behind him.

Lacy fell onto the pillows and cried.

Nothing eased the pain in her heart. Edith stole up often during the day to see if Lacy needed anything and to take the untouched trays away. Lacy sat and stared at the gray clouds, trying not to think.

By evening her throat was raw, and her head was pounding. Edith bundled her beneath a multitude of quilts and forced Lacy to drink broth. Doctor Nichols was sent for and, after a cursory examination, ordered bed rest for the next few days. Before seeing the doctor out, George Travis strode uneasily to Lacy's bedside and took one small hand in his large one. "This should make you feel better, little lady," he said kindly.

When he and the doctor left, Lacy found she was clutching the key to her room.

She was no longer a prisoner, yet she no longer had any desire to escape. She had finally forced a showdown of her own, facing her emotions and admitting to herself how she felt about Benjamin Paradise.

She was feverish throughout the night. In the morning she felt little rested. When Travis and Pearl arrived to inquire after her health, Lacy had but one thought. "Ben?"

Pearl exchanged a frightened look with Travis.

"He ain't here, Lacy," the giant said uneasily.

"Where?" Her voice was a barely audible croak.

Pearl gathered the untouched tray and left the room in a hurry. Travis waited until the door closed behind her. "Don't know. Ain't seen him since yesterday mornin'," he admitted.

Lacy struggled to sit up in bed. "The duel."

"It ain't taken place yet. Don't worry. He's probably coolin' his heels at one of the hotels."

"Yes," she said, grasping at straws. She would not think any further. She would not picture his beloved face staring blankly at the heavens as so many she had seen enroute to California.

"Travis. When is the duel?"

He hesitated only a moment. "In an hour. He ran an advertisement in the newspaper and sent out invitations ta the other saloon owners."

Lacy knew it was a common practice to invite friends to the duels that were such a frequent occurrence in San Francisco. But it seemed so callous. Ben and Ian Hawthorne would be facing each other with loaded pistols. It was not a turkey shoot. A man could lay dead within minutes.

She threw aside the heavy quilts and struggled out of bed.

Travis caught her by the shoulders.

She struggled weakly. "I have to be there. They're fighting over me!"

"Ya ain't goin' nowhere," the big man insisted.

"But he doesn't know!"

"Ya can tell him when he gets back," he soothed.

She looked up wildly. "Suppose he doesn't come back."

"He'll come back."

"Travis." Lacy clutched the trapper urgently. "He has to know before the duel. Tell him."

The big man lifted her and gently tucked her back in bed.

"Promise you'll tell him," she pleaded. "Leave now."

He patted her hand, and her fingers closed over his in a desperate attempt to make him understand.

"Promise!"

Her hands were like claws. He pried her loose gently. "All right, Lacy. I promise. I'll leave this minute. What is it ya want him ta know so bad?"

Her strength exhausted, Lacy lay back on the pillows. "Tell him . . . tell Ben I love him, not Ian Hawthorne," she said, her voice soft. "I love him," she repeated wonderously.

When she awoke late that afternoon, Lacy felt much better. The fever had broken and she had to contend with a sore throat. Pearl had spent the morning concocting home remedies which she forced down Lacy's throat.

But the only thought on the young woman's mind was the outcome of the duel.

"Any word?"

Pearl shook her head, straightened the quilts, and fluffed the pillows. "Not yet. Mr. Travis ain't returned yet."

Lacy gently touched the pillow that had held Ben's head so many times over the past months. If only he was safe and able to share the four-poster with her again.

Pearl went to the door. "I thought I heard somethin'. Ya stay put and I'll go see."

Lacy looked at the pillow. "Oh, Ben," she prayed, "please come back to me."

Pearl ran back into the room out of breath. "He's back! I think he's hurt!"

Lacy struggled out of the confining quilts. Pearl had her robe at hand. She kept a tight arm about Lacy's waist as if to support the young woman down the endless corridor.

They reached the head of the staircase and looked down into the main room. Ben was stretched out on an old, weathered door. There was a rough bandage tied around his right thigh, caked with dried blood.

With a cry, Lacy shook Pearl off and flew down the steps, unmindful of her nightgown and robe.

Men fell back before her. Travis was supervising the placing of the makeshift stretcher on the top of one of the tables.

"Ben!" She grabbed one of his hands. His head

rolled slightly as the door was tipped.

"Take it easy, Lacy. He's all right. It's just a little cut," Travis said.

"But all the blood." She looked at the darkly soaked bandage.

"Mostly mud."

Lacy did not really hear him. "What happened? Did you get there in time?" Her voice was still a hoarse rasp.

He met her worried eyes. "Yes, I got there in time. They both devolved."

She tore her eyes away from Ben's faintly flushed face. "Devolved?"

"Fired in the air."

"I don't understand. I thought they were going to kill each other."

Travis laughed and called for a round of drinks. "Damn near did, too, the young hotheads. This here's gotta be the only duel of its kind in Frisco. Usually end up carryin' both opponents ta the undertaker."

Lacy did not care to be reminded of the usual results of gun fights in the city. "What happened, Travis? Why did they fire in the air?"

"Search me, little lady. Among gents I hear it means each thought he had been in the wrong. 'Tween those two? Who knows? If this were England or even Virginny, where Ben's family hails from, I could understand either of 'em actin' the gent. But this here's Frisco. Thought they was out fer blood the way they both been carryin' on the last few days.

"Ben woulda had Hawthorne though. The boy's got a real quick draw. But he fired in the air 'fore

Hawthorne even cleared leather. When Hawthorne did the same, Ben got mad."

She could picture it in her mind's eye. The two men facing each other across the field, their guns in holsters at their side, their hands dangling, awaiting word to draw.

"They jest threw down their guns," Travis said, "and started swingin' at each other."

"Then how . . ." Lacy looked back at Ben's bandaged leg.

"Cut it on a rock. That Hawthorne has got a murderous right."

The men standing around the table laughed.

Lacy's concern was quickly being replaced by resentment. After all her apprehension, nothing had happened. She looked down at Ben sleeping soundly on the door. "What else happened?"

Travis grinned boyishly. "Nothin' much. He jest got dead drunk on the way back."

"I have seen Benjamin Paradise drink everyone else under the table," Lacy said. "So how did he reach this unconscious state?"

Travis smile broadened. "He put his mind ta it, Lacy. Jest put his mind ta it."

"And Ian Hawthorne?" she rasped.

"Heard he was leavin' fer Sacramento," Travis said. "Other than a black eye, he's fine."

Lacy looked disgustedly at the face of the man she loved. She had been worried sick while he had been getting drunk.

"I suggest you dump him in a horse trough, Travis. I am going back to bed," she said, and, taking Edith's handkerchief, blew her nose.

CHAPTER XXIV

Around San Francisco's perimeter, the glories of spring moved from bud to bloom as the days lengthened toward summer. But in the city itself the dismal prospect of mud and shacks remained. The glitter of the opulent saloons couldn't disguise the fact that San Francisco was built on dreams. Fires raged through the flimsy structures often, but, like the mythical phoenix, a new and more permanent town rose from the ashes each time.

There was no rebirth in Lacy's relationship with Ben. Although she had confessed her love to him, Lacy did not find that Ben's deliverance from harm in his duel with Ian Hawthorne had brought them any closer. Love him she might, but Lacy was still distrustful of Ben's relations with Jeanne.

He had never told Lacy that he loved her. Did he see her only as a pretty bauble that other men desired? Since she was one of the few American women in California, having Lacy on his arm, in his bed, lent Ben Paradise status in San Francisco. But was it love he felt for her or merely pride in possession? Lacy doubted that Ben was capable of loving anyone. If he did, wouldn't he have shown that he was willing to change his life so that it included her? All it would take would be a declaration of affection from him for her to stay.

Or would it? How long had she insisted to Ben and to herself as well, that her destiny was with the Puritan Line? Was she willing to forsake her dream in favor of love?

Did it matter now? Words had been hurled with vicious intent the evening she had gone off with Ian Hawthorne, which Lacy feared had rung with truth. "You belong to me," Ben had declared. Yet being a man's possession meant relinquishing her will, and Lacy had already run from the Quires in Boston to ensure that she remained her own person, in control of her own life.

It didn't matter that the situations were far from similar. Lacy knew she had made a mistake. She had admitted to a weakness where Ben was concerned. To love.

Love. Poets hailed it as the most glorious sensation of heart and soul. They were dreamers, Lacy thought in derision. Love was a cage. It was a set of shackles that bound her. Or it would if she weakened.

Most women were prisoners of their emotions, unable to escape because they believed there was no future for a woman without a man. The cult of true womanhood was a religion of men. They placed their wives, sisters, daughters in a neat niche as if they were rare art objects to be admired but never utilized. As gentle as she had been, Amelia Wainwright Phalen had not liked being classified. She had passed on her individuality to her daughter, adjuring Lacy to fight for whatever she wanted. That spark smouldered, waiting for the clouds that shrouded the course of Lacy's future to lift.

In the meantime, Lacy was comforted by the fact that, unlike other women, she had the means of deliverance.

Ben understood that. Lacy read the knowledge in his somber eyes. Had heard him admit it, inadvertently placing a time limit on their relationship. She was his, he'd informed her grimly, *until the time her father came to claim her.*

Exactly how much time remained to them? Lacy wondered. Although the easy camaraderie she and Ben had enjoyed was now submerged in hurt, there was a desperation in their exchanges when they did meet.

Was it her imagination, or were his caresses more often distracted than amorous? He had returned to her bed, sleeping with her nearly every night. Lacy savored the feel of his lean, muscled body next to her but she mistrusted his intentions. Her body welcomed him and, at the crest of passion, so did her heart. It was her mind, tormented by suspicion, that saw danger in his actions.

He had always been considerate, charming, sensual. He knew her so well, her likes, her dislikes, her moods. To combat her new reserve, he used tenderness as a weapon. It set his seal on her, branding her as his property.

He had been inordinately successful in doing so.

She watched the harbor daily, at times nearly frantic for a sight of the familiar tall masts of the *Paramour*. The captain's voyage to China should be almost at an end and Lacy's time was running out. As weeks turned to months, she knew that the queazy sensation she had experienced nearly every morning made her departure critical. In a very short time, she would no longer be able to hide the fact that she was going to have Ben's child.

In the event that the *Paramour* did not reach San Francisco soon, Lacy had considered her options. She could forsake her dreams, both of the Puritan Line and of love, and stay in California. Or she could weave a fiction to cover the last two years and return to Boston as a widow, protected by the name of an imaginary man.

She was no longer dependent on the charity of Polly MacGuire or the fortuitous Martha Haskell's schoolmarm positions to survive. Her salary as housekeeper at the Paradise Palace was as exorbitant as the sums the visiting miners lost at the tables nightly. It would see her safely back to Boston and keep her comfortably until her father returned. It would also allow her the protection of legal counsel if necessary. When she had run from the Quires, she had been a girl, unfamiliar with the world outside her narrow social circle. Now she was a woman. Her majority had been reached on her last birthday. No one would ever force her to do anything against her will again, Lacy vowed.

As much as she cared for Ben, she could not

remain near him without having him return her love. If her father's ship did not drop anchor soon, she would have to book passage on a ship bound for the East coast. Leaving San Francisco was imperative. Despite the lies she would protect herself with, Boston was preferable to Ben's learning of their child.

The apple tree in the rear garden at the narrow red brick house in Boston would be heavy with fruit when she arrived home. Home. The word had a nice sound, but she had been away so long that Lacy wondered what the word meant. Was it the chatter of friends like Celia Clary? Was it a round of evenings at balls, musicals, card parties, smiling at people she barely knew and rarely liked? Or was it the burning glow in a pair of blue eyes? Of a man who made her shiver with the softest touch of his hand?

Lacy shook herself mentally. Home would be what she made it. Home would be where her child was. As long as she left by mid-June, she would reach Boston in the fall, a little more than two months before her baby was born. As for love . . . she would have her memories, and they would have to suffice.

All the same, Lacy felt a pang of regret.

Unaware of Lacy's secret plans, Ben whistled cheerfully as he entered her room that evening. A glow of desire deepened the cool color of his eyes when he looked at her. She was lovelier every day, he thought, and every day he grew closer to losing her.

There were times when Ben cursed the existence of the Puritan Line. But for it, he could tell Lacy of his love, ask her not only to stay in San Francisco, but to become his wife. But the specter of her ambitions hung between them.

He hoped that his news would relieve some of the sadness that haunted her eyes. Her welcome was tempered by a reserve he hated. It reminded him only too well that their relationship was deteriorating. He wanted to turn back the clock, to live once again the joy-filled spring a year ago in Missouri, before George Travis had come with his tales of California.

But the bond had been broken. Perhaps time would heal it, but time was not something of which he had a sufficient supply. When Captain Phalen arrived, Ben was afraid he would lose Lacy forever.

She was seated before her dressing table, putting the finishing touches to her hair. Was her dress new? He couldn't remember. It had never been her gowns that attracted him. It had been the scent of her skin, the nectar of her lips. The straightforward way she looked at him.

"Didn't you tell me once that your father's ships were all named *Puritans?*" he asked, resting his hands lightly on her bare shoulders.

Lacy surveyed his tall form in her mirror. Even in the conservative clothing he chose, no one would ever take Ben Paradise for anything other than the gambler he was. There was something in the way he held himself that proclaimed him a man who lived by his wits.

Her own dress was a rich burgundy silk, off the

shoulders and daringly low-cut. The style was not the fashion but it suited her life as hostess of the Paradise Palace.

Lacy nodded. "The captain has a strange sense of humor. All our ships are *Puritans* but with unlikely second names. Like the *Puritan Paramour* in which he sailed." She watched his fingers in the mirror. They caressed her neck and slid further down to the rising mounds of her breasts. Lacy stored the memory of his touch to take back to Boston with her.

"Why?"

"Oh, no particular reason," he said, bending to kiss her naked shoulder, "except there's a *Puritan* ship in the harbor."

Lacy turned in her seat. "A *Puritan!* Is it the *Paramour?*"

"The *Puritan Belle.*"

"The *Belle!*" She jumped to her feet excitedly.

Ben put his arms around her. "Where do you think you are going? Not to the wharves at this time of night."

"But when did she come in?" Lacy demanded.

"She? Oh, the ship. This afternoon. Travis just got back with the news."

Lacy frowned. The *Belle* was part of the English packet line. "I wonder what the *Belle* is doing here?"

Ben's finger under her chin tilted her face up. "Your cousin Harry's trying to make some money. It came loaded with passengers and goods. I'm surprised we haven't seen one of your line in the bay before this."

Elizabeth Daniels

"Harry's very cautious," Lacy said. "Or rather timid. He wouldn't want to instigate a venture of his own."

"How unlike myself," he said. "I was thinking of instigating something this very moment."

Lacy looked at the teasing smile curving the corners of his mouth. "We really haven't the time, Ben."

"I'll make time," he declared, and stopped any further argument with his lips.

As she kissed him, she thought about the changes that had occurred between them. The evenings he did not share her bed had become very rare, and she knew he no longer visited Jeanne from the looks the Frenchwoman threw her way. She ignored the fact that Jeanne was a dangerous adversary. Lacy was so pleased she had won the battle, she turned a cold shoulder to reason.

An hour later when she and Ben descended the staircase, Lacy had almost forgotten the arrival of the *Puritan Belle.* Ben moved off to join a poker game in the corner, and Lacy circulated, greeting regular customers and seeing to the needs of newcomers.

She had just come out of the music room when a man in an ill-fitting suit and soiled shirt stopped in front of her. From habit, Lacy moved to one side without looking at him. He moved with her.

"If you will excuse me," she began, glancing up at the stranger's face. Recognition caused a pulse to beat in the hollow of her throat and she felt as if she was choking.

"Hello, Lacy," said William Quire.

Her mind raced. How had William found her? How had he gotten to San Francisco? Had she somehow left a trail that he had been able to follow? He could not have come straight across the country. It was the wrong time of year. No one could get over the mountains in the dead of winter. Although it was now nearing the middle of May, the snows would not have melted enough to allow travel through the passes. Therefore, he had come by sea. Had he followed her to Paradise and then taken a ship from New Orleans?

"You seem surprised to see me, Lacy. Not nearly as surprised as I was when I heard there was a golden-haired minx named Lacy at the Paradise Palace. It's a shame you haven't a common name, my pet."

Somehow she managed to find her voice but fear made her hoarse. "How did you find me?"

He smiled satanically. "Why, as I said, my dear, by the merest chance. My dear brother-in-law finally decided to venture your father's money in shipping merchandise to this uncivilized part of the world. Feeling an urge to travel, I accompanied said goods."

"The *Puritan Belle!*" she gasped.

"But of course. I thought perhaps I would find a fortune trying my hand in the gold fields. Instead, I've rediscovered the fortune I lost when my bride vanished on the eve of our wedding." His smile faded, leaving his face harsh, cruel. He looked at her hard. "I don't intend to let her get away a second time."

Blood pounded in Lacy's ears, as she fought the inclination to faint. "How much do you want,

William? I'll pay you any amount if you just leave me alone."

Quire reached for her, but Lacy shrunk away from him. "Why should I be content with a pittance when I can have control of the whole Phalen fortune and you as well, my sweet?" His arm fell around her shoulders.

Lacy looked around wildly for help. All the fear she had experienced in Boston two years ago washed over her, leaving her incapable of even trying to defend herself against Abigail's brother.

A tall shadow fell on her cheek. Lacy looked up thankfully into the grim face of Jock McDonald, one of the large men hired to discourage fights at the gaming tables.

"This gent botherin' ya, Miss Lacy?"

She felt William's hand on her shoulder tighten threateningly.

"Why, Lacy and I are old friends from Boston," he said. "You needn't fear for her in my care. Why, we're almost family, isn't that right, my dear?" His tone dared her to refute his statement.

Jock looked uncertain. "That true?"

Lacy's eyes pleaded for rescue, but Jock did not understand. He waited patiently for her answer. William's body stiffened. She could feel the muscles of his arm tighten.

Lacy was suddenly afraid for Jock. Although he towered over William, she felt that the Bostonian would have the advantage. Jock was not expecting a fight.

"Yes," she said, her voice almost a whisper. "Mr. Quire and I were acquaintances in Boston two years ago."

"Intimate acquaintances," William struck in.

Jock looked confused.

"What about a toast to those days?" William said jovially. He patted her bare arm companionably. "We certainly have a lot to talk about. I believe I saw a nice quiet table in a corner." He nodded to the room she had just left.

Lacy thought briefly of the events that had followed her last intimate drink at a corner table in the music room, and shuddered.

"Cold, my dear? Perhaps your large friend here would be kind enough to bring you a wrap?" William looked pointedly at Jock.

"Miss Lacy?" the big man appealed.

William's grip on her arm tightened until Lacy almost gasped with pain.

"Yes, if you don't mind, Jock. It's on the chair in my room," she directed.

Jock relaxed visibly and with a slight nod left her to William's unwanted attentions.

"This way, my dear," Quire said.

"You are hurting my arm."

He smiled again. "This is only a sample, Lacy. Don't try to run away from me again. I'd hate to ruin that beautiful face of yours. Then no man would ever want you again, my dear. Especially not the gallant Mr. Paradise."

He forced her into the corner chair, maneuvering the table so that the only way out was past him. "I would say this occasion calls for champagne, but if I remember correctly, you have a taste for brandy. Isn't that right?"

Lacy remained silent, reliving an episode in Abigail's dining room not long after their return

383

from Quire Farm and the announcement of the engagement. William's breath had been hot on her cheek, his hands eager in their pawing. Abigail had insisted Harry walk with her in the garden, leaving Lacy alone with her brother. Her courage had waned in the face of his lust. Almost to the point of panic, Lacy had grabbed the glass of brandy on the table, hoping it would numb her senses.

William continued as if Lacy had answered him. "I'm glad you agree, my dear." He relayed the order to the waiter. "Miss Lacy is buying," he added.

The waiter looked at her for confirmation. Helpless, Lacy nodded.

"I see you are learning," William said. "And may I say you are looking quite beautiful? More so than you did in Boston. The life of a whore must agree with you."

Lacy felt a bracing warmth course through her veins as her temper flared. "I am amazed that you would want a woman you describe so as a wife."

"True," he agreed. "But where there is a fortune as well, I believe I can forgive your past."

The brandy arrived, and Quire instructed the waiter to fill Lacy's glass to the brim. "You look a little pale, my dear," he added.

For a moment Lacy thought the waiter would question the choice of brandy over her usual champagne. She pushed her goblet toward him as if eager.

"Have you seen Jock?" she asked as the waiter poured the golden brown liquid into her glass. She tried to keep her voice light and gay. "He was bringing me a wrap."

"Yes, ma'am. I saw him. He was talking with Mr. Paradise. If you wish, I can tell him you are waiting."

Lacy shook her head and smiled at him. "No, that won't be necessary. I see Mr. Paradise is bringing my shawl."

William twisted around in his chair. Ben had paused in the archway but was now coming toward them. Lacy gave him a dazzling smile of welcome.

"Jock tells me you've caught a chill, my heart," he said, "and that you've discovered an old friend among our guests." His artic blue gaze swept over William as the man got slowly to his feet.

Lacy felt the last of her fear seeping away. From the look in Ben's eye, she could tell he had guessed the identity of the visitor from Boston. "I don't believe you were ever properly introduced," she said. "This is William Quire, my cousin Abigail's brother. William, you remember Benjamin Paradise, I'm sure."

"Pleased to renew your acquaintance," Quire muttered stiffly.

"Pleasure's mine," Ben said, and gave Quire a hearty slap on the back. William almost doubled over the table.

Lacy felt an irrestible urge to grin and fought it.

"Your wrap, my heart." Ben moved between William's chair and hers. "How did this table get pushed back? Here, let's move it so you can breathe." He gave the solid oak table a shove that sent it into William's midrift. Lacy heard a whoosh of air as Quire's breath left him. Gasping, he glared across the table at Ben's tall, dark-clad form.

Elizabeth Daniels

"Sorry." Ben grinned. He spun a chair around from the next table and placed it between Quire's chair and Lacy's in the space he had created by moving the table.

"Tell me, Quire, what brings you to San Francisco? Gold?" Ben asked, straddling the chair.

William looked across the table at Lacy. "You might say so."

She felt the dizziness threaten again.

Ben reached over and took her hand in his, holding it lightly on top of the table. His thumb rubbed caressingly against her palm.

"Heading for the Mother Lode?" Ben asked.

Irritated, Quire frowned. "No, my fortune lies here in San Francisco."

Ben smiled at Lacy, blatantly ignoring Quire. "That's interesting," he said, offhand. "I'm sure quite a number of men would like to know your secret. It's back-breaking work panning for gold."

William's eyes burned as he stared at the couple's locked hands. "To tell the truth," he said, "my fortune is tied up in my bride-to-be."

Quire was pleased to note the flash of anger in Paradise's face.

"And you said you came to California for this fortune?" Ben's eyes narrowed imperceptibly. "If it's a wife you've come to find, let me warn you, women are so rare in this section of the country that we kill over them," he drawled.

"Is that so?" William asked. "This woman is promised to me though."

"Odd." Again Ben turned purposefully to the silent woman. "Do you happen to know this fortunate young woman, Lace? I can't recall hearing of

386

such a lady in Frisco. Sure you got the right town, Quire?"

The New Englander's face turned purple with anger. "You know very well who my intended is, Paradise," he growled. "And I intend to have her."

"Never," Lacy declared. "I'd rather be dead."

William's eyes met hers across the table. "If you wish it, my dear, I'm sure it can be arranged . . . after the nuptuals. I intend to gain control of the Puritan Line one way or another."

"You'll never get it," she hissed. "Never!"

The vivid color in Quire's face began to fade. He smiled mirthlessly at her. "Don't be so sure, Lacy. After all, Harry had agreed to our betrothal. If you hadn't decided to run away on the eve of our wedding, we could have presented the captain with a grandchild upon his return."

Under the table her free hand went protectively to her growing child.

"When the *Belle* sails, you will be on it," William continued. "The captain shall marry us at sea."

"Captain Ransom has the *Belle*. He would never perform the ceremony with an unwilling bride," Lacy declared. "Even if I were aboard, which I will not be."

Quire's expression was confident. "You forget the circumstances surrounding our engagement, my dear Lacy. You have no option."

Ben sighed. "It looks like you have no choice, dearest heart."

Lacy looked at him aghast.

"You'll have to marry me," he said. "After all, Quire became engaged to you for simply trying to wean you from your virtue. I succeeded."

Lacy blushed.

Neither man noticed.

"You and any other man with a bag of gold dust in his pocket," Quire jeered.

"On the contrary. She's been mine and mine alone. And will remain so." Ben's eyes were tempered steel.

"In that case," Quire said softly, "I'll have to kill you."

"Or I you," Ben said agreeably.

The two men measured each other, then Ben turned his back on Quire and brought Lacy's hand to his lips.

"I'm sure," he said, his voice dangerous, low, "that Mr. Quire will excuse us while we celebrate our betrothal, dearest heart." His fingers played along the intricately woven surface of the ring she still wore on the third finger of her left hand.

"You won't live to see your wedding night," Quire growled.

Ben smiled at him, the look challenging Quire. "Since my wife and I have experienced many nights of delight, I would die happy," he said. "Will you?"

Quire ground his teeth. "She isn't your wife yet, Paradise."

Ben's smile widened. "Isn't she? If memory serves, Lace, you've been called Mrs. Paradise before, haven't you? And answered to it?"

Quire's hand shot out and gripped the front of Ben's shirt. Lacy had been waiting for him to make a move. She jumped to her feet and shoved the table with all her strength, sending it into Quire's legs. At the same moment Ben tossed her untouched glass of brandy into the man's face. William fell backward, as the alcohol dripped down his face.

Jock and Travis were in the room immediately, looming over the fallen man.

"How clumsy of me," Ben said. "It seems Mr. Quire will need to return to his lodgings for a change of clothing."

Travis smiled grimly. "I'd be glad ta escort the gent."

Ben returned the smile. "I knew I could count on you, George." He took Lacy's hand and drew her from behind the table. "I believe we've been away from our guests long enough, don't you, my little wildcat?"

She placed her hand on his arm. "I hope you will remember me to your sister when you return to Boston, William," she said.

Ben patted her hand in approval.

"I won't forget this, Paradise," Quire growled.

"I didn't intend that you should, Quire," Ben said, and led Lacy from the room.

CHAPTER XXV

The confrontation with William Quire was tame compared to relations between nationalities in the Mother Lode. The white men looked down their nose at the Mexicans or "greasers" as they called them. The Mexicans terrorized the Chinese. Class wars raged frequently in the mining towns. Disputes were fewer in San Francisco where districts grew up, each man seeking his own kind. Fights among the rough customers had always been quelled quickly at the Paradise Palace. The tales of racial unrest and death originated in the other saloons.

But Lacy had become immune to them. The shootings and knifings weren't part of her world, which centered around the continued absence of her father.

It was growing imperative for Lacy to leave San

Francisco before her condition became known. The bouts of nausea were difficult to hide in the close quarters of the saloon. She fancied the other women looked at her curiously. If they guessed the state of her affairs, it would not be long before Ben discovered that he was to be a father.

The ring on her hand was a talisman. She hoped it warded off further harassment by William Quire. She would not hold Ben to his proposal. He had made it only to protect her. If he learned of the baby, Lacy was afraid he would insist upon marrying her for the child's sake and that she did not want.

She was beginning to lose confidence in her belief that the *Puritan Paramour* would dock in San Francisco. It was strange that she had been unable to hear word of the clipper at the docks. After months of inquiring, she was well known on the wharf. Even the crew of the *Puritan Belle*, those few who remained in San Francisco rather than heading for the gold fields, could give her no hope.

The bay was becoming so blocked with deserted ships that it was difficult to find passage out of California. If she could not find passage within the next month, Lacy would have to consider traveling by stagecoach down the coast, hoping to find an Atlantic-bound ship.

Pearl stopped by Lacy's room before going down to her monte table for the evening. Lacy's health had become a frequent subject of conversation of late. Her beauty was still unparalleled, almost enhanced by a new pallor.

"Is there anything I can get ya, Lacy?"

The room was dark, lit only by lamps in the hallway. Lacy lay stretched across the bed, her dressing gown loosely tied for comfort. At Pearl's inquiry she sat up, supporting herself on one elbow. "No, Pearl, I'll be all right in a little while. It's just a slight headache."

Pearl looked at her suspiciously. "Ya sure that's all? Ya haven't been lookin' so good lately. At dinner ya had a green tinge."

The gagging sensation returned, and Lacy closed her eyes in an effort to fight it.

Even in the half-light, Pearl noticed. "When ya goin' ta tell him?"

"Tell him what?" Lacy snapped.

Pearl smiled. "'Bout the little one."

"There is no 'little one,'" Lacy lied.

"He has a right ta know. He'll know soon 'nuff."

Lacy saw Ben's tall form come up behind the lovely dealer. "Who'll know what?"

Pearl cast a glance toward the young woman on the bed. "Lacy's ailin'."

Ben peered into the dark room. "Just a headache, right, my heart?"

"More 'n a headache," Pearl said.

His brow furrowed in concern. "Should I send for Doc Nichols?"

"No doctor," Lacy snapped. "I just need a little quiet before I come down stairs. I won't have the doctor dragged over here just for a little headache. I'm fine."

Ben grinned and put a hand on Pearl's shoulder. "But in a fine temper," he said. "I wonder what I've done now?"

Pearl winked. "Ya'd be surprised."

"Pearl." Lacy's voice carried a threat.

"I'm goin'," the woman said, and disappeared down the hall.

Ben continued to block the light with his broad shoulders. "Lace?"

"I'll be fine," she said, her voice calm once again. "An hour's rest is all I need."

"But no doctor."

"No, no doctor." Patrick Nichols was far too astute. He would know her secret immediately.

Ben chuckled at the adamancy of her reply. "Whatever you wish, my heart," he said. "Come down when you're ready."

Lacy smiled weakly. Despite the darkened room, she saw the flash of his strong white teeth, then the door closed behind him.

"Thank God," she breathed, and lay back wearily on the pillow.

Exactly one hour later Lacy descended the grand staircase, tightly gripping the hand rail. She had used the paint box to put color back in her pale cheeks and dressed in a gown the same shade as her forest-green eyes.

She was pleased to see the women were all safely occupied, their attention diverted from her by the boisterous miners. Jeanne smiled complacently at the two men at her table, who regarded their cards with blank faces. Pearl's laughter rang out amid the group of miners surrounding her at the monte table. Rita and Consuelo were at the bar, the arms of burly Mexicans tightly about their narrow waists.

"Feeling better, dearest heart?"

Lacy found Ben awaiting her at the bottom of the staircase.

She brightened at the tender warmth in his eyes. "Yes, an hour's rest was the answer," she assured him.

Ben surveyed her slowly, his glance taking in her heightened color and the bright, almost feverish gleam in her eyes. She was a game little thing. Obviously, she felt no better yet she had taken special care of her appearance to disguise the fact. "Good. Come down and join me for a drink."

Descending the stairs carefully, her skirts held above her ankles, Lacy smiled at him. "Are you trying to get me intoxicated already this evening, Ben Paradise?"

His eyes dipped appreciatively to the display of her slim ankles. "So that I can have my evil way with you, Miss Phalen?"

Lacy reached the bottom of the staircase and laid a slender hand on his proffered arm. "That's exactly what I mean, Mr. Paradise."

He laughed, a rich, deep sound. "Tom," he called to the bartender, "a drink for the lady."

"I'm going to be terribly spoiled when I get back to Boston," Lacy said. "How can Papa possibly compete with nightly champagne?"

"As long as it's the captain competing, not our friend Quire," he murmured.

Tom placed a glass of champagne and a tumbler of whiskey on the bar. Lacy's hand shook as she reached for the glass.

"If he's still in town," Paradise said of Quire. "At least he hasn't shown his face around here."

"You will be careful?" Lacy turned toward him.

"He'll never forgive you for championing me."

The light in Ben's eyes flickered over her possessively. "I know. He certainly didn't appreciate my claiming you for myself."

Fear stabbed Lacy's heart. Afraid to meet his eyes, she contemplated the bubbles rising in her glass. "Thank goodness he doesn't realize you didn't mean it," she said.

Ben studied the fall of her gold curls, the graceful curve of her throat. Had he heard regret in her voice? "Maybe I did mean it," he said solemnly.

Surprised, Lacy glanced up at him. "You know we always planned I'd go home when the captain returned."

"Plans can be changed," he suggested carefully.

Confused at the tenderness in his voice, she stammered, "I don't know . . . I hadn't thought . . . about that."

Ben smiled teasingly over his whiskey glass. She hadn't refused him. That was encouraging. Perhaps the future he envisioned for them was possible. He had to be patient though and not rush his fences when she appeared willing to accept him.

"We'll talk about it later," he said. "Now, if you'll excuse me, Lacy, there are some gentlemen anxious to lose their dust to me."

She laughed cheerfully. What would she do if he said he loved her and wanted her to stay?

Lacy looked across the room to where he now sat, leaning back in his chair, cards stacked negligently on the table before him.

She smiled to herself and took a sip of champagne.

* * *

At the lasquenet table Jeanne caught Lacy's eye,
her look full of hate. Ever since the duel between
Ben and Ian Hawthorne, Jeanne had acted as if
Lacy were invisible. She had done everything
possible to attract Ben's attention, but he had
ignored her and gone to Lacy. It was a slight
Jeanne could not bear. Rather than hate him
though, her hostility was directed at Lacy Phalen.

A slight smile appeared at the corners of
Jeanne's painted red mouth, which made Lacy
uneasy. Lately the Frenchwoman's attitude had
changed. She looked cunning, as if she knew
somehow she would win the battle and Ben. If
Jeanne had known Lacy planned to leave, she
would have had no trouble waiting. With Lacy out
of the way, she would have clear claim to Benjamin Paradise. Jeanne's new attitude puzzled Lacy.
It was almost as if the woman knew something was
about to happen.

Edith had reported that Jeanne rarely slept in
her room anymore. She was of the opinion that the
woman had found a protector and spent her nights
in his arms, in his lodgings. Lacy had not noticed
Jeanne favoring any of the customers. All the same,
she wondered.

Jeanne was the first to turn away, the game
recalling her attention. Lacy's gaze wandered past
Jeanne to the far table where Ben sat.

Should she tell him of the child growing in her
womb? His child. Their child. She still found it
hard to believe. Would it resemble its father? She
hoped so. She would have a handsome son to
inherit the Puritan Line. He would grow up strong,
tall, and daring. He would sail the world over,

discovering new markets for the Line.

"Slant eyes!" The growl came from the large Mexican at the other end of the bar. Before anyone could move, the man had pulled his gun and fired.

A few feet from Lacy, a young Chinaman jerked as the bullet entered his back. He slumped forward then slid to the floor, his lifeless hands upsetting a whiskey bottle on the bar.

The Mexican fired two more shots into the body and turned, peering about the room suspiciously.

Pandemonium broke loose. Men made for the door in a mad rush, preventing Jock and Travis from reaching the gun-toting man.

Lacy found herself pushed to the floor behind the bar. She heard bullets hit the sturdy oak. Bottles broke, splattering her with glass and whiskey. Beside her, the bartender bound the graze on his hand and reached for the rifle beneath the bar.

More gunfire erupted. She heard a Mexican swear and the sound of metal dropping to the floor. Ben's voice rang out, ordering others to drop their guns.

Lacy dragged herself up to see what was going on. Jock and Travis trained guns on the disarmed men. Across the room, Ben was returning his smoking gun to its holster. He glanced across the room, noting the disheveled young woman behind the bar.

"Lacy!"

She tried to smile to assure him that everything was fine, but the room began to spin. She grabbed at the counter to steady herself and winched as a pain shot through her shoulder.

Ben was across the room. Then he was near, his

hand on top of the bar. He vaulted over it, but he seemed to be moving very slowly. Everyone was moving so slowly. Lacy swayed on her feet and again made the effort to smile. The throbbing in her shoulder increased. Turning her head, she stared at the dark red stain on the bodice of her gown.

"Lacy," Ben said, landing lightly beside her.

She turned toward him, her vision blurred. He was all right. All right.

"Ben," she murmured.

He caught her as she fell.

The familiar face of Doctor Patrick Nichols hovered above her. Lacy's lashes fluttered trying to dispel his stern face. She didn't want a doctor. He'd discover her secret and ruin everything.

The doctor's solid form remained. She winced and moaned as something burned on her shoulder.

"I'm glad you're awake, young lady. I have a few questions to ask you," Nichols insisted.

Lacy closed her eyes tightly. Perhaps he would keep her secret. She would reason with him, pay him.

She opened her eyes and saw Ben at the foot of the bed, smiling warmly at her.

Lacy glanced to the doctor at her bedside as he finished binding her right arm in a sling. His was a kind, but stern, face. His uncombed hair fell over his forehead. His jawline was grizzled with a day's growth of beard. As usual, his shiny, well-worn suit was wrinkled. A nightshirt was pushed haphazardly into his trousers.

"I'm sorry I got you out of bed, Patrick. Is my shoulder very bad?" she asked softly.

"Bad enough." He fixed her with an inscrutable stare. "I'm more interested in learning how long you've been experiencing the dizziness and nausea."

Lacy tried to pull herself together. This was exactly what she had feared. Doctor Nichols's eyes were far too keen.

"I . . . I haven't . . ."

"And why didn't you tell this young man he was going to be a father?" the doctor continued ruthlessly.

"But I—"

"You couldn't keep it a secret much longer. Been letting out some of your dresses already I'd say."

Lacy took a deep breath and struggled up on one arm. "Mind your own damn business, Patrick Nichols," she growled. The effort taxed her strength, and dizzy again, she fell back against the pillows.

Ben's chuckle echoed in the room. He raised her hand to his lips and kissed the ring on her third finger. "Looks like I'd better replace this with a solid gold band in a hurry."

"No," Lacy whispered. "Not now."

A frown creased his brow. "We'll talk about it later."

"Drink this," Dr. Nichols commanded, and pressed a glass to her lips. "It will help you sleep. That arm is going to give you a lot of pain in the next few days, but you'll heal."

Lacy made a face as the foul-tasting liquid was forced down her throat.

Ben leaned over and brushed her lips with his. "Sleep well, my heart. Take care of my son."

She lay in the dark and tried to think. There had been a special light in his eyes that she had not seen there before. A glow that brightened perceptively when he said "my son." Now that he knew of the baby's existence, he would try to keep her in San Francisco. He would follow her if she tried to leave, yet leave she must.

The laudanum began to take effect, and Lacy drifted into a deep, troubled sleep.

He still hadn't told her he loved her.

CHAPTER XXVI

The month of June found Lacy irritable. Her shoulder had healed and rarely bothered her. Daily she went to the wharves to inquire after ships bound for the East. She had nearly forgotten the *Puritan Paramour* in her desperation. Out in the harbor the crewless *Puritan Belle* still rode the waves, stranded like so many.

During her convalescence, Pearl had assumed the duties of housekeeper and hostess, leaving Lacy free to pursue her quest for a ship. The few sea captains who hadn't followed their crews to the gold fields were trying to enlist men. But the available men, once content with a monthly salary of fifteen dollars, were now demanding one hundred to one hundred fifty dollars a month and preferred only short voyages such as those to the

Sandwich Islands. They had no desire to ship back to the east where wages were low.

The miners who frequented the Paradise watched after Lacy with a gentleness she found very touching. These were the same men who had stood in the streets, hats in hands, staring at her the previous fall. She had seen the same treatment accorded quite homely women and had heard a miner had paid a homesteading family just for the pleasure of looking at their children. To these men, so far from their homes and families, the birth of a child was truly a miracle.

Jeanne remained the only member of the staff who was unimpressed.

Avoiding Pearl, Lacy drove down to the docks, seeking information once more. Surely one captain had been able to gather a crew.

The information was the same. No ships were due to sail. No one had any word concerning the *Puritan Paramour* recently out of China.

"You are leaving us, *n'est-ce pas*, Lay–see?" a husky female voice with a French lisp sneered.

Lacy spun around angrily. "Are you following me, Jeanne?"

"*Je suis intriguée*. Why does the so wealthy *Mademoiselle* Phalen visit the docks?"

"And is your curiosity sated?" Lacy demanded.

"*Mais, oui*." The Frenchwoman idly twirled the handle of her open parasol. "Why is it you wish to leave now that Ben speaks of marriage?"

Lacy climbed back onto the carriage seat and picked up the reins. Jeanne, with a graceful twist of her rich skirts, swung herself aboard.

Lacy paused, studying the woman. "I don't

believe I offered to drive you back to the Paradise, Jeanne."

The Frenchwoman smiled humorlessly. "Ah, but I believe I can be of assistance." She tilted the angle of her sunshade carefully. "Are you not perhaps a little curious, *chérie*?"

Lacy regarded her solemnly. "It depends upon what you have in mind."

Jeanne nodded at a staring sailor. "Could we perhaps drive as we speak?" she asked as still another man slowed his step to gawk at the two lovely women. "I do not believe you wish anyone to know you plan to run from Ben as you once ran from your *fiancé* in Boston."

Shock drained all color from Lacy's face. "Who told you that?" she snapped.

Jeanne smiled complacently.

In Lacy's mind she saw once again Jeanne locked in Ben's arms. Who *but* Ben Paradise could have told her?

Lacy snapped the reins over the horses' heads. "Very well, Jeanne, we will talk."

"It seems to me, Lay–see, that it is *trés difficile* to find a ship. *Les capitaines*, they know you are Paradise's woman. When such men have taken a little too much wine, their tongues are loosened and soon Ben would know. *Je me trompe*?"

Lacy stared out over the backs of the horses. "No, you aren't mistaken."

"How else are you to return to your home? *Le petit* prevents you from traveling overland. The trains they come to California. They do not leave it." She paused. "So I ask myself, is there another way one may reach New England?"

"Did you find an answer?"

"*Oui*. A coach to Los Angeles. It is but a small trip but from there one might find a ship to Boston."

Lacy was amazed. "You have certainly done a lot of thinking on my behalf, Jeanne."

The woman's smile was condescending. "Ah, but it is on my behalf, *chérie*," she insisted.

"I see," Lacy murmured. "With me out of the way, you hope to entice Ben."

"But of course," Jeanne insisted smugly.

Lacy stared out over the horses' broad backs, a frown creasing her brow. "A plan does not help, Jeanne. Have you taken into consideration that Ben will come after me?"

"*Certainement*!" Jeanne nodded. "Already he plays the proud papa. He will wish the little one even if he does not wish you. But he will not find you. You will have vanished as the fog in the morning sun."

Lacy glanced her way. The woman was too confident. Yet she readily admitted she wished to remove her rival for Ben's affections. "And how is this to be accomplished?" Lacy demanded, suspicious.

Jeanne was nonplused. "*Chérie*, if you wish it, a private coach will set out three days from now for Los Angeles. A gentleman will accompany you. To all appearances, you will be husband and wife. He will do this for you and remain silent for a price."

"And the price?"

"Will be discussed later," Jeanne said.

"And if I agree," Lacy pursued, "how am I to know this man?"

"He knows you, *chérie.*"

Lacy was silent, considering. The man could be any one of the many miners who came through the Paradise's swinging doors. A man in search of an easy grubstake. "I'll think about it, Jeanne."

"Do not wait too long," the Frenchwoman warned dangerously. "Or you will find a real wedding band on your hand. And perhaps a dagger in your back?"

Three days later Lacy dressed in drab poplin. She packed another serviceable dress and extra petticoats into a portmanteau.

Sadly, she looked about her room for the last time. It was the room where her child had been conceived. A room that had echoed with the sounds of laughter, of anger, and of love. On the floor of the wardrobe were the moccasins she had worn on the journey from Missouri.

Tears blinded her and she wiped them away with the sleeve of her dress. The moccasins would shock Eastern society, but she would not leave them behind. She reopened the portmanteau and pushed them in. In the future she would show them to her child and tell him about his father and the adventures they had shared.

It would not be the familiar streets of Boston to which she sailed though. Jeanne was wrong in believing she would return there. It would be the first place Ben would search for her. Or rather, for his child.

How different everything would be if he only loved her. But she would not marry him merely for her child's sake. Instead, she would lose herself in

New York. Under an alias, she would rear her child quietly. Fate had played her false. She had prayed for love, had worked to be a viable part of the Puritan Line. Now she had lost both her dreams.

Lacy twisted the ring on her finger then took it off, wrapping it in a handkerchief to place in her purse. Perhaps she would wear it again one day. It was too painful to have a bright reminder of Ben Paradise on the day she left him.

A commotion in the streets drew Lacy to the window. Pushing it wide, she could hear the cries of the bucket brigade. Smoke rose a few streets away. She leaned further from the window in an effort to see exactly where the blaze had broken out. The wind blew toward the fire, fanning the flames away from Portsmouth Square. Only if the wind changed would the Paradise Palace be in danger.

San Francisco was so very fragile. It was a combustible city, not merely where men's tempers were concerned, but through the very composition of the canvas and wood structures. On Christmas Eve, fire had destroyed a number of buildings. Again in early May, merchants in the Plaza had been wiped out in a second blaze.

As Lacy watched, the wind dipped playfully, teasing her with a wafting scent of burning canvas.

An abrupt knock at her door reclaimed Lacy's attention. Quickly, she hid the portmanteau and closed the window. With a last look around the room, she decided there was no evidence of her imminent departure.

"Cherie?" Jeanne called.

"Coming." Lacy pulled the door open. A man

stood behind Jeanne, his broad back turned toward the door.

Jeanne smiled, an icy grimace. Had there ever been any warmth in the woman?

"This is the gentleman," Jeanne said smoothly. "He has a carriage below. But he would like to agree upon the price of his silence before you leave, *cherie*. That is why I brought him to you."

Nervous, Lacy glanced down the hall.

Jeanne's expression was smug. "You need have no fear, Lay–see. Ben and the others have gone."

"To fight the fire?"

She shrugged elegantly. "Should you not invite *m'sieur* in, *cherie*? They may return, *tout de suite*."

"Yes, of course," Lacy agreed anxiously. "Won't you come in, Mr. . . . ." She paused, awaiting an introduction.

"Quire," the man said, and turned to face her.

"William!" Lacy gasped.

He smiled at Jeanne who stepped aside for him to enter the room.

Belatedly, Lacy attempted to slam the door and bolt it. He blocked the attempt with his shoulder and thrust his way into the room. Lacy fell back against the bed and slid to the floor, winded.

"*Bon voyage, chérie*," Jeanne said from the doorway, and closed the door after her.

William leaned back against it, his arms folded over his barrel chest. "You seem surprised to see me, Lacy."

"I thought you had left San Francisco," she said. Without taking her eyes from him, Lacy got slowly to her feet.

"Without you?" He laughed. "Things have changed a little though."

"Have they?"

"The child," he said.

Her chin came up defensively. "I intend to rear it myself."

Quire's eyes glittered dangerously. "But I can't afford to have another man's child in my household."

Lacy moved toward the dressing table where she had left her bag. In it was the comforting weight of her small derringer. "I don't understand." She bargained for time. "This is my child. He will be heir to the Puritan Line."

"Exactly why I must get rid of it," Quire said.

Lacy froze, looking at him fearfully. "What . . . what do you . . . do you . . ." she stammered, her mouth dry. "What will happen to my son?"

"So sure of its sex, Lacy? You have what, just a few months until the birth?"

"Five, six. I'm not sure."

"That long," he mused. "What was Paradise doing? He's had two years. Did he wait this long to insure that you'd stay with him? What a disappointment it will be for him to find you've gone. You're making it a habit, aren't you, Lacy? Running away."

"What will happen to my child?" Lacy repeated.

Quire continued to lean against the door. "Who knows? A foundling home? The harbor?"

She paled, her hand going protectively to her abdomen. Lacy stepped nearer the dressing table and sank wearily to the chair before it. Cautiously, she felt behind her for the bag and eased it open.

"You couldn't be so cruel," she said.

"Couldn't I?" He smirked. "I've gone to a lot of trouble over you, Lacy. You collect men very easily. Men who tend to get in my way."

"I don't understand you, William."

"Don't you?" Quire laughed harshly. "There are many men in Frisco who would think nothing of killing a man for a bag of dust."

Her hand had stopped its exploration toward the derringer. "You are mad," she said. "Insane."

William took out his pocket watch and consulted it. "Get your things together, Lacy. It's time we left."

Her voice was steady, belying fear. "I'm not going anywhere with you," she said quietly.

Quire replaced the watch in his vest pocket. "Aren't you, my dear? I'm afraid you have no choice. If need be, I will take you from this room unconscious. But come with me you will."

Quire studied her carefully. Her bravado was chilling. She had changed considerably under the gambler's tutelage. The Lacy he remembered would have tried to lure him into believing she acceded to his plans.

"Ben will kill you," she stated calmly.

"I doubt it."

"I've seen him kill one man already." Her hand resumed its path toward the small derringer, her fingers inching their way inside the handbag toward the comforting touch of steel.

"Over you, Lacy?"

"He's very fast with a gun," she warned.

Quire was complacent. "Oh, I don't doubt it. Living on the frontier necessitates familiarity with weapons, I believe."

The smooth handle of the gun was within her grasp. The metal work was cool to the touch. Her finger found the trigger.

"Did you become a sure shot on the frontier as well, Lacy?" he asked conversationally.

"Yes!" she screamed, and swung the derringer in his direction. Her one shot thudded harmlessly into the door where Quire had been standing. Her wrist was twisted, forcing her to drop the tiny gun. Then he threw her onto the bed.

"You still haven't learned, have you, Lacy?"

Hatred licked at him from her eyes. "I'll never go back with you!"

Quire's arm swung in a stinging blow to her cheek, and Lacy's head snapped back.

Abigail was right. His ill luck had begun the day he met Lacy Phalen and tasted the lure of her fortune. The last two years had been hell. Without immediate bolstering from the Puritan Line's coffers, Quire's finances had deteriorated quickly. Abigail's plot had been useless, impotent in the face of ruin. Creditors had descended like vultures. Doors shut quickly in his face as word spread through Boston of his failure to meet his debts. Mortgaged heavily, the farm had gone. Even the oblivion of a brandy bottle had been denied him, for nightly he saw Lacy Phalen's face in the bottom of his glass. For two long years he had hated and desired her. Now she stood a few yards away, his for the plucking.

"You'll marry me," he said, "or I'll kill you."

She raised a hand to her burning cheek. "You'll never get the money that way."

He smirked. "Won't I? Perhaps you didn't know. Jeanne is an excellent forger. She can sign your name to a marriage contract. With Harry and Abigail as witnesses to our betrothal, why should your precious father suspect it as a forgery?"

She glared at him. "Anyone in Boston can tell him I ran away from you."

"Can they, Lacy?" His confidence was frightening. "You weren't there. How do you know Abigail hasn't told a different story? She's a very capable woman, as I believe you already know."

Lacy could well imagine Abigail inventing a sick relative or a sudden illness to cover her absence. A quiet wedding in the country, she could hear Abigail say. Just the family. Dear Lillian has been so melancholy since her father left, you know.

"I'll sign over my share of the Line," Lacy said quickly. The Line meant little to her compared to the lives of Ben and their child. "Leave me here, William. You don't want me. You want the Line."

He leered. "What makes you think I don't want you as well, Lacy?"

Within her womb, Lacy felt the child flutter. Or perhaps it was fear.

"I've always considered you a very desirable woman, my dear," he continued. "I remember the night I went to your bed exceedingly well. I'm sure you do, too, and what can happen if you don't cooperate with me."

She remembered only too well.

"Get your bag, Lacy. It's past time we left. Fortunately, this fire is distracting your admirers.

413

We should be well on our way by the time they return."

In the street below, the sounds of commotion had been growing steadily closer. Quire stepped to the window to investigate. Just as quickly, Lacy was off the bed and into the hall.

The smell of smoke was thick in her nostrils. The wind *had* changed! The fire was heading for the Paradise!

"Fire!" The word rang in her ears. The call had been very near. In the street out front! "Fire!" The Paradise Palace was on fire!

Choking, Lacy ran down the hall toward the women dealers' rooms. The smoke was a little denser there, but the air was still breathable. How much longer it would remain so, she could not tell. She only knew it was imperative that they leave the building and get help. She could not let Ben's beautiful saloon burn to the ground.

A thick cloud of smoke hung in the corridor, causing Lacy to gasp as she moved toward the grand staircase.

She could hear William in the hall behind her. Overcoming her fear of him in the face of the fire, Lacy shouted for him to see if any of the women were still in their rooms.

But Quire had other ideas. Blind to the danger they faced, he grabbed Lacy, pulling her into his arms. She fought him, kicking and scratching. Yet, all the time, Quire's face loomed closer. She could hear flames crackling nearby. With a strength gleaned from the urgency of the situation, Lacy broke free of William's arms. "We've got to get out of here!" she shouted. "The building is on fire!"

Quire was deaf to her warnings and lurched toward her.

Jeanne appeared in the doorway of her room, wearing the loose white robe, her rich auburn hair flowing around her shoulders. She stared at Lacy blankly, a faraway look in her eyes.

"Jeanne," Lacy gasped, "the building is on fire. We must get out!"

As if in a daze, Jeanne took a step out of the room, coming between Quire and Lacy. Quire grabbed the Frenchwoman by the shoulders and looked at her closely. "Don't expect to get any help from this quarter, Lacy. She won't save you. She's secure in her opium dream." He thrust Jeanne back against the doorjamb sharply. Her head hit the oak with a sickening thud. Jeanne sank to the floor without a sound.

Lacy stared at the woman whose robe had fallen open over her shapely legs. One arm was thrown out. The other was under her at an awkward angle. Her eyes were half-open, the lids drooping as they often had as she sized up the miners in the saloon downstairs.

William looked down at Jeanne a moment. Lacy took advantage of the distraction, moving slowly toward the stairway. A sixth sense told her Jeanne was dead.

Quire's face was completely impassive. Jeanne had been merely a tool. He had enjoyed being her protector, the man to whom she went each evening. Together, they had planned Lacy Phalen's demise.

Lacy noted the mad glitter in his eyes and quailed before it. Dear God, he *was* insane!

"Lacy!" a voice shouted from the main floor.

Her heart jumped with renewed courage. "Ben!" she cried, and turned to flee.

But Quire came back to life, and, catching her arm, dragged her back into a crushing embrace.

Lacy was suffocating. The smoke was becoming thicker. Her eyes watered, smarted. She coughed as she gulped at the smoky air.

It would have been so easy to give up the fight. To let William kill her as he had Jeanne but she could not. Lacy had a reason to live. She struggled, fighting Quire.

Footsteps echoed up the stairs.

Quire's grasp slackened and broke as Ben spun him around. The madman fell back against the wall as a powerful right fist made contact with his jaw.

"Lacy!" Ben shouted. "Get out of here!"

She had wanted to run from him once. Now she was determined never to leave the side of the man she loved.

Ben's voice rang through the empty rooms. "The fire is spreading too fast. We can't contain it. The whole place may go any minute."

Lacy took one last look at Jeanne.

"Lacy! For God's sake," Ben swore, "think of the baby!"

Lacy turned toward the stairs, undecided.

Quire dragged himself up and threw himself at Ben, and both men slammed into the far wall.

Lacy reached the top of the staircase but could go no further. William's hands were pressing on Ben's throat. Ben was trying to break the hold of those deadly fingers, as he gasped in the smoke-filled air.

Once the Puritan Shipping Line had been her life, filling her every waking hour, supplying all the stimulation she had needed. Yet she had been ready to forsake the Line, to trade it to Quire in exchange for Ben's life.

Desperate, Lacy raced back down the hall and threw herself on Quire's arm, pulling backwards with all her strength. The hold was broken, and Ben managed to throw a weak blow.

Quire staggered back toward the stairs. He still did not seem to realize the danger they faced. "I'll kill you, Paradise. I promise I'll kill you!" he cried, again backing toward the stairs. Lacy saw him fumble in his coat pocket, then caught the flash of metal as he found the gun.

She screamed a warning.

Ben had seen the danger and had already drawn his Colt.

Quire hadn't managed to level his weapon before Ben's bullet found its mark. A surprised look came into Quire's eyes. He stumbled toward the staircase, one hand clasped to his side where blood from the wound already stained his clothing. He tried to level the gun once more, but it wavered, never finding its target. He took a step down the staircase.

Lacy felt Ben's arm around her waist, holding her closely against his side.

Quire's eyes narrowed, staring down the corridor at them. "I'll kill you both!"

The hammer of Ben's Colt cocked.

The barrel of William's weapon wavered. He took another step back and stumbled.

"My God!" Lacy breathed.

Quire's pistol exploded, shattering the main chandelier. Coal oil trickled to the floor, over the bar. The liquid incited the fire which was reflected in the tall mirror, dancing hungrily, consuming the room below. It was a raging inferno in seconds.

Quire moved down another step.

"No! The fire!" Lacy cried.

William didn't hear her. He took another step and stumbled, falling over the railing to the bar below.

"Quick!" Ben shouted. "The liquor will go any minute!"

Bodily, he dragged Lacy down the corridor to the farthermost room. He closed the door. "Open the window. It's our only chance of escape!"

She did not stop to question the order.

"Can you see Travis?" Ben demanded.

Lacy leaned out the window. The whole area was filled with smoke. Men working in a bucket brigade fought a losing battle against the flames licking at the building.

At the edge of the crowd she saw George Travis and Jock McDonald towering over the heads of the mob.

"Yes!" she yelled, her voice hoarse. She coughed as she inhaled more smoke.

Ben tore strips of cloth from the bed sheets and soaked them in water from the bowl of flowers Edith had placed in the room earlier. "Hold this over your nose and mouth," he instructed.

"Jeanne," Lacy said. "He killed Jeanne."

418

Ben shook his head. "Don't talk. Just breathe through the cloth."

Below, Travis had spotted the open window and quickly organized a group of men.

Ben leaned out to watch their progress, then looked back anxiously toward the door. Lacy followed his look. How long before flames began eating away at the thick lumber?

"Ready!" came a shout from below.

Lacy stared down. A blanket was being stretched taut in the hands of the men.

"Jump!" Ben shouted in her ear. "I'll follow."

She looked down at the small strip of cloth. "I can't!"

Ben glanced back toward the door again. In a flash he scooped Lacy up in his arms and held her out the window. Before she realized his intent, she was falling toward the group of men below.

"That's a girl," Travis said, sweeping her off the makeshift sling, and pushing her into the waiting arms of a spectator.

Lacy tried to tear away. "Ben!"

The stranger forcefully pulled her back into the comparative safety of the crowd.

Lacy struggled all the more, twisting in his arms wildly. "Let me go!"

"It's all right, Lacy," the man said. "You're all right now."

Startled, she stopped fighting. "Papa!"

Behind her Lacy heard the sound of an explosion. The shock threw them to the ground. "The whiskey," she breathed, and struggled from the safety of her father's arms only to see part of the roof of the Paradise Palace collapse.

419

CHAPTER XXVII

Lacy stared in horror at the flames as the men fell back from the heat. "Ben," she whispered. "Ben." He had not escaped in time, and she would never see him again.

The captain cuddled his daughter to his chest as he had when she was a child. "Everything's all right, Lacy. You're safe."

She was dry-eyed, haunted. "Safe," she said wearily. "I'm safe, but Ben . . ."

"What about Ben?" a beloved voice said behind her.

Whirling, Lacy flew into the outstretched arms of Benjamin Paradise. Her hands moved over his face, his shoulders, assuring herself that he was real.

"I thought you were—"

"Dead? I am very much alive, dearest heart," he

said, and proved it with a long drawn-out kiss.

When they parted, Lacy was loath to release him. She kept her arms tightly around him. She had come so close to losing him that she knew she would never let him go.

He smiled down at her. His clothes were singed, as was his hair. He seemed unaware that his hands were burned.

"I was bringing your father back to the Paradise when we got involved in fighting the fire," Ben explained softly.

Lacy glanced at the captain's soot-streaked face then back to the burning saloon.

Ben followed her direction.

"We can rebuild it," Lacy said.

His arm tightened about her. "We?" he asked carefully. "Does that mean you're staying?"

Her eyes glowed. "If you want me to."

He smiled down at her, the fire reflected in his eyes. "I want you to. I need you here beside me."

"You do?" she asked, foolishly happy.

"Of course I do. I love you, Lacy Phalen."

I love you. He had said it. His voice was sure and strong as if it were an emotion of long-standing.

She gazed up at him, her eyes awash with unshed tears.

He said it again, quietly, his tone low and intimate. "I love you, Lacy."

She kissed him joyously, pledging the rest of her life to him.

"When do you want to get married, Miss Phalen?" Ben asked. "I warn you I won't be put off any longer. I refuse to wait until after the birth of my son."

"Son!" Sean Phalen's voice boomed over the hungry crackle of the fire.

Reluctantly, Lacy eased from Ben's arms. "That's right, Papa." Chin up, she challenged him. "You are going to be a grandfather whether you like it or not. A grandson who will inherit the Puritan Line."

"A grandson!"

"Benjamin Phalen Paradise," Ben said.

The captain eyed the lovers carefully. "Awfully sure of yourself."

Ben smiled down at Lacy as his arm slid easily about her waist. She leaned back against him happily.

"And when is this blessed event expected?" the captain asked.

Lacy blushed, thankful for the erratic shadows the flames cast on her face. "November."

"November." His face was stern. He rubbed a hand along his beard. "From the details in Polly's letter," he said, "I half expected to be able to rock my grandson's cradle when I docked." His eyes twinkled. She loved the way they gleamed, so like Ben's eyes.

"But I didn't tell Polly," Lacy protested.

"She knew you followed this young man across the country," the captain said. "For my Polly, that was enough to tell her how you felt."

"Oh, Papa," Lacy said, and went into his arms.

It was comforting to be in her father's embrace again. But Lacy knew she no longer needed him as she once had. Now she had Ben Paradise. A gambler, a frontiersman with the veneer of a gentleman. In his arms was where she belonged.

"We'd better leave the area," Travis said, rejoining the group. "The fire is spreading. Perhaps the safest place would be at sea?"

"Aye," Phalen agreed.

Lacy turned to Ben. He stood watching the flames dance along the remains of the Paradise Palace. She placed a hand in his. As they watched, the wing where her room was collapsed into the ruins.

"Come, my heart. There's nothing left for us here," he said.

The days following the fire were busy ones. Ben and Travis fretted, impatient for the ashes to cool so they could construct another canvas Paradise Palace and be back in business. Their days were spent scouring San Francisco for fittings for the new saloon. It would rise again, another of San Francisco's many phoenix legends.

Lacy remained on board the *Paramour*, discussing the advantages of having a Puritan office in San Francisco with her father. Her dreams had also been reborn in the fire. The fates had given her the gift she most cherished—love. Now she had no intention of forsaking the Puritan Line either. She would merely shift her theater of operation. San Francisco was now her home.

Lacy felt very confident as she leaned on the rail of the clipper watching the choppy waters of the bay slap against the prow. The captain hadn't actually agreed to open a branch of the Puritan Line in San Francisco but he'd always respected her opinions. For now she was content to let him stew over her proposal. Her future success was guaranteed by Ben's presence and by their child.

Ben pulled back on the oars, maneuvering his small craft to the rope ladder dangling over the side of the ship. His burns had been minor, but he still wore the bandage she had lovingly wound around his left hand. It pleased her that he did.

"Ahoy there," Lacy called down cheerfully.

"Ahoy, *Paramour*." He smiled. Even from her place on deck, Lacy could see his eyes sparkle like the sun on the crest of a wave. Cool, enticing, mesmerizing.

Ben had brought a stranger out to the ship with him. A thin gangly man who needed a push to start him up the swinging rope ladder. Ben followed easily, scrambling on board as if he had been around sailing ships all his life. Lacy's heart swelled with pride.

"Everyone aboard?" he asked, kissing her lightly.

Her smile was radiant. "Yes. Why do you ask?"

Mischief danced in his eyes. "Go get them," he urged.

Below decks the displaced staff of the Paradise Palace were expecting the summons. Lacy was surprised at the speed they displayed mounting the companionway. Captain Phalen was the last one topside. He took her hand in his, staring at it a few moments, fondling it.

"Lacy," he murmured, "are you happy, colleen?"

Her dark eyes softened. She reminded him sharply of her mother at the same age. So painfully lovely. So young.

"Papa, of course I am."

Sean wasn't assured. "You've been through a lot these past years."

She linked arms with him companionably. "Yes," she said carefully, considering.

Her eyes found Ben and a warm glow of contentment suffused her face, heightening her resemblance to Amelia Wainwright Phalen. The pain of losing Amelia surfaced briefly for Sean, then was laid to rest.

Lacy laid her other hand on her father's arm. The white mark on her finger where the intricate little ring had been was stark against her skin. Lacy touched it tenderly, a gentle smile lighting her face. It didn't matter that she had lost it and her possessions in the fire. She had gained something much more precious.

Her gaze returned to Ben's tall straight figure. "I love him, Papa," she said softly.

The captain patted her hand. "That's all I wanted to know. I believe they are waiting for us."

She was puzzled as he led her forward. In the bow of the ship stood the stranger, a black book clutched in his hands. Before him stood Ben flanked by Travis. Pearl stood to one side, her eyes glistening with tears, a trembling smile on her lips.

Sean lead Lacy down an aisle formed by the remaining staff. He paused at Ben's side and, with great ceremony, passed his daughter into Ben's keeping.

"Dearly beloved," intoned the stranger.

Lacy shot Ben a look of surprise. He smiled down into her eyes. The preacher's words washed over them, nearly unheard.

"Do you, Benjamin, take this woman for your lawfully wedded wife?"

Ben's hand tightened on Lacy's. His answer was strong, resounding over the deck, echoing in the rigging. "I do."

The stranger turned to Lacy, but she saw only Ben's beloved face smiling into hers.

"Do you, Lillian, take this man for your lawfully wedded husband?"

"Oh, I do," Lacy breathed.

Without waiting for further instructions from the preacher, Ben slipped a wide gold band on her hand, covering the pale circle with the ring that bound him to her. He couldn't think of a more worthy or enjoyable fate. Hungry for their future together, Ben pulled her into his arms and their lips met.

"I now pronounce you man and wife," the minister mumbled nervously.

The captain chuckled.

Lacy wrapped her arms securely around Ben's neck and gave herself up to the heady intoxication of her husband's embrace.

Kathleen Herbert

WINNER OF THE GEORGETTE HEYER MEMORIAL
PRIZE FOR BEST HISTORICAL NOVEL OF THE
YEAR!

In warring post-Arthurian England, King Loth seeks to
cement an alliance with his Cumbrian rival by presenting
his lovely daughter Princess Taniu to Owain, his rival's son.
But Taniu is haunted by a brutal pagan ritual from her
childhood, one that prevents her from loving any man except one, the huntsman whose life she saved. Sentenced to
death by her father for her rebelliousness, Taniu discovers
that she must fight for her life—and for the life of the
huntsman whose love she thought she'd lost.

__2961-8 $3.95 US/$4.95 CAN